Full Circle

Also by Mary A. Larkin

The Wasted Years
Ties of Love and Hate
For Better For Worse

Full Circle

Mary A. Larkin

PIATKUS

Copyright © 1998 by Mary A. Larkin

First published in Great Britain in 1998 by
Judy Piatkus (Publishers) Ltd of
5 Windmill Street, London W1

This edition published 1998

**The moral right of the author
has been asserted**

*A catalogue record for this book is available
from the British Library*

ISBN 0 7499 0448 8

Set in Times by Intype London Ltd
Printed and bound in Great Britain by
Mackays of Chatham PLC

To my beautiful grandchildren
Louise, Coleen, Declan and Joseph

Acknowledgements

I would like to express my sincere gratitude to:

Shirley Peacock	Ontario
Miss Martin	Lisburn
Louie Hartley	Belfast
The late Winnie Larkin	Glengormley

whose special assistance was invaluable.

Author's Note

The Geographical areas portrayed in *Full Circle* actually exist and historic events referred to in the course of the story are, to the best of my knowledge, authentic. However, I would like to emphasise that the story is fictional; all characters are fictitious and any resemblance to real persons, living or dead, is purely coincidental.

Chapter 1

Belfast 1952

Great dark thunderous clouds hung over the Cave Hill, a prelude to the advancing storm. Annie Devlin looked at them through narrowed eyes as she nestled in a comfortable padded cane chair, fanning herself with a newspaper to alleviate the oppressive summer heat. She always experienced deep pleasure sitting in her back garden and enjoying the beauty of the hill that loomed over the houses like a guardian angel – sometimes in breathtaking beauty; at other times, as today, dark and menacing. The weather could often be predicted by a glance at the hill in the early morning. A hazy distant impression foretold good weather ahead, whereas if the hill loomed close, as it did today, rain was in the offing. Their house was situated in an ideal spot. High up on a bend on Serpentine Road, it had great privacy and wonderful views. From the front there was a panoramic view over Belfast Lough and the distant County Down coastline stretching as far as Bangor, and from the back the hill formed a splendid vista, especially when it was silhouetted against a bright sky and the protruding rock that was called Napoleon's Nose was prominent – aptly named for its resemblance to the Little General's profile.

The hill always brought to Annie's mind happy memories of bygone times. A few years ago Bellevue Zoo, which ran along its side beside Hazelwood, had been a yearly outing for her. From a very early age their parents had taken her and her sister Rosaleen to the Cave Hill each year to roll their painted Easter eggs and visit the zoo. It had been a great treat; looked

1

forward to with avid anticipation during the six long weeks of Lent when they were expected to give up at least one of their simple vices. Annie had always refrained from eating sweets and taking sugar in her tea during the Lenten season, feeling guilty when she succumbed to temptation and indulged in the odd toffee. As teenagers Rosaleen and she, accompanied by their mutual friends, had kept up an annual pilgrimage to Bellevue and visited the hill and zoo each Easter.

It seemed to her that most of the population of Belfast seemed to gather on the hill at Easter, particularly Easter Monday. It was where you had the chance to meet most of the city's talent, instead of just those from your own locality, and there was hope in the hearts of romantic teenagers as they eyed those of the opposite sex and wondered if today would prove fruitful. Indeed, many a long-lasting romance had started from a chance meeting on the Cave Hill.

If anyone had told her then that one day she would be living in the shadow of the hill she would have laughed outright at the very idea of being so far away from the bustle of her beloved Springfield Road, where she had been born and reared. That, however, had been before Sean Devlin entered her life, turning her world upside down with those flashing blue eyes and black curly hair of his. However, they had not met on the hill! Oh, no . . . she had met her fate one Sunday night at a dance in the Club Orchid ballroom on the corner of King Street in the city centre. That chance meeting had changed her life completely. In no time at all she had fallen head over heels in love with him. It had been during the war, and when Sean had asked her to marry him she had jumped at the chance; astounded that out of all the girls he could surely have had, he had chosen her, Annie Magee, eight years younger than he.

Had she been a naive young fool to believe that he loved her? If he had truly loved her, would he have been attracted to her sister? Annie squirmed restlessly in the chair as other memories from the past assailed her. What difference did it make? Sean loved her now, surely that was what counted. These past five years he had never given her cause to doubt his love. So why now was she torturing herself by remembering that in the early years of their marriage, her husband had brought her great unhappiness? Annoyed at herself, Annie

2

determinedly pushed all thoughts of that troubled period from her mind. It still cut her to the quick if she allowed herself to dwell on it. She must bear in mind that he loved her *now*, that was all that mattered.

If the truth be told, it was probably because her sister Rosaleen was about to make a flying visit home from Canada, that the past was plaguing Annie; making her restless and uneasy. Rosaleen, her only sister; the sister she had always loved and looked up to, the one who had betrayed her trust. Rosaleen, the mother of Sean's son. Even in the stifling heat, Annie shivered and hugged herself for comfort as uninvited memories came flooding back. Would Rosaleen bring her children home with her? Bring young Liam who was probably the picture of Sean? Oh, surely not! She couldn't be so thoughtless.

In the telegram that had been delivered to her mother early that morning, Rosaleen had said that she and her husband Andrew were coming home for a week with May and Billy Mercer. Billy's mother had died and being an only child he was coming home to attend to the funeral arrangements. May and Rosaleen had been close friends right from the day they had started primary school. At fourteen they had left St Vincent's School and gone to work in the local Falls Flax weaving mill. In their free time they had attended beginners' classes together to learn ballroom dancing and had remained staunch friends ever since, even after Rosaleen's marriage to Joe Smith.

During the war, and in spite of incurring her father's wrath, May had dared to marry a man from the Shankill Road. Not only had Billy Mercer been a Protestant, but a divorced one to boot. The union had caused a real furore as mixed marriages often did in Northern Ireland, and when it seemed about to founder, May and Billy had emigrated to Canada, to restore their faith in one another and to salvage their relationship. It was just after the war when they left, and a few short years later Billy had returned on the sad occasion of his father's death. That was when Rosaleen had first met Billy's cousin, Andrew Mercer. Andrew had accompanied him home to pay his last respects to his uncle and had fallen in love with the beautiful young widowed friend of his cousin's wife.

Did Rosaleen really have to come over? Surely she must

3

realize that Annie would not be overjoyed to see her; but then, Annie was not the only one to be considered. Her mother was over the moon at the idea of seeing her other three grandchildren. Perhaps Rosaleen had no choice. Maybe Andrew had insisted that his wife accompany him back for the funeral.

Annie had yet to meet Andrew Mercer. He had come on the scene at the time that Annie, in despair and unhappiness, had estranged herself from the family circle. A few months before, Sean had bought this house on Serpentine Road and they'd planned to move into it on his next leave from the Merchant Navy. Distraught by the discovery of her sister's betrayal, Annie had needed to get away. The house on Serpentine Road beckoned and she had sought refuge in the big empty place; somewhere far away from the Springfield Road, where she could lick her wounds in private.

All the admiration and respect that Annie had always felt for her elder sister disappeared at a stroke when she discovered that Liam had been fathered by her own husband. The horror of that betrayal almost sent her out of her mind, and if Sean had not been at sea at the time it would surely have brought about the end of their marriage. In her anger and bitterness, she would have shown her husband the door and he would probably have been only too glad of the excuse to run off to Canada with his mistress.

For didn't Annie know in her heart, even though her sister always vehemently denied it, that Rosaleen had loved Sean? And hadn't Annie at that time been making life unbearable for him? Hadn't she been blaming him because she could not conceive? And all the time neither of them had been to blame; it was just Mother Nature taking her time. It was to Rosaleen's credit that she had promised never to tell Sean the truth about Liam; never to put any pressure on him. In the face of Annie's great distress her sister had even made arrangements to emigrate. Shortly afterwards had come the news of her marriage to Andrew Mercer in Canada. What was he like? Did Annie's sister really love him or had she married him on the rebound?

Fortunately, with Sean being at sea at that time, Annie had learnt to live with the pain of her discovery before she had to face him. Oh, she had eventually challenged him about his adultery; had lashed out at him with a tongue sharpened by

4

months of pain and misery. But somehow she had managed to keep silent about Liam; had helped Rosaleen pull the wool over Sean's eyes so far as his son was concerned. In time Annie had let Sean convince her that he loved her; had learnt to trust him again. They were happy together, especially since the arrival of the children. Was all her newfound tranquillity to be ruined now? How would her husband react to Rosaleen's reappearance? From the lack of photographs featuring young Liam sent home by her sister, Annie hazarded a guess that he resembled Sean. Was it not because of his eyes, so like Sean's, that she herself had guessed the truth?

Now Rosaleen was coming home, albeit for a short visit . . . but would she bring her children with her? Their mother was always lamenting the fact that Rosaleen lived so far away and was expecting her daughter to bring the children home to see their grannie. Laura, the daughter from Rosaleen's first marriage to Joe Smith, was now thirteen years old; Liam, supposedly Joe's child but in reality Sean's, would have celebrated his sixth birthday in February; and the youngest, three-year-old Patricia, was born of Andrew and Rosaleen's union.

Deep down in her heart Annie knew that it was wrong to heap all the blame for Liam's conception on her sister, but how would she have been able to cope with it otherwise? How would she have been able to live with Sean if she hadn't piled all the blame on Rosaleen? One thing she was sure of: Sean must never, ever learn the truth. He would never forgive them for deceiving him. How on earth he hadn't twigged, Annie would never know. Of course, at that time the idea that he was capable of fathering a child wouldn't even have entered his head. Thankfully, they now had two daughters, Rachel and Rebecca, on whom he doted. Annie's hand patted her flat stomach. She was convinced that she was once again pregnant. Hopefully, this child would be a boy. Sean came from a family of five, but he was the only son. His parents looked to him to carry on the family name. She must bear him a son. She must!

With a start of surprise, Annie realized that she had been daydreaming a long time. A glance at her watch confirmed this. Quickly she hoisted herself to her feet and, bringing the chair indoors, locked up the back of the house. It was time to get Rebecca ready to go down and collect her sister from school.

Annie's eldest daughter Rachel had only recently started primary school in Greencastle village, and much to Annie's relief had taken to it like a duck to water. She was such a complex child it could easily have gone the other way. Pausing inside the back door Annie exchanged her sandals for a pair of slippers. As she padded along the hall she caught sight of herself as she passed the hall mirror. Slowly she returned to stand in front of it to examine her reflection. Normally she would have been quite pleased with what she saw. A cloud of unruly chestnut curls framed a face lightly bronzed by the sun, and clear green dark-lashed eyes gazed solemnly back at her. Today, though, she grimaced in distaste at her own image and pictured the way Rosaleen had looked the last time she had seen her: thick silver-blonde hair, high cheek-bones and wonderful skin. Rosaleen would not have a broad band of freckles marring the beauty of her nose. Ah, no! Rosaleen had always been lucky. If she fell in cow's dung, she would come up smelling of roses.

With a deep sigh Annie dragged herself away from the disappointing reflection and climbed the stairs to wake her youngest daughter. As she went her eyes took in the beauty of the hall and landing; the last part of the house to be decorated. The dark oak panelling along the lower half of the walls had cost the earth, and pale green and silver striped wallpaper above contrasted well with it. The mirror, large and ornate, had been purchased at a country house sale as had the two gilt-framed pictures of rustic scenes that adorned another wall. A brass-faced grandfather clock with roman numerals stood elegantly in the corner, patiently ticking the time away. It was all very pleasing to the eye. They had managed to capture the elegance and grandeur of a bygone age, thought Annie, sighing contentedly.

A lot had been accomplished in the last five years. After the birth of Rachel, Sean had left the Merchant Navy and had got a job in the television studios in the city centre. They enjoyed a quiet social life with only the odd night out with friends; or sometimes on a Saturday night Thelma Magee would babysit and they would accompany Annie's brother George down to McVeigh's pub for a drink. Otherwise they were content to stay at home with their children. Any available money had been spent on making the house comfortable and Annie was proud of her beautiful home.

Before awakening Rebecca, she entered her own bedroom and opened the wardrobe, brushing a hand along the dresses and skirts hanging there. With a shake of the head she turned away in despair. There was nothing suitable for a night out with Rosaleen. It was a long time since she had indulged herself, but now she must have a new dress and get her hair styled. This morning, when her mother had arrived unexpectedly to show her the telegram, she had warned Annie to arrange for a babysitter as George was planning a family night out.

She just had to find time to go into town to buy a dress. Knowing that her next-door neighbour, kind Minnie Carson, would babysit, Annie decided she would insist on her mother accompanying her on the shopping trip. Thelma too would need a new outfit. They must do Rosaleen proud. No doubt her sister would be dressed to kill. And why not? Hadn't her first husband, Joe Smith, left her comfortably off? And hadn't Andrew Mercer his own small publishing company? Annie's sister wanted for nothing except perhaps . . . Sean? Oh, she must stop torturing herself.

Where would they all stay? A couple of years ago, George, the previously unknown half-brother who had come on the scene just after the war, had bought a house in Serpentine Gardens, just down the road from them. How he had managed to persuade Thelma to move away from the Springfield Road and all her old cronies and share it with him, Annie would never know. But he had and she was indebted to him. Both he and her mother were wonderful company for her; her mother ever ready to look after the children at short notice when Annie had occasion to go into town or to visit the doctor or whatever. And one of them always willing to oblige in the evening if the need arose. Still, compared to her fine house, the one in Serpentine Gardens was small. Her mother had tentatively suggested that perhaps Annie would put up her sister and brother-in-law, saying that if the children were with them, she herself would be delighted to look after them. Thelma had failed to hide her annoyance when Annie quickly declined. Her mother had muttered something about blood

7

being supposed to be thicker than water, and that it was the least Annie could do for her own sister.

She had remained adamant however and her mother plaintively replied that the visitors would probably have to book into a hotel and that would cost them an arm and a leg. Assuring her that Andrew could well afford it, Annie was nevertheless perturbed. What if Sean, when he heard of their arrival, offered to put them up? He was very family-minded and could very well insist that they stay at his house. The very thought of her sister being under the same roof as him, even for a few short days, sent fear coursing through Annie. So much for my faith in Sean's love, she derided herself. But Rosaleen was so beautiful, Annie could not help but feel apprehensive. After all, Sean had been tempted – and fallen – once before.

A gurgle of laughter quickened her step towards the nursery. Rebecca always awoke in such good humour. For a moment Annie smiled indulgently down on her eighteen-month-old daughter. Rebecca grinned back at her, small white milk teeth gleaming in a rosebud mouth. The child stretched up her arms to be lifted and quickly Annie obliged, hugging the small precious bundle close to her breast. Her daughters were as different as chalk and cheese. Rebecca, with her black curly hair and bright blue eyes, was the spit of Sean, bubbly and affectionate by nature. Rachel, on the other hand, was a mixture of both sides of the family. Chestnut-haired like her mother and blue-eyed like her father, she was a quiet, independent and solemn child.

'Come on now, love, let's get you something to eat and then we'll go down and collect your big sister from school,' Annie said, and hoisted the excited child high in the air, delighting in her squeals of joy.

Twenty minutes later, she locked the front door behind her and started on her journey down Serpentine Road. The road was aptly named as it twisted and turned, but it was all downhill and soon Annie reached the Whitewell Road. From there it was another good fifteen minutes to the school but at last she was standing on the Shore Road at the gates to the steep drive. She smiled a greeting to the other mothers gathered there whom she knew by sight. One of them, Mary Moon, a girl of about her own age with whom she had struck up a friendship, joined her and they stood making desultory conversation until the children appeared, stampeding down the hill with whoops of joy.

'How's your Rachel getting on at school?' Mary asked.

'Great! I was surprised. She's such a quiet child, I was quite worried about how she would settle in, but she loves it. Of course she's a very independent little madam. What about your Jenny, has she settled in all right?'

'Well . . . she was great at first, but this morning she cried . . . said she didn't want to go to school. It nearly broke my heart leaving her in tears, so it did.' At this point the worried pucker on Mary's brow disappeared and a huge grin of relief spread over her face. 'Just look at that!' she exclaimed. 'To think that I worried all day about her.'

Following the direction of her gaze, Annie laughed softly. Running down the incline towards them were Rachel and Jenny, hand in hand, clutching their efforts at drawing proudly aloft, faces wreathed in smiles.

'That will teach you a lesson, Mary! Jenny must have been playing up this morning. What did you promise her, eh? Come on now, be honest.' Annie cocked an enquiring eyebrow at her friend.

Shamefaced, Mary admitted, 'Well, I did say that I would buy her some jelly babies on the way home.'

'You'll have to put a stop to that or she'll act up every day,' Annie warned.

'Don't worry, Annie. I realize that now. This will be the last time she'll pull a fast one on me,' Mary vowed as they started off. At the corner of Graymount Road she stopped outside Stewart's Grocery Store. 'Are you doing any shopping in the village today, Annie? I'm going in here then over to Grogan's to pay my papers.'

Usually they accompanied each other around the shops and then walked up Whitewell Road together, as Mary lived not far from Annie in Veryan Gardens. Today Annie decided not to delay. 'No, I'll hurry on, Mary. I'm calling in to see me mam. Our Rosaleen is making a short visit home from Canada and I want to find out just when she's arriving. Our George is planning a family get-together so I'll need to get into town for a new dress.'

'Oh, how lovely. How long has your sister been away?'

'Let me think, now.' Annie pondered for a moment; not even to herself would she admit that she knew almost to the hour just how long Rosaleen had been away. 'It must be all of five years.'

'I'm sure you'll be pleased as Punch to see her again after all that time. If you need a babysitter, feel free to give me a shout,' Mary offered.

Touched at this spontaneous gesture, Annie answered, 'That's very kind of you.'

'Ah, away with ye! I'll be only too happy to oblige. Now, remember . . . any time.'

'Thanks, Mary.' Annie glanced up at the darkening sky. 'I hope that storm doesn't break before we get home or we'll be soaked climbing that hill. I'll rush on. So long for now, Mary, hope you get home dry.'

Thelma Magee was sweeping her front path when thunder heralded the beginning of the storm, turning her startled gaze to the hill which seemed to rumble deep in its bowels; low at first then rising to a deafening crescendo. The sky was now so overcast it was almost purple and as large spots of rain splattered the path and plastered the thin cotton of her dress to her shoulders, she hastened inside with bowed head. Just as she was about to close the door against the elements, Annie's voice reached her.

'Hey, Mam . . . keep the door open.'

'Good God, Annie, I didn't see you there, so I didn't. Come on in, love.' Sweeping Rachel up in her arms, Thelma backed into the living room and watched her daughter manoeuvre the push-chair into the small hall just as the heavens opened.

'You just made it in time!' she exclaimed, and hurried to shut the front door.

For some moments mother and daughter stood side by side at the big bay window watching the deluge. Visibility was practically nil as the rain bounced off the road and gurgled its way towards drains that were fast becoming waterlogged. Thelma nodded approvingly. 'The ground needs that badly,' she said with a pleased smile. 'The plants are dying for want of a good drink. But it won't last long, you mark my words. It's far too heavy. Meanwhile I'll make us a cup of tea. Take off your cardigans, they must be damp.'

Annie removed the children's cardigans and then her own and spread them over the back of the settee. Once the two youngsters were engrossed in some toys, kept at their grannie's for that purpose, she followed her mother into the small kitchen. 'When exactly is Rosaleen due home, Mam?'

'You know as much about it as me, Annie. But it will have to be soon. They can't delay a burial long in this warm weather.'

'If I get Minnie Carson to mind Rebecca tomorrow morning, will you come into town with me, Mam?'

Thelma looked at her daughter as if she thought her daft. 'What do you want me with you for?' she exclaimed. 'You've no need to ask Minnie, I'll take care of Rebecca for you.'

'Look, Mam ... I'm going into town because I must get a new dress if we're going out with Rosaleen. And, if you don't mind my saying so ...' Annie appraised her mother's figure in its washed-out cotton dress '... you could do with something new yourself. After all, we'll want to look our best, won't we?'

'Catch yourself on, girl! I've still got that suit I wore for your wedding. That will be good enough for me. Why, I've only worn it a few times.'

'Mam, that suit is ancient!' Annie cried in exasperation. 'Besides—' her eye ran critically over Thelma's thickening figure— 'I hope you won't be offended ... when was the last time you tried it on? I bet it won't fit you any more.'

With a downward glance, Thelma sighed and reluctantly agreed with her daughter. 'You're right, of course. OK! What time are you going into town?'

'If you walk down with me in the morning, we can catch the bus at the bottom of Gray's Lane after we leave Rachel at school. There's a sale on at the Co-op. It's been advertised in the newspapers. Maybe we'll be lucky enough to get something there. What do you think?'

'Good idea. If we can get something in the Co-op we'll get our dividend too. I'll be ready about half-eight. Now ... pour that tea before it gets cold and I'll butter these scones.'

11

Sean Devlin was whistling as he left the car in the drive. He paused to admire the rockery, rising from the neat hedge to the path along the front of the house. He had laboriously built it during their early years here and made a good job of it. When it wasn't a riot of summer colour, green and grey foliage still caught the eye and except for infrequent weeding it required very little attention.

He had been working overtime a lot lately in an effort to earn enough extra money to build a garage, the next item on their agenda. A lean-to garage built between the side of the house and the boundary hedge would make the back garden completely safe for the children to play in, whether Annie was with them or not. And since money didn't grow on trees, it would have to be earned. Still, it was good to be home early for a change. He would be able to help sort out the back garden instead of leaving it all to Annie. Great though it was to have about seventy feet of space to run about in, it was hard work keeping it in some kind of order. He paused for a moment to examine his domain. The flower beds, a mass of vivid colour, refreshed by the recent downpour, were a sight to behold. However, the grass needed mowing and the borders could do with a bit of weeding. There was no sign of his daughters.

His wife was at the sink and swung round with a start when he entered the kitchen.

'This is a surprise,' she cried in delight, and willingly entered his arms, raising her face for his kiss. The kiss lengthened. At last Annie reluctantly pushed him away.

'The children will be here any minute now,' she warned. 'Minnie took them next door for some ice cream.'

Pulling her back into his arms, Sean teased, 'They aren't here yet, so how's about you and me slipping upstairs, mmm? We don't often get a chance like this.'

Annie willingly pressed close to him but demurred. 'I don't think that would be a very good idea, Sean.'

Once more their lips met and they swayed together for long moments. This time it was he who gently pushed Annie away. 'If we can't go upstairs, I'll have to get out of this kitchen. I'll go up and change into some old clothes and then do a bit of gardening. That should please you,' he jested, a twinkle in his eye.

'I'd be forever grateful for any help out there! What would you like to eat, love?'

Annie's voice followed him into the hall. Putting his head around the door again, he said, 'You ... but if I can't have that, I'll settle for something not too heavy. It's so hot. This weather puts me right off my grub.'

'How does a nice chicken salad grab you? It can be ready in no time.'

'Our own scallions and lettuce?' He was very proud of the vegetable plot at the foot of the garden. At her nod of the head, he smiled. 'That will be smashing.'

Whilst Sean changed into old trousers and shirt, Annie carried a small table outdoors and placed it in the shade of the apple tree. The storm had raged fiercely for an hour, with thunder crashing and lightning flashing electric blue zig-zags across the darkened sky. Afterwards the skies cleared and the sun blazed down, drying all before it; undoing all the good her mother had prophesied. Quickly, Annie tossed a salad and set out the chicken, pickles, beetroot and chutney. Hughes' baps, a large pitcher of iced squash for the children and a pot of tea for her and Sean completed the meal.

He smacked his lips in anticipation when he saw the spread. 'That looks very tasty. Shall I fetch the kids?' he inquired as he joined her at the table.

'That's a good idea. When Minnie gets them in there she hates to part with them. There's plenty here so you can invite her in for a bite, if you like?'

'You know what Minnie's like, Annie. Afraid of intruding. I bet you she won't come, but nevertheless, I'll ask her.'

To their great surprise their neighbour agreed to join them. 'Are you sure you have enough to go round us all, Annie? Sean insisted that I come in,' she asked, a worried tone to her voice, as she followed the two children through the gap in the hedge that served as a shortcut between the two houses. Sean had offered to mend the gap ages ago but Minnie would not hear of it, protesting that the children were welcome to wander on to her property any time they liked and sure, her garden was secure and they could come to no harm there.

With a wave towards the table, Sean exclaimed, 'Look for yourself, Minnie! There's enough there to feed an army.'

'We are very glad of your company,' Annie assured her with a fond smile. 'Grab a plate and help yourself.'

The meal was eaten in companionable silence, with just the odd teasing remark thrown at the women by Sean – remarks that quickly rebounded on him and soon had him laughingly calling a truce. Once he had eaten his fill he excused himself and headed for the garden shed, followed by Rachel and more slowly by Rebecca. Soon he was taking advantage of the rain-softened earth to weed the flower beds, the two children being more of a hindrance than a help to him. Rebecca, following her father's example, was pulling up the flowers instead of weeds and could not understand why he was scolding her. The women watched them fondly for some time then rose to clear the table and retire to the kitchen.

Silence reigned as Annie washed and Minnie dried the dishes. It was their guest who broke it. 'Is anything wrong, Annie?' she asked tentatively, and hastened to add, 'Tell me to mind my own business if I'm being too nosy.'

Annie turned to her with an apologetic smile. 'Forgive me, Minnie. I'm so used to doing the washing up alone, I got carried away with my thoughts as usual. Actually, I meant to ask a favour of you. Could you possibly look after Rebecca tomorrow morning? That is, if you've nothing planned. I know it's short notice.'

'Well now . . . let me think.' Minnie pretended to ponder. 'Yes, I can take her tomorrow. None of my fancy men come on a Thursday,' she jested.

Annie smiled at her wit and said, 'That's a relief. I'd hate to come between you and one of your men.' After another short pause, she asked, 'Do you remember my sister Rosaleen? You met her once, didn't you?'

Annie was too preoccupied to notice Minnie's gaze sharpen. She remembered Annie's sister only too well, and what she remembered of her, she did not like. However, she was prejudiced; she was very fond of Annie, and her dislike of Rosaleen was based on a conversation overheard one day when the sisters had been sitting in the garden, unaware of her next door. 'I didn't actually meet her,' she replied. 'But I remember seeing her in your garden once.'

'You'll remember me telling you that she and her two

14

children emigrated to Canada, and about her getting married again out there?'

When Minnie nodded, Annie continued, 'She's coming home on a short visit. Billy Mercer – he's the husband of her best friend, May – well, his mother has died so he and his wife are coming over to see to the funeral arrangements. Rosaleen and her husband Andrew are coming over with them for a bit of a break. I don't know when the funeral will be but our George is planning a night out after it and I really need a new dress.'

'Are they bringing the children with them?'

'I don't know, Minnie. Mam showed me the telegram but it gave only the barest details.'

'Will they be staying here with you?'

'No!' Annie was unaware how curt she sounded but Minnie was quick to notice.

'Just you bring Rebecca in to me in the morning,' she said kindly. 'I'll be glad to have her, you know that.'

Annie smiled at her friend. 'I know. I'm very lucky to have a neighbour like you, Minnie.'

Drying the last of the cutlery, Minnie closed the drawer and hung the drying cloth on a hook. 'I'd better go now . . . but remember, I'm just next door if ever you need me.'

'I know that, Minnie.' Annie put an arm around the smaller woman's shoulders and hugged her close. 'And it's a great source of comfort to me, to know that.'

The children were long in bed and a red sky threw the hill into stark relief, forecasting good weather for the next day, before Sean and Annie at last put away the gardening tools. They sat outside, cool drinks to hand, to watch as dusk approached. Annie was about to broach the subject of Rosaleen's intended visit when the peace and harmony was broken by the shrill ringing of the telephone. With a sigh of annoyance, Sean reluctantly rose to answer it as most calls were for him. The phone was in the hall but his voice carried out to Annie on the still air. Her heart sank when she realized it was her sister he was talking to. Why had she delayed telling him that Rosaleen was coming home? Had fear held her back? No, not really. They so rarely got an evening to themselves, she had wanted to enjoy the peaceful companionship. She had not wanted tension,

15

imagined or otherwise, to break the tranquillity that surrounded them. But now what would Sean think?

'Hello, Rosaleen. This is a surprise!'

There was a few seconds' silence and then Sean spoke again. 'No, she didn't tell me, Rosaleen. Perhaps it slipped her mind. Here . . . I'll give her a shout. See you soon, by the sound of it.'

Annie avoided his eye as she took the receiver from him and raised it to her ear. 'Hello, Rosaleen. Yes, Mam got your wire this morning. Sean was late home from work and I haven't had the chance to tell him yet,' she lied. 'What? What did you say? You'll be home tomorrow afternoon? Does George know? Is he picking you up at the airport? Oh, I see . . . he doesn't know yet. You want me to go down and ask him to pick you up? Let me get a pen and write down your flight number so he can phone and check that it's arriving on time.'

Annie rummaged in the drawer of the hallstand and at last unearthed a pen. 'Sorry about that, Rosaleen. Every pen I leave handy soon disappears. There . . . I'm ready. Fire away! Right, mmm. I've got all that. I'm looking forward to seeing you too.' Once again she lied in a bright voice. 'Are the children coming over with you?' Relief flooded through her when her sister told her that only her eldest daughter would be accompanying them. 'I'll look forward to seeing Laura. She must be quite a young lady by now. Goodbye for now, Rosaleen. See you soon. 'Bye.'

After replacing the phone in its cradle, Annie slowly made her way outside again. Sean was gazing down into his drink but looked up as she approached. Bravely, she met the disapproving look in his eyes and cried defensively, 'I didn't get a chance to tell you, Sean. They'll only be here about a week. Billy's mother has died and he's coming over to arrange everything.' Her husband didn't speak; just kept that accusing look fixed on his face. Annie felt fear pluck at her heart. Why was he so annoyed? Did he still care for Rosaleen? Oh, she couldn't bear this; he had no right to look at her like that. Didn't he realize she needed reassurance, not condemnation? Was all the old uncertainty about to rear up again? Were the old wounds to be reopened? Stifling a groan, she turned and entered the house, talking the stairs in a rush.

Sean sat for some minutes deep in thought. He was worried.

16

Annie must think that he was still attracted to Rosaleen, otherwise she would have been excited by the news she was going to see her sister again after so many years. Why was his wife acting like this? Had he not proved over and over how much she and the kids meant to him? I wish to God Rosaleen had stayed in Canada, he lamented inwardly. Everything was going so well. We've been so happy. Still . . . apparently she was only coming on a short visit. He would be working most of the time and would see very little of her. So why was Annie acting like this?

Slowly he rose to his feet and followed his wife. True to form, he found her dry-eyed and straight-backed, standing at their bedroom window, gazing out over the lough. Annie always met things face on. That was why he was surprised that she had fled from the garden so abruptly. Now, having regained her composure, she turned and looked at him.

'What's all this about, Annie?' he asked softly. 'Don't you trust me?'

'Oh, I do, I do!' she cried vehemently. 'Indeed I do.' She stifled the accusation hovering on her lips. No use raking up the past. No use reminding him that she had trusted him before and he had let her down.

He laughed lightly and replied, 'Methinks the lady doth protest too much. Eh, Annie?'

Slowly he approached. Taking her unresisting figure in his arms, he kissed her. At once she erupted into fiery passion, twining her arms tightly around his neck and kissing him with an abandon that made him draw back and gaze at her in surprise.

'Do you love me, Sean?' she whispered, voice shaking with emotion.

'Annie, have I not proved it over and over again?' he cried in frustration. 'Have I ever so much as looked at another woman? Tell me now . . . have I?'

'It's not *other* women I fear. It's our Rosaleen . . .' Her voice trailed off and she muttered, 'You know what I mean. I hate her for what she did! She almost ruined our marriage. I'm so afraid that everything we've built up together is about to crumble.'

'Listen, Annie, believe me, you have nothing to fear. And

17

don't put all the blame on *her*. Remember, it takes two. But, honestly, she never really cared for me. It was just one of those reckless flings that happen on the spur of the moment.'

He pushed guilt to the back of his mind as he remembered that it had happened twice, and would have happened again and again if he'd had his way. Annie must never learn of that other time! She would never believe that about seven years had elapsed between each encounter, and who could blame her? She would be sure to think they'd been having an affair. And to be truthful he had tried to talk Rosaleen out of marrying Joe Smith. Had tried to persuade her to go away with him. But that was all so long ago. He continued in haste, 'Rosaleen regretted it immediately. She never had any deep feelings for me, so you have nothing to worry about on that score.' Hand under her chin, he tilted her face and gazed into her tear-filled eyes. 'Annie, only you can spoil what we have. I love you.'

Inwardly she cried, Oh, but Rosaleen did care for you! She cared all right. That's why I'm so frightened. Please, Sean, she begged silently, tell me what I really want to hear. Tell me that *she* never meant anything to you.

He pressed her close, murmuring endearments, trying to find words to reassure her. But the words she longed to hear eluded him and fear continued to gnaw at her. If she asked him outright he would, of course, tell her what she wanted to hear, but she would still doubt him. She shouldn't have to put words into his mouth!

Disappointment brought tears back to her eyes. Pushing herself away from him, she headed for the door. 'I must go down and tell George the plane is arriving at Aldergrove at about one tomorrow afternoon. Rosaleen wants him to pick her up there. I might be a bit late getting back. Mam will be full of plans for her coming home and I might find it difficult to get away. Don't wait up for me, Sean.'

His shoulders slumped in despair as, without a further glance, she left the room. He was aware that he had not managed to allay her fears, but what more could he do? He remained at the bedroom window and watched as Annie left the house and strode off down the road. Once she reached the bend and was out of sight, he sank slowly down on the edge of the bed, tense and uneasy.

It was a long time since he had given any thought to Rosaleen Magee. Now he was remembering as if it was only yesterday the first time he had set eyes on her: pale blonde hair lifting in the breeze, green eyes sparkling and white teeth gleaming. Even in her old work clothes, coming through the mill gates, she was the most beautiful girl he had ever set eyes on and he had been completely bowled over. He had made it his business to get to know her, only to find that she was on the verge of marrying Joe Smith. After a passionate encounter with her up at the Springfield Road dam he was aware that she was sexually attracted to him and had done all in his power to make her change her mind. He had failed, hampered as he was by the fact that he was in the Merchant Navy at the time and had to go to sea.

Although Annie was only seventeen, on his next leave he had deliberately cultivated her acquaintance in order to find out if Rosaleen still had the power to thrill him. To his dismay he discovered when he next saw her, even though she was big with her first child, that he did still desire her with a yearning that threatened to tear him apart.

But life goes on, and Annie was sweet and kind and in love with him. When Britain declared war on Germany, Sean asked her to marry him; he wanted to have someone to come home to, perhaps a son to carry on the family name should he fail to return. Then the war ended and he was devastated to learn that Joe Smith had died and Rosaleen was a free woman. Too late for him! Far too late! He was tied to her sister and Rosaleen would not hear of his leaving Annie, even though she had turned into a bitter nagging woman who had convinced him that he was sterile. After another brief passionate encounter, Rosaleen once again sent him packing.

However, long before she had emigrated Sean had discovered how much he really loved Annie. He had been devastated by the very thought that he might have lost her. To this day he had never found out how she became aware of his association with her sister but somehow he'd managed to convince her that he loved her and her alone. They had built a good life together since and now he could not imagine life without her and his two lovely wee daughters. While Rosaleen was here, he would just have to make sure that he gave his wife no cause for complaint. That shouldn't be too hard to do. Soon after she arrived in Canada, Rosaleen had married again. The man was some years older than herself and had his own business apparently. Rosaleen had probably long since forgotten the passion that used to flow between herself and Sean at the slightest provocation. On her side it had been all physical. He knew she had never loved him. Hadn't she sent him away in despair? And she had been right to do so! Hadn't he changed now? Didn't he now love his wife above all others? So what was there to worry about?

With a sigh Sean rose to his feet. After looking in on his daughters, he slowly descended the stairs. He would wait up for Annie, ensure that she knew just how much he loved her.

Once out of sight of the house Annie's steps faltered. She needed time to think before facing her mother and George. The horror of that night when she had discovered that Liam was Sean's son was recurring over and over in her mind, tormenting her. Her sister had denied it! Had tried to lie her way out of it; had pretended that she thought Annie was daft. However in the face of the evidence the truth could not be denied for long, and at last, in defeat, Rosaleen had admitted that she had committed adultery with Sean; had confessed that after Joe's funeral he had comforted her and things had got out of hand.

Devastated, Annie had fled to the Serpentine Road. God, but she would not have believed it could still hurt so much. All these years she had managed to keep at bay thoughts of Sean and her sister together; naked bodies entwined in a passionate embrace. Now the image was vividly seared across her mind. To think that Sean . . . her husband . . . had done *that*, and with her *sister*. She forced her mind back from the pain-filled mist and swallowed a sob. Dashing a hand across her eyes to stem the flow of tears, she chastised herself: Don't you start carrying on, girl! Remember, Sean loves you and the kids. The past is over and done with. He won't do anything to risk hurting you again. Still, she dreaded the thought of the week ahead.

Her mother lived near the top end of Serpentine Gardens

where it met the Serpentine Road and with averted head Annie hurried past. She intended going on down the road and cutting through Vandyck Gardens to approach her mother's street from the Whitewell Road end; to give herself some respite before facing Thelma and George. She needed time to bring her emotions under control. Her luck was out. As she was passing the end of the street she saw George in the front garden and even though it was now quite dark he recognized her.

He chided her. 'Hey there, Annie, are you not going to speak to me?'

With a wry smile she turned into the street. 'Actually, it's you I'm coming to see,' she confessed. Once more lies tumbled easily from her lips as she offered her excuse for passing by. 'I was so lost in thought I completely forgot where I was going. It's a good thing you saw me or God knows where I'd have ended up. Probably in the lough!'

'Oh, and what's so important it brings you out at this time of night?' George's eyes were scanning her face; her forced gaiety had not escaped his notice. With an effort Annie kept her smile fixed in place, but for a moment was afraid to risk speaking. After a pause, during which she dithered on the footpath, he said, 'Are you not going to come in?' Reaching for the gate, he swung it open and stood aside for her to enter.

Not really wanting to go inside where she would be exposed to bright lights, Annie broke her silence and was surprised to find that her voice was clear and steady. 'It's late. I won't bother coming in. I've just come down with a message from our Rosaleen. That's why I'm out so late. It's about time you got a phone installed, George,' she chided him gently.

He was not to be deterred. 'Come in for a few minutes at least,' he insisted. Reluctantly, Anne followed him inside. In the the living room George eyed her closely and then gently pushed her down on to the settee. 'Sit down and relax. Your mother has gone to bed. She has been scrubbing and polishing all day and she's exhausted. You'd think that Rosaleen was going to inspect the shelves and under the beds with white gloves. Not that it would make any difference! As you well know, your mother doesn't give the dust time to settle. I'll pour you a wee brandy.' At Annie's wide-eyed surprise he laughed

21

softly. 'It's been left in for Rosaleen's benefit, and the chances are she won't even be staying here. *You* look like you could do with one.'

While he was pouring the drinks Annie watched him and warned herself not to give in to the temptation to cry on George's shoulder. Many a time she had confided in him, knowing that whatever she told him would go no further. She could tell him things that she could not disclose to her mother or anyone else. But never about Sean! No, where her husband was concerned everything was kept strictly private.

Her brother was so kind and understanding it would be easy to talk it over with him, but the fewer people who knew the truth about this matter the better. Besides, she felt belittled by the sin committed against her, as if it had been her fault that Sean had strayed. And she did not want to drop in her brother's estimation.

Although George had arrived into their lives out of the blue about eight years ago, Annie felt that she had known him all her life. Her father had been one of the casualties during the blitz on Belfast in 1941. When the war ended George had arrived on Rosaleen's doorstep with a letter written by her father, claiming that he was their half-brother. For a while Rosaleen had not said a word to anyone about who he was, not wanting to bring more heartache to her mother. Of course everybody, Annie included, had thought the worst. They had assumed that he was Rosaleen's fancy man, and as Joe had died just a few weeks beforehand, the gossip had caused her great pain. Annie realized how hard a time it must have been for her sister. Rosaleen had confided in Sean and, under pressure from him, had agreed at last to introduce George to their mother.

Annie remembered the sense of outrage she had felt when Rosaleen had arrived in Colinward Street with her 'fancy man' as she had thought him. To their astonishment Thelma had guessed who he was and had welcomed him with open arms, proclaiming to one and all that he was her stepson. It appeared that George's mother had died in childbirth but Thelma had refused to consider adopting him when he was a baby, so he had been reared by his grandparents. She had been glad of the chance to make up for all the hurt she had unwittingly caused

22

by her refusal to adopt her husband's illegitimate son. His mother had been an only child, born late in life to her parents. With his grandparents now dead and no close relations, George eventually moved into the house in Colinward Street.

He and Annie had become close friends, she just six months older than him. George was the result of a one-night stand her father had been weak enough to succumb to when her mother was carrying her. His arrival into their lives after the war had proved to be a godsend.

Pushing the glass of brandy into her hand, he sat in the armchair facing her. Leaning forward, arms on knees, he asked kindly, 'Is anything wrong, Annie? You look as if you've seen a ghost.'

'No, there's nothing wrong. I'm just a bit tired. Sean was home early today and we've been working in the garden all evening.' She thrust the piece of paper on which she had jotted down Rosaleen's flight number towards him. 'Here . . . as I said, Rosaleen phoned. She wants you to pick her up at the airport tomorrow. Check before you go and make sure the plane is arriving on time. You won't want to be hanging about up there.'

George took the paper and scanned it. 'I'll phone from work in the morning. It will be nice to see her again. Is she bringing the children with her?'

'Only Laura. She's thirteen now and judging by her photographs, she's the picture of Rosaleen. As you probably already know.'

'Your mother tells me you've managed to get her to buy some new clothes for the big occasion.'

'You mean I've managed to get her to go into town with me tomorrow. Whether or not I can actually persuade her to buy anything is another matter entirely. But really . . . we must look presentable if we're going out with Rosaleen. I'm sure she will be dressed to kill.'

'You always look presentable, Annie. You needn't worry about that. Why, you would look good in rags.'

She laughed aloud at these words of praise. 'Ah, George. You can always make me laugh. Me look good beside our Rosaleen? You must be forgetting just how beautiful she is.'

'No, I remember her vividly, and you could hold your own

23

against her any day. It's the truth, Annie, and don't you ever forget it. No one . . . especially a man . . . would notice what you wore.' A smile curved his mouth as he endeavoured to make her laugh. 'Although, mind you, the less the better.'

'George, stop it! You're embarrassing me. It's just as well you're my brother or I might get the impression that you fancy me.'

A wry smile twisted his lips. 'Half-brother, Annie,' he reminded her gently. 'But still, it would never do! Think of the scandal that would cause,' he teased, and was glad to see the gloom lift from her countenance. Deftly he changed the subject, asking after the children and Sean. By the time Annie had finished her drink, she was relaxed and composed.

'Will you have another one?' he asked, rising to his feet and reaching for her glass.

'Good Lord, no. Are you trying to get me drunk, George Magee? There was more brandy than lemonade in that glass. Why, I'll be crawling up that road on my hands and knees if I have another one.'

'I'll walk you home, Annie. I'll be glad to stretch my legs.'

'No, George, there's no need for you to come out. It's late and you have to get up for work in the morning.'

'I really do want to stretch my legs, Annie. I'll take a dander along the Antrim Road before I turn in. It will help me sleep. So come on . . . no more arguments.'

They travelled the short distance up the road in companionable silence. When they arrived at the gate she turned to him. 'Thanks, George. I don't know why, but you always have a soothing effect on me.' Impulsively she reached up and kissed him lightly on the lips. She was startled and embarrassed when he moved abruptly away from her. 'I really am glad you came into our lives,' she finished lamely.

'I'm just glad you all accepted me.' His voice was warm and normal and inwardly she chided herself for thinking she had somehow offended him. 'I know it wasn't easy for your mother to admit that Father had sinned against her,' he added.

'I still find it hard to believe me da, God rest his soul, would have an affair.' Annie's voice was sad. This was the first time that George's parentage had ever been mentioned between them.

24

'Annie . . . believe me when I tell you it was a one-night stand. Dad told me so, and I had no reason to doubt him. He was a wonderful man, you know that. He would never have deliberately hurt Thelma. He was drunk the night it happened and my mother was weak and willing. Not that I blame her, mind! From all accounts she must have been very lonely.'

'I suppose it's because I found it hard to conceive for so long that I can't take it in that once is enough.'

'Well, I believed Dad. What about those poor women who are raped and conceive? Eh, Annie?'

He watched her turn this idea over in her mind and was glad when at last she admitted, 'You're right as always, George. I never thought of that. Good night. Thanks for seeing me home.'

He waited until Annie entered the driveway and then secured the gate. With a final farewell he headed on up the Serpentine Road.

As she let herself into the kitchen Annie pondered on his words. Both Sean and Rosaleen had told her that intimacy had occurred only once between them. Because Rosaleen had conceived, Annie had never really believed them. However, if George were the result of a one-night stand . . . why not Liam, eh? Why not him too? She was glad now that she had gone down with Rosaleen's message, feeling more relaxed and at peace with herself.

As she hung her jacket at the foot of the stairs, Sean's voice hailed her. 'Annie? I'm in here, love.'

Surprised that he was still downstairs, she pushed open the door and entered the living room.

'Come here, I've a drink poured for you.'

Her husband was sitting on the settee and patted the place beside him. With a contented sigh Annie sat down and relaxed against him. She laughed softly. 'The two men in my life seem to be intent on getting me drunk tonight. George just insisted on my having a brandy. It was a big one too. I feel quite tipsy.'

'Well, I'm afraid we don't run to brandy. Will you settle for the remains of the Bristol Cream?' Sean's arms gathered her close. 'I have my reasons for offering you something stronger. I have designs on your body. Do you mind, love?' He opened her blouse and his lips trailed her throat and the hollow between her breasts. 'I'm determined to show you once and for all just how much I love you.'

Eagerly Annie pressed closer still. 'Not in the slightest.' A happy laugh rose in her throat as she added, 'And you don't need any sherry. I'm all yours.' All else was forgotten as he claimed her lips.

The trip into town next day was a success. Bearing in mind that she might be pregnant, Annie settled for a loose flowing dress. Made from georgette over a taffeta underskirt, it was a hazy mixture of pastel colours with a narrow velvet band that tied below the bust. To her surprise, her mother, without any undue prompting from Annie, splashed out and bought a light-weight two-piece suit. It was powder blue and she chose a snowy white blouse to wear under it. All were purchased in the Co-op store on York Street and they were out again in less than an hour, Thelma happy to have received the dividend on their purchases.

Annie's next port of call was to her hairdresser, also in York Street, to make an appointment to have her hair cut and styled. To her great joy, due to a cancellation they were able to take her right away. Thelma, settling down with a magazine, graciously agreed to wait for her.

Annie was anxious as she watched the scissors snip away at her curls, saw her long tresses fall to the floor. She had decided to take the plunge and had placed herself at the mercy of the young hairdresser. She was pleased with the result when she examined her image in the mirror almost an hour later. Her thick hair was now short and sleek. Shaped close to her head and neck, it shone like burnished chestnut, throwing into relief the delicate curves of her cheek-bones and lending mysterious depths to the green of her eyes.

'You have done me proud, Rita. I actually look quite presentable for a change, so I do,' she complimented the young girl.

A blush rose in Rita's cheeks. 'Hah! I can only enhance what's already there. I've longed to go to town on your hair for ages now, but was afraid to suggest you part with your long tresses,' she confessed. 'I knew you would suit it short. You look absolutely stunning.'

26

'Thanks, Rita. I'll ask for your advice in future.' Annie showed her appreciation with a generous tip, bringing a delighted smile to the girl's face.

Apprehensively Annie approached her mother. Would she like this changed appearance? She need not have worried. Thelma's warm words of approval were a joy to her ears and a rosy glow enveloped her as they left the shop and headed for the bus stop.

When Sean arrived home from work at tea-time she could see that he too was impressed by her new image. During the meal he kept peering at her intently and when she tentatively questioned him, admitted that it was like looking at a new, younger image of his wife. Annie fervently hoped he would still think so when Rosaleen arrived back on the scene.

The storm had cleared the air and Thursday dawned warm and sunny. George had asked for the afternoon off and, leaving his office, headed for Aldergrove to pick up Rosaleen and her friends. As he drove along the country roads his thoughts returned to the last time he had travelled along this same route. It must have been about five years ago. Then he had actually been dropping off Rosaleen's friends at the airport on their return journey to Canada. That occasion had been a sad one also. Billy Mercer's father had died, and Billy and May had been accompanied home by Andrew Mercer who had come to offer his condolences to his aunt. It had been obvious to George that the man had been smitten with Rosaleen during his stay, and he was pleased when the romance apparently blossomed. Rosaleen was vulnerable; needed a man to look after her. A short time later Andrew had returned to take her back with him to start a new life in Canada.

There had been some kind of disagreement between his sisters shortly before Rosaleen had emigrated. George had never managed to get to the bottom of it. Now, faced with Annie's obvious unrest at the idea of Rosaleen's return, he was inclined to think that perhaps she had left Belfast because of some irrevocable dispute between the two of them. Could that possibly be true? Could it have been that serious?

He was still mulling over past events when the airport loomed near, bringing him back to reality. Pushing all thoughts of the past from his mind, he parked the car and made his way to the passenger terminal. Assured that the plane would be in on time, he ascended the stairs and took a seat in the lounge near a window to watch for its arrival. When it was announced over the intercom that the Canadian flight was approaching he rose and moved to stand by the window. The plane, easily recognizable by the red maple leaf on its tail fin, circled around like some huge bird before making its final approach. It negotiated the length of the runway and eventually came smoothly to a halt. There was a lot of activity on the ground around it before a portable stairway was driven into position against the open door. After another short wait the passengers started to disembark.

The plane was some distance away. George's eyes were strained intently on the door. He was not sure at first if he would recognize Rosaleen from this distance but he was mistaken. He knew her at once! She stood out from the others; her bright hair caught the sunlight and called attention to her. Once he recognized Rosaleen he was able to identify the rest of them. The young blonde in front of Rosaleen must be her daughter, Laura, and the dark-haired man preceding them was of Andrew's build. He assumed that May and Billy came next, but they were separated by a young lad. Could he be their son? This caused George some dismay. If there were six of them how would they all fit into his car? It would be risky enough carrying one extra passenger, but two? George was a careful driver and did not take kindly to overloading his car. And what about their luggage? There was sure to be a lot and the boot of his car would not afford much room.

A frown on his brow, he slowly made his way downstairs to the waiting room. He knew it would take them some time passing through customs and sat down to wait. Eventually the first of the passengers filtered into the waiting room, pushing trolleys laden with baggage. At last Rosaleen appeared and paused in the doorway, eyes eagerly scanning the waiting crowd. Then, with a whoop of joy, she was in George's arms and holding him close.

'Oh, it's great to be back, so it is, George!' She stepped back from him and gazed up into his face through a mist of tears. 'How are you?'

'I'm fine . . . never better. And you look wonderful.' His eyes took in the cloud of silvery blonde hair, the bright green dark-lashed eyes and pale cameo face. 'Wonderful!' he repeated, and glanced kindly at the tall thin young girl hovering quietly nearby. 'This must be young Laura.'

She blushed and nodded shyly. Full of pride Rosaleen announced, 'Yes, this is my daughter. Isn't she lovely? It's great to be here, so it is. I'm so glad to be home.'

When Rosaleen relinquished her hold on him Andrew stepped forward and gripped George's hand in greeting. 'It's good of you to meet us, George. I'm obliged.' He observed his brother-in-law's anxious look as Billy joined them with the young lad who was obviously his eldest son Ian. George had guessed right. Andrew was perceptive enough to gauge what was worrying his brother-in-law. 'One of Billy's nephews is picking them up,' he assured him, and laughed aloud at the relief on George's face.

'I was wondering how on earth I was going to fit you all into my car,' he admitted with a wry smile. Indicating the trolleys stacked with luggage, he added, 'And there's no way that lot would have fitted into my boot.' He stretched his arm in Billy's direction. 'Sorry to hear about your mother, Billy.'

He gripped the proffered hand and sadly nodded his head. 'It comes to us all. It's the only thing we can be sure of these days but she had a good innings.' He nodded at his son. 'Ian, this is George . . . George, meet my son.' A smile crossed his face as May hurried towards them. 'I think you already know my wife.'

May grinned at him. 'Anything strange or startling happen lately, George?'

'Afraid not, May. We live very quiet lives over here.'

'Huh! You probably just don't notice what's going on under your nose.'

With a laugh George agreed with her. 'You could be right. Aye, you could well be right at that.'

Billy waved a hand in greeting to someone behind George. 'Hello there, Arthur. Glad you could make it. Folks . . . this is Arthur Boyles, my nephew and our lift.'

All the introductions over, George lifted two of the cases Andrew had removed from the trolley and led the way across

29

to the car park. Soon the luggage was loaded into the boot and they were all settled in the car. Andrew sat in front with George. As he nosed the car out of the car park and headed back in the direction of Belfast, George glanced over his shoulder at Rosaleen. 'To our house?' Sensing that she was about to demur, he added quickly, 'Your mother is expecting you there.'

'All right, but we have booked into a hotel so we won't be staying too long.'

George failed to keep his voice neutral as he chastized her. 'You should have let Thelma know your intentions, Rosaleen. She's been in a right state. You'd think the Pope was coming to visit, instead of her daughter.'

It was Andrew who answered him. 'We felt it would be wrong to impose on you at such short notice, George. But you're right, we should have made our intentions clear. Sorry about that. If you would just drop us off at the hotel we'll freshen up and catch a nap before meeting Thelma. Perhaps she will cook us an Ulster fry? If it's not too much trouble, that is. It's so long since I've had one I've almost forgotten what it tastes like.'

Rosaleen flashed her husband a grateful look. He was such a fine man! He would never make her mother feel unhappy. She knew the real reason why he did not want to stay with her mother and George in Greencastle. He did not want her to be too close to her old flame, Sean Devlin. Surely he knew he need not worry? That was all in the past. Why, it was long and many a day since she had last given Sean a single thought. Andrew was her husband; he was devoted to her and she would never do anything to offend him. She was glad that he knew all about her past and still loved her in spite of it all.

She had always worried about her sister finding out. Eventually Annie had guessed and in spite of all Rosaleen's protestations had not believed that it had only happened once. A slight grimace distorted Rosaleen's face as she recalled that, in fact, it had happened twice. It had cost her dearly. Two children had been born from her encounters with Sean. It was strange to think that he didn't know that he had fathered the two of them. But he didn't, and must never find out. It was bad enough that Annie had guessed about Liam. Andrew

30

was the only person to know all her terrible secrets, and with him they were safe.

George agreed with Andrew that it would please Thelma to make them a meal, so he dropped them off at the hotel and, after making arrangements to pick them up at six, returned home.

Thelma was in her glory as she put the pan on to cook for her eldest daughter and son-in-law. She had met Andrew only a couple of times before he whisked Rosaleen off to a new life abroad but he had won her over. In spite of the terrible wrench of being parted from her daughter and two grandchildren, she had given them her blessing. When George left to pick them up at the hotel, she hovered between the front window and kitchen, unable to stand still and wait. Seeing the car stop outside, she hastened to open the door. She was through the gate and waiting on the pavement before Rosaleen had a chance to get out of the car. Then they were in each other's arms and the tears flowed freely.

'I thought I was never going to see you again, love! You look wonderful.'

'So do you, Mam. You haven't changed a bit!'

'Huh! You must need glasses or something. I've put on a couple of stone.'

Rosaleen laughed and declared, 'Well, it becomes you. What do you think of your granddaughter?'

Thelma took Laura in her arms and hugged her. 'She's lovely. The picture of you when you were that age. Come on in, love. I do wish you had brought all the kids with you,' she lamented. 'It's awful to think that I've never met young Patricia. She looks cute in the photographs you sent me.'

'Mam, why don't you come out and visit us? There's nothing to stop you. We'd pay your fare over, you know.'

Thelma was scandalized at the very idea. 'What?' she exclaimed. 'Go up in one of those big planes? Ah, no . . . you'll never get me to go up in one of those things. Thanks all the same.'

'Well then, don't go blaming me if you never see Patricia.'

They entered the house and after greetings were exchanged and tears wiped away, the conversation was fast and furious as

31

George and Thelma brought Rosaleen up to date on all the local gossip. When at last they had eaten their fill of the delicious fry, Andrew raised the glass of wine, specially bought for the occasion, and said, 'My compliments to the chef... that was a wonderful meal. You did us proud, Thelma. Thanks very much.'

Colour warmed his mother-in-law's face and she airily waved a hand. 'Oh, it was nothing.'

George choked on a bubble of laughter and Thelma threw him a reproachful look. Gallantly he backed her up. 'She's right, of course. The pan's never off the stove in this house. That's why she's put on so much weight, Rosaleen.' He ducked to avoid the cushion that came sailing through the air towards him. 'Sorry, Thelma... sorry.'

They dallied for another hour, reminiscing and looking at snapshots of Rosaleen's other two children; Thelma remarking that Patricia was indeed lovely but that she had yet to see a descent photo of Liam. 'Will he not sit still for you or something?'

Her daughter fondly assured her that Liam was a real live-wire and hated being photographed. It was Rosaleen's rising reluctantly to her feet, preparing to go, that caused George to ask, 'Are you not going to pop up and see Annie? She will be disappointed to have missed you.'

He was quick to notice the glance that passed between husband and wife. It was Andrew who answered him. 'Yes, I think it's about time I met your sister. Don't you, Rosaleen?'

'Yes, of course,' she agreed. 'We can go up now, before we go back to the hotel.' She turned to George. 'There's no need for you to come out. We can call a taxi from Annie's, or perhaps Sean will give us a lift. He does have a car, doesn't he?'

'He has and would certainly give you a lift. He's very obliging, so he is. But it's no bother to me! I'll come with you and then drive you to your hotel afterwards.'

At these words Thelma rose to her feet. 'In that case, I'm coming too. Hold on until I fetch my cardigan. I don't want to miss anything. Not if I can help it.'

Thus it was that Sean opened the door to a crowd a few

minutes later. 'Why, hello there,' he cried. 'This is an unexpected pleasure, so it is. Come in, come in.'

He stood back and Rosaleen stepped forward, closely followed by her husband. Sean gave her a brief hug and then eyed Andrew. 'You must be Andrew. It's a pleasure to meet you at last,' he said. His words were sincere and Andrew warmed to him immediately. Annie, who had followed him into the hall, could find no fault with his greeting of her sister. Be careful, she warned herself as she moved slowly forward. Don't let your imagination run away with you.

From his position on the doorstep George silently observed the scene unfold before his eyes. Although everything seemed normal enough on the surface, he sensed undercurrents. Thinking back, it did seem strange that Annie and Sean had never met Andrew. But then, he had really courted Rosaleen by letter and then had arrived unexpectedly one Boxing Day and in no time at all Rosaleen and the kids were gone.

Annie was quickly won over by Andrew's charm and warmly made him welcome. Then she turned to her niece. Tears filled her eyes as she gazed on the young girl. 'My, how you've grown. It seems like only yesterday that I pushed you up and down the Springfield Road in your pram.' She reached out and gently touched Laura's cheek. 'Do you know something, Rosaleen? Our Rebecca resembles Laura ... except she's dark like Sean.'

The breath stuck in Rosaleen's throat and she tried to still her racing heart. She had thought it safe to bring her daughter over with her; there was so little of Sean in her. Forcing a carefree tone in her voice, she steered the conversation away from danger. 'How on earth did you manage to get Mother to move from her beloved Colinward Street?' she queried, as she followed Annie down the hall.

'Oh, that wasn't me. Mam never listens to a word I say. It was George who persuaded her.' Annie paused and said hesitantly, 'We were sitting out the back. Would you like to come on through ... or perhaps you'd prefer to stay indoors?'

'No. It would be nice to sit outside for a while. Lead on.' Over her shoulder Rosaleen asked her brother, 'Why, George? Why did you leave the Springfield Road? I thought you were sweet on Mary Mitchell.'

'You thought wrong then.' George sounded abrupt. Why couldn't people mind their own business? 'Mary was married a couple of years ago, as a matter of fact.'

Thelma's voice reached Rosaleen over George's shoulder. 'Aye . . . she got married! But she was sweet on our George, and the fool let her slip through his fingers.'

George adroitly changed the subject; he did not want to dwell on his reasons for not marrying Mary Mitchell. She would have had him all right! This he knew. Hadn't she practically said so? At the beginning when he had pursued her, he had been keen. Then gradually, against his will, his feelings towards her had cooled as someone else caught his attention. Had he been a fool? The one he wanted was out of reach. Why hadn't he married Mary? Surely he could have made her happy? Would he ever find happiness with anyone now? 'I forgot to ask, do you know yet when the funeral will be?'

Rosaleen was about to persist with her questions but her husband cautioned her with a look and answered as he took a seat facing the bench where Annie and Rosaleen sat side by side. 'Billy phoned the hotel while we were there. Saturday morning at eleven, the City Cemetery.'

At the mention of the hotel Sean's eyes swung to Thelma. 'Are they not staying with you then?' he asked, obviously surprised.

Afraid of what her mother might say, Annie quickly forestalled her. 'They're staying at the Midland, Sean.'

'That will be expensive.' He was frowning in bewilderment, and feeling that she was being criticized for not putting them up, Thelma retaliated.

'My house is too small, so it is. Otherwise I would gladly have put them up.' Her lips closed in a hard straight line and her glance swung reproachfully in her younger daughter's direction and away again.

More bewildered than ever, Sean cried, 'They could have stayed here.' He turned towards his wife but, seeing the embarrassed blush on her face, with difficulty stilled any further words.

'We wanted to stay in a hotel.' Aware of the growing tension, Andrew intervened. 'We'll be coming and going a lot until after the funeral. It was my choice to stay in a hotel and Billy Mercer suggested the Midland as it is very central.'

Annie sent him a grateful look and felt confident enough to offer, 'You can move in here after the funeral, if you like?'

Andrew acknowledged this with a slight shake of the head and turned to Sean. 'Rosaleen tells me you were in the Merchant Navy, do you miss the sea at all?'

'Not in the least. I love being at home with Annie and the kids. And I enjoy working in the TV studios.'

'You must have got in at just the right time. Television's the thing of the future.'

'Yes, I did. I was very fortunate. I'm slowly climbing the ladder of success but it will take a long time before I'm even halfway up.'

After that the tension eased and conversation flowed smoothly. Andrew found himself liking Sean. Years ago when Rosaleen had confessed all her secrets to him he had been inclined to think that the man must be an idiot. However, this was no fool he was talking to, so Rosaleen and Annie between them must have really duped him. But he was also glad that he and his wife were not staying under this roof. Much as he trusted Rosaleen, he wasn't going to tempt fate. He knew how strong a first love could be; especially a blighted one. And he would be the first to admit that Sean Devlin was a handsome man, and charming into the bargain! It was better that they stay in a hotel.

On the bench the sisters conversed quietly. Annie noted that Rosaleen's fine skin was still unlined. It was pale and translucent; she obviously protected it from the sun. She was still beautiful. Anyone meeting her for the first time would never guess that she was thirty-five years old. Her hair was as silvery as ever; if it was helped to remain bright, there was no indication of it. The silk dress she wore was so simple, yet it must have cost a fortune. A dark green colour, it clung to every curve and darkened the colour of Rosaleen's eyes. As usual when in the presence of her sister Annie had a feeling of inferiority. She was very conscious of her freckled nose and as she noted Rosaleen's pale hands, the long fingernails painted a deep pink, she endeavoured to hide her own work-roughened hands. She glanced across at the man Rosaleen had married.

35

Not very tall but well-built; swarthy with dark brown eyes. Charming, very charming, but not in the least bit handsome! In fact, if she had been describing him, she would have classed him as nondescript. Did her sister really love him?

'Andrew seems nice,' she said, and ventured to ask quietly, 'Do you love him?'

Rosaleen turned, eyes wide with surprise. 'Of course I do! Why shouldn't I? Didn't I marry him?'

Sorry she had opened her big mouth, Annie blundered on. 'Oh, I just thought . . . you know . . . sometimes marriage on the rebound . . .' Her voice trailed off.

'What makes you think I married him on the rebound, eh? You're daft! If you'd listened to me five years ago, instead of making everybody miserable, I'd have told you that I had fallen in love again. But no, all you could think of was your own hurt feelings. That's why I emigrated. I was in love with Andrew and wanted to marry him. Why, he's a wonderful man, so he is.'

Annie was flabbergasted. Hurt feelings indeed! How would Rosaleen have reacted if things had been the other way round and Annie had conceived Joe Smith's son? About to retaliate, the words trembling on Annie's lips faltered and died. As she looked into eyes so like her own she realized that she didn't believe one word Rosaleen had just said. Could it be because her sister was studiously avoiding looking in Sean's direction while Andrew seemed to be covertly watching his wife? Would a couple in love act in such a way? All these tensions bewildered Annie. Was her imagination running wild again? For the life of her she couldn't be sure. One thing she was certain of – Sean was totally relaxed and apparently oblivious to the uneasiness about him.

Dragging her eyes away from Annie's probing look, Rosaleen changed the subject. 'It's hard to believe this is the wilderness I sat in years ago. You've this garden set out lovely. Did you have it landscaped?'

'Yes, we have worked hard on it,' Anne said proudly, 'And, no, it's all our own handiwork.' Glad of the chance to show off her beautiful home, she added impulsively, 'Come inside and I'll give you a tour of the house.' She raised her voice to reach the others. 'You can come too, Laura, if you like.'

Rosaleen was sincere in her admiration of the ground floor,

pleasing Annie by complimenting her on the fine quality of the furniture and the tasteful decor. With a finger to her lips, Annie quietly escorted them upstairs and ushered them first into the small room where Rebecca slept.

Gazing on the peaceful cherubic features of her small niece, Rosaleen smiled wryly. 'You're right, she really is the picture of Sean. You couldn't mistake her for anyone else's child. Laura, this is your wee cousin Rebecca. Isn't she cute?'

After Laura had oh'd and ah'd over the sleeping child, Annie quietly led them into the room where her eldest daughter lay. Rosaleen's heart give a lurch of dismay when she gazed at Rachel. The child was the spitting image of her own son Liam! Feeling quite faint, she dutifully admired her niece. Rachel was smaller in stature, of course, but as far as Rosaleen could see the children could easily be taken for twins. One thing was certain, she would never ever be able to bring Liam to Belfast; it would be tempting fate.

To her dismay, Laura also noticed and innocently commented on the resemblance. 'She looks just like our Liam, Mam.'

Hearing Annie's sharply indrawn breath, Rosaleen met her eye and said with more assurance than conviction, 'That's very likely! They're cousins after all, and both resemble your Grandad Magee.'

Nevertheless, she had received a shock, and when they descended the stairs was glad to find Andrew and George preparing to leave.

'Are you not going to stay for a cup of tea or . . .' Annie's eyes sought Sean's. 'Have we any drink at all in the house, love?'

'I offered them some refreshments, Annie. But Thelma has already filled them to the brim and Andrew's worn out after all that travelling and is ready for bed.'

Andrew smiled ruefully at these words. 'You're making me feel old, Sean.'

At the door George reminded them to keep Saturday night free as he was arranging an outing. Suggesting that they go for a meal and a drink somewhere. Saying that he would arrange everything.

Voice bright, Annie cried, 'Oh, don't you worry! I've already

37

asked Minnie to babysit whichever night we go out. I'm looking forward to it.'

'I look forward to seeing the kids when they're awake, Annie. I'm sure they're lovely.'

'You'll see them all right, Rosaleen. Look, all of you ... May and Billy ... Ian as well ... will have to come here some evening before you return. We'll have a bit of a buffet and a drink. How's about that?'

'That will be lovely. Of course, I can't speak for May and Billy.' Rosaleen turned to her husband. 'What do you think, Andrew?'

'I think they'll come. Anyway, we'll pass on the invitation. Thanks for asking us, Annie. See you on Saturday.'

After waving them off, Sean closed the door and put his arm around Annie, drawing her close. 'You go on up to bed and I'll lock up.' He kissed her and gently pushed her in the direction of the stairs. 'I'll be right behind you.'

As she creamed her face, Annie critically examined her features in the mirror. In spite of the new hair-do she had felt overshadowed by Rosaleen's beauty. As for her sister's figure ... wow! Did she work at it or was it all natural?

When Sean entered the room, she voiced her thoughts. 'Our Rosaleen looked wonderful, didn't she?'

Afraid of giving the wrong impression, he paused to consider his answer. 'Yes, she did look smart.'

Annie noted the hesitation and immediately thought the worst. He did still care for Rosaleen after all. Else, why have to think before he answered?

Seeing the hurt expression on his wife's face, Sean cried aloud, 'For heaven's sake, Annie, what do you want me to say, eh? Would you believe me if I said I hadn't noticed? No, of course you wouldn't. You'd call me a liar. I don't know why you invited them here for an evening if you're going to be watching every move we make.'

Blinking furiously to contain the threatening tears, Annie muttered, 'I thought I was doing the right thing. After all, she is still my sister. I couldn't very well do otherwise, could I? What would Andrew think? Don't you want them to come?' she finished plaintively

'Not if it's going to make you miserable.' Going to her, he

38

put his hands on her shoulders and held her eye in the mirror. 'Annie, can you not put the past behind you? While they're here you could at least pretend that Rosaleen and I never . . . you know?' He shrugged optimistically. 'Eh, love?'

She twisted round on the stool and gripped him tight. 'I'll try, Sean, I'll really try!' she promised.

Rosaleen and Andrew left George's car after thanking him for all his hospitality and entered the Midland Hotel; Laura, forgetting to be lady-like, swung on their arms. Rosaleen smiled indulgently after her daughter, as, relinquishing her hold on them, she dashed to the reception desk, collected her key and bounded up the stairs. 'Where does she get all that energy from?' she asked wistfully. 'I'm dead beat!' Wearily she brushed the hair back from her brow. 'I must look awful.'

Retrieving his key from reception, Andrew assured her, 'You look great, love.' He sounded abstracted and immediately her glance swung questioningly to him.

'Is anything wrong, Andrew?'

'Nothing that a good night's sleep won't cure.'

'You're sure?'

They entered the lift and as the doors slid closed, he gathered her close. 'Absolutely.'

Leaning back in his arms, Rosaleen anxiously scanned his face. 'I wish now that I hadn't promised to share Laura's room. I don't know what I was thinking of. I just thought she would be lonely in a strange country. Shall I tuck her in and when she falls asleep, come to you?'

'No, it doesn't matter. Give her a big kiss for me.' As the lift door opened, Andrew kissed his wife chastely on the brow. 'I'll come for you before breakfast in the morning.' He watched her enter her daughter's room before closing the door of his own.

He was feeling a bit down. It was over five years since he had seduced Rosaleen. He had told her then that it didn't matter that Sean Devlin held her heart. That it was up to him to make her love him. And until now he had been confident that he had. Knowing how she longed to see her mother, Andrew had been surprised at his wife's reluctance to come home. Then tonight he had watched her put on a wonderful act of being at ease, when all the time she had avoided looking directly at Sean. Could she possibly still care for him, after all the good times she had shared with her husband? That was something he might never know. Besides, did he really want to?

As for Laura ... was it just because he knew that Sean had fathered the child, or was there really a likeness there? He had always thought her the picture of his wife, but tonight he had seen Sean in her. Not in the features or colouring but in the mannerisms; the tilt of the head; the lift of a brow. If so, hopefully it would go unnoticed. Luckily they would be here such a short time and would see so little of the Devlins it should not cause any problems.

Of one thing he was certain: he intended sticking close to his wife's side. If you take away the temptation, you eliminate the danger. That would be his motto for the remainder of his stay in Belfast. With this thought he started to undress, feeling a little easier in his mind.

Rosaleen undressed slowly as she waited for Laura to vacate the bathroom. She was confused. How come she had been unable to look Sean straight in the face? Was she afraid that somehow, something remained of the passion he had once so easily aroused in her? Surely not? Andrew was a good husband and a wonderful lover, but he had been perturbed. Had he noticed her evasiveness and thought the worst? Did he imagine that something might still remain of her first love affair?

'Mam, I love Belfast!'

Rosaleen smiled fondly as her daughter left the bathroom and skipped across to the bed in baby-doll pyjamas that made her look all elbows and knees. 'How can you tell?' she chided. 'You haven't seen anything of it yet.'

'I just know that I'm going to love it here. Grannie wants me to stay with her on Saturday while you and Dad are at the funeral. Can I, Mam?'

'I don't see why not. She might even take you up to the zoo at Bellevue. You'd love that. But now you must be tired, so get some sleep, love. We will make plans in the morning.'

'Good night, Mam.'

'Good night, love.'

Soon Laura was fast asleep and, kissing her daughter on the brow, Rosaleen slipped into her négligé. Leaving the room, she locked the door behind her. Her place was with her husband. Laura would probably sleep through the night. Besides, they were just across the hall. She was glad she had made the decision to join him. When he opened the door to her knock the joy on his face was plain.

He was in his dressing gown. Pushing the door closed with her foot, she entered his arms. 'Why are you not in bed?'

'I couldn't sleep. I hoped you would come. But what about Laura?'

'She's sound asleep.' From the circle of his arms she urged him towards the bed. Willingly he stretched out on it but when he would have embraced her she gently pushed him away. Standing some distance from the bed she slowly removed her négligé and then slipped the straps of her night dress from her shoulders, letting the soft white silky material billow around her feet. She knew Andrew loved to gaze on her naked form. His eyes feasted hungrily on the curves of her body. Only when they rose once more to meet hers did Rosaleen slowly go to him. He reached out for her and drew her down beside him. Against his lips she whispered, 'I love you. And don't you forget it!'

'I love you too. And thanks, love, for reminding me that you are mine. I must admit I was a mite concerned back there, but not any more.'

His lips devoured her and his hands began their journey of arousal. Their love making was fierce and fulfilling.

When at last he slept Rosaleen gently extricated herself from his arms and left the bed. Going to the window she stared blindly into the night. She loved Andrew! So why had Sean Devlin's face filled her mind while they had been making love? She couldn't find any logical reason for this and shivered slightly. Surely she couldn't . . . no, of course not! Now she was being silly. Besides . . . her presence had made no impression at all on Sean earlier that evening. Was that why her thoughts kept returning to him? Was it just pique because once he had been unable to tear his eyes away from her? Creeping back in beside her husband, Rosaleen snuggled close. Andrew was her life. And Sean? He was the forbidden fruit.

41

Chapter 2

Much to her relief, Rosaleen discovered that her fear . . . no, that wasn't the right word! Shyness? Uneasiness? Whatever it was that had made her afraid to look Sean Devlin straight in the eye, was unfounded. Perhaps it was because Andrew was ever present at her side, attending to her every whim; not giving her time to dwell too much on anyone else, or anything else for that matter . . . or maybe it was Sean's laid back attitude towards her. He was so casual and cool even she could be forgiven for doubting that he had ever passionately loved her. Whatever the reason, the outing on Saturday night was a happy, light-hearted affair with no visible sign of tension whatsoever. The five-course meal which they ate at the Midland Hotel was delicious. Everyone ordered different dishes and compared them.

Afterwards, full to bursting point and swearing that they would have to go on a strict diet after all this self-inflicted gluttony, they made their way to the lounge to relax and enjoy a drink. George had chosen the Midland for the venue because Andrew had spoken so highly of the cuisine there, and everyone soon voiced their agreement. It also meant that Laura could retire to her bedroom when she felt like it and this she did shortly after dinner, with a book to read. The six adults drank and talked until the early hours of the morning, discussing living standards in Canada and all the local gossip in Belfast.

Sunday had passed pleasantly enough, renewing acquaintances of Andrew's and visiting his few remaining relatives. The visit to Annie's on the Monday night had also gone off without a hitch. That was except for one incident which Rosaleen had since convinced herself was all in her mind. After all, hadn't Sean been completely unaffected by it?

May and Billy, with young Ian in tow, had accompanied them to Annie's. After helping themselves liberally from the lovely buffet she had set out on the dining-room table, they settled down in the sitting room with drinks. Due to May's ability to imitate characters from the past there was soon laughter, sometimes verging on tears, as someone much admired but now dead was recalled and affectionately aped. Especially when she took up a stance with one hand spanning her hip, leaned forward with jaw stuck out in an aggressive attitude and delivered a speech: 'Now you listen to me, my girl! I've knocked my arse out of joint fixing you and May up on a farm and you'd better go. Do you hear me, Rosaleen? You had better go! Or there'll be wigs on the green.' Everybody except Andrew, who had never met him, and Minnie who had been invited in, at once recognized the stance and voice as Tommy Magee's. Not a man to swear lightly, his words had had the desired effect of making Rosaleen meekly agree to be evacuated to the comparative safety of Dungannon, away from wartime Belfast. But, becoming aware that Thelma was quietly crying, May brought her brilliant performance to an abrupt end. Falling on her knees beside Thelma, she was all apologies.

'Ah, Mrs Magee, I'm sorry. I got carried away, so I did. Please forgive me? I was way out of line, but I didn't mean any harm. It was only a bit of fun.' Her eyes, full of regret, anxiously sought Rosaleen's.

Before her friend could intervene Thelma gripped May's hand and cried sincerely, 'No ... don't you apologize. You had him off to a T! That was my husband all over again. It brought him close to me for a minute and I thank you for it.'

She turned to Minnie and Andrew. 'You never met Tommy, but you have just seen him mimicked to perfection. This girl here should be on the stage, so she should!'

Relieved that no serious damage had been inflicted, May retorted, 'Ah, I'm not all that good. It's only a few I can take off. Now it's someone else's turn to entertain us. How's about you giving us a song, Sean?'

'Me? Are you trying to clear the room or something?'

Annie and Thelma, knowing that Sean had a fine baritone voice, added their pleas to May's and soon the strains of 'Danny Boy' filled the room. Rosaleen sat with head bent, listening attentively to the haunting words of her father's favourite song. Imagine! She and Sean had been so close yet she had never heard him sing before. Had not known that he had such a fine voice. What other hidden talents had he that she was unaware of? Had it just been sex between them, after all? No personal feelings whatsoever?

There was complete silence when the song came to an end and Rosaleen was not surprised to find that she was not the only one to have shed tears. Glancing around the quiet room, Sean gave an embarrassed cough. 'Ah, come on ... surely it wasn't all that bad?' As the silence stretched, a bit perturbed, he queried, 'Was it?'

This broke the spell that bound them and everyone clapped and spoke at once, congratulating him on his fine performance. To distract their attention and dispel the sadness he had unwittingly evoked, Sean called on George to do his bit. Without further persuasion his brother-in-law produced a mouth organ from his inside pocket and soon feet were tapping to the sound of Irish reels. Within minutes they were all up on the floor dancing. Rosaleen, glad to throw off the sadness that had threatened to engulf her, dismissed Andrew's cries that he couldn't dance and pulled him up to join the others.

Annie was delighted at the success of her 'do' and very relieved at the harmonious atmosphere that prevailed throughout her sister's visit. She had been a bit on edge after Sean's reaction when she had issued an invitation to them, afraid that perhaps she would spoil the party with her jealousy, but thankfully everything went with a swing. When Sean, accompanied by George, had attended the funeral on Saturday morning, Annie had longed to ask him if he had been in Rosaleen's company but had curbed her tongue, knowing full well he would guess that jealousy triggered her interest. She was to be glad that she had not questioned him. On Saturday night as they had prepared for their evening out he had volunteered the information she sought, without any prompting.

'I hope Rosaleen feels well enough to come out tonight.'

'Why shouldn't she?'

'She wasn't at the funeral this morning. Andrew made her excuses and explained she wasn't feeling too good after all the travelling and excitement.'

'Oh . . . so you didn't see her then?'

Leaning across, Sean kissed her lightly on the lips. 'Annie, love, I can read you like a book.' He shook his head in mock despair. 'No, I didn't see her.' He reached for her hand and pulled her closer. Gazing intently into her bright green eyes, he reminded her, 'Now remember, love, you promised you would try to forget the past, mmm?'

'I will, Sean. But . . . you'll help me, won't you?'

'I'll not leave your side, love. I promise.'

He had kept his word and Annie could find no fault whatsoever with his behaviour. His attitude towards her sister, so far as she could see, was friendly and nothing more. She could detect no hidden nuances. Even when Rosaleen and Sean were absent for a time in the kitchen, she was relieved to find she did not worry unduly.

When her sister entered the kitchen to further dilute the large brandy George had poured for her, she had been unaware that Sean was alone there. Everyone had been too liberal with their measures when pouring the spirits. That, and twirling around Annie's sitting-room floor to Irish reels, had her feeling quite tipsy; hence her search for something to weaken her drink. Sean had just finished pouring himself a pint of beer and a glass of wine for Annie. He'd started towards the door when it opened and Rosaleen entered the room.

For some moments they stood face to face, gazing into each other's eyes. This was the first time they had been alone since her arrival. Sean stood stock still, very much aware of Rosaleen's cloud of shining silver hair, soft trembling lips and green eyes darkened with emotion. In spite of himself his eyes drifted to the pale skin of the cleavage which the low-cut blouse exposed and suddenly, inexplicably, he remembered her naked in his arms.

The image was so vivid he was dismayed to find beer trickling over his hand from the shaking glass. Disconcerted, he closed his eyes for a moment to break the spell and sought to gather his wits. This would never do! He had honestly thought that all the feelings that had tortured him in the early years of their acquaintance were gone forever. From the very first time he had set eyes on her, Rosaleen's sensuality had triggered off answering emotions within him. But all that was in the past. Now he loved Annie. He was contented with his lot; his wife was all he needed. Why then was he standing here gawking at his old flame?

Mesmerized, Rosaleen gazed raptly back into the dark blue eyes that had once thrilled her to the core. Without realizing it she swayed dangerously close and her well-remembered perfume wafted around Sean, bringing back haunting memories and reawakening forgotten desires. Her action brought him to his senses. With difficulty he dragged his eyes away from the beauty of her, warning bells ringing in his head. He was dismayed that in spite of all his efforts to show indifference towards her that old feeling was still there between them, like electricity in the air. He must not dally here too long or God knows what might happen. One wrong word, one wrong movement, could cause so much damage and undo all that he had built up with Annie.

Even now, if she should look askance at him when he returned with her drink, he would probably look as guilty as hell, although nothing had happened. But what if they were really alone? What then? He must make sure that never happened. He must never be alone with Rosaleen. At all costs he must not give Annie any cause to doubt his love! The old wounds must not be reopened; he had hurt her enough in the past. He was only too aware that his wife would not be able to cope with doubts, and life would not be worth living if he, in any way, betrayed her trust.

Confused by the charged emotions coursing through her, Rosaleen gushed into speech. 'I've just come to put some more lemonade in this brandy.' She held up the glass and was annoyed to see her hand was also trembling. She giggled with embarrassment and explained, 'See ... I'm beginning to feel quite tipsy already.'

With hands that shook Sean carefully put down the glasses he held and reached for a cloth to dry his hand, all the while warning himself to be careful. With averted eyes he diluted her drink still further, jerking back when his fingers accidentally brushed hers. Afraid to look into the dark green pools that

46

were waiting to trap his glance; afraid of what he might see reflected there. Surely she could not still care for him after all this time? Hadn't she sent him packing? Still afraid to meet her glance, he lifted the glasses again. The past was over and done with. It must stay that way. Muttering an apology, he squirmed around her in the confined space, taking care not to brush against her as he left the kitchen.

Shame reddened Rosaleen's cheeks. What on earth had come over her? She hadn't meant to sway towards him like that! It hadn't been deliberate! Still, she had wanted him to look at her; had wanted to see if he still cared . . . well, just a little. Was that asking too much? He had been the great love of her life for so very long. She had betrayed Joe and Annie because of her intense feelings for him. Had borne him two children. Not that he knew that, of course! Had he been aware of her sudden discomfort? Did he think she was giving him the come-on signal? He must have else he wouldn't have left her so abruptly and apologetically, and like a frightened rabbit into the bargain.

Shaken by the heightened emotions coursing through her, she put her glass on the table and left the kitchen, making her way along the hall. Everyone was having a rest after dancing. With head averted from the sitting-room door which stood ajar, she quickly passed by and climbed the stairs to the bathroom. She needed a respite to compose herself before facing Andrew again. Only once since they had arrived, had she been away from his side and look what had happened. In the bathroom she gazed at her reflection in the mirror and was glad she had not returned to the sitting room straight away. Red cheeks and bright eyes betrayed the tumult that beset her. Andrew would have been sure to notice. Pressing her forehead to the cool glass, she took deep gulping breaths. Slowly her composure returned and she grimaced wryly as she set to, toning down the rosy hue of her cheeks with some of Annie's face powder.

'Just what did happen, eh?' she chided herself. 'You're a big girl now, Rosaleen, so catch yourself on! Nothing happened.' For a moment the past had seemed so tantalizingly near. Every nerve end had come alive as it had when first they met and she had been thrilled to the core with the wonder of it. She hadn't asked for these emotions to be rekindled, but they had and it frightened her. In the past her inability to control her emotions had cost her dearly. It was a good thing she had never been alone with Sean for any length of time during these past few days; on her side passion still flared whenever she looked into his eyes. Was it really all one-sided?

Andrew, whilst trying not to watch his wife's every movement, nevertheless noted her following Sean into the kitchen. Had she done so deliberately? A sigh of relief escaped him when, within a matter of minutes, his brother-in-law returned to the sitting room, a glass in each hand. He saw the furtive glance Sean directed at his wife as he placed her drink on the small table by her side. He noted the way he relaxed when Annie, deep in conversation with May, seemed apparently unaware of him. Andrew frowned down into his beer. Sean looked guilty as hell! There was no other word for it. What had he to feel so guilty about? Warning himself not to jump to conclusions he made an effort to remain calmly in his chair, but in vain. He had to see his wife's face; see if the guilt was also reflected there. Rising to his feet, he made his way from the room and along the hall to the kitchen. He opened the door quietly and was immediately ashamed of himself. Was he trying to catch her off guard? He noted the full glass of brandy on the kitchen table but of his wife there was no sign.

An arm circling his waist caused him to turn with a start. Rosaleen reached up and kissed him lightly on the lips. 'Were you looking for me, love?'

Her action pleased him but did not allay his fears. Intently he examined her face. Did she look too serene? Back in control, Rosaleen gazed innocently back at him. 'I wondered where you had gotten to,' he admitted finally. 'I didn't see you pass along the hall. Are you feeling all right?'

'Yes. I was in the bathroom.' She reached across for her drink. 'I came back for this. I got Sean to dilute it for me. I don't want to have a hangover in the morning. I've a lot of shopping to do before we go home and I want to have a clear head during my last few days in Belfast.' Her eyes tenderly held his. 'Are you enjoying yourself, love?'

'Mmm, very much. Still, I'll be glad to get back home and

see Liam and Patricia. I miss them, you know. What about you? Are you enjoying yourself?'

She nodded. 'Yes, but as you know, I'm not used to all this drinking and jumping about! I'm glad you persuaded me to come over though. But . . . yes, like you I miss the kids. I'll be glad to get home too.'

Relieved at her obvious sincerity and the fact that she now regarded Canada as 'home', he put his arm around her waist and drew her along the hall, saying mischievously, 'Let's join the others before they start talking about us.'

'Now that would never do, a man and his wife wanting to be alone at a party?' she jested.

Andrew's eyes slanted sideways at her. 'Rather that than one of us sloping off with someone else. Eh, Rosaleen? Now that really would give them something to talk about.'

She giggled delightedly. Andrew was no mug! She felt as thought she'd had a narrow escape. She really would be glad to put the Atlantic between herself and further temptation.

'I was thinking, Rosaleen. We really must return all the kindness shown to us. We'll have to invite everybody out for a meal. Is that all right with you, love?'

'I think that's a marvellous idea, Andrew. Where and when?'

'I'll get Sean or George to recommend somewhere nice. Say, Wednesday night?'

'Mmm. Lovely.'

Minnie Carson had also noticed Rosaleen apparently follow Sean into the kitchen. She saw him return and noted his furtive glance at Annie; his relief when she noticed nothing amiss. Resentment against Annie's sister burned in Minnie's bosom. Unknown to the sisters, from that conversation overheard in the garden shortly after Annie had come to live next door to her, she had gleaned that Rosaleen's young son Liam had been fathered by Sean. It seemed that Annie, after many years of marriage and still childless, had been blaming her husband for their childless state. She had obviously been devastated when she accidentally found out that Sean was not at fault; that he had actually fathered her sister's child. To Rosaleen's credit she had vowed never to acquaint Sean of this fact and shortly afterwards had emigrated to Canada.

Now, as she witnessed the guilty look Sean directed at his

wife and noted Rosaleen furtively pass the open doorway with averted head, Minnie raged inwardly at their antics. They had no right to be carrying on out there under everyone's very nose! To her relief Andrew rose to his feet and also left the room. Now there was a man who seemed capable of keeping his wife in her rightful place. Minnie's lips twitched when she realized the direction her mind was travelling. How could she even hazard a guess at the action of others? She was acting as judge and jury. Why, I could write a book on these shenanigans, she mused. Nevertheless, she was very relieved when the couple returned to the room and noted that they were very much at one with each other. There was no sign of discord. Perhaps she was mistaken; her inquisitive mind running wild again. Though she remained alert throughout the evening there was no further indication that Sean was in the least bit interested in his sister-in-law. Later, thanking them for the wonderful time she'd had, Minnie made her good nights with an easy mind.

Such was the harmony between all concerned, Annie felt confident enough to ask Sean to take time off work so that he could drive her and her mother to Aldergrove to see Rosaleen off on her journey back to Canada, as George's car would be full.

Rosaleen's visit had stretched into ten days but Annie had not set eyes on her since she and Andrew had taken them, together with her mother and George, for a meal in the Belfast Castle on the Wednesday night. Once more everything had gone well and Annie began to regret her attitude towards Rosaleen all those years ago when she had found out that Liam was Sean's son. Obviously she had been telling the truth and it had been a one-off fling that had unfortunately led to a pregnancy.

As she hugged her sister close in farewell at the airport, Annie felt obliged to apologize for the past. 'Rosaleen, I'm sorry I didn't believe you. I want you to know that it's obvious to me now that you and Sean spoke the truth and that it only happened the once,' she whispered in her ear. 'Do you forgive me?'

Embarrassed, Rosaleen abruptly nodded her head. Here she

50

was savouring the touch of Sean's lips on her cheek, the feel of his arms around her as he kissed her goodbye and fighting for control at the effect he'd had on her, and Annie was apologizing for doubting her! Full of guilt, with a final hug she abruptly pushed her sister away and with tears streaming down her face, without a backward glance entered the departure lounge. It was a good thing that she was going back to Canada. Belfast would not be big enough to keep her and Sean Devlin apart for very long.

That night Annie confided in her husband that she thought she was pregnant. She was pleased when he expressed his delight at the news. A week later, when Dr Cardiff confirmed that she was almost three months gone, they opened a bottle of wine and toasted the health of their unborn child.

In the early hours of the morning the hospital was hushed. Only the muted pad of footsteps as nurses quietly toured their wards checking on their patients disturbed the silence. Sean stood by the window of the small waiting room and gazed blindly at the reflection of the room behind him. Through the mirrored images, lights from the buildings beyond could be seen as the hospital carried on quietly working throughout the night. They did not register with him. In his mind's eye he was seeing Annie's ashen face as they wheeled her away from him; out of the ward and down the corridor to the theatre where they intended delivering the baby. This worried him no end. Babies were rarely delivered there! Wasn't there a special room for mothers in labour?

His mind was in a whirl. What had gone wrong? Rachel and Rebecca had been delivered at home, Annie looked after by the midwife in the first stages of labour, and when the birth was imminent the doctor was called out. In fact, both girls had been safely delivered by the midwife before the doctor arrived. It had been all so straightforward. No problems. No cause for alarm. So what had gone wrong this time?

The evening before, when Annie's pains started, they had as usual timed them. The baby wasn't due for another two weeks but the contractions were strong and frequent and when his wife gave him the go-ahead Sean had phoned Nurse Harris; Annie warned him to say that there was no panic, but that the pains were strong. While they awaited her arrival Sean bathed the two children and settled them in bed.

The midwife had arrived some twenty minutes later. She had been upstairs with Annie a long time and Sean had sat fidgeting impatiently in the living room, waiting for the summons that would introduce him to the new member of his family; never dreaming that anything was amiss. He had heard Nurse Harris on the stairs and, rising quickly to his feet, had gone to meet her, a welcoming smile on his face; sure that he was about to hear that his wife had presented him with another daughter or a son. One look at her face and his heart quite literally sunk in his breast.

'Sean, I'm going to ring for the doctor.'

'Is anything wrong, Nurse?'

Millie Harris was about to make trite comments but he cried abruptly, 'I want the truth, mind! I can see something is wrong.'

Resignedly, the midwife nodded. 'I'll phone the doctor first and then we can talk about it.'

He stood tensely beside her in the hall and listened to every word as she spoke to Dr Cardiff, but was none the wiser. She just informed the doctor that Mrs Devlin was having contractions and she would be obliged if he would come as quickly as possible.

Replacing the receiver, she motioned for Sean to follow her into the living room. 'Don't look so worried. I'm probably being overcautious but I want a second opinion. The baby is lying in the breech position and I can't budge it. I'm afraid it's going to be a difficult birth for Annie.'

'Look, Nurse . . . I want the truth. Is my wife in any kind of danger?'

The midwife was quick to refute this. 'At the moment I can only assure you there is no imminent danger whatsoever to either Annie or the baby. I don't know exactly what's wrong. If the contractions weren't so strong I'd be inclined to think the baby would turn itself, but since they are I'll feel a lot happier if she is admitted to hospital. We don't want to take any chances, do we? Dr Cardiff will decide whether or not she should be moved. We must wait and see what he has to say.'

'I'm going up to Annie.'

Sean was already halfway up the stairs and with a shrug of resignation Millie Harris followed.

On his arrival at the bedside, Annie removed the gas and air mask from her face and smiled wanly at him. 'It must be a boy, Sean. Only a boy would make such a fuss and refuse to face the world,' she whispered. Then her face twisted into a grimace and she thrust the mask back over her mouth.

Kneeling at the side of the bed, he grasped his wife's free hand tightly in his. 'The doctor is coming, love. Everything will be all right. You just hang in there.'

She nodded in agreement and smiled bravely through the pains that wracked her body. She forgave him his ignorance. How could he know any better? She knew that something was radically wrong, and for the umpteenth time sent a prayer heavenward. Please, God, let the baby live. Please, God, please!

When the doctor knocked on the door Sean remained firmly by his wife's side and reluctantly Nurse Harris left the room and descended the stairs to let him in. They remained in the hall some minutes in muted conversation. Even though he strained his ears Sean could not distinguish one word of what they said. To his relief, when the doctor eventually entered the room he did not indicate that Sean should go. For this he was grateful. He had no intention of leaving Annie's side but didn't want any arguments either.

With a curt nod in his direction the doctor bent over the writhing form. His hands were gentle as he explored her abdomen. The examination completed, Dr Cardiff brushed the damp hair back off Annie's brow and said gently, 'I'm going to send for the ambulance. This baby is going to need more help than I can give it here. I think you will need a Caesarean section.'

'Is the baby all right?' Annie's muffled voice, weak and threaded with fear, came from behind the mask.

'Of course it is. However, you are very tired and the sooner we relieve you of this baby the better it will be for you. Nurse Harris will get you ready for the journey.'

With a comforting squeeze of her shoulder he left the bedside. A motion of his hand indicated that he would like Sean to accompany him. They descended the stairs in silence. Once the ambulance was summoned they faced each other.

53

Dr Cardiff eyed Sean intently before speaking. 'Your wife is exhausted and the baby is firmly wedged across the opening of the birth channel. At the moment it is still strong but I'm afraid an operation is imperative if we are to save it.'

'Will Annie be all right, Doctor?'

'At this stage I see no reason to doubt it. But . . .' A slight shrug of the shoulders conveyed his worry.

'What happened? Why was this not discovered sooner?'

Hearing the censure in Sean's voice, Dr Cardiff was quick to retaliate. 'It wasn't something that could be foreseen,' he remonstrated tersely. 'The baby could have changed its position at any time. The last time Nurse Harris examined your wife the child was lying head down ready to enter the birth channel. It must have changed position within the last twenty-four hours. And remember, it isn't due for another two weeks! It's all in God's hands now.'

Sean groped for a chair and slumped down.

Dr Cardiff's expression softened and he asked softly, 'Are you planning to accompany your wife to the hospital?'

'Of course I am!'

'Then I suggest you make arrangements for someone to stay with the children immediately. The ambulance will be here shortly.' With these words Dr Cardiff left the room, muttering to himself.

The opening of the waiting-room door in the Royal Victoria Hospital caused Sean to swing eagerly towards it, only to sag in disappointment. The young nurse who entered the room was obviously not the bearer of good news. She carried a tray with a cup of tea and a plate of biscuits on it. 'I thought you might like a cuppa, Mr Devlin.'

Sean thanked her politely and, taking the tray, placed it on an occasional table. The nurse wasn't to know that he didn't dare eat or drink anything. There was a great heavy weight where his heart should be and he was afraid of choking. With a long compassionate look, the nurse withdrew, leaving him alone once more with his own private anguish.

Frustrated at this enforced captivity, he left the room and prowled along the corridor, glancing into dimly lit wards where patients slept and the only bright light was at the desk where the night nurse sat writing her reports. He wished Annie was in one of these wards asleep and recovering from this terrible ordeal.

'Mr Devlin?'

His head shot round at the sound of his name. 'Yes?'

A plump middle-aged nurse approached him and tentatively repeated his name. At his nod she said, 'I've been looking for you. Your wife has given birth to a baby boy.'

'My wife . . . what about my wife?'

'She's still in theatre, but I thought you might like to see your son?'

'Yes, of course.' Sean was confused. The baby was born and Annie was still in theatre? What was going on? In a bewildered daze he blindly followed the robust figure down a corridor and up a flight of stairs to the nursery where he was introduced to the sister in charge, who in turn introduced him to the latest addition to his family.

Timidly taking the bundle from the nurse's proffered arms, he gazed down on the small wrinkled face of the baby. Suddenly Sean realized he was holding the son Annie and he had been praying for. But what about Annie? Oh, dear God, he pleaded silently, please don't let her die.

'Eight pounds he is, and just look at that head of hair.' The nurse gently touched the mop of soft dark down. With a glance at Sean's head, she smiled. 'He obviously takes after you.'

Ignoring her small talk, he asked tersely, 'What about my wife? Do you know anything at all about Annie?'

Full of compassion, the nurse relieved him of the baby. 'No, I'm sorry, I don't. But then, I'm up here all the time. My only concern is for these babies here.' Her hand swept over the rows of tiny cots.

'Of course. Thank you for letting me hold him, but now I must go downstairs again. They may be looking for me down there.' Without another glance at the baby, Sean turned on his heel and left the nursery, mind shadowed by all sorts of dark, unwelcome thoughts.

It was half an hour later that the surgeon came to him. Still dressed in his blood-splattered green robe and with a face mask hanging loosely around his neck, he wearily pushed his fingers

55

through his hair, lifting it back off his damp forehead before addressing Sean.

He stood rooted to the spot, afraid of what he was about to hear. The fact that he had blindly signed a form, giving them permission to do whatever was necessary to save the lives of mother and child, weighed heavily on his conscience. The baby was alive. Had they given it priority? Had he unwittingly signed Annie's death warrant?

Relief flooded through him, making him weak at the knees, when the big heavy-set man at last spoke. 'Mr Devlin, your wife has lost a lot of blood, but although she is very weak, I can't see any reason why she shouldn't make a full recovery.' He smiled slightly as Sean sagged with relief, and asked, 'How many children do you have, Mr Devlin?'

'This is our third, Doctor.'

'Did you intend having a large family?'

'Well, my wife wants six, but I think four is enough myself. Why are you asking me all these questions?' A premonition was sending a chill down his spine.

'Son, if you take my advice there will be no more children. Be thankful you have three. I have to confess that we almost lost your wife in there. And, to be truthful, I wouldn't give much for her chances should she ever become pregnant again.'

Sean was winded by this news. 'I'll do my best, Doctor, but my wife is very strong-willed.'

'You have three children. Be thankful for that! And remember what I said.'

Sean thrust his hand at the surgeon. 'Thank you, Doctor. From the bottom of my heart, I thank you.' For the life of him he could not remember this man's name. 'Can I see Annie now?'

'She's sedated and will be out for some hours, but no doubt they'll let you look in on her. Good night, Mr Devlin.'

'Good night, Doctor.' From the muddled layers of his brain Sean at last conjured up the man's name. 'And thanks again, Mr Montgomery.'

Annie was in a small ante-room at the entrance to the main ward. It contained two beds but the other one was empty. Sean tip-toed across and sat down on the chair. Tears spilled over and flooded down his cheeks when he saw the drips attached to Annie's arms and tubes protruding from under the bed-clothes. Her face rivalled the sheets for colour and dark shadows bruised her eyes. Icy fingers of fear plucked at his heartstrings. Apparently she'd been through the mill. Would she pull through? He certainly didn't want her to suffer like this ever again, or himself for that matter. He would see to it that there were no more children. That's if he could get Annie to agree!

Tentatively he reached for her hand and held it gently between his. Was she like this because he had given the medical staff a free hand? But how could he have done otherwise? He could not take chances with her life. And they had the much longed for son. To be truthful, Sean had a weakness for baby girls. It would not have mattered to him if this baby had been another, but Annie had set her heart on giving him a son; someone to carry on the family name. One thing he could be sure of: his da would be over the moon. Jim Devlin definitely wanted the family name carried on; had often hinted quite strongly that it was up to Sean to keep trying. Not that he was ever intimidated by his father! The number of children they had was strictly between him and Annie and if they turned out to be all girls, so what? Whether or not the Devlin name died out was immaterial. And why should it? He had plenty of male cousins. Still, it was nice to please.

Pale delicate fingers of light stealing through the chink in the curtains flitted across Annie's face, teasing her eyelids open. After some pain-filled moments as memory returned and she realized where she was, she saw her husband slumped fast asleep in the uncomfortable chair and whispered his name, surprised when only a croaking noise left her parched lips. The sound did not penetrate Sean's slumber but it alerted a nurse and brought her bustling into the room.

'Ah, you're awake already, Mrs Devlin!' she cried, stating the obvious. 'And how do you feel this morning?'

'Sore . . . very sore.' Annie tried to raise herself up in the bed on her elbows but it hurt too much and she sank wearily back. 'The baby? Is my baby all right?'

Hearing the fear in her voice the nurse was quick to reassure her. 'You have a boy. A fine, healthy eight-pound son. I'll bring him to you later. Here, I'm sure you're thirsty. Have a sip of this.'

'A boy? Oh, thanks be to God,' Annie whispered before drinking thirstily from the glass of ice-cold water the nurse held to her lips.

As their voices penetrated the fog of sleep, awareness came to Sean. He opened his eyes and gaped around him in surprise. Then all the traumatic events of the previous night assailed him. He pushed himself shakily to his feet only to sink down again as blood rushed to his cramped limbs, making him wince. Flexing his muscles and stretching his numb legs, he at last managed to rise stiffly from his cramped position and hobbled across to the bed, hovering over his wife, anxiously noting her pallor. Dear God . . . she looked like death warmed up! 'Are you all right, love?' he whispered, anxiously noting the dark haloes around her deep-set eyes.

'Just a wee bit sore.' As she moved a grimace belied her brave words. 'Who's with the children, Sean?'

'Minnie. I knocked her up. I didn't know what else to do, love. I hated imposing on her in the middle of the night. She's getting a bit old for that game. I wish George would get a phone installed.'

'Minnie won't mind. She loves feeling wanted. Have you seen our son yet?'

'Yes, last night.' Not really remembering what the baby looked like, he told her what would please her. 'He's lovely, Annie. A real beauty. He has a mop of dark hair like mine.'

She opened her mouth to question him further and the nurse popped a thermometer into it and addressed Sean. 'I'm afraid you will have to leave now, Mr Devlin. The doctor will be doing his rounds soon and I want to freshen your wife up and make her more comfortable before he arrives. You can come back later, if you like. No need to wait for visiting time.'

Planting a quick kiss on Annie's brow, he whispered, 'Thanks, love. Thanks for giving me a son. See you later. Now I've seen for myself that you're on the mend, I'll go home and relieve Minnie. I'll be back later.'

At the door her voice stayed him. 'Sean . . . have I a fresh nightie here?'

'Yes, love. Nurse Harris saw to all that while we waited for the ambulance to come last night. She packed all you are likely to need. In the clothes line, that is. Can I bring you anything else? Like a magazine or some fruit?'

'No, thanks. See you later, love.'

It was half-past seven in the morning when Sean at last wearily made his way out of the hospital. As he was nosing his car out on to the Grosvenor Road he saw George's car turning into the entrance to the maternity wing. His brother-in-law didn't see him and once out on the road Sean turned the car round and waited his chance to enter the grounds again. He caught up with George as he was about to lock the car.

'We've been worried sick, Sean! We got a terrible shock when we heard that Annie had been rushed into hospital in the middle of the night. All they would tell us on the phone was that she was comfortable, so I decided to call in and see for myself how she was before going on to work.'

'It's about time you got a phone in, George! Then I would have been able to get in touch with you and save you all this misery,' Sean chastised him. 'Annie had a Caesarean in the early hours of this morning. She came around about a half hour ago. She looks like a ghost but, thank God, they say she'll pull through.'

'Thank God indeed!' George fervently agreed with him. 'And congratulations!' He thumped Sean playfully on the shoulder. 'They did tell us that you have a son.'

'That's right. Annie's very pleased.'

'And what about you, Sean? You must be over the moon. All men want a son, don't they?'

He smiled faintly. 'You're beginning to sound like Annie. She's convinced that I want a son. But to be truthful, George, I wouldn't have been in the least bit disappointed if it had been another daughter. I love wee girls, you know. But at least it'll keep Annie happy.'

'Will they let me in to see her for a few minutes, do you think?'

'You might have to wait a while, the doctor's on his rounds, but if you can hang on for a while I think they'll let you in for a quick word. Go to the nursery and see my wee son while

59

you're waiting. I'd better get going now. Is Thelma with the kids?'

'Yes. Minnie sent a message down with the milkman and we went straight up. Thelma sent Minnie off to bed and when I left she was getting breakfast ready for the girls.'

'That's great news.' Sean swung wearily back towards his own car. 'See you later, George.'

Sean hit the works traffic in the town centre and along York Street. It was nearing half-eight when he finally arrived home. Thelma must have been watching from the window because the minute the car entered the drive she was out on the path, questions tumbling from her lips.

'Is everything all right, Sean?' she cried anxiously.

'Thanks be to God, yes. Annie and the baby are going to be all right, Thelma.'

'How come she's in the Royal? Why not the Mater Hospital? It would be a lot handier for visiting, so it would.'

'I've no idea. Dr Cardiff phoned the Royal and an ambulance was here in no time. I hadn't the chance to go down for you.'

'I've made up my mind, Sean. It's about time we got a phone in. I'll have a wee word with George about it. What would you like for breakfast, son?'

'I'm far too exhausted to eat. I'll just have a cup of tea if you don't mind. Is Rachel ready for school, Thelma?'

'Almost. She's cleaning her teeth now. Though, mind you, it wouldn't matter if she had a couple of days off. I've told her she has a new wee brother and she's all excited.'

'There's no need for her to miss any lessons. I'll run her down as soon as I've phoned work and let them know I won't be in for a few days. It's all arranged. Can you stay with Rebecca until I get back? Ah, here she is now. Come here where I can see you, love. Have you been a good girl for Grannie, Rachel?'

With a whoop of delight she threw herself into her father's arms. 'Yes, Daddy. Have you my wee brother home with you?'

Giving her a smacking kiss, he solemnly informed her, 'No, love, the baby will come home with your mammy. You see, she has to feed him. But this afternoon, when I pick you up from

60

school, we'll go up to the hospital and see your mammy and your new wee brother.'

'Can Grannie come too, Daddy?'

'Of course she can!'

'And Rebecca?

'And Rebecca! Where is she by the way?'

Thelma threw her hands in the air. 'Oh, my God! I left her sitting on her potty. I'll fetch her then I'll brew a pot of tea.'

When she returned with Rebecca by the hand, Thelma said, 'I'll stay here the rest of the day, Sean. You need a good rest. I've told George to come here for his dinner. I hope you don't mind?'

'Thelma, you're a gem! I'll be delighted to have you both here. Thanks! Thanks very much.'

Colour touched her cheeks at his words of praise. 'Oh, don't be silly. I'm only too pleased to be of use. Look, you need to eat something, Sean. I'll have a fry ready for you when you come back from school and you can tell me all about last night. Now off you go.'

Rebecca was down for her morning nap and Thelma sat across the table from him sipping a cup of tea whilst Sean ate his breakfast. Between each mouthful he brought her up to date. From the first pain, right through to the surgeon advising him that there should be no more children. He watched her reaction to this piece of information and when she didn't comment, questioned her.

'Do you think that she'll really mind not having any more children, Thelma?'

'It's hard to say, Sean. Annie made no secret of the fact that she wanted six, but if it's going to be too dangerous she'll just have to lump it. After all, you've two lovely wee girls and now a son. She will just have to count her blessings. You can't afford to take chances when you have three children to rear. Anyway, three is enough these days if you want to give them a good start in life. Everything is so expensive.'

Sean noted that birth control was not mentioned. But then, Thelma was one of the old school. Abstinence would be the only option so far as she was concerned. What the church

61

decreed was law! He steered away from the subject that was uppermost in his mind.

'Annie was determined to give me a son and heir! Heir to what, I ask you?' he jested. 'Not that I care. Wee girls are lovely! I'm sure Tommy Magee never regretted having just two daughters. I mean . . . it's out of our hands. We've to take what God gives us, don't we? I'm glad, though, that this one's a boy. If nothing else, it will make Annie happy. Make up for not having any more. We're very lucky, you know. I just hope she realizes that.'

At the mention of her husband, Thelma's face had paled. 'You forget that Tommy has a son,' she reminded him quietly.

'Ah, Thelma, I did forget completely all about that. I didn't mean to offend you. Sorry!'

'Oh, don't be silly! It's just . . . well, I'm very proud of George and thankful that Tommy insisted he took on the family name.' She smiled wryly and confessed, 'Mind you, at the time I wasn't in the least bit happy about it. In fact I played hell with Tommy. Read him the Riot Act. Accused him of putting George before the girls and me. But, I'll grant him this, he stood his ground. Said since I wouldn't adopt the child, the least he could do for George was give him his name. To tell you the truth, I'm glad now he did. I love that boy as if he was my own flesh and blood.'

Seeing sadness spread over her countenance Sean reached across the table for her hand and squeezed it sympathetically. 'Don't upset yourself, Thelma. Don't think about it,' he advised softly. 'George is one of the best.' He could see that his words fell on barren ground and sad memories from the past were plaguing her.

'I can still picture Tommy's face the night he confessed,' she muttered. 'I'll never be able to forget it till the day I die! I ranted and raved so much, I thought I'd finish up in Purdysburn. Shame and guilt was written all over his face. I couldn't believe my ears when he told me. That Tommy would stray while I was carrying my second child? Why! I was devastated! My world fell apart and I couldn't think straight for weeks on end. I was so hurt . . . that Tommy could do *that!*' Even now the memory of her husband's betrayal brought a sob to block her throat.

62

She swallowed it and continued, 'We had been so close. I trusted him completely. I just couldn't find it in my heart to forgive him. We lived like complete strangers for a long time. I even contemplated leaving him. But that would have made people pity me and I couldn't bear the thought of it. So time passed and eventually I forgave him, but I couldn't forget and I made his life a living hell.' She lifted her head and looked Sean in the eye. 'I was a real bitch, wasn't I?'

He shook his head sadly. 'You were hurt, Thelma. It was only natural to feel like that. Anyone in your position would have done the same.'

She smiled wanly and continued, 'Many a time, over the years, I wanted to ask after the boy, but I couldn't bring myself to do it. The words always stuck in my throat. I was annoyed you see, that he had stuck to his guns and continued to visit him. Every Thursday regular as clockwork he trekked up that Shankill Road to see him. I was terrified anyone would find out.' She grimaced slightly at this admission. 'All that pride! You see, I worried about the neighbours finding out. Such a waste! But when you're young, you do put on a front and I'm ashamed to admit that I did worry about what people thought. It was my stupid pride, you see. God forgive me. If I had been a stronger person I would have said "To hell with them!" I should have been more compassionate. I know that now. But then, I was weak and I made Tommy suffer for it. And then to lose him like that in the blitz! Never to be able to tell him how sorry I was, I nearly went round the bend! That's why I was so glad when George came into our lives. By taking him in and making him feel welcome I felt I was making amends. I only hope, somehow, Tommy knows that.'

'I'm sure he does, Thelma.'

Abruptly, Thelma pushed herself up from the table. 'I'm sorry, Sean. I don't know what's come over me. I've never discussed it with anyone before, you know. Please forgive me, and forget I ever mentioned it.'

'Perhaps you should have talked about it earlier, Thelma. It would have eased the pain. Got it out of your system, once and for all.'

Turning away, she dabbed surreptitiously at her eyes. 'You need to get some sleep, son. Not listen to an old fool like me rambling on. Besides, by the look of things, as far as we're concerned, the Magee name will die out anyway. As you well know . . . George never bothers with women.'

'Give him time, Thelma. He's still a young man.'

'Thirty-two is a bit long in the tooth, if you ask me. I wish he'd married Mary Mitchell. Now, that would have been a good match. And she would have had him, you know! I thought he really fancied her. Lord knows he chased her long enough. And then when she finally consented to date him, a couple of months later it all petered out. The next thing we heard she was married to John Greenwood. Sean . . .' Her voice became gruff and she appeared embarrassed as she voiced her doubts. 'You don't think he's . . . you know . . . the other way inclined?'

Comprehension dawned slowly on Sean and then he threw back his head and laughed aloud. 'Catch yourself on, Thelma! Of course he's not! How could you even think such a thing? George a daisy root? That's a good one, so it is.'

Relieved at his words, she was nevertheless annoyed at his laughter and directness. To her it was no laughing matter. 'Well then, why hasn't he got a girlfriend?' she retaliated 'A good-looking, strapping big man like him should be able to pick and choose. So why is he still single?'

'Forgive me for laughing, Thelma, but it's all so ridiculous. He obviously hasn't met the right woman yet.'

'Well, he'd better get a move on or else he'll miss the boat.' She lifted Sean's empty plate and mug and headed for the kitchen. 'Would you like another cup of tea, son?'

'No, thanks, Thelma. That was delicious. Now I'm going to take your advice and go to bed for a few hours. Will you wake me in time for me to collect Rachel from school?'

At her nod he left the room, still smiling to himself at the very idea of her concern for George, and slowly climbed the stairs. As he undressed, it suddenly dawned on him that Thelma was a very attractive woman. When Tommy Magee had been killed in the blitz the shock had turned his mother-in-law's hair white overnight. It suited her. That, combined with her pale skin and bright green eyes, made her very attractive indeed. What age would she be now? About fifty-six? She looked much younger. It was a wonder someone hadn't snapped her up long ago. But sure, he reminded himself, she never goes out anywhere that she would be likely to meet a mature man. Say a widower like . . . His mind ranged over the men he knew who had lost their wives and he smiled to himself. John McLaughlin. Now there was a likely match. Was there any way he could bring them together? He must ask Annie for her opinion. Wearily he stretched out on the bed and all thoughts of matchmaking faded into a deep sleep as soon as his head hit the pillow.

When they turned the bend on the Serpentine Road and their house came into view Annie felt tears of pride smart in her eyes. Between showers, it was warm for April and there at the open doorway stood her two young daughters. With faces scrubbed clean and hair brushed tidily and caught in big bows on top of their heads, they were a pretty picture to behold. Catching sight of the car, they threw their arms in the air, jumping up and down and waving vigorously. Thelma held on to both her granddaughters firmly until the car slid to a halt in the driveway. When she released her hold on them Rachel swooped down on the car, followed more cautiously by Rebecca.

'Mam . . . Mam, can I hold the baby?'

'Later, love. When we're inside.'

Disappointment brought a howl of protest from Rachel's lips.

'Rachel, behave yourself!'

Sean's voice was stern and seeing her little face crumple in dismay, Annie hugged her sympathetically against her legs. 'Wait until your dad carries him inside where it's nice and warm, love. Then you can sit on the settee and nurse him.'

Mollified, Rachel wiped away her tears with the back of her hands and eagerly watched every move while Sean carried the precious bundle inside. Following closely on his heels, she sat on the settee beside Thelma. Patting her dress down, she waited patiently until he gently placed the baby on her lap.

'Let's have a look at him, love.' Thelma leant across and with tender hands removed the warm shawl and hat that covered the baby. Her eyes filled with tears when she gazed on her grandson. 'My, but he's a bonny wee lad!' She had held him in the hospital but here in his own home, lying across young

65

Rachel's knees, he looked even bigger. 'He's beautiful. Have you decided on a name yet, Annie?'

She exchanged a look with Sean. 'Well, we have given it a lot of thought and decided it would be a good idea to name him after his two grandfathers, Thomas James.'

She was glad when Sean nodded his agreement. The only snag had been which name he would be called by. Sean was easy but he knew his father would hope for the baby to be called James. Still, Tommy was dead . . . surely his father would not openly object? No, this way everybody should be pleased.

A great beam split Thelma's face. 'Thank you. Tommy will be happy.' Her eyes scanned Annie's pale face. 'Now, love, I think you should go straight to bed. Remember what the doctor said . . . it will be some time before you're feeling well enough to do anything.'

'I do feel tired,' Annie admitted. 'You'd think I'd climbed the Cave Hill instead of in and out of a car.'

'Away you go, love. I'll bring you up a cup of tea.'

'Grannie, can I look at the baby's toes?'

'Yes, Rachel, let's have a look, and then he must get into his cot. Look, he's yawning. He wants to go to sleep. Come you over to this side, love.' Rebecca had been standing back watching everything in silence. When she slowly approached, Thelma put her free arm around her and drew her close. 'Now you will be able to see better. Isn't your wee brother lovely?'

Tentatively, Rebecca touched the baby's head and a delighted smile creased her solemn face when the child, at that moment opened his eyes. Thelma was contented. Both the girls had accepted the new addition to the family. At all costs no one must feel out of it.

Annie headed slowly for the stairs but with one swift movement Sean swept her up in his arms, dismissing her claims that she was too heavy: 'You're as light as a feather,' he laughed, as he effortlessly climbed the stairs. 'We will have to get you a tonic.' He laid her gently on the bed. 'Do you want to undress now, love?'

She shook her head, and reached for his hand. 'Sean, I'm so happy to have given you a son. Are you pleased?'

'Pleased? I'm delighted!' He tousled the unruly locks that spread across the pillow. 'Now you must get some rest. Are you sure you don't want to get into your nightie? You'd be more comfortable, so you would.'

'No, I just want a nap. They waken you at six every morning at the hospital. Strange though it may seem, you never get a proper rest there. I'll have a short nap and then I'll come downstairs for a while.' She stretched gingerly and then curled up, her eyes already closing.

Sean pulled the bedspread over her shoulders and bending, kissed her lightly on the forehead. 'All right, love. I'll tell your mother you don't want any tea just yet.' Drawing the curtains, he quietly slipped from the room.

Annie lay at peace, waiting for sleep to claim her. She was glad to be home. She had been in hospital ten long days following an infection to her wound. It was still a bit raw and very tender. Thank goodness her mother lived close at hand. She had been goodness itself, looking after Sean and the children. And she was certainly going to need her help in the coming months. So far Thomas ... oh, didn't that name have a lovely ring to it? She repeated it, Thomas James Devlin had so far slept between feeds but that situation would soon end and Annie knew the coming months would be arduous. Thank God her mother lived nearby and that Minnie was such a good neighbour. With their help she would soon be back on her feet again. A smile curved her lips. She had a son. Sean had someone to carry on the family name. A contented sigh escaped her lips. Rosaleen no longer posed quite such a threat. With this thought she drifted off into a contented sleep.

During the next two months, slowly but surely Annie regained her strength. Thomas was a good baby; rarely cried, slept a lot and was putting on weight daily. Why then did she feel so uneasy? She stood and gazed intently down at the child as he lay in his cot. Dark lashes fanning out on rosy cheeks, he looked the picture of health. But there was something not quite right. She couldn't put her finger on it. Was it because he was so passive? Even when awake he was content to lie looking around him. At this age both Rachel and Rebecca had been more active. But then, hadn't boys the name of being lazy? No one else had noticed anything wrong. Everybody agreed he was the ideal baby. Perhaps this time next week he would begin to make his presence felt and she would be laughing at herself. Give him time, she thought, and covered him with a blanket before leaving the room.

Another month passed quickly and still Thomas remained the ideal baby. Passive and happy, he now smiled, uttered small noises, but made no attempt to touch toys stretched across his cradle within easy reach. No matter how hard Annie tried to stimulate his interest, he remained passive. He was no way near as active as the two girls had been. They had both sat up at an early age and had walked before they were eleven months. In spite of assuring herself that boys were different, Annie was aware that she was dodging the issue. Doubts were always there, niggling at the back of her mind.

She took him to the clinic each week and they thought him a lovely baby and found no fault with him. Annie watched the nurses' faces closely as he was weighed and examined but could find no indication that these women were humouring her. And why should they? It was their job to ensure that the baby was healthy, wasn't it? After all, they were there to speak out if anything was wrong. So, convincing herself that all was well, she pushed the fears that were beginning to plague her to the back of her mind. Surely these experienced midwives and nurses would notice if anything was amiss? Who was she to doubt them? Each week she went to the clinic but was afraid to voice her fears. The nurses sounded him, asked if he slept well and took all his feeds; truthfully, she said that he did. They cooed and fussed over him and congratulated her on having such a contented child. Thomas happily beamed back at them but after each visit Annie returned home fraught with doubts.

At last, when he was five months old, she tentatively questioned her mother. 'Mam, do you think there's anything strange about Thomas?'

Thelma examined her grandson's face. Was his head slightly bigger than normal or was it that his great mop of black curls made it appear so? Was it her imagination that there was something strange about him? For some time now she herself had been thinking something was amiss but, afraid of saying the wrong thing, had held her tongue in check. He appeared healthy enough, but to Thelma, her grandson had a slight look about him of a child she once knew of who lived on the

68

Springfield Road, a little girl. Once it was confirmed that the child was backward her parents had hidden her away from the outside world. She had been kept at the back of the house, never allowed to mix with other children. With her big, bland, vacant face it was obvious that she was retarded, and children could be so cruel. Thelma didn't blame the parents. She probably would have done the same thing herself. It was for the child's own good, after all. Not for one minute did she think that the little girl had ever been neglected, but she had been kept out of sight from the neighbours. Away from prying eyes. Pauline had been her name. She must be about twelve by now. Still Thomas wasn't obviously retarded; he looked quite normal, but Thelma was worried about him. In her opinion he should be more active by now.

'To be truthful, Annie, I do think he's a bit slow. But, remember, I have only girls to compare him with . . . and you and Rosaleen were so quick at everything. You were both sitting up long before this age, and bracing yourselves on your feet, just like Rachel and Rebecca did. But no two children are the same, Annie. A girl around the corner from me actually encouraged hers to sit in the pram all day. She said once they learn to walk they get into all kinds of mischief and she saved on shoe leather into the bargain! I felt sorry for the kids but it didn't do them a bit of harm. I mean, they grew up healthy enough.'

A chill ran along Annie's spine. Her mother was being evasive. 'Mam, don't ramble! Do you think there's anything wrong with Thomas or not?'

Still Thelma dithered. 'What about the ones down in the clinic? Have they found anything wrong with him? Have you told them how you feel?'

'No, but I've noticed that other baby boys down there about the same age as Thomas are bouncing about in their prams.'

'Well then, you should have asked the nurses' opinion, since you're so worried! They would know better than me. Or, maybe you should take him down to the doctor, if you're so concerned about him.'

Annie sighed and admitted, 'I'm afraid. I keep assuring myself that they'd be sure to notice anything and advise me

69

what to do. Surely I shouldn't have to question them? It's their job to notice such things, isn't it?'

'I agree with you there. I'm sure someone would have twigged if there was something obviously wrong. After all, as you so rightly say, that's what they're paid for. It's their job to notice these things.'

'I know, Mam. But, you see, they just examine him for all the usual baby symptoms and Thomas lies there smiling at them. I don't blame them for not noticing. It's when I'm working with him, when I'm bathing him and changing his nappy . . . He's just limp in my arms. Mam, I really *am* worried.'

'What about Sean? Has he noticed anything?'

'No . . . but he sees so little of him. Thomas is in bed before his dad comes home from work and even at the weekends Sean is always preoccupied. To be truthful he thinks that I'm neglecting the girls and spends all his spare time with them to make up for it. It's not fair! I do my best, what more can I do?'

'Ah, Annie, love, what a burden to carry alone. You shouldn't have bottled all this up inside you. Look . . . let's you and me take him down to see Dr Cardiff tomorrow morning. Set your mind at rest. Eh, love?' She was glad that her daughter had spoken out; it would also set her own mind at rest.

'I'd like that, Mam. I'd like that very much. And thanks.'

In bed that night Annie cuddled close to Sean. She must get through to him how worried she was. He thought she was just being overprotective. She must prepare him for the eventuality that Thomas might be backward. Surprised, Sean held her near, but he was apprehensive. As far as he was aware it wasn't the right time of the month and he had been unable to persuade Annie to condone artificial contraception. They were both passionate people and used to love making when they pleased, but fear of another pregnancy had put paid to that now. Instead there were certain times of the month when it was assumed safe, but even then Sean worried in case there were consequences. To make matters worse he knew that Annie would never refuse him. She did not worry about another pregnancy the way he did. But what if she conceived and he was to lose her? No, that was unthinkable! He would never forgive himself. He was willing to curb himself so long as Annie was safe.

'Sean?'

'Yes, love? Is this the safe period?'

'No, but don't worry about that. I want to talk to you about something.'

'Annie, I think we'll be able to talk better if there's a wee bit of space between us.' Gently he started to disentangle her arms.

Fiercely, she clung to him and burrowed her head against his chest. 'Sean! Listen . . . I have to talk to you! I think there's something wrong with Thomas.'

'What do you mean . . . wrong?' he cried in bewilderment. 'I've never noticed anything.'

'I think there's something wrong with his legs. He's making no effort to use them. When I try to to hold him upright they just buckle beneath his weight. He's limp in my arms all the time.'

'In the name of God, Annie, do you expect him to walk at five months?' Sean laughed at the very idea. 'I know you think our kids are quick, but surely even you don't imagine they're that clever?'

'No, of course I don't expect him to walk. But surely he should be using his legs more by now? He should at least be bracing himself against me. He just lies there all the time. And . . . surely he should be making some kind of an effort to play with his toys? Sit up on his own? Make some attempt to stand? But no, he just lies there smiling at me.'

'Give him a chance, Annie, eh? He seems a very contented child. Besides, if there were anything wrong with him, surely they would have noticed when he was born?'

'I hope you're right, Sean. Mam and I are taking him down to the doctor's tomorrow.'

His ears pricked up; his interest was roused. 'Does Thelma think there's something in it then?' He was not so sure now. He'd thought Annie was too taken up with the child, but if Thelma was also worried that was a different kettle of fish entirely.

'No, not really. I think she wants to set my mind at rest so she's offered to accompany me.'

71

'Phew! Thank God for that! Maybe you're just a bit paranoid about him, eh, love? You've wanted a son for so long, it's playing tricks on your mind.' Determinedly he put her from him. 'Now I think you had better stay on your own side of the bed.'

'Sean, please hold me. I need you. I need to be close to you.'

'Ah, love . . . it's not fair on me! I'm only human, you know.'

'Well then, why not? I'm willing! I feel fine.' She pressed closer still, lips seeking his, urging him on. 'Come on, love. Let's chance it, eh?'

'Annie, you know what Mr Montgomery said. It's far too dangerous. Unless you've changed your mind about . . .' He hesitated, eyeing her hopefully. When he had told her the surgeon's views on another pregnancy he had suggested artificial contraception but she would not hear of it. Now he watched her shake her head in dismissal.

'No, Sean . . . it's wrong! It's a sin! And you know it is!'

'Listen, Annie,' he pleaded, 'I'll take all the blame. It will be my decision. All you have to do is play along with it. What about it? Eh, love? If necessary I'll go to hell for our actions. Because you see, Annie, in our circumstances I don't think it would be morally wrong. I really believe that, love.' He held his breath hopefully. If only she would pay heed to him! He was finding it extremely difficult to stick to the safe period. What made it worse was that he had never seen eye to eye with the church in this matter. In his opinion there were far too many unwanted children in the world and his answer to the problem would be birth control.

However, he pleaded in vain. He may as well talk to the wallpaper for all the good his preaching was doing. With another determined shake of the head, Anne withdrew with an exaggerated flounce to her side of the bed. Sean's expression was bleak as he gazed at her rigid back. It was all up when you had to refuse your wife the comfort she needed. He would have a talk with the priest and explain their situation. See what he had to say about it. Maybe there would be some compromise after all. But knowing the strong stance the church took on birth control, he wasn't very hopeful.

* * *

Dr Cardiff was poker-faced as he examined Thomas. He had listened in attentive silence as Annie explained her misgivings in great detail, then told her to remove the child's clothes. Annie and Thelma watched his every move as he examined eyes, ears, nose and throat. Then he sounded Thomas's chest. Lastly, he stretched the child out on the couch and first manipulated his arms and then his legs.

Suddenly he broke the silence. 'Has he ever had a fit, Annie?'

She came out of her trance. 'No, never. He's never been any bother at all. He's goodness itself!'

'Mmm . . . strange.' After further pulling at the baby's limbs, he said, 'Right, that's me finished. You can dress him now.'

He sat lost in thought, twiddling his lips between forefinger and thumb, as Annie put on Thomas's clothes. Afraid to question him, she let the silence stretch. It was Thelma, from the corner where she sat waiting, who dared break it.

'Well, Dr Cardiff, is there anything wrong with him or is it all in Annie's mind?' she asked apprehensively, at the same time trying to show some authority. She had hoped the doctor would pooh-pooh Annie's fancies; prove them wrong in their assumptions. That he hadn't done so sent fear to the very core of her.

Dr Cardiff knew these women well. He had been new to the doctor's surgery when Annie first came to Greencastle and she and her husband automatically became his patients. Then, when her mother had come to live nearby, Thelma and her stepson had also registered with him. He liked and respected this family, but was apprehensive about the condition of the child. 'Thelma, Annie . . . I'm in no position to do tests on him here so I wouldn't like to express an opinion. I'll make an appointment for you at the hospital.'

Terror clutched Annie, making her voice hoarse. 'Then there *is* something wrong?'

'I honestly don't know, and that's the truth. But like you, I'm a bit perturbed. Let's see what the specialists have to say. After all, that's what they're there for. They're the experts! I'll get in touch with the hospital and they'll let you know when they can fit Thomas in.'

He rose and courteously opened the door but he could find no words of comfort for them. He too thought that something was not quite right with Thomas. He recalled the difficult time Annie had had at the birth and could only hope that he was mistaken, but from past experience he doubted it very much.

Two weeks later, Annie and her mother sat in yet another doctor's office and watched him examine Thomas. The specialist had introduced himself as Jim Dixon and asked Annie if she would object to some students being present. When she shook her head he called in two young white-coated men and a girl from another room. Annie sat with her hands clasped between her knees to keep them from twitching and listened attentively as Thomas was examined. A running discussion went on between Mr Dixon and the students but all the medical terms used were above and beyond her ken. At last the students smiled diffidently at them, thanked them and wished them good day before filing from the room.

'You can dress Thomas now, Mrs Devlin.' Jim Dixon could see that Annie was tense and said kindly, 'I should like to admit him for some further tests. Will that be all right with you?'

She nodded mutely and it was Thelma, once again promoting herself to spokeswoman, who voiced the question. 'What do you think is wrong with him, Doctor?'

'I don't really know at this stage. You see, there's nothing obviously amiss. He looks all right, but he's not progressing as he should by his age.'

'But you have some idea what's wrong with him, haven't you?' Thelma was persistent.

The consultant was not to be drawn. 'I must wait until we have carried out further tests and assessed him.' He turned to Annie. 'Can you bring him back tomorrow and I'll make arrangements for a bed to be ready for him?'

So soon? She was taken aback. He must suspect something serious if he was admitting Thomas straight away. Close to tears, she once more nodded and soon they were standing on the Falls Road outside the Royal Victoria Hospital for sick children. Annie turned big watery eyes full of dread on Thelma.

'Oh, Mam, I'm frightened, so I am,' she sobbed.

74

'I know how you feel, love. So am I. But listen, obviously there's a chance that the doctor is wrong. After all, Mr Dixon wouldn't commit himself one way or the other. If he was positive then I'm sure he would have told us there and then. Don't be getting yourself all upset, love. There's still hope.'

However, Annie was not to be consoled. She clutched Thomas fiercely to her breast, glad that the faint drizzle hid the tears that overflowed and spilled down her cheeks as they crossed the road to join the queue at the bus stop outside St Paul's Church; sending prayers in its direction. Please, God, help us. Don't let it be serious.

That night Thomas had his first fit. The family was all gathered in the living room. Sean had that weekend purchased a television set and he and Annie were watching the six o'clock news when sudden choking sounds brought them hastily to the pram where Thomas had been gurgling happily. One minute he was lying relaxed and happy, the next his body was contorted and his limbs writhing out of control. His back arched, his eyes bulged like some giant toad's, as if they were about to pop from ir sockets, and his tongue protruded from blackening lips.

Terrified at the sight of his son's shaking body and jerking limbs, and the foam that had gathered around his mouth, Sean grabbed him from the pram. He tossed him over one shoulder and started slapping him on the back, at the same time shouting for Annie to ring the doctor. She raced to the phone and rang Dr Cardiff. He gave her instructions what to do and as he lived on the nearby Antrim Road himself arrived within minutes to take control of the situation. He worked over Thomas until the jerking limbs were limp and the contorted face calm. When he heard that the child was due to be admitted to hospital the next day, the doctor decided to have him taken in immediately. An ambulance was summoned and Thomas, accompanied by a badly frightened Annie, was whisked away. Full of dread Sean watched the ambulance out of sight and then returned to his daughters. During all the commotion Rachel and Rebecca had scurried to a corner of the room where, wrapped in each other's arms, they'd watched the fearful scene unfold before their terrified eyes.

Now he held out his arms to them. 'Come here, girls. Don't

75

look so worried. Thomas was sick and now he's away to the hospital in that big ambulance to be made better. Soon he'll be all right and they will send him home again. How's about I give you two a bath and then we'll watch the tele while we wait for your mam to come back?'

Gratefully they ran to his arms to be comforted and soon they were splashing and playing in the bath. Sean wished he too could shed his worry, but the sight of his son's wee blue face plagued his mind and it was with trepidation that he awaited his wife's return from hospital.

It was well after nine and the girls were long asleep before she returned. She was accompanied by George. 'I phoned him to come and pick me up,' she explained.

Sean had forgotten that George had recently had a telephone installed. 'That was kind of you. I forgot you were on the phone now or I would have let you know sooner what was going on. Well, how is he, Annie?'

'They gave him some sort of injection and don't expect him to waken before morning. I wanted to stay but they wouldn't let me.'

With a wave of his hand George indicated her face. 'Look at that, Sean. There's more colour in a bag of flour. She needs a good strong cup of tea to settle her nerves.'

Glad of the excuse of something to occupy him, Sean headed for the kitchen. 'I'll put the tea on. Would you like a cup, George?'

'No, thanks, Sean. I'd better go home. Thelma was down the street seeing someone's new baby when I left and I never thought to leave a note. I told her I wasn't going out tonight so she'll wonder where on earth I am.'

He sat beside Annie on the settee a moment and sympathetically patted her knee, trying to comfort her. 'Don't meet your troubles halfway, Annie,' he entreated. 'Wait and see what results the tests bring then we'll all face it together. You know you're not alone, love. We'll all rally round.'

Impulsively, she turned and buried her head in his shoulder. She needed to be held; to be comforted. And Sean? Huh! He was out making tea!

'I'm so afraid, George. I don't know how I'll bear it if Thomas is severely handicapped.'

He held her close. 'As I say, Annie. You won't be alone. We'll all help out.'

Hearing Sean coming along the hall he put Annie firmly from him. She looked at him in bewilderment, but he was up and fussing about, meeting Sean at the door, taking a cup of tea off the tray and handing it to her. Her eyes questioned him. She needed his comfort.

George kept his eyes averted. Annie must never come to rely too much on him. After all, he was only her half-brother. Sean must not be usurped; he was her husband and should share the responsibility that went with rearing a handicapped child. It was his place to comfort his wife in her distress.

Taking the seat that George had vacated, Sean made a futile effort to comfort her. He felt so inadequate. 'Don't worry, love. Lot of babies have fits in their early months. As you well know, our Betty's youngest had them for about a year. Once he passed his first birthday they stopped as if by magic.'

Annie was not to be convinced. Babies could, she was aware, develop fits for various reasons but in her heart she knew that it was more serious than that. She held her tongue. Let Sean live in a fool's paradise for a little longer. Her carefree days were gone forever.

'Put a drop of whiskey in that tea,' George advised. 'That is, if you have any, and make her go straight to bed. Thelma will come up early in the morning. I'll head on down now. See you tomorrow night.'

'I'll see you out, George.'

'No, you stay with Annie. I'll let myself out. Good night, Annie.'

The only reply he received was a nod of the head and he sighed deeply. If only Sean would admit that there was a problem maybe Annie could relax a bit. While he chose to believe that everything was hunky-dory, Annie would only get more wound up. She needed help. They both needed help. But George felt that he must be careful not to tread on anyone's toes. If the occasion arose, he would help all he could, without any hesitation.

After another three weeks, and numerous tests, it was confirmed that Thomas had cerebral palsy. Three long weeks

77

during which Annie spent most of her time either at the hospital or on her knees praying. It was Mr Dixon who broke the bad news to both of them. He asked specifically to see them together and Annie guessed the news was bad. Nevertheless, although she was prepared for the worst, she almost collapsed with shock when the doctor put it into words. Her world fell apart. The specialist explained that Thomas had what was called a bleed. It covered a small area of his brain and the extent of Thomas's backwardness would not be known for some time. He told them that the child would not develop normally. The part of his brain that was damaged was small, but they had better be prepared for the worst then any improvement would be a bonus. He might never walk or speak. Only time and patient therapy would tell. Annie was devastated. Life had become a bottomless pit. All kind of unwarranted thoughts raced through her mind as she pictured how limited her son's life might be.

'Whose fault is this?' Sean asked accusingly. 'How did it come about?'

Mr Dixon paused and considered before replying, thus fanning Sean's suspicions that something was being withheld. 'Cerebral palsy can be caused by many different things. For example, if the mother has rubella or some other infection while she is carrying the child it can result in this condition.'

'My wife didn't have any illness while she was pregnant,' Sean protested.

Annie felt obliged to back him up. Her pregnancy had been normal until she went into labour. 'He's right, Doctor. I sailed through this pregnancy without any bother. It was only when I went into labour that things started to go wrong.'

After another thoughtful pause the doctor confessed, 'I must admit it can also result from a difficult birth. However, it isn't something that can be foreseen.'

In an endeavour to ease their anguish and give them some hope he went on to explain that there were organizations that would be able to give them professional assistance. He said great strides had been made in these clinics and that someone would get in touch with them soon.

Automatically they made the necessary replies and eventually found themselves standing outside the doctor's office.

Excusing himself, Sean abruptly left. Annie gazed after him in bewilderment. Where was he off to? In a daze she made her way back to the ward and sat down by her son's cot, gazing blindly at him, jumbled prayers going round and round in her tortured mind. Please God, help me to face up to this trial. Please make Sean understand. I can't face this alone. I need someone to talk to. What have I done to deserve this?

As if in answer to her prayer George and her mother arrived. She turned to them in anguish. 'Mam, oh, Mam . . .'

George placed a comforting arm around her shoulders. 'We know, Annie. We have been talking to Sean. He's devastated. But remember what I said? We're all behind you in this. Thomas is not the first handicapped child to be born. You'll find the strength to rear him.'

George was right. Annie soon got into a set routine. She divided her time between home and hospital. It was hard work but somehow she managed. Her biggest problem was Sean. He simply refused to accept that there was anything wrong. He insisted that the doctors had made a terrible mistake; that Thomas was just slow, and when he was ready their son would show everybody just how wrong they were. After all, he didn't look backward. In Sean's opinion backwardness meant Down's syndrome.

Perhaps when Thomas was allowed home from hospital he would wake up to reality. Annie prayed that this would be so; she needed his support. Meanwhile, her husband's way of dealing with the problem was to work all the overtime he could get. It was left up to George to ferry Annie to and from hospital while Thelma and Minnie between them looked after the two girls.

Diffidently, she tried to excuse her husband's apparent indifference to his young son's plight. George was quick to assure her that he understood. He said that at first rejection was normal. He convinced her that Sean would soon come to terms with the dismay and anger he was harbouring at what fate had done to him. Annie could only hope and pray that her brother was right.

'Still, it's not fair on you, George!' she lamented. 'I'm taking up far too much of your spare time. You've your own life to live. You shouldn't have to troop up and down to the hospital with me. You're a young man. You should be out enjoying yourself and meeting people.'

His grin was wide and infectious. 'You sound like Thelma. She's forever urging me to get a girlfriend. You'd think they were all lined up, waiting for me to choose one to honour with my attentions. She doesn't seem to realize that maybe no one will have me.'

'For once I agree with her! You'll have no bother getting a girlfriend, but not if I take up all your time.'

'I honestly don't mind, Annie. What are family for, if not to help out in time of need? Besides, I'm really not interested in anyone else.' A slip of the tongue. Would she notice?

They had spent the evening together at the hospital and now as the car drew up in her driveway Annie impulsively reached across and grasped his hand. 'I'll never forget your generosity, George. I hope one day I'll be able to do you a favour in return.' She held his gaze intently.

He sat rooted to the spot. What did she mean? He dragged his eyes from hers and gazed mutely down at her hand but did not return the pressure of her fingers. Instead, after some moments, he gently released her grip and, getting out of the car, went round to open her door. 'I'm glad to be of assistance, Annie. That's the truth. Away in and get yourself to bed. You're exhausted, so you are!' With a slight push he sent her on her way towards the house, and without another glance got back in the car and drove off.

She stood for some time in confusion, gazing after the car. Had she somehow or other offended her brother? He had gone away looking so bleak and sad. A perplexed frown on her brow, she slowly climbed the steps and entered the house.

'Did you not invite George in for a cup of tea, Annie?'

Sean's voice reached her as she hung up her coat at the foot of the stairs and her lips tightened angrily. Entering the sitting room, she said sharply, 'No. Strange though it may seem, I didn't. We're both tired. But then, you wouldn't understand how tiring it can be sitting beside a cot for hours on end.'

Sean's eyebrows came together at her tone of voice. 'He doesn't have to go every day,' he said mildly. 'Neither do you, for that matter. We could divide the visiting hours out between the lot of us . . . but you . . . you want to spend every single spare minute at the hospital. So, George has decreed you must have company. And it doesn't make any difference to Thomas. He's too young to understand. Meanwhile, someone has to look after our two daughters. Remember those little girls asleep upstairs?'

'Don't you patronize me, Sean Devlin. If you would shoulder your responsibilities like a man, certainly we could share the visiting. But you bury yourself in your work.'

'I'm trying to earn some extra money. More than ever now, we'll need a garage to make the back secure for the kids to play. And *if* Thomas is retarded . . . mind you, I don't think he will be, I still think he's just a bit slow. But *if* he is, we might have to make some alterations to the house. You know, widen doors and build a ramp if he is confined to a wheelchair? Build a bathroom downstairs? That all takes money! A lot of money. And that's why I'm working all the overtime I can get my hands on. That's why I'm not sitting in the hospital every spare moment I have.'

Blinded by tears, Annie slowly approached him. 'I'm sorry, Sean,' she lamented. 'I didn't understand. Please hold me. Hold me tight, I need to be reassured.'

With a sigh he gathered her close. 'It's all right, love. It's all right,' he said softly. But in his heart he was aware that it would never be all right again.

Time passed slowly and even after saying he needed to work to earn extra money for the renovations, when Thomas came home Sean still acted as if he was a normal baby. Annie decided to let him live in his deluded world. She devoted every waking moment to her young son. Sean was very annoyed at this. He pointed out that she had two other children who also needed her love and attention, accused her of neglecting their young daughters. He stressed that since Thomas was quite content to lie in his pram, he should be allowed to do so and that she should pay more attention to her girls. Annie did try but she couldn't please everybody all the time and worry kept her hovering protectively over her son. Rachel, as if aware that something was wrong with the baby, was in her own sweet way helpful. Rebecca, too young to understand, became withdrawn,

81

watching wide-eyed as Annie lavished all her time and apparently all her love on the new addition to the family.

For Sean it was the last straw when he heard Rachel trying to console her sister with the words, 'Mammy will love us tomorrow.'

That night when his two young daughters were asleep in bed, he cornered his wife in the nursery where she was as usual. Sometimes he thought Annie actually tried to will the child awake so she could attend to him. He was convinced that she was cracking up.

Taking her by the elbow, despite her whispered protests, he manoeuvred her out of the room and down the stairs.

In the sitting room he pushed her, none too gently, down on to the settee and sat down beside her; forcibly holding her when she struggled to throw off his restraining hand. 'Annie, we have to talk.'

She stiffened, guessing what was coming. He hated the time that she spent with Thomas. Didn't he realize that she was all Thomas had? *He* still blindly believed that all would be well. For a man of such intellect she could not fathom how he could be so blind to the situation. But then, he saw very little of his son. Well, he would just have to get used to it. Normal married life for them was over. However, when Sean quietly told her of the conversation he had overheard between Rachel and Rebecca, Annie sank back on the settee in dismay and buried her face in her hands to hide the tears she could not control. She did not want him to see the guilt that she was feeling.

He watched her through narrowed eyes. At last she lowered her hands and, wiping her eyes with the corner of her apron, looked at him with remorse. 'I'm sorry. I'm so sorry. I'll be more careful in future. You know I love the girls dearly, Sean . . . but I feel so guilty about Thomas. He didn't ask to be born and I feel I'm responsible for his being the way he is. You see, when I was carrying him, I kept asking God to let it be a boy. I was so obsessed with the idea of a son, I just kept thinking that so long as it was a boy I would be eternally grateful. Perhaps I was flying in God's face, eh? If I had just prayed as usual for a healthy child perhaps I would have had another girl. Do you see what I'm getting at, Sean? This could be all my fault!'

Aghast at her wild reasoning, he fell to his knees beside her

82

and gripped her hands tightly in his. 'Now, Annie, I don't want to hear you talk like that. That's nonsense and you know it is. It's nobody's fault! There's no way we could have prevented him being born ab—' His voice trailed off and she urged him on.

'Abnormal? Go on, Sean, say it! Please, admit it!'

Much as he wanted to comfort her, he found that he could not admit openly that his son was not normal. He pushed himself abruptly to his feet and ground out, 'You're smothering him, woman! Give him a chance and see how he develops. Wait till then. He's just a bit slow. By the time he's five he'll be as lively as any other wee boy.'

Sadly, Annie rose to her feet and faced him. 'I might be smothering him with love, Sean, but you ... you're afraid to look too closely at him. Afraid of what you might see there. Well it's about time you woke up to reality. He will never be normal and we can only do our best for him. You're missing out, Sean! He's so lovable. Such a wonderful baby.' She approached him and tentatively placed a hand on his arm. 'I'd have no qualms about trying again, love. Please let's try again, eh?'

Angrily he pushed her hand to one side. 'Are you daft or something? Have you not enough on your plate as it is?'

'Sean, I want another child before I'm too old. It's my decision too, you know!'

'No! Do you hear me? There will be no more children. You can just forget about carrying on the family name. Why is it so important to you anyway that the family name is carried on? I'm not in the least bit worried about it.'

'What about your father? Does he not count?'

'Annie, my da would rather see you alive and well than have someone to carry on the Devlin name. I've stacks of male cousins, ye know. Besides ... what if you survived another pregnancy and we had another child like Thomas? Or – perish the thought – what if you died in childbirth and I was left with two like him to rear? No, Annie. There's no way I'll risk it. So content yourself.' With these words he swung on his heel and stormed from the room, leaving her frustrated and unhappy.

In 1948 when the Labour Government had introduced the

National Health Service to Britain, and eventually Northern Ireland, it had taken over the care of disabled children, thus releasing a lot of voluntary bodies who had until then attended to these children's needs. They in turn began to focus their attention on children who were suffering from brain damage. Back in 1945 the special needs of children with brain damage had become more widely known and centres had been set up in America and Australia to pioneer work with cerebral palsied children. Great Britain followed suit. Successful team work between the government and voluntary and statutory bodies had eventually led to the purchase of a big house on Ulsterville Avenue and in 1952 a pre-school clinic was opened on these premises for such handicapped children.

In due course Annie was directed to take Thomas to Malcolm Sinclair House on Ulsterville Avenue. She had not known that such a place existed and it was with trepidation that she first attended the clinic. Further tests made in hospital had revealed that Thomas was spastic at the top of the legs. At the clinic he would receive the therapy required if he was ever to walk at all. Annie was relieved to discover that for those mothers without transport the Red Cross or Knights of Malta collected and returned the children in specially adapted mini-buses, free of charge. Thomas was booked in to attend two afternoons a week and to Annie's relief mothers were encouraged to remain with their children and learn as much as possible about the massage and exercises their child needed.

There were children older than Thomas at the clinic and Annie was pleased to note that most of them were able to walk. Some quite well, others not so well, but they could at least get about; they had some independence and that was the important thing. Only one child was so badly handicapped he had to be strapped securely in a wheelchair. Perhaps one day Thomas would walk; Anne fervently hoped that her son would eventually be able to get about the garden, get some kind of joy out of life. She was taught how to exercise Thomas's legs to help strengthen the muscles, and on the days that she didn't attend the clinic, sometimes assisted by her mother, sometimes by Minnie, she massaged and manipulated her small son's legs. She was determined to do all in her power to help him stand and one day walk. It would be some time before they knew how badly his mental powers had been impaired. They could only pray he would be able to communicate at least with his family and carers.

Since his birth, their social life was non-existent. Annie, bearing in mind that her mother and Minnie shared the responsibility of taking care of the two girls when needed, showed great reluctance when asked to leave the children again with Minnie for even a short time to go down to the pub for an hour or two. When Sean and Minnie between them managed to convince her she needed to relax away from home for a while, she allowed herself to be persuaded but always spoiled the outing by being on tenterhooks until they returned home.

Sean saw no reason to fall in with his wife's pattern of spending all her free time at home. If she refused to let Thelma or Minnie care for Thomas, that was her choice. He worked very hard and thought he deserved a break, so every Saturday night saw him down in McVeigh's pub in the company of George.

One night as they sat in the bar conversing over their drinks, he confided in his brother-in-law his idea of introducing Thelma to some eligible older bachelors or widowers. He was pleased when George agreed with him that Thelma should have a chance to meet someone of the opposite sex. Between them they sized up all the eligible men of their acquaintance and soon whittled them down to two. Next they set about persuading her to accompany them to what she had always considered a den of iniquity.

Thus, to her great surprise, Thelma found herself accompanying the men to the pub. She was amazed at herself! Thelma Magee, who had seldom been in a bar and considered that those who frequented them were up to no good, sauntering down the Whitewell Road to McVeigh's pub? After a couple of Saturday night outings, however, no more coaxing was necessary. She was a convert. Indeed she would have been affronted if the men had suggested going without her. She was also surprised to find herself the centre of attention amongst the senior citizens and blossomed prettily with all the attention she received in McVeigh's lounge on a Saturday night.

The relationship between Sean and Annie became more and more strained. He was still obsessed with the idea that one day Thomas would show them all how mistaken they had been. He became more and more wrapped up in his job and took all the overtime he could get.

Annie prayed that soon he would accept that his son could never be the same as other children, then perhaps they would achieve some sort of normality within their family. But Sean was coming home later and later from work and she bitterly resented the way he was, as she saw it, shirking his responsibility. Money wasn't all that important.

Loath to criticize her husband to George, her usual confidant, or anyone else for that matter, she felt weighed down with the worry of it all, quite literally at her wits' end. She was helped through this awful ordeal by the head of the clinic, a young woman dedicated to the children in her care. With practised intuition Miss McAteer sensed Annie's deep unhappiness and set out to win her confidence. To her surprise, one afternoon after the other parents had left Annie found herself mournfully pouring out all her fears and worries into a sympathetic ear. Silently, Miss McAteer let her get it all off her chest. This was nothing new to her; she had counselled many a man and woman in her time.

Over a cup of tea she confided that Sean was not the only man to have refused to accept his child's plight. Indeed most men found it hard to face up to the fact that their child would be just that, a child, all their lives. She explained how one man in particular refused to allow his wife to bring the baby home from the hospital because it was retarded. He said that it couldn't possibly be his! Accused the hospital of a mix-up. When blood tests proved beyond doubt that the child was his, he left the family home. It was some time before he returned, sorry and ashamed at the extra burden he had placed on his wife's shoulders.

Recalling to Annie's mind the young lad who had to be strapped in a wheelchair, Miss McAteer said, 'Tony is that lad. Look at him now. Although confined to a chair and unable to use his arms much, he's happy and very gifted. He can actually paint by holding a brush between his teeth and I don't doubt that one day he will be a great artist. And no one will be prouder then than his father. In fact, I would be prepared to bet he'll be the first to tell people that Tony is his son.'

Tentatively, Annie had asked, 'Do you think that Sean will ever come to terms with Thomas being backward?'

'Your son isn't all that backward, you know. I think in time you will be able to communicate with him and that will be a great blessing. If the child can communicate in any way at all, it is a wonderful release for them. It's so frustrating for them not to be able to make themselves understood. In time we will know how responsive Thomas is. Meanwhile, try to get your husband to come along to the clinic some afternoon. I bet you he will go home a reformed character, once he sees what goes on here.'

It was only with great reluctance that Sean agreed to take an afternoon off work and accompany Annie to the clinic in Ulsterville Avenue. He felt that he had been shanghaied and hadn't really had a say in the matter. If he had refused to go, Annie had vowed she would ask George to go in his place and he was beginning to feel ashamed at how often his brother-in-law was called upon to act as a surrogate husband and father. Thomas was not George's problem so Sean finally decided it was about time he shouldered his own responsibilities.

There was dread in his heart as he drew the car up to the entrance of the great big house. With feet that dragged he followed his wife up the steps and through the front door, acknowledging to himself that he was a coward. Afraid to come face to face with all these handicapped children. He was aware that he was about to see how his son might turn out. Once inside, however, his reluctance gradually evaporated as his interest was aroused and held. He was to be forever grateful that he had attended the clinic that day, and overcome with emotion to see the care and attention patiently lavished on the children by all the staff and voluntary helpers and parents. He was also amazed at the abilities displayed by the children themselves. Hope rose in his breast as he realized that the future probably held some kind of meaningful existence for Thomas. To Annie's delight, he offered his services in fund raising for the centre.

As they bade their good nights Annie's eyes spoke volumes

to Miss McAteer. Thanks to her, Sean was well on the road to being converted.

Chapter 3

All the overtime and hard work Sean had put in eventually paid dividends. A few weeks after Thomas's first birthday he moved up another rung on the ladder of success, earning a substantial pay rise. They would be able to upgrade the car as well as get a garage built, and if Annie could be persuaded to leave Thomas in the very capable hands of Thelma and George, they could afford to take the two girls on holiday abroad.

He arrived home from work in a state of euphoria. It was a beautiful sunny day in May and Rachel and Rebecca were playing in the back garden with some of their young friends. Minnie sat and knitted in the shade of the big apple tree, at the same time keeping an eye on the children. Caught up in their own activities, they just waved affably to him.

Entering the house, he discovered Annie attending to their son as usual. Some of Sean's happiness dimmed. What had gone wrong? Why was his son like this? They could have had such a great future to look forward to. The world at their feet, as it were, if only ... Pushing these self-pitying thoughts away, he bent and tousled his wife's unruly curls. She had let her hair grow again and the sun streaming through the window shot it with chestnut highlights. It was warm and silky to the touch and his hand lingered, moving to caress the nape of her neck.

For some moments she savoured his touch, moving her head sensuously beneath his hand. Then she drew slowly back and gazed up into his eyes. Great shining green pools filled with love and yearning slowly scanned his face. They gazed at each other for some moments as if hypnotized and Sean felt an awakening of the deep emotion that used to be constantly there between them. How had they drifted so far apart? He must make a greater effort to get their marriage back on the old footing. He just had to wear Annie down! They could not go on like this. He must be allowed to take precautions. How else could you be close to the one you loved?

Although now fully aware of his son's condition, he was still loath to admit that Thomas was disabled. The child's looks were more or less normal. Head slightly bigger than usual, a squint and slowness of awareness all that was noticeable to the eye. But so far, in spite of all Annie's endeavours, Thomas made no attempt whatsoever to sit up or use his legs. Was he destined to spend his entire life propped up just watching life pass him by? It broke Sean's heart to watch him lying there so helpless, day in, day out.

Full of pity, he looked on as Annie, after a warm smile to him, returned to her task and continued to massage one of the child's thin spindly legs, fingers gently kneading and smoothing, all the while talking softly. With an effort Sean moved forward. Going to the other side, he knelt facing Annie. He hadn't really any faith in this massage therapy; if the child could not sit up, how then would he ever be able walk? In spite of these doubts, gently lifting his son's other leg, he followed his wife's example.

Annie started back slightly in surprise at his action, and gaped at him in delight. 'This is a pleasant surprise!' she cried, eyes luminous with tears. 'What has you home so early?'

'Aye, it does make a change, doesn't it?' A slight grimace accompanied the words. He was ashamed of how little help he gave her where Thomas was concerned. 'I've some good news. Very good news. That's why I'm home early. I couldn't wait to tell you.'

She smiled happily at him. He did his best to hide it but Annie knew that he still bitterly resented what fate had thrown at them. Tears threatened to fall, seeing him there on his knees beside Thomas. 'Well, tell me then! I'm all ears,' she exclaimed, blinking to hold the tears at bay.

'They are a bit big.' Sean leant across and mischievously wriggled the lobe of her ear. 'But don't let it worry you. I still think you're lovely.'

Her heart swelled with happiness. Why, he sounded like his old self! 'What brought about this wonderful change?' she asked quietly.

'I'll tell you later when we're finished here.' He nodded towards Thomas and the child grinned back at him, displaying eight good strong white teeth. Sean's breath caught in his throat. He really was a good baby, always content. So far he had sailed through the teething stage without giving them any broken nights. If only he could move about instead of just lying there. Suddenly he decided that they should take Thomas on holiday with them too. How could he even have considered leaving him behind? Besides, if truth be told, he knew full well that Annie wouldn't hear tell of going anywhere without him. Not abroad then, that would be out of the question with Thomas in tow, but somewhere nice down South. That would please Annie no end. It would be worth all the extra work involved.

When she thought that enough massage had been applied she gave him a nod and he moved to the settee while she changed Thomas's nappy. Lying prone, he let his eyes roam slowly over his wife's figure. She really did look good, much younger than her thirty-two years. She wore no bra and the firm thrusts of her breasts against the fine lawn material of the brief blouse and the swell of her generous hips as she bent over the child teased desire into play. Careful! he warned himself. Don't take any chances. If he once got going there would be no stopping him. It was so long since they had been together, he could not make an attempt to gauge whether or not it would be safe. If only Annie would be reasonable.

He had talked their problem over with the priest but, although sympathetic to their plight, he had told Sean that the rhythm method was the only contraception allowed by the church. In spite of this, Sean would have no scruples whatsoever about birth control. Surely Annie could not be held accountable for his sin? He just had to cajole her round to his way of thinking. If all else failed he would have the operation. It would be a big step, but if Annie wouldn't hear of alternative methods then it was up to him. Surely his wife could not object to that? Her voice interrupted his daydreaming.

'Sean, will you carry Thomas upstairs, love? These exercises tire him and he'll sleep for a while.'

As she climbed the stairs ahead of her husband, Annie prayed that at last he was about to take his proper role in their lives. Following her up the stairs, Sean was very aware of her long slim bare legs and swaying hips, shown off to advantage by the brief cotton skirt she wore. Annie arranged the pillow and blanket, and placing Thomas in his cot Sean covered him with another light blanket. Fired with desire, he slowly turned to face his wife. She gazed mutely back at him and then they were in each other's arms and kissing hungrily.

They clung together for a long time, savouring the feel and touch of each other. Then, lifting her bodily in his arms, he entered their own bedroom and kicked the door shut.

Away from his touch her passion abated slightly. She met his look, a worried frown on her brow. 'Sean, what about the kids?'

'They're safe enough. Minnie's still with them. She won't leave them alone.' He hovered eagerly above her, his gaze intent. 'But tell me, Annie, are we safe? Is there any reason why we shouldn't make love?'

It had been so long since he had wanted her, she decided to take a chance. To put him off now by telling him that it wasn't safe could do so much damage to their marriage. She'd often pondered on the way they were forced to live. At a time when they needed each other so badly, they were expected to count the days. Besides, she was almost thirty-three! If she didn't conceive soon she might never stand another chance of giving Sean a healthy son. So what did it matter if she did get caught? It was a risk worth taking.

'Yes, Sean, it's safe,' she lied. After all, it was her life that was at stake.

With a sigh of relief, he joined her and for the next fifteen minutes all was forgotten but their urgent need. At last, passion spent, they lay content and happy in each other's arms, completely sated. Rising on his elbow, Sean gazed down on her flushed happy face. 'Ah, Annie, I've missed you so much. Sometimes I think that you don't love me any more.'

Her hands cupped his face. 'Don't you dare talk like that, Sean Devlin! I love you more than life itself. I'll always love you. There has never been anyone but you, and there never will be.'

'If you mean that, Annie, please let me take precautions? I need to be close to you like this, often, not a couple of times a month. You know that! Sometimes I feel that I'm in no man's land. I know Thomas is a full-time job, but I need you too, Annie.'

'I know, Sean. It's so unfair. I know how you feel. So why can't you forget what Mr Montgomery said?' she entreated. For the umpteenth time she wished that the surgeon had held his tongue. 'Eh, love? Let's go on as normal. I'm getting a bit old for conception. Even so, it doesn't matter if I do conceive! I want so much to give you another son.'

With a muffled exclamation he pushed her aside and rose from the bed, to stand glowering down at her. 'I don't want another son! I don't want to lose you, can't you understand that? Besides, as I said before . . . I won't risk another child like Thomas. And that's that. I'm not going to argue any more about it.'

Annie knelt on the bed to retaliate. 'Sean, to hear you talk anyone would be forgiven for thinking you weren't a Catholic. You were brought up in the same faith as me. You were taught the same rules. How can you even consider using birth control? And you know that the chances of having another child like Thomas would be very slight. Mr Dixon said that Thomas's condition probably arose during the birth.'

'If that was the case, why did you put me off when I considered suing them?'

'Because blame can't be attached to any one person. It can happen to anyone. It's just one of those things!'

'Anyhow, Annie, we've been through all this before. I'm not going to put your life on the line. I'm not going to risk it. I'm the one who has to provide for our children. Me!' He dug his finger into his chest to emphasize his point. 'Not the clergy. Oh, no! I'm the one who will have to see to their education. I'm the one who will have to plan and provide for Thomas's care after we die. Have you ever thought about that, Annie?' Her face went blank with surprise and he laughed harshly. 'No, I can see that you haven't, but who's going to take him, do you think? Some nights I can't sleep with the worry of it all.

The girls will probably marry and have children of their own. Their husbands won't want an extra burden. Think about it! It's all very well you talking, but you know the long hours I work to give us a decent living. Tell me this ... who would look after the kids if you were to die? I'd still have to work, you know, to provide for them.'

'I could still die! There's no guarantee that either of us will live to see the children grow up, you know that. If you're destined to die young, there's nothing you can do about it. And anyway, you'd soon find some other girl to fill my shoes.'

'Annie, you're talking rubbish and you know it. No matter what you say, I'm not taking any unnecessary chances. If you die young it won't be because I gave you another child. I couldn't live with that. So forget it!'

With these words he abruptly cut short the conversation by leaving the room. It was no use trying to get Annie to see sense. She had another child on the brain. Another Thomas? God forbid! How could he make her see reason? What in the name of God was going to become of them?

When the door closed on him Annie gazed at it in dismay. Everything had been fine until another pregnancy was mentioned. It was a long time since they had been so close. Sean had been so excited. Why hadn't she held her tongue? She should have enjoyed just being so close to him; lying beside him, encouraging him to tell her his good news. Now she might never find out, he could be so stubborn at times. But he was right. They couldn't go on like this. He had been so adamant she feared now that there might be consequences to their recent actions. He would never forgive her if she became pregnant again. Oh, she shouldn't have this extra worry. Hadn't she enough on her plate? Why couldn't he just take things as they came? Put his trust in God. A long exaggerated sigh escaped from her. She had to admit that she lived from day to day. Not once had she thought how their deaths would affect Thomas. Sean was right not to want to take chances. How could she have been so stupid? Would he leave her? Surely not? She only hoped she didn't live to regret her reckless abandon.

It came as a terrible shock to Annie to learn of Sean's intention to be sterilized. He broke the news to her as casually as if

94

discussing the weather; as if it had nothing whatsoever to do with her.

'I've made arrangements to visit the hospital next Thursday afternoon to see about the *operation!*'

He had deliberately stressed the word 'operation' to catch his wife's attention. Sure enough, her head rose and her mouth gaped. 'What operation? I don't understand,' she cried in bewilderment. 'What on earth's the matter with you, Sean?'

They were having breakfast. The sun spilling into the kitchen and setting alight the brilliant white ceiling and walls had sent her mind racing ahead. The hill looked far away today, a promise of good weather ahead. All the signs pointed to a fine sunny day.

Whilst keeping an eye on Rachel to make sure she ate enough to last her till lunchtime at school, and feeding Thomas, her mind was further alive with thoughts of all she could accomplish on such a day. So, occupied with visions of bed-clothes swaying in the light breeze while she mowed the lawn, her reception of his news was a blank confused look.

Exasperated, Sean cried, 'Have I got your attention at last?'

He certainly did have her attention. 'What operation?' she repeated. There was fear in her heart. Surely he couldn't mean what she thought he did? He would never take such a drastic step.

'I'm going to have the snip. You know, be sterilized?'

The bubble of happiness that engulfed Annie burst as Sean's words brought her upright in her chair. Thomas started to whinge as the spoon missed his mouth. Hurriedly wiping porridge off his chin, she filled her son's mouth, before repeating yet again, 'What on earth are you talking about?'

'I'm going to have the snip . . . you know, sterilization?' he explained again, slowly this time, making sure that she didn't miss a word. Leaning back in his chair, he watched her from under drawn brows. She reacted exactly as he had imagined.

'I know what they call it! But you can't do that, it's not allowed. You know that.'

'I don't need permission. It's my body and I'll decide what to do with it.'

'Sean! That means that you'll never be able to father another child.'

95

'Exactly.'

'Don't I have any say in the matter? After all, I'm your wife. Surely you need my permission too?'

'Be reasonable, Annie. How could I ever discuss anything like this with you, eh? You're terrified of the church, so you are. I'm not. So you have nothing to worry about. It's my decision. I'm the one who will have to answer for it. And if I do require your signature it won't be too difficult to forge. I know you won't have me charged. In your heart you must know I'm doing the right thing.'

'But, Sean, if you would just wait until Thomas is a little older we could try for another son.' Seeing that he was about to reject this, she quickly added, 'Look, don't do anything rash! We must talk this through. When did you say you were going?'

'Thursday. But ... there's no danger of my changing my mind, Annie.'

She was not to be deterred. 'We can at least talk about it tonight.'

Rising from the table, he went through his morning ritual of kissing his family goodbye. First Rebecca, her chubby face covered with porridge. She was a wonderful eater, never had to be coaxed at mealtimes. Then a sticky marmalade kiss from Rachel. He dropped a kiss on Thomas's head. Lastly he took his wife's face between his hands and gazed earnestly at her. 'Annie, believe me, it's all for the best. No more fear of pregnancies. We'll be able to enjoy love making again. Won't that please you? It will certainly make me happy.'

She returned his look, an anxious frown on her brow. 'Sean, it's not as easy as that. What happens if, say in another year or so, you come to regret it? You might want another child, you know.'

'Look, Annie. I haven't got the time to go into all the ifs and buts right now. I'll have to run or I'll be late. We'll discuss it tonight. But remember, I didn't reach this decision lightly. God knows, if Thomas were normal and another pregnancy wouldn't endanger your life, I wouldn't mind another couple of kids myself. But as things stand I'm convinced I'm doing the right thing. My mind's made up.'

When the door closed on him Annie sat in a daze for some moments before giving herself a little shake. All was not yet lost. She would try to talk him out of this wild notion. In the meantime she still had the children to feed and dress for the day ahead.

Thelma looked after Rebecca every morning while Annie walked Rachel down to school, taking Thomas along with her in his pram. Her mother was of the old-fashioned opinion that her grandson should be kept out of sight; said it was for his own good; said that the older he got, the more people would gape at him. She had offered to look after him as well as Rebecca but Annie was determined that her son would not be hidden away from the world at large. She was proud of him and wanted everybody to know it. He was already missing out on so much. It wasn't his fault that he was slow. Besides, the clinic insisted that every child should live life as fully as possible. Soon Rebecca would be starting school, and then perhaps she would have no choice but to leave Thomas behind. Three children would be more than a handful going down that busy Whitewell Road.

All the plans that she had been making at breakfast time had receded in the face of Sean's revelation. That was the only way she could think of it: revelation. He had been so blatant! 'I'm going to have the operation.' To hear him, you'd think it was no concern of hers. But it definitely was! She still hoped for another son. She'd put her foot down, tell him that he couldn't do this terrible thing. He must be made to listen to her point of view.

The beauty had gone out of the day for her. The sun still blazed down and the air was permeated with the scent of freshly cut grass. Neighbours along the road vied with each other to create the best laid out gardens and normally she would have rejoiced in all the colourful displays that their efforts yielded. Today her mind was elsewhere. After leaving Rebecca with her mother she continued on her way in morose silence, ignoring Rachel's chatter until the child gave up asking questions and trooped glumly along beside her, guessing in her own intuitive way that all was not well with her mother.

As usual Annie fell in with Mary at the school gates. After they had waved their daughters off and watched them run hand

97

in hand up the drive towards the school, the two friends turned their prams and headed back towards the village.

Aware of Annie's mood, Mary stole a glance down into the pram. She pitied Annie, having a child like Thomas. She eyed her own baby, already sitting up without assistance, babbling away and tugging at the string of rabbits strung across the pram. At home she was already crawling into all kinds of mischief and she was but eight months old, but Thomas just lay there all the time! He couldn't even sit up on his own and he was much older than Emma. It must be heartbreaking for Annie, she thought, watching him day in, day out. Thomas squinted up at her and gave his lopsided grin. Relieved to see him apparently well, she ventured to ask, 'Is anything wrong, Annie?' in a tentative voice.

A wide smile stretched across Annie's face; if it was a bit exaggerated Mary pretended not to notice. 'No. No, just a little dispute I had with Sean this morning. It will resolve itself,' she said confidently.

Mary's eyes were round with wonder. It wasn't like Annie Devlin to admit that she and Sean could have anything as common as a '*dispute*'. Sometimes Mary thought that Sean Devlin must surely be a saint from the way Annie spoke about him, but she'd had her eyes opened lately; Sean was no different from any other man where a pretty girl was concerned. A frown puckered her brow. Perhaps she should keep her little titbits of gossip to herself since Annie seemed a mite perturbed at the moment? Or was it her duty to worry her friend still further by relating the rumours that were going round the village? Yes, better that Annie hear it from her than from someone else. With this thought Mary piously stilled the voice of conscience and went over in her mind just how she could put Annie wise, without actually naming names.

Seeing her friend at a loss for words, something unheard of, Annie questioned her. 'Is there anything wrong with you, Mary?'

With a sideways glance, she confessed. 'I'm wondering if I dare tell you the latest bit of gossip, Annie.'

'It sounds juicy. Why wouldn't you tell me, for heaven's sake? You haven't suddenly developed a conscience, have you?'

'That would be the day!' Mary joined Annie in laughter at the very idea of it. 'But . . . well you mightn't be too pleased, seeing as it concerns your own family.'

Annie's heart gave a little thump in her breast. About her family? What could possibly have Mary so embarrassed? What was she on about?

'My family? What on earth could anybody find interesting enough about us to cause gossip?'

'Maybe I shouldn't say, Annie. But it's for your own good!'

Annie's lips twisted in a wry smile as she prepared herself for bad news. Didn't people always think it was for your own good when they were about to disturb your peace of mind? Although she imagined Mary's intentions would be far from malicious. Still, obviously something was bothering her.

'I think you should know,' Mary continued. 'Although my Joe says I should mind my own business. He says you won't thank me for poking my nose in where it's not wanted. I told him if the positions were reversed, I would rather hear it from you than anyone else.'

Really worried now, Annie snapped at her, 'Well, go on! Just who is talking about us? And what exactly are they saying?' She didn't like Mary's Joe and the very idea that he had cause to discuss her family angered her. She knew she was being unreasonable, but this coming on top of Sean's bombshell earlier on had set her nerves on edge.

Still Mary hesitated. She was having second thoughts now. It wasn't like Annie Devlin to lose her cool. She was the most even-tempered person Mary knew. Perhaps she should heed Joe's warning after all, and back down? However, Annie was glowering at her, expecting a reply. After some moments of indecision, Mary at last blurted out, 'As you know, I work in McVeigh's behind the bar in the lounge on Tuesdays and Thursdays. Well, this past couple of Saturday nights I've also been relieving one of the other barmaids who was on holiday and . . .'

Annie's heart missed a beat. Were they gossiping about Sean? Was he perhaps flirting with someone?

Relief seeped through her when Mary continued, 'It's this man who's chatting up your mother. Everybody thinks his wife's dead but Joe knows him and thinks that the wife is still alive. Mind you, they're probably separated. When he moved here a couple of years ago he let everyone believe he was a widower. I wouldn't have mentioned it, Annie, but he's paying your mother an awful lot of attention and she's lapping it up. Not that I blame her,' Mary hastened to add. 'He's a fine handsome man and they say he's not short a bob or two. He's there, regular as clockwork, every Saturday night, so I'm told, and most times his daughter is with him.'

'She's very attractive, so she is. Joe says a lot of the men are giving her the eye. Even the married ones, who should know better. She lives up in Glengormley but from what I hear she's with her father most Saturday nights. As I said, it's none of my business, but I thought perhaps you might like to drop a wee word of warning in your mother's ear.'

Annie turned Mary's words over in her mind. Just what lay behind her friend's concern? Surely Mary realized that her mother was old enough to look out for herself? If this was the case, then reading between the lines as it were, it was reasonable to suppose the daughter was the one that Mary was actually warning her against. Mildly she said, 'I'm surprised at you, Mary, passing on unsubstantiated rumours.'

She regretted her words immediately. She could see that her friend was offended. A dark flush spread painfully over Mary's face. Annie hastened to make amends. 'I'm sorry, I know you meant well, Mary. Tell me, who's doing all this talking?'

But Mary was hurt and not to be drawn further. 'No, you're quite right, of course! I should have heeded Joe and minded my own business. Well, it won't be the first time he's been able to say "I told you so!" One day I'll learn to keep my big mouth shut. Look, I'd better run on, Annie. I'm calling in to see Joe's mam. See you later on.'

Annoyed at her own awkward handling of the situation, Annie watched her friend scurry along the Shore Road and turn up Gray's Lane where her mother-in-law lived. Just what had Mary been trying to tell her? There was only one way to find out. Saturday night would see Annie down in McVeigh's. She would find out at first hand just what was going on. She grimaced. Where was it all going to end? As if she hadn't enough to worry about. Her gloomy mood deepened, hanging over her like a dark cloud.

* * *

Saturday dawned fine and warm, with a clear blue sky devoid of clouds promising even better things to come. Annie and Sean spent the morning in town booking their holidays. When Sean had at last relented and acquainted Annie with his good news, her excitement had known no bounds. She was delighted and touched when he suggested taking the three children on holiday. After weighing all the pros and cons, they decided Butlin's Holiday Camp at Mosney would be best suited to their needs. Glad that the TV studios staggered the staff's holidays and they didn't have to stick to the regulation fortnight's holiday that embraced the twelfth of July in Northern Ireland, they booked for the first two weeks of August. The future looked bright. The rise in Sean's wages would make their life much more comfortable.

The only blot on Annie's horizon was Mary's tip-off about the goings on in McVeigh's on a Saturday night. She had further questioned her friend but, still nursing a grievance, Mary had remained tight-lipped.

The afternoon was spent pottering about the garden. They had a picnic meal and by seven o'clock Rachel and Rebecca were bathed and in bed. As was usual on a Saturday night, Sean helped Annie bathe and prepare the girls for bed, and once they were settled he retired to the bathroom to dress for his night out with George and Thelma.

In the nursery, settling Thomas for the night, Annie could hear her husband humming away to himself as he showered and shaved. He so looked forward to his night out, you couldn't anger him on a Saturday even if you clobbered him. She had never begrudged him his freedom. Now she was depressed at the idea that there might be an added reason for his pleasure. Today was the happiest she had seen him since their showdown on Tuesday night. All her pleas had been in vain. Very much against her wishes, he had kept his appointment at the hospital on Thursday morning. On his return he had told her that in two weeks' time he would get the *snip* and a month or so later he should be given the all clear. From then on it would be 'all plain sailing and no more worries', as he put it.

Annie could not understand how he could be so carefree about it. It weighed heavily on her conscience. Although she

101

had refused to sign the paper Sean presented for her perusal, she still felt guilty. Unperturbed, he had attended to that matter himself. Determined to go through with it, with or without her approval.

Once Thomas was settled for the night, Annie paused at the bathroom door and watched her husband splash aftershave on his hands and then vigorously rub them over his face.

'Mmm . . . that smells nice. You'll have all the girls after you tonight.' To her ears she sounded coy and hated herself for it.

She need not have worried. Sean didn't even notice. He grinned from ear to ear, displaying teeth that were still white and even in a lean tanned face. 'Chance would be a fine thing! In McVeigh's most are spoken for, and the rest aren't worth a second glance.'

It had been a long time since he had tried to cajole her into accompanying him. Now she waited hopefully but an invitation wasn't forthcoming. She wanted to invite herself along but the words stuck in her throat. If she had mentioned it casually earlier on in the day it would have been all right. But to suggest it now, when he was almost ready to leave . . . well, that would surely set him thinking.

Going to the bedroom, he donned blue slacks, a white shirt and dark tie. A dark blue Harris tweed sports jacket completed the outfit. Annie had helped him choose his clothes, loving the way the colour deepened the blue of his eyes. Was someone else admiring their blue depths now? He straightened the tie, smoothed his hands over his hair and turned to face her. 'Will I do?'

Forcing a smile to her lips, she assured him, 'I should think so!'

Pausing in front of her, he pressed a brief kiss on her mouth. 'Well, I'll see you later.' A quick look in on the sleeping children and he bounded down the stairs and out the front door.

From the bedroom window Annie watched his lithe figure leave the drive and stride down the road. Clothes sat well on Sean's broad shoulders and tapering waistline. There wasn't an ounce of fat on him. She had to admit he was still a fine figure of a man. Given the chance, girls probably did chat him up, but she could not see him returning their compliments.

102

Slowly she sank down on the edge of the bed and let her mind back track. It was long and many a week since she had gone down to the pub, or anywhere else for that matter, with him. At first he had coaxed her to accompany him, but not any ore. Never one for drinking, she had been relieved, just wanting to stay at home and enjoy a nice long leisurely soak in the bath. He hadn't seemed to mind, so long as he got out for a couple of hours. And she had always believed he would never stray.

To her astonishment, her conscience argued with her. And why not? Why wouldn't he be tempted? What was there for him at home? She was always preoccupied with Thomas. As for their love life, it was practically non-existent. But that wasn't her fault! She didn't make the rules. Still, she would have to bend a bit if she wanted to keep his love. She was daft sending him out on his own. But then, he wasn't alone! Her mother and George were always with him. She couldn't wish for better chaperones. Their presence would surely keep him on the straight and narrow?

Remembering how handsome he had looked and his eagerness to be off, she rose resolutely to her feet, her mind made up. Earlier in the day she had asked Minnie if she would keep an eye on the kids for a couple of hours, should Annie wish to go out. Well, Sean hadn't asked her to go with him but there was nothing to stop her from joining him. A glance at the clock showed her that Minnie, not having been put off, would be arriving soon. There was no time for a bath, a shower would have to do. Quickly Annie set to work and when Minnie arrived was ready and waiting.

'Oh, you do look lovely!' her neighbour exclaimed. 'It suits you, your hair loose about your face like that. It's time you caught yourself on and went out more often with Sean. You're only young once, Annie. There's nothing to stop you going out every Saturday night, you know.'

She was pleased at her friend's warm compliment, aware that she did indeed look well. Thick chestnut hair framed a face tanned the colour of honey from her long hours outdoors. Light make-up darkened the green of her eyes and enhanced her cheeks and lips. She wore the dress bought in Rosaleen's honour and even its fullness could not hide her firm bust, while the low neckline called attention to a long unlined throat. A white cardigan, bag and sandals finished off the outfit.

'Where's Sean?' Minnie asked when she became aware of the silent house, because one was always aware of Sean Devlin's presence.

'He went on down. Him and George are becoming old fuddy-duddies. They like to get the same table every week, so they go down early.' She rolled her eyes at Minnie in mock despair, amazed at the lies dripping effortlessly off her tongue. 'I never thought I'd see the day!'

'You should go down with him too, Annie. You know I don't mind babysitting. I'm very attached to that TV set of yours. Besides, Sean's too handsome to be allowed out on his own.'

Annie's gaze sharpened. Had Minnie heard the same rumours? Surely not? She never went anywhere. 'I trust him, Minnie,' she said, still watchful.

To her relief, her friend was unruffled; no sign of any warning now. 'Well now, I'm not saying anything against him. But girls will be girls, you know. Some of them will go to any lengths to get a man interested in them. Whether the men are married or not doesn't bother them. Look, I'm holding you back! Away you go or you'll be meeting them coming home.'

'Thanks, Minnie. You're a dear. I appreciate your kindness.'

As she neared the bottom of the Whitewell Road Annie's feet faltered and she almost turned back. Why was she doing this? If Sean was flirting with someone, did she really want to know? Did she really want to confront him? One thing she was sure of, he would never leave her to rear the children on her own, and she couldn't really see him having a bit on the side. When would he get the opportunity, for heaven's sake? So wasn't she getting all worked up about nothing? Still, where there was a will there was a way. Resolutely, she squared her shoulders and crossing the road entered the pub; she had come this far, so she may as well join the others. If there was any truth in the gossip, she would soon find out for herself.

A couple of men she knew hailed her from the open side door that led to the public bar. 'Hello there, Annie,' cried one and raised his pint in greeting. 'Nice to see you out,' shouted another above the din of the crowd.

Annie lingered to answer their good-natured greetings with a quip and a smile. Eventually, passing the door, she climbed the stairs to the lounge. It was quieter up here where the ladies were entertained. It was also packed as was usual on a Saturday night.

She paused at the door to get her bearings and survey the clientele. Sean, George and her mother were seated at a corner table at the far side of the room. A tall grey-haired man and a small fair-haired girl shared their table. They were all bent across listening while Sean held court and didn't notice her entrance. For some moments Annie took stock of the company. Her eyes passed quickly over the man but rested consideringly on the girl. She looked about twenty-two. A cloud of soft pale hair framed a pert tanned face and tumbled down her back in carefree disarray. Large hazel eyes twinkled at her companion and a slight smile hovered around full sensuous lips. A very brief top displayed tanned shoulders and cleavage. She was very pretty; very pretty indeed, Annie admitted to herself, and so young. Any man of forty would be flattered to have her attention. She was leaning across the table towards Sean who had his back to Annie. It was obvious that his words were directed at her, and Annie could see the admiring way the girl hung on his every word.

Slowly she made her way between the tables, speaking to those she knew well and nodding to people she knew by sight. She was almost at the table before George looked up and caught sight of her.

'Annie, this is a surprise!' he cried, rising quickly to his feet. He looked in bewilderment at Sean. 'You didn't say she was coming down or I would have waited behind for her.'

He turned a look of amazement on his wife. 'I didn't know she was coming either or I'd have waited for her myself,' he cried defensively. Annie could see that he was disconcerted. Hot colour flooded his face. Rising to his feet, he curtly beckoned for her to sit on his chair but George had already found a vacant one and swung it round to the table, between her mother and him. Greeting a surprised Thelma, Annie chose to sit on the chair between them. From here she could get a better view of the girl.

It was George who made the introductions. 'Annie, this is

Dan Wilson and his daughter Marie.' He grinned at them. 'You two will already have guessed that this is my sister, Annie, Sean's wife. You've heard us speak of her often enough.'

Dan was gallant and did not miss a chance to flatter her mother. 'Sure you're a sight for sore eyes, Annie. But then, with such a lovely mother, how could you be anything else?'

Marie nodded and smiled across at her, a twinkle in her eye at the antics of her father, but Annie's look was cool. If Marie was flirting with her husband, there was no way she was going to befriend her. Sean must not be allowed to assume that they got on well and invite her and her father up some night for a drink. Oh, no! Marie Wilson must, at all costs, be kept at arm's length.

Sean went to the bar to get her a drink and Annie addressed Marie. 'I have to confess I don't recognize you. Are you from around here?'

Before Marie could open her mouth, Dan answered the question. 'Marie takes pity on me every Saturday night.' He smiled fondly at his daughter. 'I tell her a pretty girl like her should be out with friends her own age, not with an old fogey like me. You see, we live up in Glengormley and as Marie is teetotal and has a nice wee car, she drives me down and then home again.'

'Not very exciting for you, Marie. Is this crowd not too old for you?'

The girl's eyes narrowed but after a momentary pause she retorted, 'Oh, but I find the company here very stimulating.' She slanted a look in George's direction and winked. Although he looked a mite surprised at her gesture, Annie suddenly realized she might be mistaken. After all, George was a free man and a handsome one at that. Why shouldn't Marie make a play for him? It looked like Mary had got her wires crossed. Annie still didn't like the idea of this girl with George, but if it had to be one of the men in her own life, rather her brother than her husband. Relaxing slightly, she managed to enjoy the rest of the evening.

Last orders were being called. Annie frowned when Sean went to the bar for another round. She had never known him to drink so much before; she also sensed that in spite of his friendly chatter, he was in a surly mood. Although he was genial enough so far as the others were concerned, he was offhand with her, rarely looking her full in the face. Obviously he was annoyed at her dropping in on them like this. Why? she thought in bewilderment. What had he to hide?

Half an hour later saw them on the pavement outside the pub. After saying good night to Marie and her father they dandered up the Whitewell Road in comparative silence. Much to the chagrin of Dan, another man had waylaid her mother outside the pub and, drawing her to one side, had whispered in her ear for some moments. Thelma had been in a bemused state ever since. George was also preoccupied, shooting the odd worried glance in Annie's direction. Once he made as if to speak but seemed to think better of it. What was he worried about? Was he thinking of Marie? Why didn't he ask her out if he was attracted to her? After a few attempts to get Sean talking, Annie gave it up as a bad job and retreated into silence. Did they always walk home like this? She didn't imagine so. It must be her intrusion that had put the damper on the evening.

They parted company with Thelma and George at the corner of Serpentine Gardens. Did George give her a meaningful look or was that just her imagination? She was beginning to wish she had stayed at home in blissful ignorance. As they continued on up the road, tentatively Annie questioned her husband. 'Is anything wrong, Sean?'

'Wrong? Now what would be wrong, Annie?'

'I don't know. But you're awfully quiet tonight.'

'Well, you know now . . . I think you would react in the same way if you thought that I had tried to catch you out. Especially since there's no justification for it. No justification whatsoever.'

'I don't know what you're talking about,' she blustered.

'Oh, come off it, Annie. You know damn' well what I'm on about! What else would have brought you down to McVeigh's in such secrecy?'

'Now you're being absurd!'

'Am I, Annie? How come there was no word or sign that you were coming out tonight? Why didn't you ask me to wait for you? Which I would have done . . . willingly. Instead you made me look a right eejit. You must have planned it all before

I left the house, and yet there wasn't a sign of it. I wouldn't have believed you could be so sneaky.'

Annie was in a quandary; she hadn't given any thought to how he would react. And he was right! It must look odd, her not saying a word to him and then landing down there, out of the blue. Opening the front door, she entered the house and was glad that the argument had to be abandoned while Minnie gathered together her few bits and pieces.

With an abrupt good night to their babysitter, Sean went upstairs. Minnie gaped after him, then turned a questioning glance on Annie. Afraid her pent up emotions might erupt into tears, Annie just shrugged slightly and led the way outside. At the gap in the hedge from where one of them always watched until Minnie had safely entered her home, her neighbour hugged her in silent sympathy. 'Good night, love.'

'Good night, Minnie. And thanks . . . for everything.'

Annie watched her neighbour safely indoors and then returned to her own house. She locked up and slowly followed her husband up the stairs. She was out of her depth. Sean had never behaved like this before. Why now? But then – to be fair – neither had she. Once again she wished she had stayed at home. If she had, she would be warm and snug in bed by now. On his return from the pub he would have brought up a cup of tea and some toast to the bedroom. While they ate he would have recounted different things that had happened during the evening. So far, every week he had kept her up to date on the pending romance between her mother and Dan Wilson. Making her laugh as he related the different ways Dan tried to get her mother interested. Yet not once had he ever mentioned Marie. Not once! Now that was strange, wasn't it? That wasn't a figment of her imagination. That was a fact. So why had he not mentioned the girl? No, it wasn't all in Annie's mind. She mustn't let him put her on the defensive. She deserved some kind of an explanation.

She looked in on the children, pulling the kicked aside bed-clothes over them again and kissing each one on the brow. As she gazed at their sleeping faces some of the tension left her and once again she wished she had remained at home. Still feeling loath to face her husband, she restlessly descended the stairs again. After making tea and toast she once more

108

ascended the stairs. She would act as if nothing had happened and take it from there.

Sean lay with his back to the door. 'Would you like a cup of tea?' she asked.

Slowly he turned towards her, a resentful expression on his face. Then, sitting up, he silently reached for the tray, holding it steady until she was perched on the side of the bed.

Annie willed him to speak but he ate the toast and drank his tea in silence. They were almost finished when, in spite of her resolution not to speak first, unable to stop herself, she asked, 'Why the big silence, Sean?'

'Silence?'

'Yes, silence. You know this thing that's hanging like a blanket between us?'

He nodded towards the tray. 'Are you finished?'

'Yes.'

Setting the tray to one side he leant across and gazed into her eyes. 'Annie, let's see if we can make any sense out of this. For months I've begged you to come out with me, haven't I?' At her nod he nodded back in satisfaction and continued. 'Why then did you not tell me that you wanted to come out tonight? I mean, we've been together all day and you never even hinted you'd like to go out for a drink.'

'I know that! I willed you to ask me, and when you didn't I decided to stay at home. Then, at the last minute, I changed my mind again, so I asked Minnie to babysit.'

'I don't understand. Why could you not say? Did you think I wouldn't want you with us? Was that it, Annie?'

She shrugged slightly, at a loss for words to explain. 'Not really.'

'Then there must be some other reason.'

She sat with bowed head and he continued, 'What was it, Annie?' After a short pause he asked tentatively, 'Have you have been listening to rumours?'

This was the opening she'd been waiting for and she latched on to it right away. 'So you admit there are rumours going about?'

'I admit nothing of the kind!' he cried indignantly. 'Get that into your head. I've done nothing wrong. But you'll always find someone ready to make a mountain out of a mole hill. I bet I

109

know who's been filling your ear with this nonsense. It's that Mary Moon, isn't it? I saw her watching our table like a hawk when she was working behind the bar last week. The nosy wee cow!'

'Yes, it was Mary! But she never named names. That's why I went down tonight . . . to find out for myself just what was going on. She told me about this auld lad who's trying to get off with Mam. She thinks he still has a wife somewhere.' Annie knew she was babbling and was angry at herself. It was Sean who was being talked about. He was the one who should be making excuses.

'And what did you find out, Annie?'

'*You* put me in the picture, Sean. You know all about it.'

'What do you want me to say?'

'Tell me the truth!'

He held up his hands in exasperation. 'There's nothing to tell where I'm concerned.'

'Then why are you so annoyed with me?'

'Because you tried to catch me out and I wasn't doing anything wrong.' Her head was swinging from side to side in denial as he insisted, 'Oh, yes! I know the way your mind works, Annie.'

'I didn't! I'm sorry if that's how it seemed to you. I realize now that Mary must have got her wires crossed. It's George, isn't it, that Marie's interested in? But why have you never mentioned her to me? Eh, Sean? You mentioned Dan Wilson every Saturday night when you came home . . . why not his daughter?'

'I never thought to mention her. I told you about Dan because he was making advances to Thelma. Mary Moon is right in that department. Whether or not he has a wife, I don't know. I didn't for one moment think you'd be interested in Marie.'

No, I'm sure you didn't, she thought resentfully and sat silent, looking intently at him, desperately wanting to believe him. He reached for her hands and held them against his breast. 'Annie, I'm forty years old. Why would a lovely young girl like Marie be interested in a grumpy old bugger like me, eh?'

A lovely girl like Marie. For some reason these words frightened Annie. She gazed back into Sean's eyes and could

110

understand perfectly why any young girl would be interested in him. She would have to tread softly. Choose her words with care. She laughed lightly and, keeping her voice even, agreed with him. 'You're right, of course. About Marie,' she hastened to add. 'I'm sure she has plenty of young men queuing up to date her. But I must admit I still got the impression that she fancies our George. I saw her winking at him. Of course he's a free man, so why not? Do you think he's interested in her?'

'That's something you'll have to ask him yourself. He hasn't confided in me.' Sean drew her closer and kissed her. As the kiss deepened and he started to release the zip at the back of her dress, she gently shrugged his hand away. 'It's not safe, Sean,' she whispered against his lips. She waited breathlessly; would he realize that she lied? He drew back and looked down the length of his nose at her, a frown puckering his brow. Whatever he read in her face, his lips tightened in a hard straight line and without another word he turned his back on her and lay down. He knew all right. She had never refused him before.

A sadness filled her, that it should come to this. She reached out to touch his shoulder, but found she couldn't. What would be the point? She could not bear for him to touch her. Not tonight. She was too hurt and confused, and needed time to think things out. It was obvious that he admired this Marie Wilson. And it was obvious to her that the admiration was returned. Why would Marie fawn over a married man? Was she a serious threat to their marriage? They had drifted so far apart Annie wasn't even confident of his love any more. For the first time she was glad that he was going to have the operation. Sex was so important to a man and who, after all, was she to decide what was right and what was wrong? Everybody had their own ideas about things like that. Yes, the operation might well prove a blessing in disguise. It would at least bring them closer physically.

Her mind was filled with a mixture of troubled thoughts as she slowly undressed and slipped between the sheets. She was tempted to renege, and moved closer to her husband's body. He stiffened. Afraid of a further rebuff, she moved away and hoped that sleep would soon claim her.

Annie didn't usually have time to delay for a cup of tea when she collected Rebecca on her way back from school but that Sunday morning George had dropped a word in her ear that perhaps she should have a chat with her mother as she was worrying about something. Her curiosity roused, on her way home from school on Monday Annie called at the local bakery for one of their delicious rhubarb tarts. Presenting it to her mother, she said, 'It's a long time since we've had a good natter, so it is. So how's about a cup of tea, Mam?'

'Oh, I'd love that, Annie. Funny, I was hoping to have a word with you. I'll put the tea on.'

They sat out in the back garden to drink it. While the girls played and Thomas slept in his pram, Thelma confided in her daughter.

'I'm really pleased you have time to stay for a while. I want your opinion on something.'

Noting that her mother looked embarrassed, Annie inched to the edge of her chair in anticipation. When Thelma appeared to be having difficulty finding the right words, Annie encouraged her. 'Well then, what do you want my expert opinion on, Mam?' she teased.

With bowed head, she muttered, 'Would you think me unfaithful to your father's memory if I were to go out with another man?'

Annie's jaw dropped in amazement. Then she managed to gasp, 'Ah, Mam, catch yourself on! Me da's been dead over ten years. You can't mourn for the rest of your days. You have your own life to get on with.'

'I know that! But . . . well, I never imagined I would even think of another man, let alone want to go out with one. I'm in two minds. I don't want to be a laughing stock, you know.'

'Well then, believe me, you can go out with him with an easy mind. All your friends will be happy for you.'

'You don't think your father would object, then?'

Annie's eyes widened at the very idea. Seeing her mother was serious, she patted her gently on the arm, and said softly, 'No, Mam, I don't think he would mind one bit. After all, he's dead. And remember, he had an affair. So he wasn't exactly lily white himself. Bear that in mind. After all, George isn't your son.'

'That was a one-night stand, Annie. And I shouldn't have held it against your da all those years.'

'Why not? It upset you no end at the time. Made you miserable for long and many a day.'

'I know all that, Annie. And I never really got over it. It was always at the back of my mind. But still ... you should never hold spite all that time. Life's short enough as it is without being bitter towards anyone, let alone your own husband.'

'That's easier said than done, Mam. They're the ones who can hurt you most!' Even to her own ears the words sounded more bitter than the conversation warranted. Seeing her mother's attention perk up, Annie continued, 'Who's the lucky man, then? Is it Dan Wilson?'

To her surprise her mother quickly refuted this. 'Indeed it's not! That man gets on my nerves. Him and that Marie monopolize our company every Saturday night. We never get a chance to meet anybody else. No, it's John McLaughlin. I don't suppose you noticed but last Saturday night he collared me outside McVeigh's?' Her brow was raised as Annie quickly thought back. 'He asked if he could take me to the pictures some night. I told him that I'd have to think about it. He's phoning today to find out if I'll go with him.'

'I was under the impression you were being wooed by Dan Wilson?'

'Oh, yes. To give him his due, he tries, but he just won't take no for an answer. He's full of himself, that one, thinks he's God's gift to women.'

'Why do you sit with him then? Is that not giving him false hope?'

'Because they're always in first and keep the seats for us. That's why. I don't even want to sit with them. He talks the greatest load of rubbish. His mouth seems to go into overdrive from when I sit down until I get up to go home. I can't hear myself think straight when he's about.'

'I suppose you put up with him because George and Marie are interested in each other?' Annie held her breath, willing her mother to agree with her.

113

But no, Thelma pulled a face. 'Our George, interested in that one? You've got to be joking! He can't bear the sight of her ... thinks she's dying about herself. Says she's a trouble maker. The only one that girl's interested in is herself. I hear she's fond of married men. Maybe she doesn't a want real commitment! Well, all the married men down in the pub are too wise to get involved with the likes of her.'

'Then why ...?' Afraid she might hear something she wouldn't like, Annie changed her question. 'So you like this John McLaughlin, do you?'

Colour came and went in Thelma's face as she confessed, 'I do, actually. I like him very much. As a matter of fact he reminds me of your da. Not in looks like, but in manner. Does all this make me sound like an overgrown schoolgirl? Do you think I'm being an old fool?'

'Not at all, Mam. Not at all. You're still a very attractive woman, you know,' Annie kindly assured her. 'And you're young enough to get married again,' she added fondly.

Thelma immediately became flustered. 'Oh, well now,' she cried in dismay. 'I wouldn't go so far as to say that. I'm just going to the pictures with him.'

'You never know where it may lead, Mam. And good luck to you. There's a Glen Ford picture on in the Ritz this week. Get him to take you there.'

'Thanks, Annie.' Thelma was still embarrassed as she confided, 'I'm really glad you had time for a cuppa. When he phones, I'll tell him he can pick me up on Saturday night at six, and I'll suggest the Ritz to him. I like Glen Ford. His films are always good.'

'What about McVeigh's?'

'Oh, I don't mind missing that! I'm fed up with Dan Wilson and his daughter.' Her laughter was like that of a young girl as she admitted shyly, 'I can't wait for John to phone now. Thanks for helping me make up my mind, Annie.'

That night Annie relayed all this news to her husband. He appeared surprised.

'You know, I honestly thought Thelma was keen on Dan. Still, I myself prefer John. He's a grand man. Dan, I imagine, is a bit of a womaniser.'

'And suspecting this, you set him up for Mam?'

'Hey, hold on. I didn't do anything of the kind,' Sean cried indignantly. 'George and I invited Thelma down to McVeigh's with us to give her a chance to meet some eligible men. Your mother is a very attractive woman, you know. And still young enough to marry again. That's why we invited her down. Dan Wilson did the rest. One look at your mother and he invited himself into our company.'

'Do you think our George fancies Marie Wilson?'

'I'm afraid you'll have to ask him that. As I've already said, he hasn't confided in me.'

'She must think he does. Why else would a lovely young girl like her frequent McVeigh's where most of the men are married and getting on a bit?'

Leaning back in his chair, Sean sighed. 'I don't know, Annie. Why do you think she goes?'

'If there're rumours, aren't you adding fuel to them, sitting with her every weekend?' she accused.

'Annie, I like to get out on a Saturday night. Good God, I work long hours and it's the only break I get. So I don't intend staying put just because some people have nothing better to do than spread malicious tales. Why don't you come with me every week, eh? That will soon put a stop to the gossip!'

His eyes were fixed on her face and she realized he was giving her an ultimatum. Slowly she nodded her head. 'Why not?'

If he was disappointed at her decision, he didn't show it.

'That's settled then! So let's not hear another word about Desperate Dan or Rose Marie,' he said tersely.

The weather was unsettled during the first week of August and they were glad that they had chosen to go to Butlin's. There were plenty of outdoor amusements for the children, and when a shower of rain sent them all running for shelter, indoor games and contests were laid on by the Red Coats. In the evenings, after high tea for the children, they were put to bed, leaving their parents free to enjoy themselves. For their peace of mind, Red Coats patrolled the rows of chalets and if a child was heard crying or seemed disturbed a message was relayed over

115

the Public Address System to all the different places of entertainment.

Rarely was a parent called back to the chalets. The youngsters were up so early and running about so much during the day that they slept throughout the night, with the odd exception. Afraid that Thomas might wake up and not kick up a fuss but perhaps be in distress, Annie or Sean kept nipping back at regular intervals to their chalet to check up on him.

The second week the weather was brilliant and a lot of time was spent on the beach. They choose a quiet spot where Thomas would not be subjected to the curious gazes of older children. While Sean splashed about in the water with Rachel and Rebecca, Annie stayed on a grassy slope on the sand dunes on a blanket with her son. She was flicking through the pages of a magazine when a movement caught the tail of her eye. To her amazement she watched as Thomas rolled over on his tummy and made an effort to move forward. Realizing that he wanted to be near his sisters, Annie cried excitedly out to Sean.

'Sean! Sean, come here quickly!' She was jumping up and down in her excitement.

There were tears in his eyes as he watched his son try to crawl along, using his elbows. Lifting him high, Sean cried, 'Come on, son. Let's see how you like the water.'

Annie followed him to the water's edge and watched intently as he sat with Thomas and let the waves ripple over the child's legs. Thomas splashed excitedly with his hands and even as they watched he moved his legs. Seeing them move he tried again, harder this time, and squealed with delight. Sean and Annie looked at each other and cried spontaneously, 'Thanks be to God!'

'Oh, isn't it wonderful, Sean? There's hope for him yet. Wait till they hear about this at the clinic. This is a great step forward.'

And Sean had to agree with her. It was certainly more than he had anticipated.

Back home, the staff at the clinic were indeed very pleased with the good news. Now that they had discovered that Thomas preferred to be on his stomach, they laid him face down and encouraged him to raise himself up on his knees until eventually he was crawling about the floor. Next came the long task

116

of encouraging him to stand. Favourite toys were placed just beyond his reach. Soon, if he wanted something badly enough he could drag himself to a standing position to reach it. It was a long hard haul but after many weeks he started to move to one side or the other. So long as he had something to hang on to, he managed to get about fine.

The first time he stood erect was a sight to behold and all who saw him were in tears. It hadn't been easy to stand aside and watch him struggle to pull himself to his feet but they did, knowing that he had to learn to fend for himself as much as possible. It had been particularly hard for Annie, who suffered every effort along with him, weeping sometimes when he had to give up because of fatigue. But eventually he was quite accomplished at it. At the clinic they were delighted with his progress and a small sturdy walking frame on wheels was made for him by the resident handyman. With its aid Thomas was able to get about the room. Miss McAteer assured Annie that the future now looked bright for her son.

The romance between Thelma and John blossomed into love. A year later her blushing mother asked Annie if she would be their matron of honour. George had already agreed to be best man.

Annie clasped her close and quickly assured her that she was honoured to be asked. 'I'm so pleased for you, Mam. John's a good man and it's obvious that he dotes on you.'

'He is very kind and considerate, Annie. I have no qualms about marrying him. And that wee house of his on Orange Row is like a palace. Sure I've fell on my feet, so I have. But what about George?' she lamented. 'He'll be on his own in this house.'

'Mam, he's an adult! Not a wee boy. You have no need to worry about him. He's very capable. In fact, your getting married might even give him the nudge. It mightn't be long until he's up the aisle behind you. Sure, isn't he seeing someone?'

'Who's he seeing?' Thelma looked at her daughter in bewilderment.

Taken aback, Annie blinked at her in surprise. 'I don't know.

I thought you would. I just somehow or other got the impression that he was courting.'

As comprehension dawned on Thelma, her lips tightened and hot colour flooded her face. 'Oh, you mean that hussy he visits every now and again? I should hope he wouldn't think of marrying her! She's nothing but a prostitute, that one. I don't know how he can do it. He should be ashamed of himself, going to the likes of her. You'd think he couldn't get a good girl of his own. She's a slut that one. I've heard tales about her. Lots of men visit her,' she finished derisively.

Annie was taken aback. George visiting a prostitute? She didn't believe it. Her mother must have got the wrong end of the stick. She herself had been aware that he was seeing someone . . . but a prostitute? Never! A handsome compassionate man like George could have anybody he wanted. He would have no need to pay for services rendered. No, not George. He would have no trouble getting himself a nice girl. But even if he did choose to visit someone of ill-repute . . . well, it was none of their business. He would be mortified if he found out they were gossiping about him.

'I think you're wrong, Mam.'

'I wish I was, Annie. I wish I was, but I'm not. I've been told by a friend who lives near her and recognized George as my son. She's seen him come and go and I'm worried stiff about him. Do you think it could be serious?'

Annie gripped her by the shoulders and gave her a slight shake. 'Listen, Mam. George would be annoyed if he thought he was causing you any worry, so just you think of yourself. After all, what he does is his own business.' She let go of her mother and changed the subject. 'Tell me, what would you like for a wedding present?'

'Nothing! I don't need anything.'

'Oh, we want to buy you something. Do you intend having a reception?'

'No, no. We want as little fuss as possible. We're going to have the banns called and then get married straight away. All John's family are dead. He never had any children, you know. There's no reason to hang about.'

'That's wonderful!' Annie did a quick calculation. 'That means we can look forward to a wedding early in August. I know what we'll do. Sean and I will have a reception for you in our house. If the weather is good we can have it outdoors. How would you like that?'

'That would be smashing, Annie. Do you think that maybe Rosaleen and Andrew might fly over for it?'

'I don't know, Mam. Phone her tonight and ask. You never know, she might just come over.'

To Annie's relief Rosaleen declined the invitation to the wedding. It transpired that Andrew had had a slight attack of angina a month earlier; nothing to worry about, they were assured. That's why they weren't told about it at the time. He was recovering well, but in the circumstances Rosaleen did not want to leave him. She sent a sizeable cheque with her regrets, telling her mother to buy something nice for her big day.

The Nuptial Mass was held in St Mary's Church in Greencastle at eleven o'clock. It was a Saturday and there had been a fine drizzle early that morning but by ten o'clock the sun was out. Thelma wore a pale grey suit and small white hat with an eye veil; Annie had bought a new blue suit for the occasion and a hat that was a concoction of feathers. They both carried a spray of yellow roses. Rachel and Rebecca wore long white flowing dresses and carried small posies. They looked delightful and proudly presented a horseshoe and a figure of a chimney sweep to their grannie and new granda.

Both Thelma and John were popular figures in the village and the little church was packed. All of the McVeigh's crowd had turned out to wish them well. Even Dan and Marie put in an appearance with a present for the happy couple. When they had signed the church register and emerged into the grounds, Annie saw Sean talking to them as he waited to take some photographs and silently prayed he would not ask them up to the reception. Sean had indeed intended to invite them but, catching sight of his wife's warning look, decided against it.

There were twenty-four people at the buffet lunch Sean and Annie had arranged. Some were old friends from the Springfield Road and some friends of John's from the village. Thelma had also invited Rosaleen's first mother-in-law, Amy Smith, and her new husband Bobby Mackay. Thelma and George,

119

with Annie and Sean, had been at their wedding a few years earlier.

To leave themselves free to enjoy the occasion, Annie and Sean had brought in outside caterers and bar a few minor hiccups everything was a great success. There was a slight breeze but the weather remained dry. Long tables brought by the caterers were covered with snowy white cloths and decorated with vases of flowers. By the time they returned from church, the tables were spread with all sorts of appetizing dishes, with a two-tier wedding cake baked by Minnie as a wedding present holding pride of place.

Sean had arranged for a sherry reception and soon afterwards the caterers left and everybody was invited to help themselves from the groaning tables. Meanwhile Sean and George brought out bottles of spirits and beer. Later, George moved the gramophone close to the kitchen door so that the music could be heard outside. Soon everyone was up dancing to a medley of rock and roll, waltzes and Old Time dancing.

Thelma was overcome by the generosity of her daughter and son-in-law and shed a few tears as she tried to express her thanks. John's voice was gruff as he seconded her. After the cutting of the cake, the newly-weds left to go South on their honeymoon and soon afterwards the guests offered their thanks to Annie and Sean for a wonderful day before drifting off in different directions.

When the last guest had departed Annie ran a weary hand across her brow, reflecting that it had indeed been a wonderful day all round. She decided to seek out George. The caterers had yet to return to collect their delft, cutlery and tables. Minnie had taken the girls and Thomas into her house for an hour or so to give Annie a chance to unwind, saying that she must be utterly exhausted. Sean was driving Thelma and John to the train station. Now was the chance for a heart-to-heart talk with her brother. After much soul searching Annie had decided that he must be told about the talk circulating about him and that woman. She would be very careful not to mention the word 'prostitute'. Discreet questioning had revealed that Josie Stafford was the woman's name, and although she did not live in Greencastle, her name was well known in the village.

Arming herself with two long cool drinks Annie wandered

120

through the house, expecting to find him in the sitting room, but he was nowhere to be found. She hadn't noticed him in the garden but his car was still outside the house so he must be about somewhere. At last she came upon him sitting at the top end of the garden, contemplating the hill. His back was against a tree trunk and he had been hidden from her view. An empty beer glass was on the ground beside him. He was unaware of her and she paused to examine him. Thick chestnut hair, so like her own, tumbled down over a wide brow; at this age he looked the way she remembered her father when she was growing up. In repose sadness etched his fine features. He looked tired as well. It still confounded her that this good-looking brother of hers should visit Josie Stafford. Not that she was a prostitute in the real sense of the word, but over the years she had certainly built up a reputation for herself.

Slowly Annie approached him and when he at last looked up and blinked in surprise, she asked, 'Am I interrupting anything? Do you want to be alone?'

He shook his head and, relieving her of one of the glasses, smiled his thanks. Waving at the ground beside him, he invited, 'Draw up some grass and join me. I'm just thinking how lucky we are to be able to see this beautiful hill every day. Although, I confess, most times I forget it's here. It's true what they say about familiarity.'

Sitting down beside him, she returned his smile and gazed up at the hill. The sky behind it, glowing pink, threw it into stark relief. The hill's covering of grass was dark and velvety-looking and you felt that if you reached out your hand you would be able to touch its softness. 'I never tire of it,' she admitted. 'Or the lough, for that matter. I love watching the sun rise over the water on a morning.'

'You're very lucky, Annie. You have all your wants.'

'Well, I wouldn't go so far as to say that,' she laughed, but in the next breath contradicted herself. 'But, yes, I consider myself very lucky.' Her eyes searched his face. 'Why so sad, George?'

His head jerked and he gazed at her. 'Me, sad?' he cried in mock amazement. 'What have I got to be sad about? Oh, I admit that I'll miss Thelma. But sure Orange Row isn't a stone's throw away. I bet you she'll be up every other day to see how I'm getting on.'

Annie smiled and retorted, 'I don't bet on sure things.' A lovely peace had descended on them and he returned her smile. That was one of the things she loved about George, he could always inspire a calm serenity within her. They sat in silence for some time listening to the drone of the bees and the twittering of the birds, lost in their own thoughts. It was Annie who broke it.

'I hear you've got yourself a girlfriend?'

He brought his attention back to her, brows furrowed. Slowly his head swung in denial as he eyed her warily.

'Josie Stafford?'

'Well now, who told you that?'

The coldness in his voice warned her not to continue; not to interfere. She ignored it. 'You do know she has gotten herself a name for entertaining men, don't you, George?'

In an instant he was on his feet, glaring down at her in red-faced fury, knocking his glass over in the process. 'How dare you! How dare you meddle in my affairs? Do I ever tell you how to live? Josie Stafford happens to be a very good friend of mine, but not in the sense you are obviously implying. She's a very nice person and not at all the way you gossipy women paint her. And how the hell would you know what she's like? She doesn't even live in Greencastle.' With a hand he indicated the glass and mumbled, 'I'm sorry about that.' She stretched out a hand as if to deter him but he growled, 'Go to hell! And I warn you . . . don't go sticking your nose in where it's not wanted.'

With these words he turned on his heel and stormed off. Annie sat in a bemused state. George swearing? And at her into the bargain! He must be smitten. Did he really believe that Josie was lily white? Had this woman successfully pulled the wool over his eyes? Was there a chance, however remote, that Josie Stafford would one day become Annie's sister-in-law? The very idea appalled her. Oh, no, it mustn't be allowed to happen. Heaven forbid that such a thing could be allowed to come about!

Later that evening, when the children were in bed and they

were clearing up the last of debris in the garden, Annie voiced her doubts to Sean.

He rounded on her in amazement. 'You mean, you actually questioned George about Josie Stafford? Are you daft? Have you no sense at all, woman?' He turned from her in disgust. 'Huh! Don't expect to see him around here again. The man must be mortified.'

'Then it's true? He does go to see her?'

'As a friend. At least, that's what he tells me. But ... you know, she's a fine-looking girl. Why shouldn't he be serious about her?'

Annie's nostrils flared and her mouth was tight as she derided Josie Stafford. 'She's not the kind of woman that men marry. She doesn't even live in Greencastle but they still know all about her. I hear there's been a lot of talk about her this past few years.'

Sean moved closer and bent down to peer closely into his wife's face. 'And I bet you that those who talk the most about her are the very ones whose husbands secretly visit her. What does that tell you, Annie?'

'It tells me she's a cheap whore, to sleep with other women's men! That's what it tells me. And you tell me this, Sean Devlin. How come *you* know what she looks like?'

'Ah, well now, Annie, it tells me a different story. To me it looks like there are many dissatisfied men about or why else would Josie be so popular, eh? But I bet you it's more talk than anything else! As for how I know what she looks like ... I've had the pleasure of meeting her. What do you think of that? I ran into her and George in town one Friday night. They were on their way to Tommy McCarthy's. George is learning ballroom dancing and enjoying it, so he tells me. He introduced me to her. And do you know something? I liked her. She seems like a nice caring girl.'

'You never mentioned it to me.'

'Because you would have been shocked. That's why I didn't say anything. I knew you would have to meddle ... and I've been proved right. Besides, I'd already heard tell of her.'

Remembering the time before his operation when he had been frustrated for so long, terrible unspeakable thoughts crossed Annie's mind.

He watched her intently then swung his head from side to side in mock despair. 'Annie. I can still read you like a book. And the answer is no, I didn't. But don't you be so quick to write Josie off. If George is serious about her, I for one will make her welcome in my home.'

Before Annie got a chance to apologize to George, he sought her out. She was on her way home from school a few days later when he came to his gate and hailed her.

'I've been watching out for you, Annie. Could I have a word, please?'

'Why are you not at work today, George?' she questioned him as she ushered Rachel and Rebecca into the house ahead of her, leaving George to look after Thomas who was asleep in his pram.

'First let me settle the children, Annie. Rachel . . . fetch your colouring books from the drawer in the kitchen, love. I bought some new crayons for you. Look how thick they are. You can show Rebecca how to colour in.' He spread some papers on the kitchen table and, piling cushions on the chairs, lifted the two children up to sit there.

Every time Annie started to speak, he held up a hand for silence. 'Patience.' When at last the girls were absorbed in colouring their books, or in Rebecca's case, scribbling, he turned to Annie with a smile. 'Would you like a cup of tea?'

She shook her head but he frustrated her further by insisting on pouring them all cool drinks. At last he sat down facing her, smiling at her impatience.

'About time,' Annie said and managed a smile. 'First I want to apologize humbly for last Saturday. I don't know what got into me. It's none of my business who you see. Can you ever forgive me?'

'You took me unawares. I shouldn't have been so touchy otherwise. You see, I was sitting thinking about my relationship with Josie. Trying to come to a decision. You helped me to get things into perspective.'

'Oh, then thank God I spoke out when I did.'

Now George was laughing at her. 'No, Annie, you don't understand. I've decided to court her. She pretends to be as tough as nails but really she needs someone to look out for her.'

'It doesn't have to be you!'

'No, that's true. But why not me? I'm getting on. It's about time I settled down.'

'You mean . . . you might actually marry her?' Annie cried, aghast.

'Perhaps. If she'll have me. I wanted you to be the first to know. I would like to bring her to meet you. Break the ice. I know Sean won't mind, he's already met her.'

Annie was speechless. He could *not* be serious. At last she laughed aloud in obvious relief. 'You're having me on. Here, pull the other one!'

Now George's face was still, his eyes watchful as he solemnly assured her, 'No, I'm deadly serious, Annie. Will you not agree to meet her?'

Leaving her chair, she sat close beside him on the settee. 'George, listen to me. You're a handsome man and there are lots of girls out there just hoping someone like you will take notice of them. So why her? Why Josie Stafford of all people?'

'She's very attractive and a good listener. I can tell her anything and I know it won't be repeated. There's not many you can say that about.'

'You can always talk to me,' Annie cried. 'Don't you trust me to keep my mouth shut?'

'Annie, there are things that I could never discuss with you. You're my sister, for heaven's sake!'

'I'm only your half-sister and we are more like friends than relations. I tell you everything.'

'Not everything. Be honest now, Annie. You know there are things you could never discuss with me, for the simple reason that I'm your half-brother.'

She saw the wisdom of this, realizing she could never talk to him about Sean. However she wasn't willing to give up that easily. 'There must be other girls you can confide in. What about Marie Wilson? You could have had Marie.'

'You never cease to amaze me, Annie. I thought you didn't like Marie. Wouldn't want her in the family.'

'Not for . . .' She dithered. 'You're free to date her. Why don't you like her?'

He shrugged. 'Right from the start, Marie and I just didn't hit it off. She wasn't the least bit interested in me.'

He watched her turn this over in her mind and said, 'Now, don't go jumping to conclusions, Annie. I wanted to warn you but didn't see the sense in worrying you. It was just a harmless flirtation and once you started coming along with Sean on a Saturday night, Marie soon moved on, as I'm sure you've noticed.'

Yes, she had. But what if Mary Moon hadn't dropped hints? What then? How far would Sean have gone? And would George have intervened?

As if aware of her bitter thoughts, he said, 'Annie, Sean would never hurt you, he cares too much for you. And I would have warned you if I had thought it might get out of hand.'

Pushing her own bleak thoughts to the back of her mind she brought her attention back to the matter in hand. 'George, what if you commit yourself to this woman and then fall in love with someone else, eh? What will you do then?'

'There's no chance of that happening, Annie. I discovered a long time ago that I'm a one-woman man. That's why I never married. The woman I love is out of reach.' Unconsciously a deep sigh accompanied these words.

Annie was round-eyed with wonder. 'Who is she? What do you mean . . . she's out of reach?' she cried, bewildered at this turn of events. Who would have dreamed that George carried a torch for some woman? 'Is she married?'

He nodded in confirmation and watched in silence as she digested his words.

'It was Mary Mitchell, wasn't it? Did you find out after she married John Greenwood?'

'Something like that. Just hold on a minute. Let me think . . . get things sorted out in my mind.' He sat collecting his thoughts together and she waited patiently for him to explain. 'It's like this. I don't think it would be fair to marry a woman while I love someone else. Now Josie . . . I can tell her how things are and she'll understand, I think she'll have me anyway. I certainly don't expect her to fall in love with an old fogey like me.'

'Why not? Anyone could love you!'

'Annie, she's twenty-two years old, and as you well know

I'm thirty-five. But she needs someone older. Someone she can trust. I think she'll still have me.'

'Of course she will! And be glad to get you,' Annie snorted.

'Hush now, let me finish. You have no idea what Josie's like. She's kind and honest, and to be truthful, since Thelma got married I'm very lonely. I need someone to care for. To grow old with. I know she has the name of being a loose woman, but she assures me that she's only ever slept with two men and I believe her.'

'More fool you! Even so . . . that's two too many,' Annie interrupted bitterly.

'I really believe her,' he said quietly. 'And since I'm no angel myself, I would have a cheek expecting a virgin to fall for me. Haven't we all done something in our lives that we're ashamed of? I think it could work out for us, Annie. In fact, I know it could, but you and Thelma and Rosaleen are the only family I have. I don't want to lose any of you. Please don't let Josie come between us.'

'Oh, George, don't put me on the spot like this. Mam will have kittens when she hears about it.'

'If you and Sean befriend Josie, Thelma will take her cue from you. And as for John . . . he wouldn't know how to be anything but nice. Please meet her at least, Annie. If you care for me at all . . . do you, Annie? Do you care for me?'

'Of course I do. You know that!'

'Well then, try and befriend her, please.'

When he put it like that, how could she refuse? 'Oh, George. If it means so much to you, all right, I'll meet her. But, mind you, I can't promise to like her. But I do promise not to make any judgement until I've run my beady eye over her.'

The tears that had threatened during their conversation at last overflowed. To Annie it seemed all such a waste. She turned towards him and pressed close for comfort. George cradled her in his arms. Above her head his eyes were bleak. Perhaps what he was proposing was not such a good idea after all? The sensible thing to do would be to move somewhere far away from Greencastle. But would that solve anything? How then would he survive?

Josie Stafford was at her kitchen window when she saw George

127

Magee enter the yard via the back entry. She hastily wiped her hands on her apron and, going into the hall, ran a comb through her curly black locks. She had a few minutes to tidy herself. George would play in the yard with Tiger, her pet labrador, before knocking. Her stomach was in knots. George Magee was the only man who had ever shown her respect. Oh, she had plenty of men friends and they promised her the earth, but they were only after one thing. George had been coming to her house for three months now and not once had he tried it on. Not once! Now surely that was some kind of record? She examined her face in the mirror. Her eyes were too big; they looked as if they were about to pop out of her head. She wrinkled her short snub nose in distaste. She was so plain! Why did he still come?

His knock on the door was firm and confident. Slowly she opened it and stood looking at him. 'I didn't expect you tonight.'

'I was passing and thought I might as well pop in and see you.'

They both laughed at the very idea of this. He had to come to the other side of Greencastle, go well out of his way, to get near the back street where she lived. 'You look lovely.' His eyes scanned her face and hair.

Embarrassed, she ran her fingers through her hair, sending it back into disorder. 'And you tell such lovely lies.' She smiled but it was forced and he eyed her closely.

Sensing that she was out of sorts, he asked, 'What's wrong, Josie? You're not your usual happy self. Aren't you going to ask me in? Or . . .?' The words 'Is someone with you?' hung unuttered in the air between them and suddenly he was hot with embarrassment. He should have waited until tomorrow night. In any other circumstances the words would be innocent enough but considering the gossip that circulated about her, he felt as if he had put his foot right in it.

'There is no *or*! I do have my off days the same as everybody else. I can't always be smiling.' Her voice was sharp. 'I didn't expect you so you'll have to take me as you find me.' She led the way through the scullery into the only other downstairs room.

Closing the back door, he followed her inside and through

to the other room. It was clean but cluttered. A small range that ran almost the length of one wall was well black-leaded and set with sticks and papers for easy lighting should the weather break. There were snowy white net curtains at the window and a bright rag mat in front of the range. A treadle sewing machine stood in the centre of the room and remnants of various materials were strewn about the floor.

'Are you cold? Shall I light the fire?'

She sounded distant, and he remained standing by the door, unsure of his welcome. Perhaps he should have waited until tomorrow night when he usually visited her. Suddenly uneasy, he shuffled his feet. 'Are you expecting anyone? If you like, I can come back tomorrow night.'

Vexed, she swung a hand towards the sewing machine. 'Does it look like I'm expecting company? And just what kind of a question is that, eh? Do you think I keep an open door every night of the week? Is that what you think, George?'

'No, I think no such thing! It doesn't have to be a man. You could be waiting for a friend to come.'

'But that's not what you were really thinking, now is it? Huh! Give a dog a bad name and it sticks.'

He approached her warily. 'What on earth has you in such bad form?' he asked in bewilderment. 'Look . . . I'll go out and come back in again and start afresh. All right?'

At this she had to laugh and the tension eased. 'Take off your coat and sit down. I don't know what's got into me. Look, it's getting chilly, I'll light the fire.'

Gently he pushed her down on to one of the small arm-chairs that graced each side of the range. 'You sit there. I'll light it.'

Tears stung the back of her eyes as she watched him remove his coat and roll up his shirt sleeves. It would be wonderful to have him about the house permanently. 'Is the coal in here?' He indicated the cubby hole under the stairs and she nodded. He was such a fine man, she was afraid of becoming too fond of him. Twice before she had thought herself in love and twice she had been disappointed. She had been young and silly and had soon got over the others, but this time it was different. George meant more to her than the other two put together. It frightened her to think just how much she had come to depend

129

on him. Could he learn to care in return? No! Men didn't fall in love with the likes of her; they tried to use her, and to her everlasting shame two had succeeded.

He used the bellows that hung to one side of the fireplace to boost the flames. Soon the fire was roaring. Laughing over at her, he said, 'I could become a dab hand at this, you know.'

'You could at that,' she agreed.

'I've a bottle in the car,' he confided. 'I'll fetch it in.'

While he was gone she swivelled the sewing machine on its pivot so that it was suspended underneath the table. With the base filling the void it now looked like a small table. It had been a present from her Aunt Martha on her eighteenth birthday. Pulling it closer to the fire, she covered it with a white table cloth folded in two. When he returned, there were two wine glasses sitting on it.

His eyes roamed the room. 'What did you do with the sewing machine?'

Lifting a corner of the cloth, she let him see what was underneath.

'My, that's handy. I always thought that was a wee table,' he exclaimed as if she had performed some wonderful piece of magic.

'A lot of things aren't what they seem.'

He held up the bottle of wine. 'Your favourite.'

Again tears stung the back of her eyes. Her favourite. Never before had anyone considered her likes or dislikes. No ... bottles of beer and sometimes whiskey had been carried in, in brown paper bags. Drink that was consumed by her male friends while they worked up the courage to try it on. She wished she hadn't been so foolish in the past, but since her mother's death she had been lonely. If only she had waited. But then, she had never been in a position to meet a man like George Magee. Had her father been like him? Oh, she would love to think so. But what would a man like George have been doing with someone like her mother? Josie had never known him; had been told that he was dead. With hindsight she realized that her mother had tried to shield her from the nature of her work. The oldest profession in the world. The men who had visited the house then were all *uncles*. Josie grimaced when

130

she thought how proud she had been to have so many uncles. Nobody at school had as many uncles as she had.

Then her mother died suddenly of a heart attack. Josie had just left school and started work in the mill at the time. Her mother's eldest sister Aunt Martha, who had visited them about once a year, had arrived and sorted out the small insurance policies her mother had diligently kept up. It still wasn't enough but Aunt Martha told Josie not to worry, she would see to things. She hadn't stinted and Sarah Stafford had gone out in style. After the funeral, Aunt Martha stayed on for a few days.

She had talked bitterly of her wayward young sister. Had explained, haltingly, that Sarah was the last of a family of six. She had been born late in life to their parents. Martha herself had been twenty-five when Sarah was born. The birth had proved too much for their delicate mother and she had died when Sarah was six months old, their father dying shortly afterwards of grief. It was left to Martha, as the eldest of the family, to rear her. Sarah had chafed against the strict religious upbringing imposed on her by her sister. At fourteen she had run away from home and by the time Martha had tracked her down was already living a life of shame and enjoying every minute of it. When Martha had told her to change her ways or she would go to her eternal damnation, Sarah had laughed in her face and cried, 'Well, all my friends will be there too.' She had refused to give up her new way of life. The rest of the family had washed their hands of her. Only Martha had kept in touch.

After the funeral her aunt offered Josie a home with her in the house she owned in Bangor, but she had declined. She had heard that they were all well to do over there and knew she would never fit in. She was happy here with the lough nearby and miles of countryside around her. Martha had explained to her that the lough was every bit as beautiful from the County Down side and that there was plenty of open country around Bangor too. But Martha was a spinster and set in her ways. She was so different from Josie's happy-go-lucky mother that she could not bear the thought of living with her. After some persuasion, Martha gave in. She explained that she had put a small amount of money in trust for Josie when she was born.

She was to have received it on her eighteenth birthday, but since she probably needed it now Martha would see that it was advanced to her. Josie had been content. The landlord had said she could continue to rent the wee kitchen house and her name was put on the rent book. She had her job in the mill, and now, thanks to her Aunt Martha, she had a wee bit of money in the building society. What more could she want? She soon found out that there was lots more she wanted. Foolishly, she went the wrong way about getting it and lost her money and earned herself a reputation into the bargain.

'Penny for them?'

'Oh, thank you.' Josie took the glass of wine from George and confessed, 'They're not worth a penny.'

He pulled the other chair closer and leant across, arms on thighs, so that he could look into her face. 'Josie, I want to talk to you.'

'That sounds ominous, but fire away.'

'I've been talking to my sister Annie about you and she would like to meet you.'

Josie froze. That prim and proper sister he was always talking about, who lived in the big house on the Serpentine Road, wanted to meet her? Not that George had said that she was prim and proper but Josie had read between the lines.

'You've got to be joking! Why, she'd have a fit if she opened the door and saw me standing there.'

'No, she wouldn't. She asked me to bring you along.'

'Ah, George, I know you mean well . . . but it wouldn't work.'

'Why? Why wouldn't it work?'

'You know very well why it wouldn't. You know what they say about me. Why, I'm infamous.'

'But it's not true!'

'Some of it is. And I'm sure there's talk about us, too. The best thing you can do is never to come back here.'

'I'd be very hurt if I thought you meant that, Josie.'

'You don't understand, George. We wouldn't stand a chance. I was born into this life. I'm illegitimate! Never knew my father. I don't know whether he's alive or dead.' He opened his mouth to protest; tell her none of this mattered to him. She quickly covered it with her hand. 'Hush! Listen to me. If you stay here you'll spoil your chances of marrying some decent

132

woman who will give you children. People will point the finger at you. Don't spoil everything. That's what would happen if you try to make your family accept me. It wouldn't be worth it.'

He gripped her hands and pulled her to her feet and into his arms. For a moment she was stiff and unyielding then she responded eagerly; her arms went around his neck and her lips met his. This was what she wanted. She might never own him but at least she could have this night; if she pleased him, maybe other nights too. She wouldn't be greedy. Raw passion flared between them. They clung together exchanging kisses and caresses. A knock at the door brought them breathlessly down to earth. It was the back door. Josie's eyes were full of dread as she hurriedly buttoned her dress and went to open the door. She could guess who it was though she prayed it wouldn't be him. George would get the wrong impression. To her dismay he followed her into the kitchen and stood there watchfully. She opened the door slightly and he heard her mutter, 'Go away. Please go away.'

A man's voice, rough and ragged, pleaded, 'Please, Josie. Please. I'll pay. Look, I've got money.' George heard the clink of coins and saw her push the extended hand away and close the door.

She stood with her back to him for some moments to regain her composure. When at last she turned to face him she wanted to weep but pride kept her head high. He was shrugging into his jacket.

'Would you believe me if I said it's not what you think?'

'Try me.' He sounded sceptical.

'That was Dosey Brown. He comes all the time but he never gets in. I honestly never let him in. I haven't been with a man for . . . oh, I forget how long.' She heard the pleading in her voice and hated herself for it, but she didn't want to lose him completely.

'How much was he offering you, Josie?' His hand indicated the wine bottle. 'Was that bottle enough? Is that why you were so willing just now?'

She was slightly built but the slap she delivered then knocked his head back on his shoulders. 'Get out,' she ground out between her teeth. 'And don't ever come back. You! With all your mealy-mouthed niceness, you're no different from the rest of them.'

Without further ado, he brushed past her and left the house. Josie moved restlessly about the room. She would not let it get to her. She would not. She was used to being alone. Then, lifting the half-full bottle of wine, she threw it against the wall. Watching it shatter and the red contents stain the wallpaper, she wailed over and over again, 'Damn you, Dosey Brown! Damn you to hell!' As she dropped to her knees, face buried in her hands, her body was wracked with uncontrollable sobs.

Chapter 4

George inched his car out of the back entry and on to the Shore Road, turning left in the direction of Carrickfergus. Putting his foot down and speeding perilously through Jordanstown and Greenisland until eventually he arrived at the old castle on the shores of Carrickfergus town. Pulling in beside the castle walls, he left the car and climbed up on to the the battlements of the castle to stand gazing out over Belfast Lough towards Bangor. To his left the lough ran on towards Whitehead before opening out into the North Channel, and in the far distance the dark blue waters merged with the horizon, swaying like some great jelly and creating a picture to which no artist could do justice. It was still early evening and the sun's reflection on the water was breathtaking, the skies above it a radiant mass of pinks and mauves.

It was beautiful here, a peaceful haven. In the harbour small sailing boats bobbing about on the gentle swell of the incoming tide were well cared for and colourfully painted. On the harbour wall a few men sat fishing, and to his left, children accompanied by their parents played along the water's edge, splashing and laughing as the flowing tide lapped around their legs. In this tranquil setting George slowly unwound. He grimaced as, relaxing against the cold stone wall, he let his mind drift back over his recent behaviour. Josie must think him a conceited, big-headed fool! After all, she had never denied she had other men friends. From the very beginning she had made no secret of her past. Even earlier on this evening she had gone to great pains to point out to him that she would not be accepted in any family circle. She had, however, without actually putting it into words, led him to believe that it was all in the past and that she had turned over a new leaf. That was what made the difference. He had believed her.

Dosey Brown. He didn't recognize the name. The voice had been that of a young man. He had sounded very eager. Over eager in fact! George cringed with distaste at the idea of Josie with a younger man; with any man for that matter. He had become very fond of her. She said she always sent this man packing. But . . . he had his money ready. Was that the act of one who was always sent away? Had Josie lied to him? Did she still do the business? His cheeks paled when he recalled asking if the bottle of wine was payment enough. In the name of God, what had he been he thinking of? Hadn't he been ready to take all that she was offering? Hadn't he felt wonderfully alive for the first time in many a long day, with her willing body in his arms? Hadn't thrill upon thrill coursed through him when she had returned his kisses and caresses? He could still feel her warm body pressed against his and writhed at the memory. It was a long time since he had held a woman so close; had felt so keyed up. It was probably the disappointment on top of that excitement that had turned him suddenly sanctimonious. He, who had always considered himself broad-minded, had come over all self-righteous. No wonder she had ordered him out of the house. She must think him a right twit! And he didn't blame her. Not one wee bit. He fingered his tender left cheek. She could certainly pack a wallop. Would he ever have the gumption to face her again?

He recalled the first time he had met Josie. On his way home from work one night he'd had to swerve at the junction of the Whitewell Road to avoid a black labrador pup that ran out in front of his car. He had almost crashed into a lamp post. Infuriated, he parked the car and marched back to where a slight girl was kneeling on the pavement, the pup in her arms, murmuring to it.

At his approach she glared up at him. 'You could have killed him, you stupid fool.'

George gaped at her in amazement. 'What about me? I don't suppose it matters that I could have been killed?'

Full of concern, she had slowly risen to her feet to face him, big velvety brown eyes begging his forgiveness. 'I'm sorry, I

136

never thought. I was so worried about Tiger, you see. He's so tiny. Are you all right?'

His lips had twitched to hear that the pup had such a savage name. 'You should keep him on a lead,' he advised more gently. She looked so vulnerable standing there, eyes huge and haunted-looking in a small pointed face.

A lead with collar attached was displayed for him to see. 'I had this on him. I'm afraid it's too big. He slipped out of it.'

'I'm not surprised. That would fit a real tiger,' jested George, and in spite of the thought of a hot meal ready and waiting for him, he crouched by the dog and gently examined the shaking animal's legs. 'He's just frightened. There's nothing broken, but don't walk him for a while. Where do you live? I'll give you a lift home with him.'

'No, that won't be necessary. It would be well out of your way. You're headed up the Whitewell. I live some distance along the Shore Road.'

He had insisted on taking her home. Once there she had invited him in for a cup of strong tea, just in case he was suffering from delayed shock. One couldn't be too careful, she had solemnly advised him. Very much aware that he was suffering no ill effects whatsoever, except maybe a quickening of the pulse as he watched her movements, and pushing the thought of Thelma's annoyance if his dinner should be spoilt to the back of his mind, George had let her persuade him to remain. For the first time he had entered her small neat home.

Sitting in the spotless scullery, at the well-scrubbed table, he watched as she put the kettle on the stove to boil. Spooning tea leaves from a tin caddy into a pot, she filled it with the boiling water and placed it back on the stove to draw. Unconscious grace was in every action as she moved about the room. He found himself thinking that she must be a wonderful dancer, and voiced his thoughts. 'Do you dance? I mean, proper ballroom dancing?'

Her eyes lit up and she confessed, 'It's the love of my life. Not that I get many chances to go to proper dances. You know . . . big bands. But I go to the Club Orchid and the Orpheus sometimes, although it's mostly records you dance to. Do you dance?'

'Afraid not, I never had the time to learn properly. I'm afraid

137

I just slouch around the floor. It must be nice to do the steps properly.'

'Oh, you should go to a learners' class. They're all over Belfast. I help out at Tommy McCarthy's. I get in free if I dance with some of the first timers, for the first hour.'

'I'm afraid I'm a bit long in the tooth to start now.'

'Oh, what a pity. You would probably enjoy it. And you're not all that old,' she consoled him.

Conversation flowed easily between them as they drank the tea. He learnt that her mother was dead and that Josie lived alone. Her father wasn't mentioned. She was young, much too young for him to get any fancy ideas about, he warned himself. Besides, she probably had a boyfriend, she was so pretty and easy to get on with. They talked about everything under the sun and he found her outspoken views on local affairs very refreshing, soon feeling as if he had known her all his life. It was with reluctance that he eventually said goodbye and climbed into his car to go home.

On the drive back that night he'd admitted to himself that he found Josie Stafford very attractive. There was something sensuous about her. Those dark eyes that smouldered when she was earnest about something, and those full red lips, were enough to spur on any hot-blooded man. Since John McLaughlin had entered their lives and seemed intent on making Thelma his wife, George had felt at a loss. He would soon be coming home to an empty house each night and didn't relish the idea one bit.

He had noticed that there were no rings on Josie's fingers. Had she a steady boyfriend? Would she come out with him some night? Would she think him too old? But some girls liked older men. It was worth a try. After all, she could only say no. But if she did agree to see him, who knew where it might lead? Not all marriages were made in heaven. You didn't have to be head over heels in love to make someone happy. With the right person he could make a go of it, and perhaps Josie was that person.

A few days later he called to see her on the pretext of finding out if Tiger had made a full recovery. He had approached by the back door as he had before and Josie appeared apprehensive as she opened the door a crack and peered out at him.

Seeing it was him, she opened the door wide, a surprised questioning look on her face. She told him Tiger had fully recovered from his ordeal and motioned him in, to see for himself. He played with the pup, trying to find the words to ask her out. When he could dither no longer he straightened up and asked her if she would like to go to the pictures one night. Gently she had refused. When he persisted she explained she had a bad name in the village and no doubt her fame had also spread as far as Greencastle. She had assured him that he would only live to regret it. The idea of her being a woman of ill repute had thrown him for a moment. To him she appeared so young and vulnerable. Not at all like a woman of easy virtue. But looks could be deceptive! Reminding himself that it didn't have to go any further than a date, he had replied that he was a big boy and was only asking her out, not proposing marriage. With a wide smile she told him that 'He had been warned and on his own head be it.' She had agreed to go to the pictures with him. They discussed the films which were on in town and decided on 'Calamity Jane' showing at the Imperial cinema on Cornmarket.

That was the beginning of their friendship and for the past few months they had dated twice a week. She had cajoled him into going to a dancing class. On Friday nights they went to Tommy McCarthy's school of ballroom dancing on Royal Avenue, where he had the joy of twirling around the floor with her held close in his arms. He discovered that once shown the basic steps, the rest came naturally to him and with her for a partner he couldn't go wrong. He was soon adept at dancing the Tango. Although older than most of the crowd, he very much looked forward to Friday nights.

Every Tuesday night he visited her at home, where they sat listening to records and had heated debates about everything under the sun. He found that she had a cynical attitude towards men, didn't trust them. When he asked if that included him, she assured him it included all men. In spite of this she continued to see him, and apparently enjoyed his company; they had a lot in common. What she did the rest of the week, she never said and he never asked. Totally in ignorance of the fact that the neighbours were speculating what a nice fellow like him could see in a girl like Josie Stafford, he continued to visit her home every Tuesday night.

The only fly in the ointment was his family. He'd had cross words with Thelma about his relationship with Josie. He'd had to curb his temper, when on more than one occasion, his step-mother had called Josie a whore. Why couldn't they mind their own business? Eventually they'd agreed to differ, and Josie's name was never mentioned again.

He lingered for a long time on the castle walls, loath to return to his empty house, watching the dusk start to darken the sky before returning to the car and heading back home. Near the turn off in the road that would take him to where Josie lived he slowed the car. Should he go and apologize? What if Dosey Brown had returned? Would he be able to face up to the fact that she was still on the game? Was he even being fair since he had never asked her not to? Should he offer her an alterna-tive? Just what had he to offer her? Certainly not love! But he was physically attracted to her and she didn't seem to find him repulsive. They got on so well together he was sure that they could make a go of it. He didn't think for one minute that she would expect love to blossom. They were just friends and that was as good a basis for marriage as anything else he could think of. Until tonight he had not made a wrong move although he was pretty sure she wouldn't have refused him. He couldn't just walk away now. Even if she refused to go out with him again he still had to see her and apologize for being such a boor. Tomorrow night he would call and plead his case, and she just might forgive him.

The following evening it took real will-power to make him present himself at Josie's front door. He had spent the whole day debating what to do and had decided that he must let her know that he had become very fond of her. He must make it clear that his intentions were serious. Then, if she was still doing the business, she would realize that it would have to stop once and for all. Tonight was the first time he had used the front door. As he waited for an answer to his knock he gazed at the brightly painted green door and shining brass knocker and questioned himself. Why had he so far always entered by the back entry? Was he unconsciously trying to be

140

secretive? Was he ashamed of his association with a woman of ill-repute? He knocked again and waited. All to no avail. Josie was not at home.

Had she guessed that he would call and deliberately gone out to avoid meeting him? Was Tommy McCarthy's open on a Tuesday night? She was very popular there. He knew a lot of noses had been put out of joint when he had started accompanying her every Friday night. He was also aware that he was called her sugar daddy, and that he wasn't expected to last long with someone as young and popular as Josie.

Should he wait in the car for a while in case she had just popped out on an errand? A slight movement of the net curtains on the window next door hit that idea on the head. God alone knew how many eyes were watching him at this very minute. Head high, he made his way back to the car, feeling as if hundreds of eyes were boring into his back. He chided himself for being so melodramatic. Probably the neighbours were too busy with their own affairs to even notice him. And even if they were watching, what difference did it make?

As he drew the car to a halt in front of his own house, for the first time in their acquaintance George was dismayed to see Annie at his door. He had an idea what she wanted and what kind of answer could he give her?

He was right. After greeting him, Annie waited until he opened the door and they were inside before speaking further.

'I was down seeing me mam and I thought I'd call in and invite you and Josie up to visit us on Saturday night. Sean says he'll bring in some drink and I'll make sandwiches and some savoury dishes. Is that all right with you?'

Relieved that it was to be Saturday he smiled warmly at her. Saturday was four days away. Plenty of time for him to see Josie and win back her confidence. 'That's very kind of you, Annie. I'm much obliged. I'm sure Josie will be pleased too.'

Her expression was apprehensive. 'So you haven't changed your mind then? You're sure that you still want to go through with it?'

'Annie, I'm a grown man, for heaven's sake! Not some love-sick kid. I know fine well what I'm doing.'

'I hope so, George. And that you don't live to regret it. By

141

the way, I haven't said anything to Mam yet. You know . . . that you might be serious about Josie. Don't mention it when you see her. She'd be worried sick. If it doesn't work out, she need be none the wiser.'

'I admire the faith you have in me, Annie. But never fear, I won't say a dicky bird. It's bad enough having you trying to save me, without Thelma joining in.'

'Where have you been?'

'Out.'

'I know that. But where?'

'That's none of your business, Annie. Have you time for a cup of tea or . . .' He eyed her questioningly. When she shook her head he opened the door again. 'Well then, if you don't mind I'm tired and I'd like an early night.' Annie was the last person he wanted to discuss Josie with at the moment.

Obviously offended, she bade him a stiff good night and briskly left the house.

The following night George left work early. Parking his car out of sight, he waited across from the mill gates to watch the workers leave. She was one of the last ones out.

'Josie?'

He saw her start of surprise and the furtive way she glanced around before she acknowledged his call and crossed the road to join him. 'Are you daft or something? Everyone will be talking about this tomorrow.'

'Let them. I came to say how sorry I am about Monday night.'

'That's all right. It doesn't matter.'

'It does to me.' She was galloping along the road, head down, towards the bus stop. 'Here, hold on. I've the car with me, I'll drive you home.'

Suddenly she stopped and faced him. 'Let's put an end to this farce once and for all, George. I accept your apology. Now, goodbye.'

Before she could move off again, he gripped her firmly by the arms. 'Does that mean that you don't want to see me again?' His gaze impelled her to look at him.

'That's right! You've hit the nail on the head.' Her gaze

wavered and she wriggled uncomfortably. 'That's exactly what I mean. Goodbye.'

He thought he detected the glint of tears in her eyes but wasn't sure. Deciding to take the bull by the horns, he bent and planted a kiss on her trembling lips.

At first she struggled, endeavouring to break his hold on her arms. Eventually he allowed her to succeed but before she could pull away his arms encircled her, gripping her closer still. At last her emotions took over and her lips moved hungrily under his. Releasing them, he laughed down at her in triumph. 'Come on. I'm taking you home.' He tucked her hand under his arm and smiled brightly at some of the mill workers who were hanging about gaping at their outrageous display. Let them all stare. He wanted Josie Stafford. He wanted her very much indeed and he didn't care who knew it! And to his great delight, all the signs said that she felt the same way.

This time he parked the car in front of the house, a fact not wasted on Josie. He followed her eagerly inside and reached for her. She warded him off.

'No, George. This isn't right. We must talk. But first I want to have a wash and freshen myself up. The mill has its own particular smell and I hate it.' She sniffed down at herself in disgust. 'You go home and come back later.' When he hesitated, she pleaded, 'Please. Give me about an hour.'

'I'm only going to please you. I never noticed any smell,' he lied gamely.

She laughed and gave him a gentle push towards the door. 'Liar! One hour. Away you go.'

One hour to the minute found him back on her doorstep. Josie looked shy as she motioned him inside. Her hair was still damp and curled in wisps about a face devoid of make-up. She smelt of roses. She made no apology about being still in her dressing gown and George took this to be a good sign. She made to lead him into the kitchen but at the foot of the stairs he hesitated, a questioning look in his eyes.

She gazed at him solemnly. 'Are you sure this is what you want, George?'

'I was never more sure of anything in my life,' he vowed.

Without another word she climbed the stairs and he eagerly

followed. He was relieved to find that her bedroom did not look as he'd imagined a paid woman's would look. It was bright and airy, with flowered wallpaper and white paintwork. The room of a young girl. The bed was covered with a brightly coloured patchwork quilt.

He smiled as he gathered her close and pressed his nose against her throat. 'I have to admit, you do smell much nicer.'

'I should hope so! I hate the fusty smell of the mill but you can't avoid it.'

'Why don't you try for a job somewhere else?'

'I can't do anything else. Come here.' She smiled wryly as she led him towards the bed. 'Although, mind you, there are those who would tell you different.'

Slowly and seductively she undressed him. As he lay in cosy contentment the thought crossed his mind that she certainly knew how to make a man relax. He pushed it away and concentrated on her performance, waiting patiently for the moment he would see her naked body. At last, slipping the dressing gown from her shoulders, Josie climbed on to the bed beside him. Anticipation shivered down his spine as he gazed at the beauty of her breasts. Her eyes, dark with suppressed passion, seemed to mesmerize him and her body felt cool and soft beneath his hands. They made love, long and leisurely, and never had he felt so alive. Lifted completely out of himself into a world of sensation and pleasure.

Completely sated, he at last rose on one elbow and gazed down on her. She was flushed and smiling. Had he pleased her? It was hard to tell with a woman. He had read somewhere that they were very good at faking. Not wanting to ask her bluntly, he tentatively asked, 'Do you still not want to see me again?'

Her fingers trailed over his face. 'You are a very persistent man, George Magee. But you know . . . it can never become serious.'

Gently he mocked her, 'You mean, you were being frivolous just now? I can't wait for you to become serious.'

She smiled, but wanly. 'George, listen to me. You can come here whenever you like. I'll always be glad to see you. Oh, yes . . . I shall always be pleased.'

'Did I please you, then?' He was eager to be reassured.

She smiled tenderly at him. He was so immature for his age. 'You must know you did! But remember, George, Greencastle isn't all that far away. My fame has probably reached there too. But if we steer clear of the obvious places – you know, the pubs and such – we might get away with it for a while. I don't want you to become the laughing stock of the village. As for meeting your sister . . . the answer is no, no, a thousand times no!'

He heard her out in silence. No need to tell her she was indeed known in Greencastle. 'Josie, my sister and her husband have invited us up for a drink on Saturday night, and I'll be very disappointed if you don't come. I hope you're not going to refuse to come with me? In fact, I won't take no for an answer. I'll be very proud to show you off.' He held her eye and at last, with a muffled exclamation, she buried her head against his chest.

'You'll regret it! I know you will.'

'Why not let me be the judge of that, eh? I promise you that no one will offend you in my presence. All right?'

She did not raise her head, but nodded. He was unaware of her tears until they wet his chest. Gently raising her head in his hands, so that he could see her eyes, he cried, 'Josie? Why are you crying? Here now, there'll be none of this. I intend to bring joy into your life, come what may, so wipe away those tears.'

'Ah, George, George. You're too good for me. I . . .' The words trailed off. She had been about to say 'I love you,' but somehow or other had received the impression that declarations would not be welcome. He was waiting for her to continue. 'I'll give it a try.'

He gripped her close again. 'That's my girl. That's what I want to hear.'

'George, about Dosey Brown . . .'

Quickly he interrupted her. 'I don't want to know! That's all in the past. It's the future that counts.'

'I want to explain. You know, George, I've never done business in the real sense of the word. As I've already told you, I've only been intimate with two men. I was foolish though no more so than some *nice* girls. But because of what my mother was, men kept calling. I suppose they thought that I would be

145

a chip off the old block. I know now that I was daft to let them inside, but to me they were just "uncles". I never entertained them, and to the last man they took no for an answer and left me alone. Except for the two I mentioned to you, and they were younger.' She was too absorbed to notice him wince. 'I fancied myself in love.' She shrugged. 'However, I was my mother's daughter, so I got a bad name. But I wasn't promiscuous. I cared. I was even stupid enough to think one of them meant to marry me. Do you believe me?'

'I believe you, and remember, Josie, we're going to put the past behind us.'

Sadly she shook her head. 'They won't let us.'

He pulled her close. 'Think positive! Trust me. Now no more confessions.'

'George, I want to explain about Dosey Brown. You see, Big Phyllis ... that's his mother ... and mine were great friends. Dosey has just turned eighteen. He isn't right in the head, if you know what I mean? That's why everybody calls him Dosey. His real name is David.' She paused, and when he nodded to show that he understood, continued. 'But everything else works all right! This past few months Phyllis has sent him to me every now and again. She says if I'm nice to him it will keep him out of trouble, and it won't cost me anything. She won't take no for an answer. Because he's a good-looking big lad, and you know how daft some girls can be. The wee young ones have no sense, but if anything happened to one of them their da would take it out on Dosey. Honestly, George, I have never once obliged him. As a matter of fact, the older he gets the more worried I am. His mother thinks it's just a matter of time before I give in, but to be truthful ... I'm beginning to be a bit afraid of him. I dread answering the back door in case it's him. And why *should* I oblige? He's not my problem!'

'Exactly! Why should you indeed?' George was highly indignant. 'I'll have a word with him.'

'Oh, no, he wouldn't understand, so he wouldn't. I've talked myself hoarse. I'll call and see Phyllis and give her a bit of my mind. Perhaps that will do the trick. George, do I have to go with you on Saturday night?'

Her voice had dropped so low he had to ask her to repeat her words. 'I beg your pardon?'

146

'I said, do I have to go with you on Saturday night?'

'I would very much like you to.'

'She won't like me, I know she won't.'

'It won't make any difference. It won't change my mind about you.'

'We'll see.' Josie didn't sound very hopeful. He gathered her close again, and as passion was once more rekindled all else was forgotten.

George picked her up on Saturday night and was dismayed to see that she was wearing a very tight skirt with a split up the front and a red low-cut top. The outfit left nothing to the imagination and he could imagine Annie's reaction to it. Josie was also wearing red stiletto-heeled shoes and much more make-up than was necessary. As she climbed into the car and stretched to put Tiger in the back, the skirt rose even higher up her thighs and although he found it very stimulating he thought it uncalled for in the present circumstances. After all, this was a serious matter; it was his sister he was taking her to meet. What on earth was Josie playing at? Was she deliberately trying to look like a tart? Did she often dress like this? So far when they had met she had always been tastefully dressed.

He edged the car out on to the main road and headed towards Greencastle. She watched him covertly and at last asked, 'Well, will I do?'

He sought words to explain how he felt without giving offence. 'You look . . .'

'Cheap?'

He shrugged slightly. 'It's you who's saying that.'

Her lips tightened. 'Believe me, this is how your sister will be expecting to see me. I don't want to disappoint her. I want you to understand just what you're up against.'

'So be it. Let's go meet her.'

'You mean, you would still take me to her house, dressed like this?' she cried in astonishment.

George was not amused. If she thought that this charade would prevent her from meeting Annie, she was sadly mistaken. 'Why not, if this is how you want to go?' he said mildly.

'Turn the car round immediately. I want to go back home and change.'

147

'Certainly not! We're already late. I told Annie to expect us about eight. It's already half-past and we have to stop to leave the dog off. You've made your bed, now I'm afraid you'll just have to lie on it.' He smiled grimly. It was going to be an entertaining night.

In fact, the night was not a success. Josie was uncomfortable in her tight clothes. In her haste to sit down she chose a chair on which she had to sit upright or display her thighs. After her first wide-eyed appraisal, Annie's endeavours to put Josie at her ease sounded false and were in vain. Sean did his best to bridge the gaps in the conversation but even he found it hard going. He had to admit that Josie was not the way he remembered her. She had never looked like a prostitute before, or at least not in his eyes. Also that split in the skirt and low neckline made it difficult for him to keep his eyes on her face.

George was non-committal. Josie had set this scene, and he could find no fault with Annie's and Sean's attitude towards her. Josie offended her hostess further by just nibbling at a sandwich and refusing anything savoury. To make up for her lack of interest in the food, George overate and washed it down with a lot of beer, guessing that in her embarrassment Josie was having difficulty swallowing. Time dragged slowly by and they all rose with alacrity when Josie tentatively said she would have to be going as her neighbour was keeping an eye on her dog for her.

The good nights were quickly over with. Once outside, Josie, with a sigh of relief made to enter George's car. With a sympathetic smile at her, he said, 'Sorry, but we'll have to walk. I've been drinking a lot, remember. Thanks for a lovely evening, Annie, Sean. I'll get the car in the morning.'

'Yes, thank you very much for having me.' Josie's voice was subdued.

Taking her by the hand, George pulled it through his arm and led her down the drive and on to the road. With a final wave he guided her towards the Gardens. He was hoping to set the seal on their relationship by persuading her to spend the night in his house.

Annie and Sean stood at the gate and watched them out of

148

sight, Josie looking ungainly as she clung to George's arm and stumbled along beside him in her stiletto heels.

Unable to resist the temptation, Annie grunted, 'Look at her! He should be ashamed to be seen with her. Why, she's nothing but a common little tart!'

Sean followed her slowly up the drive and indoors. He took his time locking and bolting the door before turning to face his wife. 'He probably doesn't see her the way we do. And really, we shouldn't judge a book by its cover.'

'I'm glad the kids were in bed. She looked as common as muck! It's only natural to judge her by the way she was dressed. We have to have some standards. And did you see all that muck on her face? She must have put it on with a trowel!'

'It wouldn't have mattered, Annie, if the kids had been awake. Kids don't notice things like that.'

'What on earth does George see in her? I mean . . . did you see the state of her, trying to sit on that chair? She didn't leave much to the imagination, did she?'

'Well, so far as looks are concerned, you've got to admit that she's quite pretty.'

'You really think so? You actually had time to notice her face, and her sitting there airing the rent book?'

Sean smiled slightly at his wife's crude choice of words, and followed her into the kitchen. As he watched her fill the sink with water he admitted to himself that she was right. It had taken some concentration. 'She's not my type, of course.'

Swishing the water into a lather, Annie thought grimly, No! They have to be blonde and beautiful. Angry with herself, she pushed this terrible thought from her mind. Why was she always allowing the past to overwhelm her? 'I did my best, Sean. You have to admit that. I did all I could to make her feel welcome. I just can't get over the state of her. What on earth can our George see in her?'

Sean's lips twisted wryly and he started to dry the dishes. 'Oh, you did that, Annie. You were very gracious and tolerant,' he assured her. 'To be truthful, she wasn't what I expected either. It was . . . well . . . as if she was putting on some kind of an act for us.'

'You only think that because you were seeing her in this setting,' Annie cried in exasperation. Men could be so blind!

149

'In those clothes, of course she looked out of place here. She looked as if she was soliciting. I wouldn't have been in the least surprised to see her price stuck on the sole of her shoe. She certainly looked the part! I've seen prostitutes with more clothes on in Union Street. You would have thought she'd have made a bit of an effort at least to look normal.' Her chin in the air she said smugly, 'Well, I did my best! I can do no more. George must realize now that she won't find favour in our circle. After tonight, he must surely see that she just doesn't fit in. I don't think we'll see her again, do you?'

'All I can say is, if tonight was meant to show George she wouldn't fit in, it was a success,' Sean agreed. 'But I'm inclined to think it won't make a bit of difference to him. I think . . .' He paused. He had been about to say that he got the feeling George and Josie were already intimate. It had been obvious in their attitude towards each other. In George's eyes that would mean they were as good as married. But that wouldn't go down too well with his wife. Annie thought there would be a break up now, so let her live in ignorance for a while. Not wanting to antagonize her, he continued, 'He's already made up his mind. You've probably just pushed them a little closer to the altar rails.'

'My God! You don't really think that, do you, Sean?' she cried, aghast.

Folding the tea towel, he put it to one side and took her in his arms. 'Don't you know that obstacles only heighten attraction, Annie?'

Her thoughts were bleak as she pressed close. Was that why Rosaleen had been irresistible? Because she was Annie's sister and a married woman as well. It was a one-night stand! she reminded herself. Obstacles hadn't entered into it. It was just one of those things. Ashamed of the way her thoughts plagued her, she gazed up at him. 'I guess I've always been too open and above board to know about things like that.'

'Yes, love. I guess you have. And don't you change, Annie. That's one of the things I love about you. Your integrity. Let's go to bed, love. George is big enough to look after himself. You've done your bit and that's all that matters.'

Comforted by these words of praise, Annie let him manoeuvre her along the hall and up the stairs. Remembering that tight skirt and low neckline, Sean gripped her close. After all he was only a man and easily turned on . . . and he was with his wife.

Arm in arm, George and Josie travelled the short distance in silence. When they entered George's living room a ball of fur hurled itself at Josie. She gripped it close, burying her face in its softness. George raised his eyebrow at her. 'I nearly burst out laughing when you said that a neighbour was keeping an eye on your dog.'

Above Tiger's head big mournful eyes met his. 'I'm sorry. I just couldn't stand another minute of being tolerated there.'

'Annie's really very nice, you know. She went to a lot of trouble tonight. She's just a bit overprotective where I'm concerned.'

'That's not unusual. Most sisters would try to keep their brothers away from me.'

'Well, with you looking like that, you can't really blame her. I think even Sean could hardly believe his eyes. You accomplished what you set out to do. You sure looked the part.'

Josie looked down at herself. Gripping her lower lip between her teeth, she frowned in distaste. 'I borrowed these clothes from a friend,' she confessed. 'I've done the wrong thing, haven't I, George?

He nodded. 'I'm afraid so. It will make things that little bit more awkward for me. Annie will be planning how she can get me out of your clutches. But it won't make any difference. I still think you're lovely.' He took Tiger from her and gently placed him on the floor. Drawing her close, his hands caressed her shoulders and back. 'And I know that you're kind and considerate and caring.'

Muffled against his chest, her voice barely reached him. 'Thank you. But any sister in her right mind would object to me associating with her brother,' she lamented.

'I'm afraid there is an extra element in our case.'

'Oh?' Big tear-filled eyes were raised to his. 'What do you mean?'

He sat on the armchair and gently drew her down on his knee. Josie listened wide-eyed as he explained that Annie was only his half-sister. He told her how his father had strayed and that it was only after Tommy's death that George had joined the family.

'You mean, they knew about you and never bothered to get in touch?'

'No, only Thelma, my stepmother, knew the truth.'

'How could she? How could she hold such spite against a little baby?'

'Ah, come on, Josie. You know it happens all the time. And in those days that was the worst kind of betrayal, for a man to have his wife and another woman pregnant at the same time. He was considered the lowest of the low. And Thelma is such a proud woman. She couldn't bear for all and sundry to know that my father had strayed. I think that's why she hardened her heart against me.'

'Still . . . when she heard that your mother was dead, she should have adopted you. Surely your father could have arranged it quietly and no one need have been any the wiser?'

'I never thought of that, but I suppose it was asking too much.'

'Did you not hold it against her?'

'No, I was too glad that she accepted me in the long run. You see, my father died during the blitz in 1941 and after the war, with him dead, I had no one to return to. I didn't really expect them to take me in. Why should they? After all, I was a complete stranger to them. It must have been an awful shock, me turning up out of the blue. Father had told me that if he should die, I was to approach Rosaleen first, and I have to admit that she was very understanding. And believe you me . . . I came at a bad time. She had just buried her first husband the week before. He was another casualty of the war, but she took control. Thelma had taken Father's death very badly and was on the verge of a nervous breakdown. Rosaleen was afraid my arrival on the scene would push her over the edge. She bided her time and eventually got me accepted into the family circle. We have all been very close ever since.'

Josie sat silently and he teased her. 'Are they worth a penny this time?'

There was no answering smile. 'I'm sorry now for the way I got on. It was childish! Annie couldn't hide the fact that she

152

doesn't think that I'm good enough for you and I agree with her. I've been a silly fool. If you persist in seeing me it's bound to cause a rift between you.'

'I know her better than you do. She'll come round once she gets to know you.'

Leaving the comfort of his arms, Josie rose restlessly to her feet and prowled about the room. Lifting a photograph off the mantelpiece, she examined it intently. 'Is this your stepmother?'

'Yes, that's her and Rosaleen, and Annie of course. It was taken when Rosaleen was home on a visit.'

'You're very fond of Annie. Her opinion is important to you, isn't it?'

He was silent for some moments, startled by her insight. 'I am very fond of them all,' he said softly. 'They're my family, after all. And as I've already said . . . Annie will come round when she realizes how serious I am about you.'

Josie eyed him closely and disagreed with him. 'Don't count on it. She obviously thinks the world of you. I'd better be getting home now.'

In an instant he was on his feet and facing her. 'I was hoping you'd stay the night,' he cried, his disappointment evident.

She laughed aloud at the very idea of it. '*Me* stay here? Ah, George, are you trying to ruin my reputation altogether?'

'I didn't think you'd mind.'

'Well, that's where you're wrong. I do mind!' she cried indignantly, and a fiery red blush stained her face. 'I mind very much. Would you have asked any other girl to spend the night with you, George?' Embarrassed colour spread in a guilty tide over his face and she grunted. 'No, I thought not. Perhaps it's these clothes that make you think you can take liberties? Now, are you going to drive me home or shall I call a taxi?'

Hating himself for his thoughtlessness, for the hurt and pain he sensed within her, George cried, 'I didn't mean to offend you, Josie.'

'No offence taken. I just don't want to spend the night here.'

Gently he took her in his arms. He must make her understand that he hadn't meant to belittle her. 'You do realize that I'm not just playing about, that I'm serious about you? I'm hoping that in due course you will consent to marry me.'

153

Waves of emotion trembled across her face. 'Be sensible, George. It wouldn't work.'

'Am I too old?

'Don't be daft!'

'That's the only obstacle I can see against our marrying. You could have many a young man, if you wanted.'

In her mind, she cried, I only want you! But she was wise enough to know it wouldn't work. 'Please, George . . . I must go.'

'I can't drive you, Josie. I'm sure I'm still well over the limit. But if it's what you want, I'll call a taxi for you. But I'm not giving up. I'll wait until you're ready.'

He bent to kiss her but she turned her head away, and a sigh escaped him as he made for the telephone.

George's association with Josie didn't exactly cause a rift – Josie just wasn't included in any activities planned by the family. It was as if she didn't exist. At first Thelma had pleaded with him until she was blue in the face. Begged him to see the folly of his ways before he got in any deeper. Eventually he had ordered her to mind her own business. John just sadly shook his head. He intended sitting on the fence. He wanted to upset no one, least of all Thelma. But to Sean he confessed to a sneaking liking for Josie. He thought she was very brave to keep seeing George in the face of all this opposition. He also confessed to having known her mother, although in what capacity exactly he did not say.

Things were cool between Annie and George. He continued to support her where Thomas was concerned, but he was deeply hurt that she had taken a stand against Josie. How could she be so cruel to someone of whom he was fond? When Josie was omitted from the Christmas festivities, it was the last straw for George. To the consternation of the family, he chose to spend Christmas Day with her. Indeed, he would have spent the entire festive season with her but she cajoled him into splitting his time between her and his family. Although very annoyed and angry at the attitude of Thelma and Annie, George knew that an open rift must be avoided at all costs. Thomas must not suffer because of the stupidity of his elders. Sean worked such long hours and Annie needed him where Thomas was

154

concerned. However, George refused to see in the New Year with them. As the church bells rang and mill horns blasted a welcome to 1956, George Magee went down on his knees in the tiny kitchen and formally proposed to Josie Stafford, confident of her acceptance.

Sadly, she refused him, assuring him that she was happy with the way things were; no strings attached. George *wasn't* so happy with the way things stood between them! The cosy Tuesday evenings spent at home had now come to an end. George, surprised at the hurt displayed by Josie when he was apparently taking her for granted, had silently vowed he would not take her again until they were married. So cosy nights at home were out of the question, now that he knew the joy of possessing her. He knew he couldn't spend long spells alone with her without showing his need. That had put paid to all their intimacy. Now their evenings were spent at the pictures or, weather permitting, taking Tiger for walks up around the Belfast Castle grounds, or Cave Hill, or along the beach at Hazelbank.

In spite of their now platonic relationship, the summer passed in a haze of happiness and he had been sure that she would agree to marry him. Her refusal threw him into turmoil. He had promised himself that he would do things decently, but with no marriage in sight how could he control his longing for her?

Josie was sad that apparently his need for her had waned. She had been enchanted by their one night together, had longed for more. But in the face of Annie's blatant disapproval, George had cooled off. It was all her own fault! She should have dressed in decent clothes. Tried to win Annie over instead of acting like a pro. But if his passion could blow hot or cold like that, could he really care for her? She thought not. How else could she explain the way he held her at arm's length? As things stood at the moment, there was no reason to marry. Better the way things were between them than allow him to enter into a marriage he might later regret.

They had been to the Troxy Picture House one Saturday night and on the way home, as they neared McVeigh's, George pleaded with Josie to go into the pub for a couple of drinks.

Loath to do so, she nevertheless allowed him to persuade her otherwise and climbed the stairs to the lounge with leaden feet. She was very much aware that heads popped out of the public bar to gape after them and could imagine the turn the conversation would take.

Annie was sipping a drink when she glanced up and to her horror saw Josie come through the door, followed by George. The shock caused the vodka to slip down the wrong way, and tears streamed down Annie's face as she almost choked on it.

Aghast, Sean thumped her on the back. 'Are you all right, love? What happened?'

Annie, spluttering and trying to regain control of her breath, waved him away and pointed towards the door.

Seeing Josie poised for flight at the antics of his sister, George kept a firm grip on her arm and led her straight over to the table occupied by his family. Sean was on his feet at once, offering his seat. 'Hello, Josie, nice to see you again. Sit down here.' Excusing himself, he went to fetch two more chairs.

With a look of apprehension Josie sat down beside Annie and nodded in her direction.

Annie wiped her face and said, weakly, 'Hello.'

This was Thelma's first meeting with Josie. She waited until George introduced her to this woman friend of his and, taking her cue from Annie, said, 'Pleased to meet you, I'm sure.' Although she looked far from pleased.

John greeted the girl warmly and said that he had been sorry to hear of her mother's death. This caused Thelma to turn a suspicious glance upon him.

After an awkward start the conversation took off again. Annie, very much aware of the furtive looks and whispers of the people around them, put on a brave face and was very polite. Thelma alone chose not to converse with this woman who threatened to ruin her stepson's life. It was only Josie who noticed that Thelma did not once address her directly.

Thelma had no intention of encouraging this friendship. Thus when they all emerged on to the pavement outside the pub, she wished George good night and crossed the road without a glance at Josie. Much embarrassed, John shook Josie's hand and wished her a good night before following his wife. George was incensed. Only a warning hand on his arm stopped him from exploding.

'Good night, George. Good night, Josie. Perhaps you'll join us next Saturday night?' Sean's voice was soft as he sought to ease the tension.

'I think not. But thanks for the offer, Sean. Good night all.'

With a face like thunder George charged along the road, sweeping Josie along beside him.

She allowed him to work off some of his spleen then breathlessly dragged him to a halt. 'Hold on, George. You're running me off my feet.'

'Sorry, Josie . . . it's because I'm so mad. How can they behave like that? Who the hell do they think they are? Why, for two pins I'd tell them all to go to hell. No wonder you don't want to marry me.'

'Well, to be fair, it was only your mother who was so ignorant, the others seemed to have accepted me. Even Annie was quite mellow tonight.' She stopped walking and gazed up at him. 'There's really no need for you to walk me home, George.'

He gaped at her in amazement. 'Of course I'll walk you home! What kind of a guy do you take me for?'

'It's unnecessary. You'll only have to trek all the way back again.'

He reached for her hand and pulled it through his arm. 'I'll walk you home!' he snapped and forged ahead, heart heavy within his breast. She was making it obvious that he needn't expect to spend the night. Was she seeing someone else?

Tears blinded Josie as she plodded along beside him. She had given him the opportunity to suggest staying the night but he hadn't taken her up on it. Now she felt cheap. Had he been only pretending to enjoy the night he spent with her? It would be better to put an end to this farce. She would never be able to comprehend just why on earth George Magee had asked her to marry him.

In spite of all her vows to end things between her and George, Josie found that the idea of life without his comforting friendship was so bleak she could not bear to send him away. When you really liked someone, just being with them was a bonus.

And who knew what fate had in store? He might even learn to care for her.

Towards the middle of 1956, work in all the mills was gradually drying up and George suggested that Josie should look around for a job before her mill closed down, which it surely would. Maybe not soon, but in the none too distant future.

'A bright girl like you is wasted in that mill, Josie.'

'I don't know anything else, George.'

'Would you not go to night school and learn a trade? Or what about shorthand and typing? You'd be able to get a job in an office. They're always looking for typists.'

Her expression was dubious. 'Do you really think I could do it? I've never worked anywhere but the mill.'

'Of course you could! I'd join a class too . . . say carpentry, or better still, motor mechanics. What I know about under the bonnet of a car could be written on the back of a stamp. If we get a class on the same night you wouldn't have to worry about transport. Not that I wouldn't be willing to run you there and back again, but you would call that using me and then you wouldn't hear tell of it. This way you'd be doing me a good turn.'

Wide-eyed with surprise, she asked, 'You would be willing to do that for me?'

He nodded. 'Like I say, you'd be doing me a favour.'

'I'd love to get away from the mill. I've thought of it often enough but lacked the initiative.'

'Next month, September, is when they enrol new students. We'll go down to Carrickfergus Tec and see what's on offer.'

'Thanks, George. You're too good to me.'

'That's settled then.'

It was Sunday night and they had been for a drive along the Antrim coast. It was late when they arrived at her door and he gave her a brief kiss on the cheek before going to open the car door for her. 'Josie, I'll not come in for tea tonight, I've an early start in the morning. The auditors are coming. And . . . I'm afraid I can't see you on Tuesday night either.'

She hid her dismay as she clambered out on to the pavement. 'That's all right! You have no need to feel obliged to come if you have something better to do.'

'I haven't anything better to do.' His voice was terse.

Sometimes he felt like shaking her. 'Our Annie's loaded with the cold and Sean is working late on Tuesday night. I've told her if she's no better, I'll take Thomas to a do they're having at the school. I'm sorry, but he's so cute I don't want him to miss out and I can't see Annie being well enough to take him.'

'Oh, that's all right.' Josie was relieved. They often took Thomas out for drives with them and she had become very attached to the boy. 'I wouldn't want him to miss out either. He really is a lovely wee boy.'

'I suppose you wouldn't like to come along? I think you'd enjoy yourself.'

'Then you suppose wrong. I'd love to tag along.'

A wide grin split his face. 'You really mean that? Wonderful! That's wonderful. I'll pick you up at about twenty to seven. And thanks, Josie. I appreciate what you're doing.'

The outing to the clinic on Ulsterville Avenue was Josie's introduction to the world of disabled children. She discovered that they were warm and affectionate and had great fighting spirit. There were tears in her eyes as she watched the older children being encouraged to display their many talents. Even Thomas, young though he was, joined in, and was flushed with triumph when they all applauded.

Miss McAteer watched Josie closely as she mixed with the children. No acting here, she was genuine in her interest. Had a word for each child and was patient when they tried to keep her attention. She helped serve tea and cakes and sat on the floor by a wheelchair to help a youngster by handing him his cup and plate, as he needed them. The kids, one and all, seemed to like her. Miss McAteer was very impressed and at the end of the evening she managed to take Josie aside. 'I hope you don't mind my saying so, but you have a natural aptitude with the disabled. You treat them as normal people and there's not many do that, you know! That's a great gift, Miss Stafford. Can I ask what it is you do for a living?'

Pleased at the remarks made by Miss McAteer, Josie blushed and said honestly, 'I work in a linen mill as a reeler.'

'Have you never considered a change?'

'Well, just recently, George . . .' she nodded to where he was chatting to one of the parents '. . . has talked me into going to

159

night school to learn shorthand and typing. We're going to see just what courses are available next month at Carrickfergus Technical College. I really would like to get away from the mill. It's a dead end job.'

'Would you not consider working with the disabled?'

Josie's eyes rounded with surprise. 'You mean, actually get paid for helping children like these?'

'That's exactly what I mean. Next year the government is planning to open a new school to educate disabled children. As you have seen for yourself here tonight, they are all gifted in different ways. If they could be taught to use all their potential it would open up a whole new world to them. There are classes you could go to, to learn how to cope with the disabled, and when you're ready I'd do all in my power to get you a job in this new school because you are a natural carer! Would you be interested?'

'Very much so.' Josie's eyes glowed and her voice throbbed with emotion. 'Thank you very much indeed.'

'Meanwhile, feel free to come here whenever you like. We're always glad of an extra pair of hands and it will all be good experience for you.'

'I will, you can count on that.'

On the journey home, bright-eyed with enthusiasm, Josie told George of Miss McAteer's comments. He was touched at her excitement but warned, 'Remember . . . it won't be easy work. Are you sure you want to go for it?'

'I was never as sure of anything in my life before. I felt at home there tonight. I got great satisfaction out of helping those children. As if I was doing something really worthwhile.' Shyly, she added, 'Miss McAteer says I'm a natural.'

'I second that! You're very kind and compassionate.'

'Ah, George.' Now she was really embarrassed. 'Ah, no.'

George smiled at her discomfort. Josie was a fine person.

He in turn passed on the good news to Annie who was delighted. 'I know they've been trying to get a school opened for disabled children. It's great to hear they've succeeded. This is wonderful news! I was wondering what was to become of Thomas. Every child will have to be assessed, of course, but I'm confident that he will qualify, he's so bright. Of course, he

160

won't be able to go until he's six. Wait until Sean hears, he'll be so pleased. He was even considering private tuition. This really is good news! It's given me no end of a lift. I feel almost well.'

George debated whether or not to tell Annie about Miss McAteer's offer to Josie and decided against it. He was in a happy mood and Annie could very easily say something to spoil his contentment. She still hadn't warmed towards Josie.

Mount Collier House, situated on the Malone Road, was large, detached, and stood in five acres of grounds. It was a white-stucco building with long narrow windows and a porch to the front door. These were the premises chosen for the new school. It opened on March 1st with a staff of two teachers, two child carers, two physiotherapists and an occupational therapist. There was also a resident caretaker and his wife. To her great delight, Josie was employed as one of the carers. She still had a lot to learn at night classes but Miss McAteer thought that her natural ability with the children was worth more than any certificate. Experience would be of greater benefit to her than anything else. Others had thought otherwise but Miss McAteer had put her neck on the line for Josie and warned her that she would be expected to work harder to prove her worth. The girl swore to do all in her power not to let her down.

Since this establishment was specialized, it would be expensive to run and might have to serve all six counties. Of the twenty-three children accepted, only fourteen were allowed to live at home. The others were accommodated in the City Hospital, the Good Shepherd Convent and foster homes, and brought to school by taxi.

Annie immediately put Thomas's name on the waiting list as a child had to be six before starting this school. She was buoyed up with hope at the thought of her son getting an education.

Josie kept her up to date on every aspect of the school. At first Annie had been sceptical that a person such as she could hold a position as a carer. She'd questioned her brother as to the girl's suitability and a very irritated George asked her to explain herself.

A bit put out by his attitude, Annie did so. 'If you must

know, I'm wondering if she told them what her former employment was.'

'Yes, she did. She admitted she had worked in a linen mill since the age of fourteen and it didn't make a bit of difference.'

'You know quite well I wasn't thinking of the mill!'

'Josie never had any other job. She went straight into the mill when she left school.'

'You know what I mean. She was on the game, so she was.'

George glowered at her. 'And you have proof of this? Eh, Annie? Remember . . . unless you have proof, Josie could have you up for slander.'

'I haven't exactly got proof, but it's a well-known fact.'

'Oh, is it now? How well known?'

'You know quite well she was on the game!' Annie was so agitated now, she was almost hissing at him. 'Remember the state of her the first night you brought her here? Why, it was written all over her.'

'You listen to me, Annie Devlin! Josie never was on the game. It was gossipy women like yourself who took away her good name because she was unfortunate enough to have a mother who, unfortunately, *was* on the game. If Josie hadn't been the strong person that she is, they might very well have driven her on to the streets with their snide remarks and knowing looks. The night I brought her to visit you, she deliberately put on those clothes. She knew you had already judged her and didn't want to disappoint you. Which she certainly didn't!'

This silenced Annie for some moments. She was remembering Sean saying it was as if Josie was putting on an act for their benefit. Then outrage surfaced. 'Hey, hold on! You're putting me in the wrong here. It's not my fault that she was foolish enough to get herself a bad name. Believe you me . . . there's no smoke without fire! She was notorious before I ever heard tell of her.'

'I'm sorry. I'd no right to snap at you like that.' George's voice was gentle now. 'Give her a chance, Annie,' he urged. 'She really is a very nice person once you get to know her.'

Annie eyed him keenly. 'You care for her, don't you?' At his nod she cried, 'Then why don't you marry her? Lord knows you threatened to. I thought you had seen some sense and that's why you didn't get married.'

'I've asked her time and again to marry me, but she won't have me. I'd be a proud man if Josie consented to walk down the aisle with me.'

'She won't have you?'

George laughed mirthlessly at the astonishment in Annie's voice and stressed, 'No, she's refused me. And why not? She's a vibrant young woman who could have many a younger man by her side and in her bed. What would she want with a grumpy old bugger like me?'

'You mean . . . you two aren't . . .'

'No, Annie, not that it's any of your business, but we aren't. It is all purely platonic between us. Now what do you think of that? I respect Josie and until she consents to marry me, that's the way things will stay.' With these words he rose from his chair and left the room. He had told Annie more than he had intended. He wanted her to get to know Josie. Find out for herself just what a fine person she was. How could this kind, caring sister of his be so blind?

That was the turning point so far as Annie was concerned. She held out an olive branch and with trepidation Josie accepted it. They became if not friends then close acquaintances. Just as George had prophesied, Thelma followed Annie's lead and if she didn't quite welcome Josie with open arms, at least no fault could be found with her attitude from then on.

However, in spite of all his pleas, Josie still refused to marry George. She thought she knew where his true interests lay and steadfastly refused to become further involved.

It was then that Josie received a letter from her Aunt Martha, requesting her to call and see her the following Saturday. She showed the letter to George and he immediately offered to run her over to Bangor. They had no difficulty finding Martha's bungalow on the corner of a street in a posh district. Both were surprised at the size of the property which was in excellent condition.

Martha had directed Josie to come to the back of the house as she had arthritis and found it painful to walk. She was sitting

163

in an upright chair in the beautiful conservatory and waved them inside.

Hiding her dismay at how frail her aunt had become, Josie greeted her with a warm kiss on the cheek. 'Aunt Martha, it's great to see you. This is a friend of mine, George Magee. He kindly offered to drive me over here.'

George was careful not to squeeze the gnarled hand with swollen joints that she offered him. 'I'm pleased to make your acquaintance, Miss Stafford.'

Bright blue eyes scanned him from top to toe and she replied pertly, 'And I yours, Mr Magee.'

'Call me George, please.'

With an abrupt nod, Martha turned her attention to her niece. 'You are looking well, my dear. If I may say so.'

Josie examined her aunt with anxious eyes. 'I wish I could say the same about you, Aunt Martha, but you look quite ill.'

'That's what I want to see you about. But first . . . Mrs Duffy, who comes twice a day to assist me, has left a tray ready in the kitchen. Make some tea and put another cup and saucer and whatever else is needed on the tray. I'm sorry, but I was expecting you to be alone.'

'I hope you don't mind my bringing George along?'

'Not at all! I'm just sorry I didn't think to suggest it. Rummage about out there . . .' She nodded to a door at the far end of the room. 'You'll find all you need.'

When Josie went to obey her aunt, Martha, with an abrupt nod, directed George to a chair adjacent to hers.

'Are you a close friend of my niece's?'

'Yes, we have known each other for some time.'

'Josie has mentioned you in her letters to me. She tells me she has changed her job and now cares for handicapped children.'

'That's right. Excuse me.' Josie had entered the room and George rose to relieve her of the tray.

As they drank their tea and ate the biscuits and cakes provided, Martha questioned her niece on her present and future plans.

Josie patiently answered her questions to the best of her ability, until she could bear the suspense no longer. Just what was Aunt Martha getting at?

164

'Aunt Martha, I hope you don't mind my asking but just why have you sent for me? Why the interrogation? What's it all about?' Curiosity was getting the better of her.

Martha gave a wry smile. 'I'm sorry, dear. I suppose I do sound a wee bit eccentric. I sent for you because I have a proposition to put to you.'

Josie sat in apprehensive silence and Martha continued, 'I'm hoping that I can persuade you to come here and live with me.' She leant back in her chair and watched her niece's reaction.

Josie looked so aghast that she cried, 'Surely the idea can't be all that bad?'

'Aunt Martha, I didn't mean to appear disrespectful, but you know that I've started this new job and I'd need transport. Besides, I'd be all out of place here.'

'Josie, hear me out. I am practically house bound, but I am not quite incapable. I can attend to my own needs. Everything about the bungalow has been adapted to make life easier for me and Mrs Duffy keeps the house clean and cooks most of my meals while a friend looks after the garden. I can afford to pay for these things and I'm happy this way. Independence is a great thing, dear. However, mine is being threatened.'

Martha paused for breath and Josie cried in bewilderment, 'I don't understand! What difference could I make? Why do you want me to live here?'

'To cut a long story short, the doctor thinks someone should be here during the night in case I fall or take a bad turn. Your Uncle William, my brother, has come up with the brilliant idea that his young daughter Cassie and her spineless husband should move in here with me, and I won't hear tell of it. You have just got to rescue me, Josie! I won't restrict you. You can come and go as you please. All you have to do is sleep here. If ever you want to go away for a few days or on holiday, we can arrange for someone to relieve you. I spend the evenings in my room watching television so the rest of the house would be yours to entertain friends and so forth. Just don't let me become dependant on our William.'

'Aunt Martha, have you no other nieces?'

'The only niece I like is you. As for transport, we have quite a regular service of buses to Belfast, but if your friend—' she nodded in George's direction, 'will teach you to drive, you can have the use of my car to get about in. That's another thing William has his eye on for his youngest son, and I don't intend he should have it!'

Josie flashed an appealing look at George. Quickly he came to her rescue. With an apologetic glance at Martha, he said, 'May I be so bold as to suggest something?' At her nod of consent he continued, 'All this is news to Josie. She's just started a new job and attends Carrickfergus Tec two nights a week. I know for a fact she is very fond of you, so why not let her sleep on it? See if she can work something out to suit you both.'

'That's a good idea, George.' There was relief in Martha's voice. She had thought that he might object as he seemed to have some influence over her niece. 'Don't commit yourself, Josie. As George says, sleep on it. Just don't keep me in suspense too long. William is wearing me down.'

Josie sat deep in thought for some moments then nodded. 'All right, I'll think about it. I'll come back later on in the week and let you know what I've decided. Is that all right?'

A grin split Martha's pale face. 'That will be great, dear.'

Amazed at her aunt's brightened demeanour, Josie cried in alarm, 'I'm not making any promises, mind! I just said I'd think about it, that's all.'

'I understand, dear. I'll not take anything for granted.'

Piling the tea things back on the tray, Josie made to lift it. George beat her to it and headed for the kitchen. Martha's voice followed him. 'Don't you dare wash those things. I pay well to be looked after. Mrs Duffy will be back shortly. She will clear up.'

Turning to Josie, Martha held out her hand. Josie held it gently between hers. 'My dear, I hope you will take pity on an old woman. I don't think it will be for long.'

'What do you mean, Aunt Martha?'

'Oh, I'm not keeping anything back from you, child, so don't look worried. Just remember, I'm an old woman and I won't last much longer. Nor would I want to. I won't rest until I hear what you have decided.'

George and Josie sat until the early hours of the morning,

drinking numerous cups of tea and debating what she should do.

Josie flashed an affectionate glance around her small kitchen. She had been happy here. 'I would have to keep on this house, or when Martha dies I will be homeless.'

'Yes, that would be a wise move,' he agreed. 'Remember, this would be a new start for you, Josie ... away from all your old neighbours and acquaintances.' He didn't mention her reputation but she knew what he meant.

'You're right, of course, but I would miss you, George. You're the only true friend I have.'

He reached over and took her hand, rapping her lightly on the knuckles. 'Don't you think for one moment you'll get rid of me as easily as all that. I intend to remain very much in the picture.'

'You mean that, George? We'll go on as before?'

Heart heavy, he promised, 'We'll go on as before.'

Suddenly she was on her feet. Throwing herself on her knees beside him, she gazed imploringly into his face. 'Am I repulsive to you, George? Can't you bear the thought of touching me?'

Aghast that she could think anything so daft, he cried, 'Repulsive? I think you're beautiful.'

Her eyes clouded with bewilderment. 'Then why do you keep me at arm's length?'

'Because you won't marry me and I've vowed I'll do things decently.'

Her cheeks were wet with tears, her smile tremulous. 'And all the time I thought you'd gone off me!'

His hands cupped her face. 'Josie, you will never know how often I've been tempted to sweep you into my arms and up to bed. But I want to prove to you how much respect I have for you.'

Her hands were opening the buttons of his shirt. 'Well, I think you've proved it long enough. I was beginning to think I was a leper or something.'

'You're the prettiest girl I know.'

'Even prettier than Annie?' she teased.

'Annie's family. She doesn't count.'

Josie didn't agree with him there. Annie counted very much. But as he said, she was family. 'You're a wonderful man,

George Magee. When they made you they threw away the mould.'

'Then you will marry me?'

'I didn't say that. But . . . I am certainly going to try to keep you happy.'

One week later Josie moved to Bangor. George hired a van and helped her pack her personal belongings and favourite pieces of furniture and drove her to her aunt's house. To their surprise there was a welcoming committee. Well, that wasn't quite the word to describe the dour-faced man who was waiting, not to greet them but to try and deter them. Josie's Uncle William, accompanied by his wife and one of their daughters whom they soon discovered was Cassie whose husband Martha didn't like, watched with disapproving eyes as George unloaded the van with Josie's help. No one offered them any assistance.

'I hope you realize just what you're taking on, Josie? Martha needs a lot of attention and if you don't mind my saying so, you look quite frail.'

'Looks can be deceptive. Besides, Aunt Martha already has a few people to attend to her personal needs.'

'Hah! So you think you're on to a soft touch?'

Aghast, Josie cried, 'I think no such thing!'

'Don't you listen to him, Josie. It's none of his business. He always did poke his nose in where it wasn't wanted.' Martha's voice was harsh and the look she threw her brother was full of wrath.

'William is only trying to save you from doing something you might regret, Martha.' His wife's voice was soft but insinuating. 'After all, dear, you don't really know this young woman. We don't know what kind of upbringing she has had.' Her lips pursed into disapproving lines and her nostrils flared with disdain. Her eyes roved over Josie's figure, taking note of her clothes, tasteful but obviously not in the same class as hers.

Since Josie's mother had not been rich by any means, George pondered on how William and his sister Martha appeared to be so affluent. He was soon to learn that William had married into money. His wife was the only child of the owner of a large engineering firm, and heiress to her father's substantial fortune. At a later date, Martha confided in him that she herself had

168

been very lucky, dabbling in stock and bonds. Having worked for many years for a firm of brokers, she had discovered that she had a gut feeling about some things and it had made her a wealthy woman. This raised his opinion of her no end. Perhaps when he got to know her better she would give him a few tips.

William kept his lips tightly pursed. He had never acquainted his wife with his youngest sister's fall from grace, the primrose path she had chosen to tread. Martha now caused him to rise to his feet in panic.

With a malicious smile she addressed her sister-in-law. 'Our youngest sister gave her daughter a fine upbringing, Isobel. Josie now works in that big house on Malone Road. You know the one that had all the write ups in the newspapers? The school for disabled children? It was Mount Collier House but because their deliveries were being mixed up with Mount Collier Secondary School some miles away, the name was changed to Fleming Fulton School. Surely you've read all about it?'

Some interest flickered in Isobel's eyes, but before she could get involved in a conversation that might give secrets away, William intervened. 'I'm sure we're not questioning our Sarah's rearing of her daughter, Martha. That goes without saying. We had better go now but I will keep an eye on you to see how you are faring.'

There was a distinct twinkle in Martha's eye as she assured him, 'I don't for one minute doubt that, William. However there's no need. Josie and I get on very well.'

'Nevertheless, I'll drop in now and again.' He was at the door when he was apparently struck by a new thought. 'Oh, by the way. About your car . . . obviously you'll not be able to drive again, and young Timmy's got his licence! He'll be pleased to keep it in running order for you. It would be silly to let such a fine car deteriorate in the garage for want of a run now and again. Perhaps he could borrow it at weekends?'

Martha smiled brightly at him; she had been anticipating this. 'I'm afraid not, William. Josie is going to learn how to drive and she will need the car for travelling to and from work, and for doing my shopping, of course.'

He gulped a few times before he could frame words suitable

for ladies' ears. 'You're going too far, Martha! You'll regret the day you thwarted me.'

'I don't think so, William. Please close the door on the way out,' she quietly replied.

There was silence until the big outer door banged, then Martha laughed aloud. 'Thank goodness that's over! But he'll be back, that you can count on. But we'll be ready for him, eh, Josie?'

'I don't know about that, Aunt Martha. I don't want to cause any trouble between you and your brother. Let Timmy have the car. As you say, there's a good bus service. Besides, I might never learn to drive.'

'If you put your mind to it you will learn. Apply for your provisional licence and George will give you some lessons. Take my word for it, you'll be driving in no time.'

Still doubtful, Josie turned to George. 'What do you think?'

'I'm certainly willing to teach you. So get your licence, you've nothing to lose.'

Still Josie dithered and with a nod at a dark oak bureau, Martha said, 'George, in the top drawer of that bureau you will find the keys to the car and garage. Take Josie out and show it to her. Perhaps that will influence her.'

All Josie's reluctance fled when he removed the dust sheet and she saw the sleek dark green Morris gleaming in the evening light. 'Oh, George, it's beautiful! Why, it looks so new. Do you think I could ever have the confidence to drive it?'

Her eyes were large luminous pools full of awe, and George thought that she had never looked lovelier. 'It is a beauty! And obviously well looked after.' He ran a hand lovingly over the sleek bonnet. He would certainly enjoy teaching her to drive in this car. 'There is no reason whatsoever why you shouldn't one day drive this.'

Gently he drew her further into the garage. 'Come and sit in it. Get the feel of it about you, and once you want to drive the rest will come naturally. You can do anything you set your mind to.'

'Only since I met you! I owe you so much. Without you behind me I would be still working in the mill and pretending I didn't care that most people thought I was a whore.'

Her skin gleamed in the faint light and her lips were inviting.

170

He silenced her by claiming them and passion between them mounted. Mindful of where they were, he gently released her and, fighting for control, eased out of the car. Slowly, she followed him and waited while he locked the garage door.

'I won't come in again, Josie. You have a lot to do before you get to bed. Besides, Tiger will be patiently waiting for his walk. Tell Martha I'll see her tomorrow night.'

Resisting the impulse to kiss her again, he climbed into his own car. She waved him off and returned to the house.

Her aunt greeted her eagerly. 'Well? What do you think?'

'It's beautiful! I can't believe all this is happening to me. I must confess that I'm looking forward to living in this luxurious bungalow and driving your lovely car, Aunt Martha. I only hope you don't regret inviting me here.' Her voice hesitant, she continued, 'I forgot to mention that I have a dog, but George says he will take him if you object to animals. Tiger's trained to sleep outdoors in a kennel, so he is,' she added hopefully.

'By all means bring your pet.'

'What about Mrs Duffy? Will she not object?'

'She can object all she likes! I'm the boss around here. But in any case she has been at me to get a dog for company, so she'll be delighted.'

They smiled at each other and Josie said softly, 'I think I'd better get a move on or we will both miss our beauty sleep. I'll make up my bed, and then I'll make you a nice cup of tea.'

'Has George gone then? I assumed he was locking up the garage. Why didn't he stay for a cup of tea?'

'He said if he lingered any longer Tiger might have a mishap on the carpet. You see, the kennel is still at my house. George says he will see you tomorrow night.'

'He's a very nice young man, Josie.' Martha hesitated then took the plunge. 'I hope you don't mind my asking . . . are his intentions serious?' Her hands rose in protest at her own words. 'I'm sorry, forget I said that!' she entreated. 'I promise you that I will never interfere in your private affairs again.'

'It's all right. I agree with you. He's the nicest person I have ever known. He has asked me to marry him, but there are problems. Maybe some day I'll confide in you. Get your advice on the matter. Meanwhile we are very close friends.'

Martha nodded understandingly. 'Don't wait too long, dear,' she admonished. 'He might slip through your fingers.'

'If that happens, I'll assume he wasn't meant for me.' And Josie turned away. She would have to learn to hold her tongue; her aunt was very inquisitive. 'I'd better go and put the tea on before it gets too late.'

'Cocoa, Josie. I take cocoa before I retire, thank you.'

When her niece left the room Martha gazed into space. What problems could keep two people, so obviously attracted to each other, apart? Perhaps one day she would find out. Until then she must respect her niece's privacy.

In no time at all Josie had settled into a routine. The bungalow quickly became home to her and under her aunt's persuasion she gave up the lease on her own small house. She was easily persuaded. In her heart she knew she would never want to return there. And after all she had a good job. No longer need she worry whether or not the mill closed. If her aunt died she would be able to afford a mortgage on a new house. Her devotion to her aunt for making all this possible was fierce. She refused to take any money from her niece towards the running costs of the bungalow, saying she didn't need any financial help and was only too grateful that Josie gave up so much of her own time to attend to her aunt's whims.

With a heart full of gratitude Josie took her advice and saved hard for a rainy day. Sometimes she even dabbled on the stock market when her aunt thought it was safe for her to do so. Slowly but surely her savings grew and, free from financial worries and in a job that she loved, she blossomed. A first-class hairdresser had cut her hair close to her head in the urchin look and careful make-up made her as beautiful as she was ever likely to be. She was at peace with herself, serene and happy. The only blot on her horizon was George.

Her new way of life put a different complexion on her friendship with him. Although she still loved him, she realized it wasn't the kind of love that should exist between a man and woman who are destined to marry. The young men she now met through work, or sometimes through her aunt, treated her differently from those on the other side of the lough. They showed her respect and admiration with no veiled innuendos.

172

She saw a whole new meaning to life and, in her honesty, tentatively tried to explain her feelings to George.

They had been to the Ritz cinema and were about to have a meal at the Carlton Steakhouse on Wellington Place.

His heart sank as he listened to her. 'Are you saying you don't think we should continue to see each other?'

Josie reached across and covered his hand with her own. 'Oh, no! I didn't mean that. You know I didn't!'

He gazed down at her hand, no longer rough and red but white and soft; the nails painted a pale pink. He made no attempt to clasp it. 'Just what do you see in store for us, Josie?'

'I hope that we will remain best friends and continue to see each other,' she said eagerly. 'In fact, go on as we are expect for . . .' Suddenly confused, she withdrew her hand and sank back in her seat. 'I think you know what I'm trying to say, George.'

'Yes, I think I do.' His voice was cold and cutting. 'Correct me if I'm wrong, Josie, but now that you have left your unsavoury past behind, have a new job and can drive your aunt's car . . . all thanks to me, mind . . . you seem to be tiring of me. Mind, you gave me quid pro quo. Why did I not see it as that? Why did I think it was mutual attraction? But forget all that! Now you think it's time to move on, isn't that it? In other words, I have served my purpose. Now I can clear off.'

She visibly flinched when he mentioned her past but George hardened his heart and continued to stare coldly at her. He was hurting inside and didn't care if he inflicted pain on her as well.

The waiter who had taken their order arrived to set the places. Close to tears Josie excused herself and headed for the cloakroom. Face set in angry lines, George watched the man in silence, bringing an abrupt end to his attempted small talk.

Josie returned to the table, pale but composed. They sat in silence until their steaks arrived. She gazed down at the succulent steak with all the trimmings and wondered how on earth she would manage to eat it. George seemed to have no such problem. Ignoring her, he got stuck in right away, digging viciously at the meat and wolfing it down. Josie picked at hers, forcing some down her throat, wishing she was safely back home where she could have a good howl.

Why had she expected George to understand? He was a man after all. He wanted to marry her. She wished now that she had let things drift on a little longer, but once she had made up her mind that she would not be content with what he had to offer her, sheer integrity had made her speak out. Sometimes she thought it would be more diplomatic not to speak her mind like that, but it was hard to change the habit of a lifetime.

At last she felt she had eaten enough and replaced the knife and fork on her plate. She met George's eyes across the table.

'Would you like a dessert?' he asked.

'No, thank you.'

He beckoned for the bill and they sat in silence until it arrived. Once it was paid, George motioned her to her feet and out of the restaurant ahead of him. They were in their respective cars, having met in town, and outside she faced him.

'Thank you for taking me to the pictures and for the lovely meal. I'll head back now, George. I'm sorry we can't remain friends, and I really am grateful for all you have done for me. But you'll have to forgive me for thinking there were no strings attached. I really am very sorry. Good night.'

Unable to conjure up any words that would erase the terrible insults he had thrown at her across the dinner table, he watched in horrified silence as she left him. Watched until, without so much as a backward glance, Josie turned the corner into Queen Street and was gone. On leaden feet he turned in the opposite direction, towards his car. She had taken him unawares! He had never dreamed that things were any different between them. There had been no signs. A sudden thought brought him to a standstill. She must have met someone else. Probably someone younger. Someone she cared for. That would account for the sudden change in her attitude towards him.

He didn't remember how he got home. It was still early so, leaving the car, he walked down to McVeigh's. Later that night it took John and a companion to help him home and into bed.

A week passed and Josie had given up all hope of ever hearing from George again. She started up every time the phone rang, but it was never him. She waited every morning for a letter in his familiar handwriting. How she missed him! Missed him terribly. But she was convinced that she had done the right thing. George could not offer her the love she craved. A love that meant a full commitment and children born of it. She was well aware that he was already committed to someone else and unless he could break free from these bonds, there was no hope for them. Perhaps it was her imagination? No one else seemed to think it strange that he had never married. Was she the only one who guessed the real reason behind it all?

She knew her aunt was having a terrible time trying not to interfere, but did not want to discuss George with her. The letter was beside her breakfast plate the following Monday morning and, blushing under Martha's questioning look, Josie folded it, unopened, and put it in her pocket.

Martha said nothing but she hoped it was from George. Her niece was losing weight and looked quite ill lately. Perhaps a letter from George would be the tonic she needed.

Throughout the morning Josie kept fingering the letter nervously. Afraid to open it; afraid he would add insult to injury. She would be unable to bear that! It would be the last straw.

It was the lunch break before she got up the nerve to read it.

Dear Josie,
Please, please, forgive me for all the terrible things I said to you last Saturday night. I don't know what got into me. That's a lie! It was jealousy that ran away with my tongue. I realize now that you must have met someone else, someone younger, and I don't blame you. But I beg you not to let my stupid jealousy ruin our friendship. It is far too precious to me. If you can still bear to call me your friend, please meet me Tuesday night at our usual meeting place.
Yours always,
George.

Tears of relief poured down her cheeks. He still wanted to be friends. Tomorrow night she would meet him and explain that there was no one else. Never had been. They could go on as before! Except he should not expect any favours from her. Not unless he learnt to love her. Was that possible?

175

Chapter 5

September 1963

George climbed the sloping drive, absently admiring the profusion of colour created by the abundant heather and Alpine plants in the rockery. He passed along the front of the garage that had been built on to the side of the house, cutting off access to the back garden and making it a safe haven when the children were younger, and walking along beneath the high sitting-room window, climbed the three steps leading up to the front door.

It was half-past seven and a fine morning in September. The family would be at the back of the house having breakfast. As he waited for an answer to his knock, he swung round and gazed out over the lough. He envied Sean and Annie this wonderful view; often wished that he had waited until one of these houses, set so high up off the road, had become available before leaving the Springfield Road. Although the houses on Glenhurst Estate had been built since they had all come to live in Greencastle, they were low-lying and did not obscure the overall view which was still breathtaking, especially on a beautiful morning like this when the lough shimmered like a diamond necklace in the morning light and a fine mist enhanced its sparkle.

However, the beauty of his surroundings did not quite obliterate from his mind his reason for visiting his sister so early in the day. He pondered how to break the bad news to the family. They had never been very close to Andrew Mercer, but he had been a fine upstanding man and Rosaleen's husband. A short time ago his young niece Laura had phoned to tell George of the death of her father. He'd had a heart attack some hours earlier. George had asked to speak to Rosaleen but Laura said the doctor had sedated her and she was sleeping. 'Please, please, Uncle George, come over! We need some family here.' His niece had been crying into the phone and he had immediately assured her that he would be there as quickly as possible.

Turning, he lifted his hand towards the knocker once more but, hearing sounds from within, let it drop to his side again and waited patiently.

Swinging the door wide, Sean swallowed the remains of his toast and greeted his brother-in-law with surprise. 'Good morning, George. Come in . . . come in!' His tone was cordial as he stepped aside and motioned for the visitor to enter but his eyes had a puzzled look. He sensed from George's demeanour that something was amiss. Besides, it was much too early for a social visit. His mother-in-law came instantly to mind. She had been poorly lately. 'Is anything wrong?' Sean asked, voice tinged with apprehension. 'Is it Thelma?'

Quickly George set his mind at rest on that score. 'No, she's fine.' He followed Sean through the hall and kitchen before continuing. All the family, with the exception of Thomas, were seated around the big table in the recently built conservatory and their heads turned to him. It was Annie who spoke first. Rising quickly to her feet, she too questioned him about Thelma. 'Has Mother taken a turn for the worse? I thought she was on the mend.'

'To my knowledge, she's fine, Annie. I came here to tell you the bad news first, before going down to break it to her.'

'Bad news?' Annie's eyes widened and filled with dread. 'For God's sake, George, you're frightening me! What's wrong?'

'Laura has just been on the phone to me. Andrew's dead. He had a heart attack.'

Slowly Annie sank down on her chair again and the colour drained from her face as she pictured her brother-in-law dead. What age was he? She wasn't sure but not all that old. He was about ten years older than Rosaleen. Her poor sister. How would she manage out there in Canada on her own? But she wasn't on her own, Annie reminded herself! Her family were with her. The two eldest children, Laura and Liam, were now of an age when they should be a considerable support to their mother. Then there was May and Billy; they were as close as family. In fact, Billy *was* family! Wasn't he Andrew's cousin? And didn't other members of the Mercer family live out there now? With difficulty she brought her racing thoughts back to focus on what George was saying.

'Of course we shall have to go over for the funeral. Not all of us, but I thought you and I, Sean, could go and represent the family.'

He was nodding in agreement and the muscles of Annie's throat went into a spasm, threatening to choke her. Sean must not go to Canada. No, he must not! It was unthinkable that he should go out there and meet his son for the first time. Discover how Annie and Rosaleen had deceived him all those years ago. She tried to form words that would put him off, but they stuck in her throat. Unaware of her turmoil, with a wave of his hand in her direction, George had said farewell and was moving through the kitchen and down the hall followed by Sean. Their voices drifted back and she heard her brother say that he would book two seats on the next available flight out. Maybe three. He would have to see how Thelma felt. Though it was doubtful that even the death of her son-in-law would get her on an aeroplane, but perhaps John might want to go. The earlier the flight the better! But not today. They would have to fly from Shannon Airport and it was about five hours' journey by car. As early as possible tomorrow.

Annie sat dumbfounded, unable to move, listening to their fading voices making plans. Plans that could expose her deceit and ruin her life forever.

'Here, Mam. Drink this.' Rachel pushed a glass of water into her mother's hand and bent anxiously over her as she sipped it. She was surprised at Annie's state of near collapse. She had not thought that her mother and Aunt Rosaleen were all that close, or else why hadn't Mother consented to visit her last year when Dad had won that small amount of money on the football pools? He had been so excited, planning how he would arrange his holidays at work and take them all to Canada for a month. Her mother's refusal had upset him. In fact, it had upset them all! They had been agog with excitement at the thought of it. As usual her dad had shrugged off his

178

disappointment and at his wife's suggestion had spent the money on building this conservatory at the back of the house. Now, seeing her mother shiver slightly, Rachel asked solicitously, 'Can I do anything for you, Mam?'

'No, I'm all right, it's just the shock of it. Your Uncle Andrew wasn't all that old, you know. He wasn't even near sixty!' Annie rose determinedly to her feet as her husband returned to the kitchen. 'Sean, I must go to Rosaleen. I'm her only sister. She'll be disappointed if I don't go, I know she will.'

He put a comforting arm around his wife's shoulders and hugged her close in sympathy. 'She'll understand, Annie. She knows how protective you are of Thomas. She knows you would never leave him.'

'In normal circumstances, no, I wouldn't dream of it. But this is different! This is a tragedy. Our Rosaleen will want me with her, I know she will.'

'Ah, come on now, Annie. You're surely not suggesting that Thomas goes with you? He would be a burden on you at a time like this.'

'Oh, don't be daft!' She shrugged his arm away impatiently. 'We couldn't afford for two of us to go. But I feel strongly that I should be the one to go with George.' There, she had made her point!

His brow furrowed. 'Annie, it would be best if I went,' he reasoned.

'Sean, please, I'd never forgive myself if I didn't go. Rosaleen and I used to be so close, remember? Let me do this for her sake. It will help to salve my conscience where she's concerned.'

Sean opened his mouth to protest further but caught the gleam in her eye. In a subtle way she was reminding him that he had been the cause of that rift between the two sisters. However, he was also remembering that just a short time ago she had refused even to consider going to Canada. Now, when money was scarce, she was electing to go. It just didn't make sense! 'Look . . . we can't talk about this now. Once we know when the flight is, we'll decide. Meanwhile, girls, if you don't want to be late for school, you'd better get a move on. As far as you're concerned, life will go on as normal.'

After George had left, Rebecca, with a few worried glances at her distraught mother, had returned to her perusal of the

179

morning paper, but Rachel had listened attentively to her parents' conversation and she disagreed with her mother. It would be best if her father went to the funeral. He was restless lately and the break would do him all the good in the world. Over the years she had watched as he made allowances for her mother's short temper, on account of the time and attention she spent on Thomas. He was a full-time job, everybody admitted that, but it must be hard on Dad too.

Realizing that her brother had yet to come down for breakfast, and that her mother in her bemused state had for once forgotten about him, she headed for the stairs to make him get a move on. Thomas was almost ten and wasn't as daft as he was made out to be. He understood every word that was said to him. He might be a bit slow on the uptake, but he eventually got the message. Or at least Rachel believed so. She thought he overdid the thick act to play on his mother's sympathy. Rachel no longer took everything at face value. She was aware that at times there were undercurrents between her mother and father and it wasn't all to do with Thomas.

'Thomas! Come on. It's time to get up. You'll miss the school bus.'

The bedclothes stirred ever so slightly and with an exasperated sigh she pulled them off him and, gripping him by the arms, yanked him out of bed.

'Up you get! No more play acting. I'm not Mam. You don't fool me.'

'Sore. Sore.' With a pitiful groan Thomas clasped his midriff.

Rachel was not to be swayed. Pushing him forcefully she managed to get him into the bathroom and closed the door on him. 'Ten minutes. Do you hear me, Thomas? I will stay at this door until you're finished, so hurry up. And don't forget to brush your teeth. It will be your own fault if you miss breakfast, but I'll certainly make sure you don't miss the bus!'

The morning dragged on and Annie's mind was in a turmoil as she tried to do the housework. At last, unable to bear her own tormented thoughts, she locked up the house and set off down to Orange Row to see how her mother was bearing up. She had phoned earlier but John had said that he'd persuaded

Thelma to lie down for a while. Now she intended finding out for herself how her mother was.

It was Thelma who opened the door. Her ashen face with its red-rimmed eyes told its own tale.

'I was hoping you would come down, Annie,' she said as she motioned her in. 'Isn't it awful? I can't take it in, so I can't. He was such a well-built man. The picture of health.'

Annie refrained from reminding her mother that it was ten years since she had last seen Andrew and that he'd already had one heart attack since then. A lot could happen in ten years. 'I know, Mam,' she agreed soothingly. 'I know exactly how you feel. Did George manage to persuade you to go over for the funeral?'

Thelma was aghast at the very idea. 'Me, Annie? Me go up in a plane? Ah, no, no. I couldn't do it! Not even for Rosaleen's sake. You know how I feel about flying. I don't know how those things stay up in the air.'

Annie jumped at this chance to get her mother on her side. 'George wants Sean to go with him.'

To her dismay, before she could elaborate further, Thelma interrupted her. 'I think that would be best, Annie,' she agreed. 'The two men of the family. I wanted John to go as well, but he won't leave me. He's away down to get some Mass cards to send over. Do you think Rosaleen will expect me to go?'

'No, no. She knows that you've been ailing lately. She won't expect you,' Annie assured her. Tentatively, she added, 'Do you not think that I should be the one to go?'

Thelma looked bewildered. 'But you would never leave Thomas, Annie. Everybody knows that!'

'In this instance, I think I should. After all, Rosaleen and I are sisters. If the positions had been reversed, God forbid, Rosaleen would have come over here at once to be with me.'

'Would Sean take time off work to look after Thomas? He's a bit much for John and me now, you know.'

'He wouldn't have to! And I wouldn't dream of asking you. I'll ask Josie to take him for a few days. She's very attached to him and has plenty of room in that bungalow since her aunt died last year. And with working at Fleming Fulton, she could take him to school every day.'

'I think you'd be a bit presumptuous, asking her. After all, Thomas can be very awkward at times.'

'But that's the beauty of it, Mam! She's a carer . . . and one of the best. She's deputy to Miss McAteer now. So he couldn't be in better hands.' Silently she willed her mother to agree with her. Josie was Annie's last hope of saving her marriage. Sean mustn't, under any circumstances, go to Canada!

To her relief, Thelma was slowly nodding her head. 'You're right, of course. Josie is the ideal person to ask.' She leant forward and gripped Annie's arm as tears poured down her face. 'And wouldn't it be great if you could be with Rosaleen at this terrible time, Annie?'

A sigh of relief escaped her. At last her mother was seeing her point of view. If the case arose, she would be an ally in Annie's arguments as to why she should be with her sister to share her troubles. 'Yes, Mam. I'm glad you agree that I should be the one to go. Come on now, love. No more tears. You'll only make yourself ill again.' She hugged her mother close but her mind was racing ahead. Would she be able to convince Sean?

In spite of her success in winning her mother over in her favour, worry still plagued Annie as she retraced her footsteps up the Serpentine Road. All the tension was upsetting her stomach and making her feel physically ill. She knew that Sean had been hurt and confused when she'd refused to visit Canada last year, but how could she go? Even the girls, young as they were, had been unable to hide their disappointment. They had all been so annoyed with her. For a few weeks everybody had practically sent her to Coventry. So now she didn't blame him for being confused by her decision to be the one to go. But she just had to convince him that it was the right thing to do. He could be very stubborn at times. In view of the stance she had taken last year it would be understandable if he insisted on accompanying George, and then what would she do? It didn't bear thinking about.

It was early afternoon when George phoned from work and told her he had reserved two seats on an early-morning flight out of Shannon. They would have to travel down to the airport that evening, to make sure that they didn't miss the plane.

'John doesn't want to leave Thelma,' he explained. 'Much as he would have liked to see Canada, he felt it was a bad time to leave your mother. I said I was sure you would have her up to stay with you while we were away, but he refused the offer. Your mother took the news very badly. I'm afraid it has set her back a bit. She was in a state of nervous exhaustion.'

Anger seethed within Annie's breast. It was typical of men to assume that women would fall in with their wishes. With great difficulty she managed to keep her voice matter-of-fact. 'George . . . I think it best if I go with you.'

After a short silence during which she could picture him staring at the phone in disbelief, he said, 'What about Sean? I thought it was all settled, that he would go in your place?'

'Sean won't be very happy about it, but I just have to go out to our Rosaleen. Look, we can't talk about it now. See you later.' Before he could argue further she hung up.

Sean arrived home from work earlier than usual. He was all excited, confiding that his boss had been very understanding and that he had arranged for some compassionate leave. Annie greeted this news in silence.

He frowned at her, perplexed. 'Any word from George? I tried to phone him before I left the office but he had already left for home.'

As if on cue there was a knock on the door. It was George. He had refrained from ringing Sean and had left work early, hoping to talk to Annie before her husband arrived home. Now he directed his question tentatively at his brother-in-law.

'I've booked two seats on the early-morning flight out, is that all right?'

'That's great, George! I've managed to get some compassionate leave. Whose car will we go in?'

'Mine, I think. It's newer than yours. We don't want to risk breaking down when we're halfway there,' George answered him absently. He was watching different expressions flit across his sister's face. She threw him a beseeching glance and he realized that she wanted him to leave. He turned on his heel at once. 'I'd better go. I want to ring Josie and explain what's happened. I'll be in touch with you later on tonight to arrange the last-minute details.'

183

The door closed on him and husband and wife gazed at each other in silence. Sean was uneasy. He had become aware that all was not well. Better ignore Annie's silence and prepare for the journey ahead, he thought.

'While you make the dinner, Annie, I'll pack a suitcase.'

His foot was on the bottom stair when she dropped her bombshell. 'Sean . . . I've decided that I should be the one to go to Canada. Not you.'

He swung round to face her, his face a study of amazement. 'What? What on earth do you mean? It's all settled. Why . . . I've even arranged time off work! I've already told you that.'

'Too bad! You should have phoned me first. Nothing was settled this morning. In fact, I told you then that I was going, but as usual you just ignored me. I may as well talk to that wall for all the attention you pay me. But no matter what you've arranged . . . Rosaleen is my sister and I intend being with her at this awful time. She'll want me there.'

'What about Thomas? And the girls?'

'I'm going to ask Josie to look after Thomas. As for the girls . . . they're not babies. Surely you can manage to look after them for a couple of days?'

His face was grim and his voice bitter as he reminded her of her refusal to visit Rosaleen before. 'Don't do this to me, Annie. Last year you wouldn't hear tell of going to Canada. You were so selfish you wouldn't even agree to me and the girls going over without you. We could have had the holiday of a lifetime and you spoilt it for everybody, so don't think you can walk all over my wishes now. If you insist on going, I'll book another seat on the plane for you.'

Despair in her heart, she answered him. 'You do that, Sean. But where will the money come from?'

'If I beg, borrow or steal,' he thundered, 'I'll get it! I have every intention of going to Canada and I don't want any more arguments from you. Do you hear me?'

Annie watched him scale the stairs in a rage. He was so angry. If he booked another place on the plane there was nothing she could do about it; the cat would be among the pigeons. Was she being overcautious? Did Liam really resemble Sean so very much that he would notice? Rosaleen never spoke of her son and Annie was afraid to broach the subject.

Sean sat on the edge of the bed, his head clasped in his hands. Why was Annie doing this? God forgive him, Andrew was dead and he had been looking forward to going over there. He had actually felt in holiday mood. It would be great to get away for a while, even in such sad circumstances. He'd felt so hemmed in lately. The future looked bleak. Imagine getting excited about going to his brother-in-law's funeral! Perhaps it really would be better if Annie went? In spite of their past differences, Rosaleen would probably prefer her sister's company at a time like this.

At the dinner table, Rachel watched her parents closely, afraid to ask any questions in case she sparked off a huge row. Rebecca was thicker skinned than her sister. Unaware of the tension, she asked brightly, 'Well, Dad, when do you set off for Canada?'

The silence was deafening. Rebecca looked from one to the other of her parents and then at Rachel who was making motions with her mouth which she rightly took to mean, 'Shut up, you fool!'

Sean had not spoken a word to Annie since his threat to book another seat on the plane. Now she waited with bated breath for his reply.

At last he broke the uneasy silence. 'Your Uncle George has booked two seats on a flight out early in the morning. Your mother wants to accompany us, so I'll go down and see George and find out the flight number and book another place for her. Now, girls, if we both go, I shall ask Thelma and John to come up here and stay with you until we get back. So be sure to be on your best behaviour.'

'What about Thomas? Who'll look after him?' Rachel cried.

'Your mother is going to ask Josie to care for him.'

'Dad . . .'

Sean was at the end of his tether. He was trying to convince himself that he was doing the right thing borrowing all that money. Really, it was such a waste! They didn't both need to go. It was just the idea of Annie's being so eager to go now . . . and last year, when they could have well afforded it, in spite of all his pleading she had not budged. It was so unfair! He would never understand her.

'No more questions now, Rebecca.' Without a glance in his wife's direction he rose from the table. 'I'm away down to see George. I won't be long.'

As he neared the Gardens, Sean felt a great cloud of desolation descend on him. He was in no fit state to face his brother-in-law. Why, the way he felt now, he might even blubber all over George and that would never do. Without a doubt George would see Annie's point of view quicker than he would Sean's. He was that close to his sister.

Veering to the left he cut through the estate built shortly after the war, known as the White City because all the houses were finished off with white pebble dash on the walls. Passing the row of shops that backed on to the Gardens, he paused, tempted to call into the newsagent's to purchase some cigarettes. This notion brought him up short. Imagine wanting to start smoking again after ten years of kicking the habit. He must be really low even to consider it. Why was he feeling so jumpy and depressed lately? Nothing had really changed over the last few years. He worked hard, earned good money. They had a beautiful home. The kids wanted for nothing. Thomas was advancing better than they had dared hope for. He should be content with his lot.

Why then was he so discontented? Was it because Annie and he were drifting apart? Although she never refused him, they rarely made love now. The old spark was diminishing. They were coming together less and less. Was it his fault? His thoughts swung this way and that and it was with a start of surprise that he realized he had made his way up on to the Antrim Road. Reluctantly he turned left and started homewards. He had reached a decision. Since Annie was determined to go . . . he would stay behind. He wouldn't feel justified wasting all that money. After all, it was a funeral he would be going to, not a holiday.

Still loath to return home and tell Annie that she had won yet again, his feet led him past the top of the Serpentine Road. He walked until he reached Gray's Lane and with swift strides made his way down its twisting slope on to the Shore Road. A short distance along the road, a car drew up beside the kerb and a familiar voice hailed him.

'Hello there, Sean. Would you like a lift? I'm on my way up to see George.'

'Hello, Josie. Thanks very much.'

He climbed into the car beside her and gave her what he hoped was a smile.

Obviously she wasn't fooled. 'Is anything wrong, Sean? Oh, I'm sorry . . . that was tactless of me. George phoned me earlier. I know your brother-in-law is dead.' She peered at him in the dim interior of the car, and what she saw concerned her. 'Can I be of any help? Is anything else bothering you?'

With a muttered exclamation he reached for her hand and gripped it hard between his own. It was like a life line to him. 'Ah, Josie, Josie . . .' Realizing what he was doing and who he was with, he dropped her hand and hurriedly withdrew to his own side of the car.

She was dismayed to notice that he was fighting tears. Quickly she came to a decision. He obviously needed someone to talk to, but this was too public a place. Easing the car out into the line of traffic, she drove on down the road until she came to a secluded spot where she parked.

Sean had his emotions under control again and when she turned to him he smiled wryly at her. 'Forgive me, Josie. I almost made a fool of myself back there, but I'm all right now.'

Her hand covered his where it lay clenched on his thigh, and squeezed it gently. 'Sometimes it helps to talk about whatever is troubling you. They say a trouble shared is a trouble halved. So come on, out with it.'

He looked at her face and was struck by the thought that she was one of those women who grew more attractive with age. In the dim interior of the car, her skin was luminous and those great eyes of hers simply glowed with compassion. How come George and she had never got married? His brother-in-law was a fool! She was leaning towards him and her wide sensuous lips were tantalizing. Without a thought he reached for her. Startled, she drew back for a second then moved over closer to him. Here was a man who needed comfort.

His mouth covered hers and expensive perfume wafted about him. The kiss was deep and full of need. To her horror Josie found herself responding with a fiery passion. It was a long time since she had felt aroused. There was also a great

187

want in her. It was when his hands started to wander that she brought herself and him reluctantly back to reality. Pushing him gently away, she looked intently into his eyes. 'This isn't what you really want, Sean. You'd only regret it later on,' she said gently. 'Tell me what's troubling you. Were you close to this man Andrew. Is that why you're so upset?'

He laughed and his voice broke on a stifled sob. He did not release his hold on her. It was comforting to have the warmth of her in his arms. 'Close to him? Ah no, Josie. I was actually looking forward to going to his funeral!'

Her eyes blinked rapidly a few times as she digested his words. 'I . . . I don't understand.'

He shook his head as if in a daze. 'How could you? I don't understand myself. I only know I desperately want to go to Canada. I need to get away for a while.'

'But . . .' She sounded mystified. 'I thought that you and George were going out there?'

'No, my dear wife has decided it is her place to go.'

'Oh, I see.' But she didn't. She knew all about the upheaval last year when Annie had refused to go to Canada. 'Does that mean that George and Annie will go together?'

'I'm afraid so.' Slowly he relaxed his hold on her. 'Thanks, Josie. Thanks for being so understanding. You know I didn't mean any disrespect just now, don't you?'

'Yes, Sean. I'm only glad I was able to help you. Shall we get a move on then?'

'Yes, please.' He wondered then just how far Josie would have been willing to go to help him and eyed her covertly. She really was an attractive woman. Why then had she never married?

Annie was in their bedroom packing a suitcase for herself when she heard him return. With ears strained she followed his progress up the stairs. Although her back was to the open door, she knew when he stopped there. Without turning, she addressed him. 'I'll pack your case in a minute, Sean. I wasn't sure just what you'd want to take with you.'

He watched her in silence. Chestnut hair swinging forward about her face, displaying the nape of a white slender neck, the long back and swaying hips. Not so long ago this would have been enough to start him off, but now he felt no interest whatsoever. She had lost some weight over the years but, slim and firm-breasted, was still an attractive woman. One part of his mind admitted this, but it was with cold dislike that he now regarded her. Lately it was as if he was invisible to her, she had so little time for him.

When was the last occasion they had been out together? About a year ago. No, not quite a year. She had, under duress, attended the company's Christmas dinner dance with him last December. Every year Woolworth's gave a Christmas party for the children of Fleming Fulton School. This year the date had clashed with the company do. Only after a lot of persuasion had she agreed that George could take Thomas, and she would accompany her husband, but she had relented with bad grace.

Tensed up, Annie paused in her task, waiting for him to say something. Why didn't he speak? She wanted to shout and rail at him, ask him what he intended doing, but managed to hold her tongue.

A harsh laugh escaped his lips as he informed her, 'You'll be glad to hear that I have decided to stay at home and look after the children.'

Relief seeped through her and slowly she turned to face him, words of gratitude hovering on her lips. They remained unuttered, she was so taken aback by the hatred etched on his stony face. Why was she always the one in the wrong? It was his past sin that had denied them a holiday last year; his sin that now stood between him and Canada. But of course he didn't know that and she, apparently, was to be the villain of the piece. Sometimes she thought it would be better to tell him the truth and get it all out into the open. Make him realize just how much he had spoilt things for her. It was only fear of his reaction that stopped her from taking this course.

'I'm sorry if you're annoyed, Sean. But, after all, Rosaleen is my sister . . . it's only fitting that I should be the one to go.'

Tentatively she moved towards him and placed her hands on his chest. Her eyes beseeched him to be kind. Abruptly he moved away, ignoring her proffered lips. He didn't want any consolation prize. Her nostrils flared in awareness and he knew she must smell Josie's perfume on him.

'You'd better finish your packing. I'll go down and see

189

George and find out all the details of the flight.' He met her eyes, his still cold and full of distaste. 'I trust you won't object if I offer to run you both to Shannon? I think, in spite of what George said, the car will hold out. And since I've pulled a lot of strings to get time off work, there'll be no need for you to trouble Josie. I'll see to Thomas.'

'I thought you had already seen George?'

He smiled grimly. 'No, I had something better to do.' With these words he turned on his heel and left the room. There! That admission and the smell of expensive perfume would give her something to think about. Where had he spent the last hour or so? He sincerely hoped she realized he'd been with a woman. *That* would give her something to worry about. Him smelling of expensive perfume and with free time while she was in Canada? She wouldn't like that! Aware that Josie had left him to go and see George, he once again passed the Gardens. He couldn't face her at the moment. He'd call down and visit Thelma and John and bring them up to date on all that had happened. Josie had remarked that she was making a flying visit to see George. If he spent an hour or so with his mother-in-law and John the coast should then be clear for him to see George alone and find out the details of the flight.

Annie held George's hand so tightly her knuckles showed white as the plane left the runway and rose into the sky. Dawn was breaking and the view was breathtaking. However, Annie's one and only time on a plane some years ago had been a stormy crossing and he knew that she was terrified of flying. So why on earth had she insisted on coming? He and Sean could have represented the family. Rosaleen would have understood.

After some moments Annie asked, 'Are we up yet?'

'We certainly are. You can even take your seat belt off now.'

Slowly she opened her eyes and peeped nervously out of the window. A gasp of pleasure escaped her lips. 'It's wonderful! Quite literally out of this world,' she cried.

'I knew you'd be impressed.'

She smiled with pleasure at him but the smile faded as memories of the past hour returned to haunt her. What must George be thinking about Sean's treatment of her? On the journey down from Belfast she had slept in the back of the car most of the time and it had gone unnoticed, but once at the airport his coldness towards her was blatantly obvious. She may as well have been a stranger for all the attention he paid her. She had noticed George eyeing him in disapproving bewilderment, but if Sean was aware of George's displeasure he did not show it. Boarding time had been humiliating. Sean had wished them a safe journey and shaken George by the hand but he had only given Annie a curt nod and turned away when she would have reached out to touch him. She had climbed aboard the plane blinded by tears.

'Are you feeling all right, Annie?'

'Oh, I'm fine.' She smiled but it wobbled a bit.

'You don't look fine to me. Remember, Annie, I would never, ever repeat anything you tell me in confidence.'

For a moment she was tempted to pour out all her worries into George's sympathetic ear. However, common sense prevailed. She must not forewarn him. Wait and see if Liam really did resemble Sean. See if George noticed the likeness ... if there was any!

The plane touched down at Toronto International Airport. A single-storey building of yellow brickwork, it reflected the bright sunlight. After passing through customs, they found Laura, accompanied by Billy Mercer, waiting for them. Many tears were shed as condolences were offered.

'Oh, Auntie Annie, what are we going to do?' wailed the girl.

'You'll get the strength to bear it, love. You have to be strong for your mother's sake.' Her eyes sought Billy's. 'How is Rosaleen?'

With a glance at Laura's bent head he grimaced and mouthed the word, 'Bad.' Out loud he said, 'She's bearing up all right. Here, George, let me give you a hand with those cases. Laura, lead the way to the car, love.'

Billy pointed to some buildings in the distance, still under construction. 'That's going to be the new airport when it's completed. The one we've just left has outgrown its use.'

Once the airport was left behind, George could not help but remark on the beauty of the countryside which stretched around them, a carpet of bright colour in the sunlight.

191

A warm smile lit Billy's sombre face. 'Yes, in my opinion this is one of the most beautiful places on earth. That's why we have no inclination to return to Belfast.'

Annie was unable to resist the opening and asked, 'What about Rosaleen, does she feel the same way?'

'Well now, Rosaleen loves it here too, but every now and again she gets itchy feet and wants to go back. May and I don't have that problem. We love the lifestyle here and the children are doing very well. Ian's in Market Research and Rosie hopes to teach English and history when she eventually graduates,' he said proudly. He had been talking over his shoulder to Annie; now he gave his attention to George. 'Have you ever seen such a mixture of colours in one place?'

They were passing along an avenue of maple trees and George gazed in rapture at the profusion of colour created by approaching autumn: rust, orange, scarlet and yellow. Every now and again they would reach the brow of a hill and a panorama of beauty opened before them in a faint veil of smoky mist. He was speechless and just nodded in agreement.

'The autumn, or the fall as they call it here, is my favourite season,' Billy continued. 'Andrew lived here since he was seven so it really was home to him. His publishing business is in Toronto but he chose to buy a house in Hockley Valley outside Orangeville. It's in Dufferin County and I suppose he chose it because it's handy to the golf course and skiing resort. He was a keen sportsman, you know, and always kept himself in good shape. That's why it was such a shock when he had the heart attack.' Billy fell silent for some moments and pondered on the pity of it. Rousing himself with a slight shake, he continued, 'By British standards Orangeville is a large village but by Canadian standards it's a small town. It has a population of about four or five thousand, but spread over a wide area.'

'Orangeville . . . what a lovely name. I can almost smell oranges. Do they actually grow them here?' George queried.

Billy couldn't help but laugh. 'Afraid not. It was actually named after one of the founder settlers, Orange Lawrence. He built the Grist Mill which still stands on Mill Street. The name Orangeville was suggested by the wife of one of his employees in his honour, and before we go any further, don't ask me how he came by the name "Orange", because I haven't got a clue. It's a very strange name for a man.'

'Have we much further to go, Billy?' Annie interrupted him. Even the picturesque countryside and the history of Orange-ville couldn't quite lift her spirits. Would her nephew resemble Sean? The worry was tying her stomach in knots.

'No, Annie. It won't be long now. It's about thirty-five miles from the airport to Hockley Valley where Rosaleen lives. We're about halfway there.'

Some time later they passed through tall gates into a broad tree-lined driveway. George informed them, 'This is Andrew's land. Twenty acres of it.' Sadness crept into his voice. 'He was very successful, you know. It's such a pity he died. He had so much to live for.'

The house, when it eventually came into view, took Annie's breath away. Imagine her Rosaleen living in a place like this. It was like something you'd see in the movies! A great rambling ranch-style bungalow nestling in the midst of all this beautiful landscape. It was set on top of a hill overlooking the valley below.

They scrambled from the car and Annie stood there, awed by the beauty of her sister's home. Not once had Rosaleen bragged about it. No pictures to show how well off she was. Why not? How had she resisted the temptation? Annie herself would certainly have done so.

The double hardwood doors were thrown open and May Mercer rushed out and clasped Annie close. Wordlessly they clung together and then May drew her forward and led her into a beautiful wide hall. A tall dark-haired woman came forward and May introduced her to Annie and George.

'This is Andrew's sister, Cissie. Cissie, this is Rosaleen's brother and sister, George and Annie.'

The resemblance to Andrew was marked and Annie felt tears once again sting her eyes as she gripped the woman's hand in silent sympathy. It was all such a sad business. Cissie told them that light refreshments were ready in the drawing room. She turned to lead the way but Laura intervened.

'Would you like to see Mam first?'

'By all means, take them along.' Cissie sounded resigned.

'But, mind you, she was asleep when I looked in on her a few minutes ago.'

Without a further glance in her aunt's direction Laura headed for the door. They followed her down a corridor that branched off the entrance hall. There were doors to either side and Annie guessed that these were bedrooms. At last Laura stopped and tapping lightly on a door, then quietly entered the room.

Annie had to adjust her eyes to the dim light when she was shown inside. Her sister lay asleep on top of the bedclothes. Even in bereavement Rosaleen looked beautiful. Long dark lashes shadowed high cheek-bones and the blush of sleep tinted them. She looked young and vulnerable lying there, a light rug over her legs.

Quietly, Laura approached the bed. 'Mam . . .'

With a wave Annie stayed her. 'Don't disturb her, love. We'll see her later on, after we've freshened up.'

After some tea and biscuits they were shown to their rooms. In the bedroom assigned to her, Annie was once again struck by the fact of how wealthy her sister must be. Everything was of the finest quality. Lack of money obviously was no obstacle here. She stood by the window drinking in the breathtaking view of the valley shrouded in a gentle haze stretching below. If only circumstances were different, she would have enjoyed a month's holiday with her family in these beautiful surroundings.

A tap on the door was followed by Laura entering the room. Sensing that her niece wanted to talk, Annie left the window and, sitting on the bed, patted the place beside her. Laura sat down and then she was in Annie's arms, crying her eyes out.

'It all happened so quickly, Aunt Annie!'

'I know, love. It must be awful for you, but you must be strong. Where is your . . .' Unable to frame the sentence, Annie stopped in embarrassment.

Laura understood. 'They took Dad away. You know how it is when someone dies suddenly.'

'Yes, of course I do, love. How stupid of me.'

'His body will be brought back here. He'll be buried from the house tomorrow. That is, if everything goes all right. I can't take it all in. When Mam collapsed, I actually ran to fetch Dad. She's in an awful state.'

194

Even in the midst of all the tears and sorrow, Annie found herself trying to find out what Rosaleen intended doing. 'Perhaps she'll come over to Ireland for a while?'

'I don't know. Liam says he'll try and get her to take a vacation after the funeral.'

Hating herself, Annie nevertheless probed, 'Will he come with her?'

'I don't know, Aunt Annie. I don't know what's going to become of us. We all depended so much on Dad.'

'There, love, don't cry. You will need to be strong for your mam's sake.'

Dabbing at her eyes, Laura rose to her feet. 'Thanks, Aunt Annie. I needed to be with someone for a while that I didn't have to put a brave face on for. Aunt Cissie is all right . . . but . . . well, she is always so aloof. I've never really gotten on with her. I'll come for you later when you have rested for a while.'

Impulsively, Annie gathered her close. 'You're a fine brave girl, Laura Mercer, and don't you forget it!'

When they next saw her, Rosaleen was wan and pale. She clutched Annie and the tears started to flow. They rocked together, both in tears, until at last George stepped forward and gently parted them.

'Here now, this will never do. Aren't you going to say hello to me, Rosaleen?'

She burrowed her head against his chest and the tears continued to fall. 'Oh, George, how am I going to live without him? I feel as if a part of me has been wrenched away.'

'That's only natural, Rosaleen. He was, in a way, part of you. But you'll survive. You have your children to comfort you. They'll be your saving grace.'

She wiped her eyes with the handkerchief that he thrust into her hand and sighed deeply. 'Where's Sean?' Her look at Annie was accusing. 'Why isn't he here?'

'He had to stay behind to look after the children.' Annie was terse. Rosaleen hadn't the right to demand his presence. 'He sends his love.'

'Are you feeling any better, Mam?'

Unnoticed by them, a young lad had entered the room. He

stood diffidently at the door, anxious eyes scanning his mother's face. All other eyes focused on him. Annie could see at once why Rosaleen had never sent any clear photographs of him home to Ireland. But for the chestnut hair, he was Sean Devlin's spitting image.

'Liam, come here, son. This is your Aunt Annie and your Uncle George.'

Annie gulped deep in her throat as she gazed up at the tall thin lad. There could be no doubt whatsoever that Sean was his natural father. And he would be so proud of this handsome boy!

Putting her arms around him, she hugged him briefly. 'I'm so sorry you've lost your father, Liam. He was a grand man.'

Tears filled the boy's eyes but he manfully held them in check. 'I know, Aunt Annie. I'm going to miss him a lot.'

He turned to George and held out his hand. 'Hello, Uncle George. Sorry to be meeting you in such sad circumstances.'

A puzzled frown was on George's brow as he acknowledged Liam's greeting. 'I too wish the circumstances were happier, son.' His eyes roved over the fine delicate features. He had never met Rosaleen's first husband but there was something very familiar about her son. He didn't resemble Rosaleen in the slightest so how . . .? Ah, he was the picture of his cousin Rachel. It must be just the family resemblance that made him appear so familiar.

Still there was something else. Suddenly the truth struck him like a punch in the face and he gaped in amazement. He was looking at Sean Devlin's double! Like the pieces of a jigsaw everything immediately fell into place. Annie's determination to avoid a holiday over here last year. Her insistence on accompanying him now. Sean must not be aware he had another son and Annie was determined to do all in her power to prevent him from finding out. Confused, he glanced in her direction.

Her eyes were waiting. She turned abruptly away from the pity she encountered in George's. She didn't want anyone's pity! She had done nothing wrong. To her relief the traumatic moment passed when Cissie entered the room and announced that dinner was about to be served in the dining room.

The meal was eaten in comparative silence. Annie, unnerved

by the resemblance of Liam to his father, schooled herself not to stare at him. Instead she let her eyes roam over the splendour of the big wood-panelled room. The table was set with the best of china and the cutlery was heavy, embossed silver. Once again she was struck by the opulence of everything. She had known that Rosaleen was well off, but had never dreamed just how wealthy she must be. And now she was once again a widow. A beautiful rich widow at that. Annie remembered how she had feared her sister when she discovered that Liam was Sean's child. Now that fear was rampant again. With Andrew gone, would Rosaleen stay in Canada? Or, horrible thought, would she come home to roost?

George and Billy, with a little help from the usually talkative May, kept the conversation flowing. The rest were silent, only speaking when spoken to. Covertly, George watched his nephew. Now he understood why Annie had so passionately wanted a son. When she had learnt that Thomas was handicapped it must have been heartbreaking for her to know that Sean had fathered a strong healthy boy. Especially when she was warned that another pregnancy might prove fatal. He found himself critical of Rosaleen. From the very beginning he had admired her courage; thought it wonderful the way she had rallied round when she discovered she was pregnant and her husband still fresh in his grave.

Yet she must have been carrying on with her brother-in-law while her first husband, Joe, was recovering from injuries suffered during the war. He wouldn't have believed that she could be so deceitful. He had figured out that Liam was the child Rosaleen was expecting when he himself had arrived out of the blue all those years ago and announced that he was her half-brother. And Sean ... what impression had he formed of him at that time? He had liked him; hadn't noticed anything out of the ordinary between him and Rosaleen. They must have planned their clandestine meetings very carefully indeed.

Still, surely there must have been some undercurrents? Perhaps he had been too wrapped up in his own problems to notice. Just relieved that the family had welcomed him into their midst. Sean had been in the Merchant Navy at the time and George did remember Annie haring off to that big empty house she and Sean had bought. And hadn't he been aware

197

that something was not quite right between the sisters? But nothing as drastic as this had ever crossed his mind. The revelation was devastating. Poor Annie! How she must have suffered. Was she about to suffer more? What, now that Andrew was dead, if Rosaleen should decide to return and live in Ireland?

Discovering that there was an open night at Fleming Fulton School, Sean was in two minds whether or not to go. He dreaded facing Josie after the fool he had made of himself. What must she think of him? How would she greet him? Still, Thomas was excited about the outing and Sean couldn't let him down. It was with heavy heart that he made the journey across town.

He need not have worried. Josie came forward at once to greet him, a welcoming smile on her face, hand stretched out in greeting. 'I'm glad you could come, Sean. Thomas loves these evenings.'

Her words brought home to him how often he missed these evenings; how often George took his place by Annie's side. He silently vowed that things would be different in future; overtime must be a secondary priority from now on.

'I know,' he agreed ruefully. 'I should be here more often.'

'It's not your fault, Sean,' she consoled him before greeting Thomas. 'Come along, let's join your friends.' Offering the lad the support of her arm, she guided him slowly across the room.

During the course of the evening Sean watched Josie closely. Every action showed love and caring. He examined her minutely. The short dark hair with its glossy sheen emphasized her pale skin and dark eyes. His eyes travelled over her lissom body and long legs, the slim ankles shown off to advantage by high-heeled shoes. He felt his cheeks redden as he was suddenly overwhelmed by the memory of the feel and smell of her in his arms, the softness of her lips. He glanced around guiltily to see if anyone had noticed. It was Josie's eye he caught and he felt like a teenager caught out in a naughty act. She smiled at him and he realized how absurd he was being.

She had blossomed since moving to Bangor all those years ago. Gone was the awkward, defiant teenager and in her place was a poised self-confident young woman. He had heard that her aunt had left her everything she possessed when she died, and that it had amounted to a great deal. There had been a lot of unpleasantness when her Uncle William had contested the will, but the court had ruled in Josie's favour. Now she was the owner of a beautiful bungalow and was apparently quite well off. Surely there must be a man in her life? If not George, then who?

Time passed all too quickly and it was with regret that Sean took his leave of the other parents and staff. He had enjoyed the evening, applauding proudly when Thomas took part in a dance routine with another child.

To his great delight Josie followed him outside. 'It's still early, Sean. Will the girls be all right if you come home with me for a cup of coffee? You've never been to my bungalow, sure you haven't?'

'No, I haven't had that pleasure. I'd enjoy that, Josie. Rachel is down at her grannie's and Rebecca is next door keeping Minnie company. They'll be all right. I'll be delighted to come.'

'Give me five minutes and then follow me home.'

Thomas had followed the conversation intently. It took some time for him to decipher the words then he cried in delight, 'Are we going to Josie's, Dad?'

Sean laughed aloud at his son's excitement. Didn't he himself feel excited? 'We are indeed, son.'

'Great! Oh, great!'

Thomas was wiggling about in his seat with pleasure and Sean realized just how indebted he was to all at Fleming Fulton. Without the school and its staff, and all the volunteer workers, where would Thomas be today? They had indeed worked wonders with him.

It was ten minutes later that Josie emerged from the building and with a wave in their direction, hurried over to her car. Sean followed the Morris saloon closely through East Belfast and along the Bangor Road and at last drew up behind it at the entrance to a bungalow.

'Very nice. Very nice indeed,' he exclaimed when he joined her on the driveway.

'Yes, it is, isn't it?' Her voice was shy and he could see that she was pleased at his reaction to the bungalow. 'My Aunt Martha was a very kind woman. I honestly didn't expect her to leave everything to me. A little, maybe . . . but certainly not the lot.'

'She must have been very fond of you.'

Blinking back tears, Josie just nodded and hurried ahead to unlock the door. Once the door was open Thomas left the support of his father's arm and loped awkwardly ahead of her and into the living room.

'Thomas! Come back here!'

'It's all right, Sean. He knows his way about the house and has a lot of toys here to occupy him. George brings him quite often.'

She had entered the kitchen whilst speaking and Sean followed her. 'Dare I ask why George and you don't get married?'

She smiled slightly and replied, 'It's very simple. He's in love with someone else.'

His jaw dropped in amazement. 'George in love with someone else? I don't believe you! You're having me on . . . aren't you?' Laughter escaped him. 'I think I'd be the first to notice if he was carrying a torch for someone else.'

Josie marvelled at the blindness of men. 'No! Truly, he's in love with someone else. Mind you . . . he wants to marry me, but I'm greedy. I want the lot. Love, lust, commitment. Everything that goes to make a good marriage.'

'I don't blame you there.' Remembering that he had married Annie whilst still carrying a torch for Rosaleen, he hastened to add, 'Although, mind you, love has a habit of growing on you.'

'I won't settle for that,' she said determinedly.

'Tell me, why doesn't George marry this other woman then?'

'She's already married. Besides it's more complicated than that.'

'Now you've really got me intrigued. Come on, tell all. Who is she?'

He moved to join her at the sink and Josie was aware of the vibes that flowed gently between them, waiting to be recognized. She turned to the table, fumbling in her haste as she set a tray. 'That's all the information you are going to get. It's not my secret.'

She was regretting her impulsive gesture in inviting him back with her. The attraction between them was elusive but nevertheless dangerous. She knew it was loneliness that was pulling them together.

Sean watched her through narrowed lids. What was she playing at? Did she or didn't she want him to make a pass at her? Time would tell. He lifted the tray and preceded her out of the kitchen and into the living room. Conversation was general as they drank their coffee, but she was acutely aware of Sean's eyes endeavouring to seduce her. She moved restlessly. She'd been a fool! She should never have invited him here. Would he be put off? He was lonely and at odds with his wife. The perfect recipe for the start of an affair. But she didn't want an affair. If an affair was enough for her she would marry George. Because there, although George didn't realize it, she would always be the *other woman!*

Coffee finished, they looked in on Thomas, now engrossed in pictures spread out on the kitchen table.

'I'll show you the rest of the house.'

He followed her from room to room, making all the necessary comments, his mind on other things. In the room that was obviously her bedroom he eyed the bed and turned to face her, brows raised, a slight inquiring smile on his face.

Hurriedly she turned aside. 'No, Sean. I don't know what I was thinking of inviting you here. I'm afraid I've given you the wrong impression.'

'I think you knew exactly what you were doing.' He blocked her escape from the room, but did not touch her. His eyes held hers as he sought to sway her. 'Would it be so wrong, Josie, eh? Think about it. A bit of excitement and pleasure. What harm can it do? We're both adults. We know what we're doing.'

'We would be giving in to lust, Sean. That's what we'd be doing. The guilt would spoil our other relationships.'

His smile widened. 'Spoil? Why, Josie, I think it would enhance our lives.' He reached for her but she stepped back.

His lips tightened in a straight line and his brows drew together. 'Are you a tease, Josie? Do you make a habit of leading men on? Or . . . is it just emotionally mixed up fools like me you dally with?'

'You don't really believe that, Sean. I like you! I like you very much, but physical attraction isn't enough. I love George.

201

And no matter what you may feel now, you love Annie. You'd hate yourself for it afterwards. And so would I!'

He turned and abruptly left the room. She was right. They both had their own commitments. 'George is a fool! He doesn't know when he's well off,' he growled, and couldn't resist a parting shot. Eyeing her over his shoulder he said slyly, 'Perhaps another time. But for now . . . I'd best be going.'

In his heart he admitted that she was right. He was very angry at Annie but he was missing her. These last few days had made him aware just how important she was in his life. Why, without her he would have no life at all. Was he really willing to risk all that for a fling with Josie? That was something that Annie, should she ever find out, would never forgive. Not in a million years.

Andrew's body was returned to the house that evening. Annie stood beside Rosaleen and gazed down on the features of the man her sister had married. In death he looked younger than his fifty-five years, and when she saw the grief etched on Rosaleen's face she no longer doubted that her sister had indeed loved this man dearly. The coffin was set on two trestles in the drawing room, alongside a pine-panelled wall decorated with Andrew's cherished golf trophies and pictures of sporting groups. His relatives and friends called to pay their last respects. People milled about quietly offering platitudes and it was the early hours of the morning before the family had the house to themselves again.

After a lot of persuasion Rosaleen retired to her room. Annie, Laura, May and Cissie quickly followed suit. The men sat up for another hour or so, their muted voices still audible when sleep at last claimed Annie.

It was after the funeral that Rosaleen received the bad news. On their return from the cemetery the family were asked to gather in the drawing room where the will was to be read. Mr Spence, the family attorney, a tall, distinguished-looking elderly gentleman, waited until they were all seated before opening his briefcase and shuffling through some papers. Just the immediate family were present: Rosaleen, Laura, Liam and Patricia.

Clearing his throat, Mr Spence fixed his eye on Rosaleen and admitted, 'I'm afraid, Mrs Mercer, that I'm the bearer of bad news. I don't know if you are aware that the business has been going through a rough patch recently?' His glance embraced Rosaleen and Laura. They both shook their heads in bewilderment. He continued, 'If Andrew had survived you would probably have lived on in total ignorance, as he would surely have pulled it out of this latest crisis. He has before, you know! But his untimely death has changed all that.'

Rosaleen moved to the edge of her chair, back straight, ready to face whatever was coming.

'First let me assure you, Mrs Mercer, that this house is yours, and your husband assured me that you have money of your own, left by your first husband, so that whatever happened you would not be left penniless on the street. However the publishing business is on the verge of bankruptcy. Andrew took me into his confidence and I know he hoped to take on a partner with a substantial cash injection in an effort to save things.'

Rosaleen sat in a daze. Why hadn't Andrew confided in her? Was the worry of this the cause of his heart attack? Surely he knew her well enough to understand that money wasn't a ruling factor where she was concerned? He had always lavished presents and gifts on her but . . . She realized that the attorney was staring fixedly at her and cried, 'I beg your pardon? What did you say?'

'I asked you if you would like to meet this man and see if you can agree to his terms and conditions in an effort to avert financial disaster?'

Quickly Rosaleen came to a decision. Turning to her daughter she said, 'I think Gordon should be present. You and he know more about the business than I do, Laura. Ask him to come in, please.'

Kind and of great repute Mr Spence might be, but she had no intention of taking his word blindly. That was one thing she had learnt from Andrew. Always to look at every angle of a proposition before coming to a final decision. Gordon Mackenzie had worked alongside Andrew for the past five years. He was engaged to Laura, and as his future son-in-law surely

Andrew would have taken him into his confidence? He would know what his boss had intended doing.

It was soon obvious that Gordon had indeed been in Andrew's confidence. He was swift to assure them that Andrew had decided against the partnership mentioned by Mr Spence. He had been about to meet someone else with the same aim in view. Had died before telling Gordon just who he had in mind.

Mindful of the fact that Mr Spence had warned them that time was fast running out, Rosaleen asked if Gordon was willing to try his hand at pulling the business through this financial crisis. Cautiously, he told her that he would use his best endeavours but couldn't guarantee any success. Rosaleen assured him that she could ask no more of him.

The following day Laura offered to take George and Annie into Toronto to show them over her dad's publishing premises and also the offices of the *Toronto Telegram* where she had worked as a journalist since graduating from Ryerson Polytechnical Institute. Liam and Patricia were on compassionate leave from their respective schools. Liam was at Orangeville Secondary School studying for his high school diploma and Patricia attended Mono Amaranth Public School. They asked if they could also go along for the ride.

Rosaleen was feeling poorly and since May and Cissie had returned to their respective homes, Annie elected to stay behind and keep her sister company. After lunch they sat out on the veranda at the back of the house and Annie admired the wonderful view.

'Yes, it is beautiful. Andrew loved to sit here on an evening.' Rosaleen's voice broke and she wailed, 'Oh, Annie, I don't know how I'll manage without him. I loved him so very much.'

Annie gripped her hand in deep sympathy, but she was bewildered. Did Rosaleen no longer care for Sean? It was reasonable to suppose that she had really loved Andrew. Hadn't he been here to lift and lay her; to lavish all that money could buy on her? Hadn't he adopted her two children and treated them as his own?

Wiping her eyes, Rosaleen confided, 'The business is in a bad way, Annie.'

'What do you mean, in a bad way?'

'It seems it's on the verge of bankruptcy. It must have been the worry and stress of it all that brought on Andrew's heart attack. He bottled it all up within himself. Never said a word to me. As if money matters! If only he'd talked it over with me, shared the responsibility, he might still be alive today.'

Annie was sceptical of this view. Money didn't matter if you had enough to cover your needs but it mattered if you were worried how you could afford to buy the kids their next new shoes or clothes. Of course Rosaleen had always been comfortable where money was concerned. Joe Smith, her first husband, had also been a businessman. Not in the same league as Andrew, of course, but he had left her quite comfortably off.

'Does this mean you have no money at all?' she asked. 'Will they repossess this house?'

'No, the house is mine and Andrew never let me spend any of the money Joe left me. He said it must be kept for the children. It's all invested.' She paused, deep in thought for some moments. 'Now there's a thought. Perhaps . . . if I am in a position to touch it . . . it will be enough to save the business? I'll have to look into that.'

Annie felt like laughing. Money didn't matter indeed! 'What happens now?' she queried.

'Gordon is going to try to persuade someone to put money into the business. He says that Andrew didn't really want a partner. He wanted to keep the business strictly in the family. It was just a case of needs must. Gordon knows the publishing business inside out, and since he's almost one of the family I'm going to wait and see what happens. I had hoped to come over to Belfast for a while,' she added wistfully. 'But this latest setback hits all that on the head. I'll be needed here to sign papers and so forth.'

'Rosaleen, I hate to bring this up now . . . but I got a shock when I saw Liam. He's Sean's double! I could see that even George was gobsmacked. Will he ever come over to Ireland, do you think?'

'He is certainly hoping to go over there one day.' At Annie's gasp of dismay Rosaleen hastened to add, 'I, of course, will do all in my power to prevent it. Did George say anything about him?'

205

'No. Not yet. But he will, you can be sure of that. He won't be able to contain himself.'

'He won't tell anyone else though . . . will he?'

'Oh, no. I'll say this about him, he can be trusted to keep his mouth shut. Tell me, do May and Billy know the truth?'

'I think May guesses, but I have shown her so many pictures of your Rachel and remarked so often on both the children's likeness to me dad that she can't be sure. As for Billy . . . he only met Sean a few times, so I doubt if the thought ever crossed his mind. So stop worrying. Later on, I would love to come over for a holiday. Will that be all right with you?'

What else could Annie do but say, 'Yes, of course it is, Rosaleen.'

The short time spent in Orangeville had been traumatic and after a prolonged tearful farewell, Annie was exhausted as she boarded the plane for the return flight home. Rosaleen's last words were still ringing in her ears. 'Remember, as soon as I can, I'll be home for a long holiday. The idea of living in Canada without Andrew is heartbreaking. As soon as I can I'll come over to Belfast for a long rest. Once everything is settled, that is.'

It certainly wouldn't be until the New Year, Annie realized. Her sister would be needed at home to keep things running smoothly. There were books to launch for the Christmas rush and authors to placate whose books had had to be postponed because of Andrew's untimely death.

George held Annie's hand as the plane left the runaway but he could see that she didn't even realize they were airborne. The stewardess came round and he ordered a large brandy for her and a Jameson's for himself.

'Here . . . get this into you. It will make you feel better.'

'Thanks.' Annie accepted the glass from him and sipped at it but he could see that she was still miles away.

This was the first time they'd been really alone since the discovery that Liam was Sean's son. Now George tried to express his sympathy. 'Annie, I can't tell you how sorry I am. It must have been awful for you.'

She didn't pretend not to understand him, but said, 'I don't want your pity! I have lived all these years with the knowledge that Rosaleen's son was fathered by my husband. How would you like to live with something like that? Afraid of Sean ever finding out the truth.'

George showed his bewilderment. 'Annie! How could he not know?' he cried. 'Sean's far from stupid!'

'Because it took me so long to conceive Rachel, I had him convinced that he was sterile. It would never have dawned on him to put two and two together.'

'Annie, would it not be better to tell him the truth?'

'It would ruin our lives! He would not rest until he went out there and saw for himself what a fine boy Liam is.' A sob escaped her lips but she bit it back. 'My poor Thomas. Oh, my poor Thomas.'

'Ah, now, Annie,' he chastised her. 'You needn't worry on that score. It wouldn't make any difference to how Sean feels about Thomas.'

'Is that what you really think? You can't see him making comparisons? Besides, he would never forgive me for not telling him earlier. You see, at that time he thought he was unable to father a child. I was blaming him! I can still recall how miserable he was. It was no wonder he strayed. When I discovered about Liam, I was afraid to tell him that he had a son.'

'You can't take all the blame, Annie. Rosaleen deceived him too. Why didn't she tell him the truth?'

'She said it was a one-night stand and she didn't think there would be any point. She knew he loved me. When she discovered that she was pregnant, she didn't want to put any pressure on him. It was assumed that Joe was the father, so she let everyone think he was. Although, mind you, at the time I knew in my heart she was in love with Sean. Still, I let her convince me. I made myself believe her. I convinced myself it was only the once because I didn't want to lose him. I really did think he loved me, you see. What a fool I was!'

It was breaking George's heart to see her in so much pain. He put an arm around her and pulled her as close as the dividing arm of the seat allowed. 'Annie, Sean does love you. I know that for a fact. He's a bitter man at the moment. But look at it from his point of view. He's in the dark; thinks you're mucking him about. But you've got a good marriage going there. Don't you go spoiling things.'

Her head burrowed into his shoulder and her voice was tearful. 'Oh, George, how would I manage without you? You've been my salvation so many times. Always there when I needed you.'

He savoured the feel of her hair against his cheek, the warmth of her body against his. If only she wasn't related to him . . . Sean didn't deserve her! But she *was* related to him. All he could do was be there when she needed him. But he must make a life of his own. If only Josie would agree to marry him, everything would be all right. With a wife and family of his own he would be able to break free from this hopeless attraction.

Fearful that in the midst of all these churned emotions he might be tempted to tell her how he truly felt, he released his hold on her. 'I'll always be here for you, Annie, no matter what. That's something you can depend on.'

'I know that, George. And thanks.'

Annie dozed fitfully during the long flight home. She dreaded meeting Sean. Had he cooled down? What would his attitude be towards her?

George lay back in his seat, eyes closed, reliving the past. He found it hard to believe that no one else had noticed that Sean and Rosaleen had been carrying on. What about Thelma? Had she turned a blind eye? No, she had been ill at the time. Still, he had been there and hadn't noticed anything. It was just as well that Rosaleen had run off to Canada. If she had remained in Ireland, anybody with eyes in their head would have been sure to notice. Liam's likeness to Sean was so uncanny.

Soon however, he found his thoughts kept returning to Josie. Why had she never married? He was aware that she had dated two other men. One, a young therapist, had proposed to her when he was offered a position over in London. She had asked George's advice. He had tried to be fair, pointing out all the advantages of moving to London, but his heart wasn't in it. He had sighed with relief when she told him that she had decided to stay on at Fleming Fulton School. The new therapist, another handsome young man, had also shown interest in Josie. And why not? She had a lot going for her.

That romance had lasted about six months and he had been miserable the whole time. He rarely saw her when there was another man in her life and missed her sorely. He was relieved and glad when she let him date her again. If only she could see him in a romantic light. He had been convinced that in time she would consent to marry him. They were such good friends! He remembered the sex had been good between them. He was sure she had enjoyed it as much as himself. Why had she changed? What had gone wrong between them?

Silently he vowed he would ask her once more to marry him. He wasn't really optimistic that her answer would change, but he had to give it one more go. The *Telegraph* and *Irish News* had been advertising that the Beatles, a group of young musicians who were the latest rave, were coming to the Ritz Cinema to do a concert in November. Josie had shown great excitement at the idea. Personally he thought they were a bit old for all that nonsense. But of course she was much younger than him! He would get tickets for the best seats. He would make it a night to remember; flowers on the day and dinner after the show. If all this failed and she refused him again, he'd have to look elsewhere. Surely there must be a woman somewhere he could make happy? One who would give him children.

From the window of the lounge at Shannon Airport, Sean watched the big plane land before slowly descending the stairs to the waiting room where his wife and brother-in-law would come once they had cleared customs. Whilst they were away, he'd had time to dwell on his treatment of Annie before she'd left, and was thoroughly ashamed of himself. He was very much afraid that perhaps he had widened the rift between them beyond repair. She had every right to be annoyed at him. At a time when he should have been supportive, he had thought only of his own selfish need to be apart from her for a while. Well, he had gotten his wish! Although not in the way he'd intended. Every day that passed had made him more aware how much he depended on her. He'd been a fool! Of course it was Annie's place to be with her sister. She was Rosaleen's closest relative. He had been a thoughtless idiot. But thanks to Josie, at least he hadn't betrayal to feel guilty about as well.

Annie passed through customs with mixed feelings. If Sean was distant with her she would ignore him. Time enough to thrash things out when they reached the privacy of their own home. George must not be caused any further embarrassment. Her husband was the first person she saw when she entered the waiting room. Her eyes met his and then dropped in confusion. She actually thought she had seen a welcome there.

Sean reached her in three strides and, gripping her very close, sank his face into her hair. She stood as if made of stone. Surely this was some wonderful dream? But no, he was whispering in her ear, begging her forgiveness. Slowly she raised her head and gazed dazedly into his eyes.

'Can you ever forgive me, love?'

Bewildered, she nodded, not trusting herself to speak. His hands cupped her face and his lips claimed hers. Bemused, she gave herself up to the joy of his kiss. Whatever it was that had wrought this change in him, she was grateful for it and was certainly not going to question the whys and wherefores.

George watched them for some moments and then claimed their luggage as it came into view. He would wait outside for them. Their renewed happiness made him more than ever determined to have it out with Josie. He would put his plan into action and plead with her to marry him. He could make her happy, he knew he could. But would she give him the chance?

The trip to the Ritz Cinema to see the Beatles was a great success. It had been harder to obtain tickets than George had anticipated, but he had contacts. By paying double the price he eventually got two tickets for the front balcony, right in the first row. Josie's excitement when he told her was reward enough for all the extra money he had spent.

On the night, having decided to leave their respective cars at home, they arranged to meet outside the Ritz half an hour before the show was due to begin. George travelled by trolleybus to the bottom of Castle Street and then made his way along Queen Street towards the cinema. To his amazement the area around the Ritz was thronged with teenagers all battling each other for a prime place to see the arrival of the Beatles. Full of dismay he stood on tip-toe and tried to see Josie. How would he ever find her in this crowd? At last he caught sight of her, waving to attract his attention. With great difficulty he shouldered his way towards her. Once assured that they had tickets, stewards channelled them into a queue. Slowly but surely they shuffled along and some time later found themselves settled comfortably in their prime seats.

With eyes aglow, Josie turned to him. 'Isn't this wonderful?'

George smiled at her enthusiasm and had to admit that the excitement was rubbing off on him too.

When the group at last appeared on stage he could not for the life of him see why the female section of the audience was in such a fever, jumping up and down in their seats and screaming their heads off in fits of near hysteria. Some actually fainted and were quickly carried out to be attended by the St John's Ambulance volunteers who were there in numbers. George thought it must surely be from the heat which was overpowering. How could four lumps of lads with weird haircuts cause such pandemonium? However, he too was soon clapping and tapping his feet to the wonderful catchy rhythm of the music. At the end of the show, to his amazement, he rose to his feet in a standing ovation with the rest of the crowd, and even found himself shouting for more.

Josie hugged his arm as they left the cinema and sighed with pleasure. 'Thank you, George. Thank you very much. I have never enjoyed anything as much as I enjoyed that performance tonight.'

He smiled indulgently down at her. 'It was a smashing show, I have to admit. However, there's more to come. I've booked a table at the International Hotel for dinner. What do you think of that?' Holding her arm, he ushered her across the road and along Howard Street.

She chuckled delightedly. 'Hey, have you won the pools or something? First the beautiful bouquet of flowers. Everybody at work was green with envy when they arrived. Then the show of a lifetime. And now you tell me we are to dine in opulence! What's behind all this?'

'I want to talk to you. I want you to take me seriously, so I've paved the way with flowers and wine, you could say.'

211

'Oh, dear. That sounds ominous. Can't you give me a hint?'

'You'll know soon enough.'

It was only a few minutes' walk to the hotel and soon they were sitting at their table.

During the meal Josie kept smiling happily at him, between courses humming 'It's Been a Hard Day's Night', one of the catchy tunes from the show. He began to think that perhaps he might just be able to change her mind about marriage to him after all. Words from another of the hit songs turned over and over in his mind. 'She loves me, yeah, yeah, yeah!' Who knows? With Josie in this mood anything might happen.

During the course of the meal they drank two bottles of wine and Josie began to giggle at silly things and he was aware that she was a little bit tipsy. After dinner they retired to the lounge and, sitting close to her on a big comfortable settee, George raised his glass. 'To success.'

She smiled and touched her glass to his, a dreamy smile on her face. 'To success.' Taking a sip of brandy, she placed her glass carefully on the table close by. She had an idea that he was about to propose yet again and was unsure what her answer should be. Gazing down at her hands clasped in her lap, she mulled over the idea in her mind. She wasn't getting any younger and she was tired of living alone. She loved him, so why not settle for second best? After all, he was never likely to run off with the woman who held his heart and she knew he would make a wonderful father. Look how fond he was of Thomas and the girls. If only he loved her it would all be plain sailing.

'Josie, you know how fond I am of you, don't you?'

She nodded, wanting to scream that fondness wasn't enough but afraid of the consequences.

'I know you are now a woman of means . . . and I also know that you are aware I am not interested in your money. I earn enough to give us a good lifestyle.' He reached down and his hand covered hers. 'Look at me, Josie.' Slowly she raised her head and met his eyes. 'Will you marry me?'

Deciding to take the plunge, she took a deep breath and nodded her head.

He gaped at her in disbelief. 'You really mean it?'

She laughed aloud. 'Yes. If you're sure it's what you want?'

212

'What I want? Haven't I been asking you to marry me for years? When? When will we get married?'

'I think we should get engaged first.'

'Oh, yes! Yes, of course. How silly of me.'

'Let's keep it between ourselves and get officially engaged at Christmas, George. Don't you think that would be a good idea?' she asked gently.

'Josie, so long as you're going to become my wife, we will do it whatever way you like.'

'Right then! Let's just enjoy ourselves tonight. We can arrange everything else later.' The lounge was practically empty and they were in a secluded corner. She pressed against him and offered him her lips. Eagerly he claimed them, unable to take in the fact that she had actually consented to be his wife.

At last they drew breathlessly apart. They were both aroused and he was tempted to ask her if he should inquire if they had a vacant room, but decided against it. He would do things decently, show her respect. Not take advantage of her tipsy state.

Josie watched him intently, willing him to ask her to spend the night with him. Obviously he didn't need her enough. He was gripping her hands and drawing her up to face him.

'Come on, I'd better ring for our taxis.'

Sadly she agreed with him. 'Yes, I suppose we must go home. But can't we finish our drinks first?' Doubt was once again gnawing at her mind. Was she doing the right thing? She knew that he found her very attractive, so was it because of her past that he could not love her? Anyway, she had until Christmas to change her mind.

'Sorry, Josie. Of course we can. You must think me very stupid. It's because you've at last agreed to marry me! I don't know whether I'm coming or going. Will you have another brandy?'

When he returned from the bar his hands were empty. 'Josie, if I'm being presumptuous, just say so,' he stammered, 'but I inquired at reception and they have a vacant room. I thought perhaps you might like your drink in private? If you know what I mean.'

He stood on edge, awaiting her reply, ready to back down if need be. With a smile, Josie rose to her feet. 'I thought you'd

213

never ask.' She moved across the floor, leaving him to follow her with the drinks. Her heart was light. There was hope for them yet!

Annie and Sean threw a party for George and Josie on Boxing Day to celebrate their engagement. It was a great success and Rachel and Rebecca were thrilled when Josie asked them to be bridesmaids. The wedding was to be in June.

'You really mean it?' cried Rebecca. 'Both of us?'

Josie smiled at their excitement and nodded. 'I'll get some wedding brochures, and we can pick the dresses and decide on colours. I will be in ivory.' She had no intention of causing any gossip by walking down the aisle in white. Besides, ivory would be more flattering to her colouring.

'Oh, I can't wait!' Rachel cried. 'When can we start looking?'

Annie rolled her eyes heavenward. 'It's going to be a long six months.' She smiled at Josie. 'I'm very pleased you have decided to put George out of his misery, Josie. You should have married him years ago. He has all the makings of a fine husband.'

Josie's eyes met Sean's and he recalled her telling him that George was in love with a married woman. Surely she must have been mistaken? Hadn't he watched George closely these last few months, looking for the slightest clue that would confirm Josie's fears, and never seen him even glance sideways at another woman? Now he raised his glass and smiled. 'To the happy couple.'

Thelma had been gracious in her reception of the news and Josie breathed a sigh of relief. That was one obstacle cleared. Now the decision as to whose house they should live in must be broached. George was taking it for granted that they would live in Serpentine Gardens but Josie was against this idea, arguing that Bangor was an ideal place to rear children, and that the bungalow was much bigger and wasn't her back garden just right for children to play in? All said with a demure twinkle in her eye. At last she won George over to her way of thinking and his house was put on the market.

It was snapped up quickly and to the great delight of Thelma, George asked if he could occupy their spare room until the big day, bringing all the excitement right into her home. The months flew past and then the wedding was upon them. Josie had agreed to be married in St Mary's Church, Greencastle, and on a beautiful sunny day in June, in a hushed church, she and George solemnly took their marriage vows. As she gazed into his eyes she was convinced that he really, whole-heartedly, loved her. Then why didn't he say so? Eyes full of love she returned his look, determined to give her all to make their marriage a success.

The reception was held in the Royal Avenue Hotel. No expense was spared; George made sure of that. It was a perfect day and everything went smoothly right down to the final farewells. Josie, looking splendid in a dark blue suit with long slim skirt that showed tantilizing glimpses of her legs, threw her bouquet into the crowd of hopeful girls who had come to wave them off, and laughingly made her escape into the car under a shower of confetti. They had decided to tour the South, stopping when and where they felt like it. It really was the perfect day.

Chapter 6

1967

Entering the house, Rachel Devlin was aware that Thomas was throwing one of his tantrums. It was his way of getting attention. Usually her mother gave in to him to keep him quiet. Not today however. Her mother's voice, low but clear, came to her above the din. 'No, Thomas, you mustn't. Now stop it this very minute! You're just being naughty.'

Rachel remembered how not so long ago she had resented the attention lavished on her disabled brother. It had not been easy to stand by and watch everything arranged to suit Thomas. Her mother had never missed an open or sports day at Fleming Fulton School, even when such evenings clashed with open days at the Dominican College she and Rebecca had attended. Oh, no! Thomas had always come first, and her father, when he wasn't working late, always accompanied her mother to keep the peace. Many a night Rachel had cried herself to sleep after receiving her prizes applauded only by her grandmother and John, or kind Uncle George and Josie. Then she had spent days hating herself for begrudging Thomas his big day.

Rebecca felt differently from her sister, she was easy-going and hard to ruffle. Against the wishes of her parents she had defiantly chosen to leave school at sixteen and had managed to get herself a job in the office of one of the big stores in the city centre. She attended night school three times a week at Carrickfergus Technical College where she was studying shorthand typing and book-keeping. It could lead to great things. Look how well Josie had advanced through night school. Why,

216

her typing and shorthand were so fast she could surely get a job anywhere she wanted, but she chose to remain at Fleming Fulton School. She was devoted to the children there. Rebecca's ambition was to become a secretary to some big nob and if her dream came true, maybe one day marry him. And with her luck she could very well do so!

Sometimes Rachel envied her outgoing, independent sister and wished that she too had left school at sixteen. It was a terrible responsibility attending Queen's University. Her father expected so much of her. Fear dogged her as she tried to revise for her exams and still see enough of Desi McKernan. She didn't dare put him off too often in case he decided to cast his eye elsewhere. He was so popular! There were numerous girls just waiting to step into her shoes. But God knows where she would end up if she failed her exams. Her father set such store by her, expected great things from her. It was all such a worry.

For the past few weeks her mother had started to prepare Thomas's meals early so that he could have time to eat at his leisure. He could feed himself by using elbow holders that stuck to the table. His arms were strong as she well knew. The weakness in his legs meant that he needed support when on the move, so when no one was handy he used his arms to propel his body about. Thus his shoulders and arms were exceptionally strong for a boy of his age. No one dared look sideways at his mother while Thomas was about or they could find themselves on the wrong end of a hard punch.

The pads were especially made so that he could control the cunningly designed fork and manage to feed himself. This was how he had been taught at school and it worked to his advantage. The only snag was that it took him such a long time to finish a meal. Rachel and Rebecca now often invited friends home to tea and it was an embarrassment to them. In his own way Thomas realized that he was being excluded from the family meal and, like the little boy that he was at heart, retaliated by being naughty.

Pushing the kitchen door open, Rachel took in the scene at a glance. Her brother sat at the table glaring at his mother. At first glance he appeared normal. His features were quite handsome except for a slight squint. He had his father's strong chin and dark, curly hair and even white teeth. Then, as he

217

moved awkwardly, it became apparent that he was handicapped. Thomas either didn't like the dinner his mother had prepared for him or he was letting it be known that he didn't like eating alone. Probably the latter as he enjoyed most food. He was deliberately scattering his vegetables and meat across the table. Rachel's lips closed in a tight angry line. He wasn't that backward that he didn't know what he was doing was wrong. Her mother was a saint to put up with him.

'It's a good slap across the knuckles he needs,' she cried in exasperation.

Annie swung around and faced her eldest daughter. 'Rachel! I didn't hear you come in.'

'That's not surprising, considering the racket he's making. You're too soft with him, so you are!'

Knowing that Rachel would keep on and on if she got the least bit of encouragement, Annie ignored her comments and patiently started to clean up the mess. It was no use explaining to her daughter that Thomas couldn't help himself. That it was the frustration of not being able to control his jerky movements, of taking longer than everyone else to comprehend things, that caused him to act up. He was well aware that he was being deliberately excluded from joining the family at meal times and wasn't the least bit happy about the arrangement. So sometimes, like now, he showed his objection. With a glare in his sister's direction, Thomas lowered himself from the chair and awkwardly propelled his body from the room.

When the door closed on him Rachel said softly, 'You're too soft with him, Mam. You've no life of your own. Lifting and laying him all the time.'

She drew back, startled, when her usually docile mother lashed out at her. 'And what about him? Do you think he doesn't understand all he's missing out on? Eh? Do you? Because he's backward doesn't mean he can't comprehend. It's all right for you and Rebecca, you can fly your kite, but him . . .' Her voice softened. 'I only wish I could help him more. I know he's better off than most cerebral palsied children, in that he can walk and watch TV. And I honestly think he can understand most of what he sees. That's what makes it so hard on him. He must desperately want to be like the lads he sees on TV. He has wants and needs just like the rest of us, you know.'

'I know that he understands a lot, Mam.' Rachel's voice was tentative. 'But do you really believe that he knows what he's missing out on? Is he not happy wrapped up in his own little world?'

'Yes, I do think he understands! He's aware enough to have he longings that any fourteen-year-old has. Still, there's nothing we can do about it. What we can do, however, is try to make life more pleasant for him and be more tolerant where he's concerned.'

Suddenly ashamed of her outburst, Rachel whispered, 'I'm sorry, Mam. I shall make an effort to be nice to him in future.'

Wearily Annie pushed the thick chestnut hair, now showing a scattering of silver, back from her brow. 'It's all right. You're only young. You don't do too badly really. Now tell me . . . how come you're home so early?' she asked, eyes roaming in admiration over her daughter's figure. High breasts, narrow waist and full hips. Clothed in a tight fine woollen sweater and the blue hip-hugging jeans that her father detested, she was as pretty as a picture, with those wide, dark-lashed blue eyes and bright chestnut hair.

Annie's thoughts strayed to her nephew. Liam must be a handsome young man by now. They could probably be taken for twins. They had exactly the same colouring and features. He would be coming of age soon. Annie could imagine how excited Sean would be if he knew he had a fine healthy son approaching his twenty-first birthday. Rosaleen must also sometimes ponder on how fate had robbed her son of his natural father.

Things had worked out all right for her. Gordon's father had financed his son to buy a partnership in the publishing business and eventually, due to the hard work put in by Gordon and Laura, it was once again a viable business and thriving. To Annie's great relief all talk of Rosaleen's coming over for a holiday had petered out. She had been too caught up in her own family affairs. Two years ago when Laura, at the age of twenty-five, had come into her inheritance, she and Gordon had married and last year had seen the birth of Rosaleen's first grandchild, a beautiful wee girl. George and Josie had gone over for the wedding but to Annie's relief Sean had just taken over a new department and couldn't afford any time off work so they had declined. If Rosaleen chose to come on holiday now, she might well be on her own. A couple of years ago Liam had got his high-school diploma at Orangeville Secondary School and was now attending the University of Toronto, studying to become a lawyer. Imagine, Sean's son a lawyer!

Rachel had moved to lean against the sink unit, her back to the window, and Annie brought her attention back to her. Her daughter's face was in shadow and Annie failed to notice the tell-tale blush that stained her cheeks. 'I felt unwell and took the afternoon off,' she lied.

'Ill? What's wrong with you? You look all right to me.'

'Just a tummy ache . . . you know what I mean.' What would her mother think if she told her that she had missed lectures to spend the afternoon with Desi McKernan? Desi who was in his final year at Queen's and with whom she was sure she was in love. Desi who was dark and intense and wrote lovely poems. They had spent hours roaming hand in hand around the Botanic Gardens, whilst he recited poetry to her. He had lifted her to great heights when he had kissed her; her first real, long, passionate kiss. She still tingled with pleasure when she remembered the feel of his body against hers. She had never been so close to a man before. Her mother would do her nut if she knew about it. Wasting an afternoon when she should be in class, and carrying on like that in the Botanic Gardens. What if someone had seen them? Rachel had been too mesmerized to notice anything but Desi. Thank goodness he hadn't put her to the test by asking her to prove how much she liked him. What would she do if he did? He made no secret of the fact that he didn't think it was wrong to kiss and pet. What if he asked her?

It would be unheard of! What if they got carried away and lost control? It didn't bear thinking about. Her da would kill her if she brought shame to their door. It was all right for Desi; the man never suffered any consequences. And, as far as she could make out, he was a genius. Didn't need to revise. Had total recall. He would sail through his exams while she would be constantly on her knees doing novenas, begging the Mother of God to help her get a pass. She really hadn't time to roam the parks listening to Desi McKernan recite poetry and worrying whether he would or he wouldn't chance his arm. It was the wrong time to fall in love. She hadn't asked for it to happen. At times she wished she had never met him. But Desi had caught her eye one day and had winked at her. He had deliberately singled her out after that, and now the very idea of life without him devastated her.

Moving closer, Annie peered into her daughter's face. 'You do look a bit flushed. Do you think you're sickening for something?'

Rachel moved restlessly away from her mother's keen gaze. 'No, I told you . . . it was just a tummy ache. I must have eaten something that disagreed with me. I'm all right now.' She stood strumming her fingers along the edge of the table. Annie waited in silence, aware that more was to come. 'Mam . . . can I bring a friend home to tea on Saturday night?'

'Oh, this one must be special. You're giving me plenty of warning.'

'Yes, as a matter of fact he is. And, Mam, could you possibly keep Thomas out of the way?'

'Now, tell me, Rachel, how can I do that?' Annie sounded reasonable but her daughter could tell she was annoyed.

'Could he go down to Grannie's for his tea?' she suggested, diffidently.

'And what if your friend becomes a regular visitor? What then, eh, Rachel?' Annie sighed and advised her daughter, 'You know, there's no need to be ashamed of your brother. He's not some kind of freak.'

'I'm not ashamed of him!' Rachel protested, aghast at the idea.

'No? Well, it sounds very much like it to me. Who is this friend then?'

'Desi McKernan.'

'Where did you meet him?'

'At uni.'

Annie silently debated with herself. The boy sounded presentable. Obviously a Catholic and at university. And Rachel didn't often ask for special treatment. 'All right, but just this once, mind you,' she warned. 'I'll get Mam and John to give

Thomas his tea. It's lucky for you he loves going down there and they're always delighted to have him.'

Rachel gave her a quick hug. 'Thanks, Mam. You're an angel. This means a lot to me.'

Sean wasn't so indulgent as Annie towards his two daughters. He'd heard the way the young men at work went on about their girlfriends. Some of them had no respect at all for the fairer sex, and from their conversation Sean judged that some of the girls had little respect for themselves. He didn't know what the world was coming to! So he tried to keep a tight rein on his daughters' comings and goings without appearing too protective. So far with very little opposition. Rachel and Rebecca did not seem interested in any particular boys. The ones they brought home were obviously just good mates. Now, however, a special young man was coming to tea. When he heard that Thomas was to be banished to his grannie's while Rachel's new boyfriend was introduced to the family, Sean forbade it.

Fully aware of the kind of reception she would receive, Annie had prudently waited until they were in bed before acquainting him of the situation. 'Sean, I told Rachel I would do it just this once.'

'Well, you had no right to tell her that! Have I no say in my own house?'

'Look, let this guy, who seems to be very important to our eldest daughter, get over the shock of meeting you first, mmm? Then he can meet Thomas.'

Sean's lips twitched. 'You make me sound like a tyrant or something.'

'Well, so you are where the girls are concerned. We want them to feel they can bring all their friends home, no matter what race, colour or creed.'

'Is he coloured? Is that what you're trying to tell me?'

'Of course not! Well . . . I don't think so. I never really asked. Even so, what difference would it make? Good heavens, he's only coming to tea.'

'Why does Thomas have to be out of the house? I'm surprised at you for allowing it. You always say he must be involved in everything we do.'

'I know that, but she must really want to impress this boy so I agreed. Just this once, I told her, he can go to me mam's. You know he loves going down there. John is so patient with him. Sometimes I think he understands him better than we do. They seem to be on the same wavelength!'

Sean had often thought the same thing. Once into his teens, Thomas had seemed to find a bond with his grandparents and it was a great help all round. Annie and Sean could go out to the pictures or to dinner without any unrest on Annie's part. Life was quite agreeable at the moment and she daily thanked God for all his goodness to them. Now Sean comforted her. 'We do our best, love. You especially. We can do no more.'

'I know that, Sean. I wasn't complaining. We've been very lucky. He could have been so much worse.' Resolutely she pushed the memory of the fine upstanding young man in Canada to the back of her mind. 'And the girls have been a credit to us,' she reminded him.

'So far, yes, they have,' he agreed.

'God forbid one of them should ever fall by the wayside,' Annie lamented. 'You'd never forgive them.'

'They've been brought up decently, Annie. They're big girls now and know right from wrong. So of course I wouldn't forgive them. They'd be shown the door.'

He sounded so adamant Annie felt fear enter her heart. Anyone could make a mistake after all. Emotions could get out of hand. Hadn't he an illegitimate son he knew nothing about, and him a married man at the time? Rosaleen had not conceived Liam by holding Sean's hand! However, she was in no position to throw this in his face.

'You don't really mean that, Sean?'

'I do, you know!'

Annie sighed and hoped he would never be put to the test. 'Well then, will you allow Thomas to go to Mam's on Saturday night?' She trailed her hand up and down his stomach.

He sighed contentedly 'Well now, I don't know . . .'

Her hand was slowly withdrawn and he pulled it back and raised it to his lips. 'Keep trying. I think you might be able to persuade me.'

223

Rachel rose early on Saturday morning and joined her mother and father in the conservatory for breakfast.

'My, my. What has you up so early?' Sean inquired.

'To hear you, anyone would think I never got up early. Remember, I'm out of the house at eight every morning, so I deserve a lie in at the weekend.'

'Exactly! I'm not refuting that. So, what's so different about today that you're up before nine?'

Rachel flashed a glance at her mother but Annie was reading the morning paper while she was getting the chance to do so in peace, before attending to her household chores, and failed to notice her daughter's plight.

'Did Mam tell you that I'm bringing a friend home to tea tonight?'

'Yes, she did indeed inform me that Thomas was to be banished to Orange Row tonight, while we entertain this friend of yours. Now why is that, Rachel? What's so important about this friend that you don't want him to meet Thomas?'

'Ah, Dad. You know how awkward he can be.'

'And what about that? Has this friend not got any compassion in him for the disabled?'

'He's the kindest person I've ever met,' Rachel cried defensively. 'He writes poems, so he does.'

Once more she sought help from her mother. Annie was turning the pages of the paper and this time Rachel managed to catch her eye. Gallantly, she came to her daughter's rescue. 'Sean, don't tease her.'

'But I'm not teasing, so I'm not! I'm dead serious. So he writes poems, does he? Does that make him something special, then?'

'In my eyes, yes.' Rachel was wary. She had a feeling there was more to come.

'And what kind of poetry does he write?'

'What do you mean?'

'Are they love poems or . . .' Sean paused when he saw hot colour flush his daughter's face. 'So it *is* love poems. Is he in love with you?'

Rachel glared at her father. Trust him to spoil things. 'We're just good friends, so we are, and I hope you won't spoil everything tonight by giving him the third degree.'

'Ah, that means that in spite of reciting love poems to you, he hasn't committed himself. It sounds to me like this guy prefers to hear himself talk. By all means bring him here tonight. I'm looking forward to meeting him. Maybe we'll be able to persuade him to give us a recital, eh?'

'Ah, Mam,' Rachel wailed in despair, and sent her mother another imploring look. Annie just shook her head at her and advised her husband, 'You'd better be careful, Sean. You might just be about to meet your match.'

He took an instant dislike to Desi McKernan. Tall, dark and handsome, he was obviously the answer to any young girl's dream. Sean could not put his finger on why he disliked him, but neither could he deny the feeling. But then, perhaps he would have reacted like this to any young man brought home by his daughter? He did so desperately want to protect them. Hiding his aversion behind a bright smile, he waited to be introduced to this young man who seemed to have won his daughter's heart.

Nervously, Rachel made the introductions. 'Mam, Dad, this is my friend Desi McKernan.' Her eyes pleaded with them to be nice to him.

Gripping his hand, Sean said politely, 'Hello, Desi. Whereabouts do you hale from?'

'Dunmore Street.'

'That's up the Springfield Road, isn't it?'

'That's right. Rachel told me that her mother was reared in Colinward Street, just up the road from it.'

Before Sean could question him further, Annie intervened. 'That's right! I know Dunmore Street well. Must have passed down it hundreds of times. I'm pleased to meet you, Desi. Welcome to our home.'

'It's a lovely place you have here, Mrs Devlin.' He looked appreciatively around the big hall and Annie could see that he was really impressed.

'It is that,' she agreed. 'Tea isn't quite ready. Sean, you take Desi into the sitting room while Rachel and I set the table.'

Reluctantly, she followed her mother into the kitchen.

Setting out the cutlery, she kept throwing imploring glances towards her mother who was unperturbed as she folded napkins and polished glasses. Annie wanted everything to be nice, but was annoyed that Rachel let this young man influence her so much.

'Mam, me dad won't interrogate him, sure he won't?'

'Has Desi anything to hide, Rachel?'

'Of course not.'

'Then I don't see what you're so worried about.'

'You know what me dad's like! He makes a mountain out of a mole hill. He'll find something wrong with him.'

'You're being a bit paranoid, love. Your dad isn't all that bad.'

Rachel didn't agree with her mother and her heart was heavy as she continued setting the table.

To make matters worse Rebecca arrived home just as they were about to sit down at the table. Normally she dined at her best friend's house on a Saturday and Rachel had taken this into account before inviting Desi home. Her sister had such a bubbly personality and Desi was susceptible to feminine charm.

'I forgot to tell you that I'd be home tonight, Mam. Moira's away to Dublin for the weekend with her cousins. Is there enough grub to go round?'

'Of course there is. I'll lift you some while you set a place for yourself.'

Desi's eyes followed Rebecca's movements as she set a place at the table. Dismay in her heart, Rachel reluctantly made the introductions.

'Desi, this is my sister Rebecca. Rebecca, meet Desi McKernan.'

Rebecca felt something like an electric shock go through her when her eyes met his. Managing to keep her cool, she pretended not to see the hand he offered her, and acknowledged him with a nod of her head. 'Hello there. Pleased to meet you.'

Slowly the hand was withdrawn. 'I've heard a lot about you from Rachel, but she never told me that you were beautiful.' His voice was soft, like a caress; he spoke as if they were the only ones in the room.

Rebecca blinked in surprise. No one else seemed to notice. Was it only to her ears that his voice appeared so seductive?

His words did have the effect, however, of bringing a frown to Sean's brow and hot colour to Rachel's face. Would Rebecca flirt with him? Oh, she hoped not! Her sister was so laid-back. Boys chased her all the time but she wasn't in the least bit interested in them. It would be just like her to fall for Desi.

Rebecca also frowned. She didn't like the effect he was having on her. She smiled sweetly at him. 'I'm afraid you need spectacles.'

For a moment he looked taken aback. He had also been aware of the current between them; had for a time forgotten where he was. This girl with the dark curly hair and intense blue eyes was to him the most beautiful one he had ever met. Quickly he regained his poise. 'I suppose it is only to be expected that Rachel's sister would be every bit as beautiful as her,' he said gallantly. Rachel lapped up the praise and smiled at him and the tension was broken.

During the remainder of the meal the conversation drifted from one subject to another. Indeed it was sometimes very witty as Sean subtly questioned Desi about his future plans in such a way that he divulged a lot without realizing it. Desi declared that he intended when – not if, but when – he got his exams to take a year off and tour America before settling down. Rachel's face fell when she heard this. He had never mentioned his intention to travel to her. Was she wasting her time? Too bad if she was! She was in love with him and could not help herself. Rebecca was relieved to hear he would not be around for long.

The following day, to Rachel's surprise, her sister cornered her in the kitchen after breakfast and offered a word of advice.

'I'd be careful if I were you. I'm pretty sure it's the same Desi I've been hearing about, and it's not all good news.'

'You're only pretty sure and you're willing to besmirch his character? How many Desis do you think there are in Belfast, eh?'

'It's not all that common a name. And the field narrows when they both live in Dunmore Street.'

Now she had Rachel's attention. 'What have you been hearing then?'

'Enough! He's a charmer. He loves the women and leaves them.'

'That's only because he hasn't met the right one yet. Girls throw themselves at him!' Rachel cried defensively.

'He also gets the name of being a troublemaker.'

'Just what do you mean, troublemaker?'

'To be truthful . . . I don't really know,' Rebecca confessed. 'But I'll find out! As you know, Moira Mullen lives in Spinner Street and I've heard his name mentioned in her house.'

'He can't help what people say about him.'

'I know that! Just be careful, Rachel. Don't give him your heart. You're young and lovely. You could have anyone you chose.'

Rachel's thoughts were bleak. It was no use being lovely if you had a retiring personality. Men wanted someone with a bit of go in them as a companion. Her shyness was ruining her chances where men were concerned. 'I wish everybody would mind their own business,' she muttered sulkily. 'I've only known him a short time. We're only friends, so we are!'

Annie had entered the kitchen unnoticed by them. Now she asked, 'Who's only friends?'

'Desi and me! Anybody would think I was about to marry him. Now will you all get off my back and let me run my own life?'

On this defensive note she flounced out of the kitchen. Annie and Rebecca exchanged worried looks.

'What did you think of Desi, Mam?'

'Let's be fair, Rebecca. He seems all right. You can't judge a person on one meeting.'

'Oh, Mam. You're so naive. He's a charmer, so he is!'

Annie gaped at her seventeen-year-old daughter in amazement. 'Me, naive?' she gasped.

'Yes, Mam. You wouldn't believe the half of what goes on nowadays! Our Rachel is too trusting, so she is.' Putting an arm around her mother's shoulders Rebecca hugged her close. 'Don't look so worried, Mam.'

'How can I help it, when a seventeen-year-old tries to put me wise?'

'Everyone is permissive now. Pressure is put on you to go with the crowd.'

'Just you remember, Rebecca,' Annie warned, 'if everyone else puts their hand in the fire, you need not follow suit. So watch yourself.'

'Don't worry, Mam. I'm too crafty to be caught out. It's our Rachel you need to worry about. She's so gullible!'

Annie latched on to the word 'crafty'. 'What do you mean, crafty? Just what are you up to?'

'Nothing! Nothing. Perhaps crafty is the wrong word to use. I mean, I'll save myself. I'll wait for the right man.'

That evening, when Annie told Sean of this conversation, she was amazed at his response.

'Rebecca said that? And here I was thinking my two daughters were still innocent young children. I don't know what the world's coming to, Annie. You should hear what some of the lads at work get up to with their girlfriends. It would make your hair curl. And they're actually proud of it.'

Annie sat in stunned silence as he ranted on. Now she asked tentatively, 'Do you think our Rachel would do anything stupid?'

'I should bloody well hope not! Why, if he so much as lays a finger on her and I hear tell of it, I'll break every bone in his body.'

Annie sat silent. What if, by the time he heard of it, it was too late? She decided that she must have a word in Rachel's ear and the sooner the better. Hadn't Rebecca said that her sister was too trusting? 'Gullible' was the word she had used. Anyone would think that she was the elder of the two, whereas Rachel was almost nineteen, surely old enough to know not to take any chances where men were concerned?

Rachel didn't take kindly to her mother's words of advice when, a week later, Annie managed to get her alone. 'What do you take me for, Mam? I'm not stupid you know!'

'That's all I want to hear. So long as you respect yourself, nothing bad will happen to you.'

Under her mother's piercing look Rachel actually quailed. She felt that her mother must somehow be aware that Desi was cooling off and of her own attempts to try to keep him interested. But she hadn't succeeded. He was definitely cooling off.

'Nothing is going to happen to me, Mam. For heaven's sake, our Rebecca is more likely to get into trouble than I am. She goes to all these dances and everything. I'm too busy studying to run about after boys.'

'Rebecca goes out with a crowd. There's safety in numbers, you know. I'd feel better if you weren't alone so much with Desi McKernan. When you like someone a lot, temptation is a terrible thing. And it is all too obvious that you are very fond of him.'

Realizing that her mother was really concerned, Rachel sought to reassure her. 'Don't worry, Mam. I'll be all right. I know what I'm doing.'

'I'm only thinking of you, love. Some men will promise you the earth to get what they want and then leave you in the lurch.'

'I know that, Mam, but Desi isn't like that. He's very kind to me.'

Oh, no? Annie thought. Weren't they all the same? The look she gave her daughter was sceptical, but to keep the peace she managed to hold her tongue.

A great believer in the old adage that trouble always come in threes, Annie's heart sank when a letter arrived from Orangeville. What now? Was more trouble, in the form of Liam, about to descend on them? She fingered the blue air-mail envelope gingerly for some moments before eventually tearing it open. A sigh of relief escaped her lips as she scanned the pages. Rosaleen was at last in a position to take a holiday and would be coming over to Belfast in a few weeks' time. She would be travelling alone and asked if there was anything in particular she could bring for Annie, and could she suggest something that would please her mother?

Grateful that her sister was travelling alone and therefore Liam did not pose any imminent threat, Annie was quite happy to break the news to the family at the dinner table that night.

'Sean, what do you think? Rosaleen is coming home for a holiday soon. She'll be staying with Mam and John but no doubt we shall see a lot of her. We will have to get her out and about a bit. A lot has changed since she was last over here.'

'What age is me Aunt Rosaleen now, Mam?' Rachel asked curiously.

'She's forty-eight, Rachel.'

'Quite old, isn't she?'

'Well, the last time I saw her she looked lovely. She's well preserved for her age. Do you not remember her at all?'

'For heaven's sake, Annie. It's fourteen years since she was last home,' Sean chastized her. 'Rachel was barely five years old.'

'Still, Dad, I do vaguely remember her. She was very blonde and had lovely bright green eyes like me mam's. Isn't that right?'

'Yes, and I bet she'll still be blonde and beautiful. She has all the time and money to pamper herself,' Sean said wryly.

Annie's heart sank at his words. Would he be smitten again?

'Perhaps if we're nice to her she'll ask us to visit her in Canada. Wouldn't that be lovely?' Rachel sighed at the idea.

'Don't count on it! She hasn't exactly bombarded us with invitations all these years, so why change now?' He sounded so bitter Annie turned a look of amazement on him. Had he resented it so badly? 'Besides,' he continued, 'your mother would probably forbid you to go.' He took the sting from his words with a wry smile at his wife.

'Oh, but Mam couldn't stop me now!' Rachel retorted. 'Sure you couldn't, Mam?'

Annie didn't raise her eyes from her plate. 'No, I don't suppose I could. But where would you get the money to go?'

'Maybe I'll go there on my honeymoon!'

All eyes swung to her. 'I'm only joking!' she cried, at their amazed expressions.

'I should certainly hope so. There'll be no wedding for you until you get your degree.'

Rachel shrank back in her seat at the threat she sensed in her father's words. 'If I meet Mr Right, I'll get married whether you like it or not!' she cried defiantly.

'Ah, so we have something to be thankful for after all,' Sean muttered. 'Do you hear that, Annie? William Wordsworth isn't Mr Right, after all. Isn't that a relief?' he asked sarcastically.

231

Thrusting her chair roughly away from the table, Rachel rose to her feet in a fury. 'I hate you! I hate the lot of you. Her!' Red-faced, her finger jabbed in a startled Rebecca's direction. 'She gets away with murder! But all I get is ridicule.' Her voice broke and tears fell. Without another word she fled from the room.

'Ah, Sean.' Annie threw her husband a reproachful look and rose to follow her daughter. 'There was no need to say that.'

Hands raised in entreaty, Sean asked his youngest daughter, 'Tell me, what did I do wrong?'

Rebecca's shoulders lifted and fell in a negative shrug and she sighed deeply. 'I think she really likes Desi, but because she isn't too sure of him, she won't admit it. Take it easy on her, Dad.'

'If he hasn't committed himself by now, she's well rid of him and his stupid poetry.'

'Dad, you don't understand. It's all right your talking like that. You and Mam met and fell in love and got married. I'm sure it was all like a fairy-tale. But these days it's different. And poetry isn't stupid. It must be very romantic to have someone recite to you.'

Her words had the effect of stilling Sean's tongue. Fairy-tale? Those first years together had been anything but magical. And it had been all his fault. So what right had he to tell other people how to act? Why, if Annie had known the half of it, she would have sent him packing.

'You're right, Rebecca. Only the people involved know the real truth. I'll hold my tongue in future and let nature take its course.' He was silent for some moments, but couldn't help adding, 'I only hope she meets someone else. I just don't like that Desi McKernan fellow.'

'Why, Dad? He seems all right to me.'

It was Sean's turn to shrug. 'To be truthful, Rebecca, I just don't know.'

With a light tap on the door, Annie entered the room shared by the two sisters. Rachel sat on the bed, arms around her knees, tight-lipped but dry-eyed. She threw her mother a resentful look.

Sitting on the edge of the bed, Annie sought to reason with

232

her daughter. 'You know, Rachel, there's no need to react like this. Your dad is only thinking of your welfare.'

'Huh! He never makes fun of Rebecca, so he doesn't. He's always picking on me.'

'He wasn't making fun of you. He only hopes you won't waste the talent that God has given you. There'll be plenty of time to marry and settle down later on. Besides, isn't Desi going to travel for a year before he seeks a post? That will give you plenty of time to make up your mind about him.'

Rachel swung her legs off the bed and moved closer to her mother. 'Mam, promise that you won't be angry at me and you won't tell Dad?'

Fear clutched at Annie's heart. What was she about to hear?

'I want to leave university,' Rachel confessed. 'I'm not good enough. I'll never pass my exams, and the worry of it is getting me down.'

Relieved, Annie assured her, 'Everyone feels like that, love. You will pass, I'm sure you will. You've got what it takes.'

'And how do you know how everyone feels? You've never been to university. You left school at fourteen and got a job as a stitcher, and it didn't do you any harm. And ... what if I don't pass? Eh, Mam? What if I fail?'

'Well, it won't be the end of the world. But you needn't worry, you will pass,' Annie insisted.

A sad nod greeted her words. 'I hope you're right. Oh, I do hope you're right. Dad will kill me if I fail. He's disappointed that Thomas will never go to university and all the pressure is put on me to prove myself.'

'Don't talk nonsense, Rachel! Your dad will understand if you fail. But, you see, you're so clever there's no way that you will.'

Rachel gave a deep sigh. What was the use of trying to make anyone understand? If she had to choose between a degree or Desi, he would win hands down. Would they be so understanding then? 'If you don't mind, Mam, I think I'll have an early night.'

Annie gazed into her daughter's drawn face and her heart lurched within her body at the pain she saw etched there. 'Is anything else worrying you, Rachel?' she probed.

The anxious note in her voice brought a wan smile to her

daughter's face. 'No, Mam, you needn't worry. I'm not hiding any dark secrets.'

Relieved, Annie rose to her feet. 'You have a good night's sleep, love.' At the door she hesitated. 'You didn't finish your dinner. Shall I bring you up a snack?'

'No, Mam, I just want to go to bed.' At the weary, defeated tone of her voice Annie felt like weeping. It was so hard to be young these days.

Slowly Annie descended the stairs. She found Sean in the kitchen up to his elbows in suds at the sink. Of Rebecca there was no sign.

'Where's Rebecca?'

'She's away up to visit Moira Mullen. She'll be packing her bags and going to live in Spinner Street if we aren't careful. She's never away from it lately. It seems she and Moira are going to the pictures. Tell me, Annie, how are we supposed to keep an eye on our daughters when they gallivant out nearly every night of the week?'

'Sean, they're young women now. We must trust them.'

'Rebecca isn't eighteen yet! You can't exactly call her a young woman.'

'Sean, I was seventeen when I met you, remember?'

'Yes, but I wasn't always trying to get you into bed the way the young lads do nowadays.'

A wide smile temporarily lifted the worry from Annie's brow. Going to him, her arm circled his waist as she reminded him, 'Maybe not bed. But I remember a couple of incidents when I had to be very firm with you.'

Drying his hands on a towel, Sean gathered her into his arms. 'That's just it. You were strong enough for both of us.' He planted a kiss on her brow. 'But what about them?'

'Rebecca's like me. She has the same nature. No one will take advantage of her.'

'What about Rachel, eh? Who does she take after?' To his dismay he was suddenly overwhelmed by a memory from the past, and buried his face in Annie's hair so that she couldn't see his guilty expression. What if Rachel was like her Aunt Rosaleen? Hadn't she succumbed to his passion and desire up at the Springfield Road dam? And as Annie had just pointed

234

out, a bed had not been necessary. He had vowed his undying
love but Rosaleen had called it lust and had berated him. She
had refused to marry him and had gone on with her plans to
marry Joe Smith. He brought his attention back to what Annie
was saying.

'I admit I worry a lot about Rachel,' she said. 'Lovely though
she is, she has no confidence whatsoever. She could very easily
be led astray.'

Pushing her gently away from him, he gazed down into her
face. 'Annie, if our daughters are anything like you, they will
be all right. Look . . . I put the remains of your dinner in the
oven to keep warm. You go and sit down and I'll bring it over.'

'No, I'm not hungry any more. But I would love a cup of
tea.'

'Right! I'm almost finished here. I'll put the kettle on and
we'll settle down in front of the TV. You see if there is anything
good on.' With a gentle push he headed her towards the door,
but his thoughts were sombre. He wished his daughters were
safely married to men who would take care of them. Was that
asking too much?

The episode at the dinner table had left Rebecca more disturbed than she cared to admit. Rachel was obviously still
besotted with Desi McKernan. Why couldn't her sister see that
Desi needed a strong woman; someone who would keep him
in line? Instead she moped about because he was seeing less
and less of her. It was no good hanging on if you weren't
wanted. At this rate she really would fail her exams, and then
what?

Leaving the bus at Willowbank Park, she hurried towards
the Broadway Cinema. Moira was already there, patiently
waiting.

'Come on. The queue went in ages ago! Hurry up, or we'll
miss the start of the show. As it is, we'll be lucky to get a good
seat,' she cried as she briskly led the way into the foyer.

'I'm sorry I'm late. I missed my usual bus.'

Mollified, Moira replied, 'Oh, it's all right. So long as we see
all of Glen Ford's picture, that's all that matters.'

'Isn't Glen Ford handsome?' Moira enthused later, as they left the picture house. 'He could put his boots under my bed any time, so he could.'

Rebecca smiled down at her petite friend. Glen Ford was too small for her taste; she preferred tall men. Gregory Peck would get her vote any day of the week. She had thought him wonderful in 'Duel in the Sun' with Jennifer Jones. Why did Gregory Peck bring to mind Desi McKernan? There was a slight resemblance, of course. They were both dark, handsome men with intensely blue eyes.

As if she had conjured him up from memory, suddenly Desi was standing in front of her, gazing down into her eyes.

'Hello, this is a surprise.'

His gaze was deep and searching; she felt he could see into her very soul and had great difficulty dragging her eyes away. Her heart did a somersault and she fought for control. 'What's so surprising about me being at the Broadway?' she retorted. 'For your information I go there quite often.'

His smile widened and she knew that he was aware of her turmoil. Moira had discreetly moved ahead and as Rebecca lengthened her stride to catch up with her, Desi gripped her elbow and drew her to a halt. 'How long are you going to keep this up?'

'I don't know what you mean.'

'You know quite well what I mean, Rebecca Devlin. You run like a scared rabbit every time you see me.'

'What about our Rachel, eh? Aren't you dating her?'

'Only because she won't let me break it off and I don't want to hurt her. Honestly, Rebecca, if she wasn't your sister I'd have finished with her ages ago. But because she is, I try to be kind to her.'

Moira had stopped and was waiting some distance ahead. Dismayed at the feeling of his hand on her arm, Rebecca angrily pulled it free. 'Look, even if you weren't involved with our Rachel, I'd have nothing to do with you. You're just not my type!'

They had stopped at Willowbank Park and, gripping her by the shoulders, he forcefully drew her over into the shadows. Before she could object his mouth covered hers. Appalled at the intensity of the passion that rose in answer to his, she struggled savagely. He must never, ever guess the effect he had on her. Rachel had met him first.

Abruptly, he released his hold on her and she fell against the railing, grabbing wildly at it to stop herself from falling. 'Have it your own way. But you mark my words . . . we're meant for each other and you know it!' With that he abruptly left her.

Rebecca gazed blindly after his tall figure striding down the road, until her friend's voice brought her back to her senses. 'Are you all right?' Moira hovered beside her anxiously. 'What was all that about?' In spite of herself she was agog with excitement. Imagine Desi McKernan kissing Rebecca Devlin like that! In public, and on the Falls Road of all places. And all those people getting off the bus to go to the second house in the Broadway had stopped to watch. 'I thought he went with your Rachel?'

Acutely aware of the curious glances being directed at them, straightening to her full height, Rebecca assured her, 'He does. He was just being obnoxious. Come on, let's forget about him. Am I still invited to your house for a cup of tea?'

'Of course you are.' Moira gave her a sideways glance. 'Our Brian would never forgive me if you went home without calling in. Mind you, Rebecca, you could do worse than our Brian. He's daft about you, you know.'

Rebecca gave her a wry smile. Didn't she wish with all her heart that she could fancy Moira's quiet, dependable but dull brother? And she *had* liked him. Had not thought him in the least dull until Desi had come on the scene and turned her world upside down. Now he plagued her every waking thought. He was always on her mind. If only Rachel could see how unsuited they were, perhaps she could . . . Pushing these unwelcome thoughts to the back of her mind, she linked her arm through her friend's and they dandered down the Falls Road in silence, each lost in their own thoughts.

'Are you all right, Rebecca?' George glanced sideways at his young niece as he guided the car through the busy evening traffic in Belfast city centre. Rebecca was babysitting for Jamie tonight and he had never known her to be so quiet. There was a bad 'flu bug doing the rounds and he voiced his concern. 'Do you think you might be sickening for the 'flu?'

'No, honestly, Uncle George. I feel fine. Just a bit tired.'

Josie met them in the hall, dressed and ready to go out. They had not been out much since the birth of their son and she was quite excited at the thought of a night at the pictures followed by a meal at their favourite place, the International Hotel. 'This is kind of you, Rebecca,' she enthused. Then her gaze sharpened and she asked anxiously, 'Are you feeling unwell? Don't be afraid to say, mind! We can always go out another evening.'

Forcing a smile to her lips, Rebecca replied wanly, 'I'm fine, Josie.'

Deciding not to look a gift horse in the mouth, George took his wife's elbow and urged her gently in the direction of the door. 'Well, so long as you're sure. Let's go, Josie. We might be late home, Rebecca, so if you're tired don't wait up. And thanks again.'

Thankfully she closed the door on them and then made her way to the small room that was now a nursery. She gazed down at the sleeping child with unseeing eyes. Why had she let Desi McKernan know that she was babysitting here tonight? He was always asking her out, so she could have declined as usual. There had been no reason to tell him that she was babysitting for Josie and George. She was well aware that he knew where they lived. It had really been an invitation for him to come. And he would! She was sure of that. They would be alone here for hours. Would she be able to handle him?

Twenty minutes later there was a knock on the door. Bracing herself, Rebecca went to open it. She had decided that her best course of action was to send him away.

He stood on the doorstep, a bottle of wine in one hand, a box of chocolates in the other. A happy grin split his face and made her go weak at the knees. Her heart thumped within her breast when his eyes met hers.

'What are you doing here?'

'Ah, now, Rebecca, I was invited. Remember?'

'I did not invite you to come here.'

'Not in so many words . . . but invite me you did. And you know it! How else was I to learn you'd be here, all on your own, with just a little baby for company? Are you not going to invite me in?'

Reluctantly she moved to one side and he entered the hall, bringing with him that warm sensuous feeling that seemed to reach out and engulf her in his presence. It was going to be a long evening. How would she be able to control him when she wanted to be close to him, to get to know him? When she wanted to be held gently against him – not like that episode up at Willowbank Park! But miracles like that didn't happen. So her only course of action was to get rid of him as quickly as possible.

She was wrong. The evening started off on an easy, friendly footing and slowly got better. It was a wonderful time. All her fears had been for nothing. Desi behaved like a gentleman from start to finish. They sprawled on the sheepskin rug in front of the fire, and drank the wine and ate cheese and crackers, and talked and laughed like old friends. The firelight cast mysterious shadows on his face and she felt more attracted to him than ever. He really did resemble Gregory Peck, as he had been in 'Duel in the Sun', dark, mean and dangerous.

They discovered that they had a lot in common, only disagreeing on one issue. Desi was caught up in the fever that gripped the youth of Northern Ireland at that time. Although 1966 had been a troubled year, so far 1967 had been quiet. Rebecca thought that Terence O'Neill should be given a chance to fulfil his promises. Had he not sworn to do great things? Would marches at this point not upset the apple cart? Desi assured her that any marches or demonstrations would be conducted in an orderly manner. He reminded her that she had a job and a beautiful home but not everyone was so fortunate. They had the right to fight for better jobs and better housing. He confessed he had joined the Civil Rights Association that had recently been formed in the International Hotel. He also assured her that all marches would be conducted in an orderly, peaceful way.

Nevertheless, she was worried. She understood his point of view but did not think that marches and demonstrations, orderly or otherwise, would make any difference. She backed O'Neill to the hilt and hoped he would fulfil his promises. So they agreed to differ. They talked and argued about everything

239

else under the sun and she fell more and more under Desi's spell. Time flew by and at eleven o'clock he surprised her by saying that he must go; a friend was picking him up in his car.

A bit disappointed, she managed to hide it and fetched his coat from the cloakroom. In the hall he took her gently in his arms and held her close, just as she wanted him to. His eyes twinkled down at her. 'I think I've surprised you tonight, haven't I, love?' he teased gently. 'You thought I wasn't capable of friendship with a woman but, Rebecca Devlin, the minute I set eyes on you, I knew that you were the one for me! I love you, and by hook or by crook, one day I'll make you admit that you love me.'

Hot colour flooded her face at this passionate declaration. 'What about our Rachel?' she cried in anguish. 'She'll be so hurt if she finds out.'

He kissed her lightly on the lips. 'Rachel doesn't love me. She's only angry that I tired of her first. Her feelings for me are only superficial. Look, if it's any easier for you ... let's keep our friendship a secret for a while. When Rachel falls in love with someone else, as she's bound to, we'll be free to tell the world about our love. Just let me see you sometimes, Rebecca, please?'

'I don't know! I don't like being sly and deceitful. It's just not my nature.'

'At least admit that you're attracted to me?' Receiving no apparent response, he pleaded, 'Even a little? Mmm?'

Head down, she thought about all the other girls she knew of that he had loved and left. Why should it be any different with her?

Hand under her chin, he raised her face towards his. 'Rebecca, I know I've been a fool in the past and I've earned myself a bad name with the girls. But I'm a changed man! I just didn't believe that I could be swept off my feet by a beautiful face. I didn't know that something as wonderful as you could happen to me. Why, if I couldn't see you again, I'd die. I mean that, Rebecca. I can't stop thinking about you. Give me a chance to prove my love for you. Eh, sweetheart?'

She raised her eyes to his and the breath caught in his throat at the love he saw there. God, he didn't deserve a girl like her; so pure and innocent. So many others had passed through his

240

hands and this he regretted now. From here on there would be only her. He would never cause her pain, he vowed silently. Never! So help him God. Slowly his head bent and she rose on tip-toe to meet his lips. Then, as her body fused against his, she knew that he was her other half. They clung together for long moments, savouring their closeness. At the sound of a car's horn outside, he resolutely put her from him. 'I'd better go now, love, before I do something we'll both regret. Will you come to the pictures with me on Monday night?'

Unable to find her voice, she nodded mutely.

'I'll see you at the bottom of Castle Street, outside Anderson McAuley's, at seven o'clock. All right, love?'

One again she nodded and then with a final brush of his lips against hers, he was gone. For some time she stood with her head pressed against the cool wood of the oak door. She was all atremble, on fire with desire. Her heart pounded and her lips felt bruised and tender from his kiss. God help her! No matter what Rachel or her father thought, no matter whom she might hurt by her actions, she was in love with Desi McKernan. Was there any hope for them? There had to be! There just had to be! In a happy daze she tidied up and retired to bed before George and Josie returned, not wanting idle banter to spoil the wonderful sensuous thread of happiness that bound her.

Although the tension of the previous evening was replaced by a relaxed happy mood, Josie was not deterred from her determination to get to the bottom of Rebecca's apparent unhappiness the night before. It was Saturday but George was going into work for a couple of hours, so once he left the house Josie questioned her niece. 'I'm happy to see you looking so much better this morning. Did Jamie wake at all last night?'

'No, he never budged. He was as good as gold.'

Mindful of the fact that there was an empty wine bottle in the dust bin, and that Josie might possibly see it, Rebecca decided to be truthful.

'I've a confession to make, Josie. I hope you don't mind, but I wasn't alone here last night. A friend called to keep me company.'

Relieved to find that it had probably been a lover's tiff that

241

had caused Rebecca's misery, Josie said, 'That's all right. Why on earth should we mind?'

'It was a man friend.'

'Well, I guessed as much. Although I wasn't aware you were seeing anyone. Not that it's any of my business,' she hastened to add. Curiosity made her ask tentatively, 'Is it serious?'

'Yes, I think so,' Rebecca said softly and Josie was surprised to see a glow of love in her eyes. 'You see, I've never felt like this before about any man,' she admitted. 'So I don't really know.' Worried eyes met Josie's. 'It's all so complicated! I don't know what to do for the best.'

Afraid of how vulnerable this young girl was, Josie warned, 'Remember, love, you wouldn't be the first to mistake infatuation for love. Especially as you have never felt like this before. Sometimes the wrong man can awaken emotions so strong they blind you to everything else. Is he married, love?'

'Oh, no! No, he's free ... well, sort of. He isn't married, Josie, or engaged for that matter. But he is in a way committed to someone else. I can't tell you anything more about it now. Later, when things get sorted out, I'll bring him to meet you and George. I would value your opinion of him.'

A cry from the nursery brought both of them to their feet. As they hurried to attend to the child, Josie warned, 'Be careful, won't you, Rebecca? You have your whole life in front of you. Promise me you won't do anything rash? You'll only regret it for the rest of your life.'

'I won't. I promise I'll be careful.'

The weeks before Rosaleen's visit passed in a flurry of excited preparations. Thelma and John had the decorators in. Every room must be freshly papered and painted in Rosaleen's honour. Remembering the opulence of her sister's home, Annie also spent a lot of time and money. All the things that they had been putting off till tomorrow suddenly took on a new urgency that had Sean protesting as his every spare moment was spent repairing this and painting that. At last Annie was able to look around her home with pride. She might not be able to compete with Rosaleen's splendour, but she could at least make sure that everything was shipshape.

The morning of her sister's arrival dawned and Annie threw

the curtains wide. It was a perfect morning. Pink clouds scudded across a bright blue sky and reflected on the still waters of the lough. She exclaimed with delight, 'Oh, look, Sean. It's a beautiful day. I'm glad our Rosaleen will be arriving in fine weather. What time will you be leaving here?'

'Well now, her flight gets in at three . . . it takes about five hours to get to Shannon. Just to be on the safe side and give us plenty of time.'

'It's seven now! I'd better get the girls up. Do you want to use the bathroom first?'

'You bet!' Sean rose from the bed with alacrity and headed for the door. 'Those two will be in there all morning. You'd think it was royalty we were going to meet, instead of their Aunt Rosaleen.'

'I have to admit that I feel excited too. I'm looking forward to seeing her.'

He paused in the doorway. 'I know you are, love. And I'm glad to see it! Glad that at last the past is over and done with.'

Annie managed to keep her smile in place, but her happiness was dimmed. How different her feelings would be if Liam was coming with his mother. But he wasn't, so a good time should be had by all.

Once the car left the driveway, Annie spent the morning fussing about with unnecessary energy putting the house in order, and the afternoon preparing the meal she was cooking in Rosaleen's honour. She was dining with them before going to stay with her mother and John. Thelma had hinted that she would like to be there when Rosaleen arrived but Annie had pretended not to notice. She wanted her sister to herself for a few hours to catch up on all the news.

During the last few days Thomas had spent most of the time in his room away from the last-minute flurry of excitement. He disliked change and was aware that something important was happening. Now he sat at the kitchen table and watched as his mother chopped vegetables and stuffed and dressed the large chicken. When Annie started to set the table, and he saw her put the elbow supports out, his eyes brightened and he gazed at her in delight.

'Yes, Thomas, tonight you're dining with us. Does that please you?' He nodded his head vigorously and Annie's eyes filled with tears. It took so little to please him. Silently she vowed that when the girls got married and left home, she would devote all her time on him.

Glancing at the clock, she came to a decision. 'Thomas, I think we shall have a break now. I'll make us a cup of tea and then we'll sit down and look through some of your books. Would you like that?' His smile brought the tears once more to the surface and as she hurried to fill the kettle, she furtively brushed them away. Definitely, she would spoil him rotten when the girls left home, no matter what. He had so little to look forward to.

Rosaleen was, as Annie had expected, slim, blonde and beautiful. Even after the long journey, dressed in a figure-hugging suit of moss green, make-up perfect, every hair in place, she managed to look like a film star. Annie immediately felt overweight and plain.

Gathering her sister into her arms, she hugged her close and exclaimed generously, 'You look beautiful, Rosaleen. And, oh, but it's lovely to see you again. Did you have a good journey?'

'It's good to see you too, Annie.' Rosaleen warmly returned her sister's embrace before replying. 'The flight was smooth and the car drive up from Shannon was wonderful.' She smiled over her shoulder at the girls. 'Your two delightfully witty daughters kindly kept me entertained all the way up here.'

'You've never met Thomas.' Annie drew her forward. 'This is our son.'

Rosaleen examined her nephew, and Annie prepared herself for the pity she was sure would follow. But no! Reaching out, Rosaleen took Thomas's hands in her own. 'My, what a fine big boy you are. I'm very pleased to make your acquaintance, Thomas.' She offered him her arm. 'Perhaps you will escort me indoors?' Her action brought a joyous smile to her nephew's face and, clinging to her arm, he shuffled proudly towards the steps.

Annie's heart filled with gratitude. So many people were embarrassed in the company of the disabled that it was great to see her sister making an immediate impression on Thomas. She glanced at Sean and saw that he too was impressed by his sister-in-law's perceptiveness. He gave his wife a nod of approval and hurried forward to lead the way into the house.

It was with regret that Rosaleen rose to her feet some time later and prepared to go down to her mother's. She stretched languorously and all eyes travelled over her slim figure. 'I've really enjoyed myself,' she declared. 'The meal was scrumptious, Annie. I'm afraid I made a pig of myself! I only hope Mam hasn't a spread laid on for me.'

Sean hid a smile as his wife smiled in pleasure at these words. 'She will have, you know!' Annie stated. 'But she can't say she wasn't warned. I told her I'd be cooking a meal for you.'

'Thanks, Annie, for everything. And thank you, for collecting me from the airport, Sean. And a final thanks to you all for making me feel so welcome.'

'We're only too pleased to have you, Rosaleen. And sure we'll see plenty of you while you're here. We'll have to arrange some outings. Is there anywhere in particular you would like to go or see? Things have changed a lot here in the last fourteen years. You won't recognize some of the places now.'

'Anything you arrange will be fine by me, Annie. Meanwhile, I'd better be on my way. But first, a kiss for my favourite nephew.'

Thomas hung his head shyly but nevertheless let her kiss him on the brow.

'I'll run you down, Rosaleen. Want to come with us, Thomas?' Sean offered his son his arm and he gripped it tightly.

'Thank you, Sean. You're very kind.'

Mother and daughters stood on the step and waved them off, then returned indoors to clear up the kitchen.

'She's very attractive, Mam,' Rachel mused as she filled the sink with water. 'And so young-looking. Why, she could pass for someone in her early thirties.'

'She certainly could, Rachel.'

'I wish I was blonde.'

'Why?' asked Rebecca. 'You have grand hair. Be content with what you have, Rachel. Aunt Rosaleen might be lovely, but I bet it costs a bomb to keep her hair that colour.'

'You think it's dyed?' Rachel asked in surprise.

'Well, if not dyed, at least brightened. She's too old for it to be natural.'

Annie intervened. 'I think you just might be wrong there, Rebecca. Rosaleen was always very fair. When she was young her hair was like pure silver.'

'OK, have it your way. But I'll find out. I'll ask her.'

'You will do nothing of the kind, Rebecca,' Annie cried warningly. 'You will mind your own business. How would you feel if someone asked you if you dyed your hair? Huh!'

'All right! All right! Live in ignorance if you must.'

As predicted, they saw a lot of Rosaleen. One or other of the girls agreed to sit in with Thomas on a Saturday night and the old jaunt down to McVeigh's was renewed. Annie found herself enjoying her new lease of life, as she laughingly called it. Sean was glad to see her take an interest in her appearance again and was quick to praise the new hairstyle Rosaleen had encouraged his wife to adopt. Her long tresses were gathered on the top of her head, wound into curls and held in place with unseen hairpins. It made her face appear thinner and younger and called attention to her long slim neck.

He arranged a week's holiday off work and, accompanied by Thomas, he and Annie took Rosaleen on a tour of Donegal. They had booked into the Port-Na-Blagh Hotel set on the hillside with panoramic views. From there they set out each morning after a scrumptious breakfast and toured the country-side, travelling through breathtaking scenery to all the nearby towns and villages. One day was spent taking in the beauty of the Atlantic Drive, finishing up watching the fishing boats in Bunbeg harbour. Another day they pottered around the shops in Dungloe and Letterkenny, returning each evening to the hotel and a perfect meal; later unwinding over a drink in the lounge overlooking a magnificent view of the Atlantic Ocean and rugged coastline. The beauty and tranquillity of it made Sean vow that they would return the following year.

During breakfast one morning, watching some golfers on the links opposite the hotel, they discovered that Rosaleen was a keen golfer. 'That's one of the things I've missed since Andrew died. He taught me how to play.'

'I didn't realize you played, Rosaleen?' A surprised Annie

246

turned a wondering look on her sister. Imagine Rosaleen being interested in golf!

'You sound surprised. But let me tell you, I'm quite proficient at it. Andrew saw to that! Do you play at all, Sean?'

'I used to, Rosaleen, but I work such long hours it's about two years since I've had a round.'

'Could we not borrow or hire some golf clubs and have a few rounds up at Fortwilliam?'

'That's a very good idea, I'll see what I can do.' However, by the look on Annie's face they were both aware that it was something that was highly unlikely to come about.

The weeks passed and although Rosaleen, no matter where she happened to be, phoned home nearly every night, she showed no inclination to return to Canada. She was content to wile away the time with her family, even going out to dances in the Orpheus and Club Orchid with the girls who gave a running commentary to their parents on their aunt's popularity. She never sat out a dance, and one night two men almost came to blows over her. She was having a great time. Convinced that she would soon tire of running about, Annie was not unduly worried by her sister's extended visit.

However, as Christmas approached, the announcement that her young niece Patricia would be joining Rosaleen for a time over the festive season did cause Annie some apprehension. What if Liam too decided to spend his Christmas break here? Sensing her sister's unease, Rosaleen explained to her and all in general that Liam would not, on this occasion, be accompanying his sister as he had met a young lady in whom he was very interested and would be spending Christmas at her parents' home. Relieved though she was to hear this, there was nevertheless fear in Annie's heart that her sister might indeed decide to stay in Belfast. All the signs were beginning to point in that direction.

Heaven knows, she was causing a big enough stir down in McVeigh's. What if she got interested in one of the young men who hung on her words every Saturday night, and decided to stay put? And why not! What did it matter that they were all younger than her? She was lonely and certainly didn't look her age, and the well-known fact that she wasn't short of a bob or two would certainly encourage any young man. She had confessed to Annie that during their marriage, Andrew had discouraged her from too much socializing. Rosaleen had realized that he did not want her to meet and mix with men her own age; men younger than him. At the time she had not worried about it; had been content with her lot. But once the funeral was over and everybody had returned to their own lives, she had realized just how isolated she was in her beautiful home, with just the children for company. 'But what if Liam decided to come too?' Annie asked in despair.

Rosaleen had hired a small car to use during her stay and each morning drove up to have a coffee with Annie. Some days they went into town and wandered around the shops, and others they would go for a drive out into the countryside. Today, they were going over to Bangor to visit Josie. Rosaleen concentrated on her driving before answering.

'I don't know, Annie! I honestly don't know how things will work out. This is what comes of telling lies in the first place.'

'You're not suggesting that we should confess to Sean now? You can't possibly tell him after all these years. Promise me you won't, Rosaleen?'

Annie's despairing wail brought quick assurances from her sister. 'Of course I won't! That will be your decision. Your decision alone. I told you that years ago and I would never go back on my word.'

'I will never tell him, Rosaleen,' Annie vowed. 'That you can count on. Why . . . he would never forgive me.'

'What if Patricia likes it here and I decide to stay, Annie? What then?' She sounded wistful and Annie's heart sank.

'But you won't do that, sure you won't, Rosaleen?'

'I don't know! I don't know what I'm going to do. I'm enjoying myself here, so I am. Liam was glad of the excuse to move to a flat nearer the university when I said I was coming over. Now that he has had a taste of freedom he won't want to live at home, especially with a girl involved. You should hear him on the phone! He's having a whale of a time. And it's only right that he should be free. Not tied to my apron strings. As for Patricia, she simply loves staying with Laura and Gordon. They live close to her school and she has friends nearby to visit. If I return, she and I will be lonely living by ourselves in that big house.'

They drove in silence for some moments, each lost in their own thoughts. It was Rosaleen who broke it. 'To be truthful, Annie, I'm thinking of putting the house on the market,' she admitted. 'I've already asked Gordon to put out some feelers on the housing front. He says we should get a generous price on it.'

Her words brought Annie upright in her seat. 'You can't, Rosaleen! You just can't do that!'

'Why not, Annie? Why not, eh? Listen to me, I've been giving this a lot of thought. If I stay here, I'll buy a house at the far end of town. Probably out at Dundonald, away from you. Sean and Liam need never meet. If he comes over on a visit, surely between the two of us we could manage to keep them apart? Once Liam meets the right girl he'll settle down and I'll probably have to fly over there if I want to see anything of him. It will work out all right, you'll see!'

'Oh, yes, that would be something wonderful to look forward to. Keeping them apart! But what about everybody else? What about the girls? And me mam? Do you think they won't notice? Catch yourself on, Rosaleen! Your desire to stay is blinding you to reality. The cat would be out of the bag in no time at all.'

Suddenly Annie's brows drew together and she gazed suspiciously at her sister. 'Or . . . is that what you want? Do you think Sean would turn his attention to you again? Is that what you think? Has he shown any inclination in that direction?'

'Don't be so silly, Annie. I think no such thing! You're getting paranoid again. And the way you've been watching us, do you think you wouldn't have noticed if we still fancied each other? I'm sick, sore and tired of the way you scrutinize every move we make. It's so embarrassing! If you must know,' she finished defiantly, 'I've met someone else.'

Annie sat silent for some moments, her mind in a turmoil. Was it so obvious that she kept an eye on them? She hadn't thought so and Sean hadn't remarked on it, and he was not one to hold his tongue. Surely he would have pointed out to her how foolish she was being? Unless, of course, he was pulling the wool over her eyes. Oh, God, she cried inwardly, help me to trust him. Rosaleen's last words resurfaced in her mind and she cried in bewilderment, 'Who? Who have you met?'

'An old friend from the past. Remember Pat McDade? I went up to visit Amy and Bobby . . . you remember Joe's mother?' Annie nodded. Of course she remembered. She wasn't senile! Rosaleen continued, 'Well, we went down to the Clock Bar for a drink and he was there. I've been out with him a few times,' she admitted. 'He's a widower, Annie. His two children are married. He says he never really got over me.' Her voice had gone all dreamy. 'Imagine that! Pat still has a crush on me after all these years,' she purred.

Annie laughed derisively. 'And you believe him? Huh! If you believe that you'll believe anything. You're a fool, so you are. If he felt that strongly about you, how come he got married then, eh?'

'Why not? People do, you know. Not everyone is as lucky as you and gets the one they want,' Rosaleen said stiffly, obviously offended by her sister's attitude.

'What about you, Rosaleen? You've been married twice. You must have loved Joe when you married him, but what about Andrew? Was he second best? I've always wondered about that. Is Pat McDade really your reason for staying?'

'You're raking over dead ashes, Annie Devlin!' Rosaleen cried in frustration. 'I can't believe that you're still jealous of me after all this time.'

Annie's shoulders slumped and she admitted sadly, 'No, not jealous. Afraid of your selfishness.'

'Selfishness? You think me selfish for wanting to stay where I was born and reared?'

'Yes, I do. Your children are out in Canada. You'll regret it if you don't return. Everything here is a novelty to you at the moment. If you stay it will become humdrum. You'll soon miss that beautiful big house of yours, and all that land. You'll not be able to find anything to compare with it over here, you know.'

They had arrived at Josie's bungalow and before leaving the car Rosaleen gripped her arm. 'That's just it, it's far too big! Look, you're just worried where Sean is concerned. In your heart you know there's nothing left between him and me. You've nothing to fear, so stop worrying. Good God, it was

250

only a one-night stand! I'm sure it happens in a lot of families and no one is any the wiser.'

'You've got it wrong, Rosaleen,' Annie lied. 'It's your utter selfishness I'm worried about. You've everything a woman could hope for. Good looks, money, two daughters and a wonderful normal son . . . and still you're not satisfied. But what goes round, comes around. If you stay in Belfast we'll all live to regret it, I know we will. So don't expect me to make it easy for you by giving you my blessing.'

She angrily pulled her arm free and left the car, leaving Rosaleen in a daze. Would she really regret it if she stayed? Oh, why did Liam have to resemble his father so much? If only he had looked like her side of the family, everything would have been dandy.

Rosaleen had first met Josie when she and George had been over for Laura's wedding. They had liked each other but had not spent much time together, what with all the hurly-burly of the wedding and George insisting that they see a bit of Canada whilst they had the opportunity, touring the surrounding countryside and even spending a couple of days at Niagara Falls. Since her arrival in Belfast, Rosaleen had visited Josie often and they got on like a house on fire. Today she was at once aware of the tension between the two sisters. 'Is anything wrong?' she asked tentatively.

Annie laughed, determined not to spoil the occasion. She could see that Josie had gone to a lot of trouble. The best china was out and some wine glasses were ready on a small occasional table. 'Never mind us, Josie. You know what sisters are like. We've agreed to differ. So let me have hold of that lovely cuddly wee baby of yours. How is he coming on at the walking?'

She took the gurgling child from his mother's arms and lifted him high. He screamed with delight. 'He's lovely, Josie. You're very lucky.'

'I know that. And, thank goodness, he's coming on great at the walking. He's going around the furniture and after all he is only eleven months. And wait till you hear this! I just learnt for sure at the weekend that there's another one on the way. I got a couple of bottles of wine in so we can celebrate the big occasion.'

251

'Congratulations! That's wonderful news, isn't it, Rosaleen?' Anne said, turning to her sister.

Rosaleen graciously accepted the olive branch. 'It is indeed. You don't mind them so close together, Josie?' she asked gently.

'No! We were beginning to think that we weren't going to have any. It gave us a scare, I can tell you. So we're absolutely delighted we will have at least two.'

'Then I'm glad for you.' Rosaleen gave her a quick hug and for the time being all their own problems were put on a back burner.

A couple of glasses of wine mellowed them and Rosaleen played contentedly on the rug with Jamie while the others retired to the kitchen to make the tea. But Annie's peace of mind was once more to be threatened.

Filling the kettle, Josie gave her a wry smile and confessed, 'You know, when you first arrived I thought perhaps you were worried about Rebecca. Have things worked themselves out then?'

A puzzled frown gathering on her sister-in-law's brow warned Josie to be wary and not open her big mouth too far. She groped about for something to say to cover her blunder. Annie was obviously in the dark where her youngest daughter was concerned.

'I don't understand? What do you mean?'

Flustered, Josie tried to retrieve the situation. 'I just thought she was a bit unhappy the last time that she babysat for us. I thought maybe a lovers' tiff was the cause?'

'She hasn't got a boyfriend. At least, no one in particular that I'm aware of.'

Josie smiled brightly and, removing the cover, lifted the tray of sandwiches she had prepared earlier. 'Well then, I was clearly wrong. Would you put that tea cosy on the pot and carry it in for me, please? Bring that plate of cakes too.'

To her relief, Annie did not pursue the matter in front of Rosaleen. Josie would have to make sure that Rebecca knew that she had almost let the cat out of the bag and that her mother would surely question her. Towards tea-time she began to panic. If they didn't leave soon she would be too late to catch Rebecca at work.

'Is Thomas not due home from school soon?' she at last ventured to ask.

'Oh, didn't I mention that Rebecca was off work today? She woke with awful stomach pains this morning and called in sick, so she'll be there for him.'

A cold sweat enveloped Josie. Sick? She herself had been sick that morning, and with good reason. Was Rebecca in the same boat? And if her boyfriend wasn't married, why all the secrecy?

Some time later, she waved them off. As soon as the car left the drive, she was back inside and on the phone. It was answered on the second ring. Disappointment clouded Rebecca's voice when Josie made herself known. 'Who were you expecting? This mysterious boyfriend?' Guilty about her disclosures to Annie, she could not keep the sarcasm out of her tone.

'There's nothing mysterious about him!' Rebecca cried defensively.

Ashamed of her outburst, Josie hurried on, 'Look, I'm ringing to let you know that I almost let the cat out of the bag this afternoon, so your mother might ask you some awkward questions when she gets home. But she knows nothing! I'm sorry if I was a bit indiscreet but I was sure all would be resolved by now.' The unspoken question hung in the air but Rebecca did not rise to the bait.

'Thank you for ringing me, Josie. I must go now, I'm pre-paring tea.'

'You've got over your sickness then?'

'Yes, it was just a tummy upset. I'm fine now.'

'I've some good news. I'm expecting another baby.'

'Oh, that is wonderful news!' Rebecca cried in delight. 'Remember, you said that I could be godmother to the second one?'

At her warm tone of voice Josie knew her fears were unfounded. If Rebecca were pregnant there was no way she could react like this to Josie's good news. Wishing her luck, she rang off.

Rebecca slowly replaced the receiver and blinked back tears. It was four days since Desi had attempted to contact her. She hadn't really thought it was him on the phone; she had warned him never to call her at home. But even at work he hadn't tried. Had he tired of her already? Was she to suffer the same fate as the others? She wouldn't have believed that he could treat her like this.

She was glad that she had been forewarned because as soon as she arrived home her mother joined her in the kitchen. She was far from discreet, coming straight to the point, as a matter of fact.

'Are you carrying on with somebody, eh?'

'What on earth makes you think that?'

'Josie mentioned you were unhappy about something. She thought perhaps it was a lovers' tiff.'

'And you immediately jump to the conclusion that I'm carrying on? Huh! The faith you have in me.'

Annie ran a hand wearily over her face. 'I'm sorry, love. I have so much on my mind lately, I don't know whether I'm coming or going. Do you forgive me?'

'Of course, Mam. What has you all upset?'

'It's a long story. Perhaps some day you will hear all about it, but meanwhile I must suffer alone.' Seeing the worried look on her daughter's face, she cried, 'Never mind me! I'll be all right. But remember, love . . . I'm here if you need me. Don't you ever forget that.'

Rebecca climbed the Serpentine Road with feet that dragged. It was now a week since she had last heard from Desi and she was in despair. If she had any pride at all she should be the one to stand him up. Near the top of the road relief flooded through her, quickly followed by anger when she recognized him standing close to the hedge. How dare he? How dare he turn up and expect her to meet him? It was unwise really to meet so close to home but Rachel always took the Whitewell Road route into town so now and again they risked it and went for strolls up Hazelwood or in the castle grounds.

He had failed to meet her in town on Wednesday night and so she greeted him tight-lipped. 'What happened to you on Wednesday night, eh? Leaving me standing like some kind of eejit at the bottom of Castle Street. Are you getting sick of me? If so, just tell me! I'm not like some others that I could mention. I won't hang on where I'm not wanted.'

He reached for her but she angrily pushed his hands away and, blinded by tears, headed along the Antrim Road. He strode beside her in silence, until at last she swung round to face him. 'Well . . . where were you?'

'Are you ready to listen to me?'

'Your excuses had better be good.'

'I was ill.'

'Huh!' Her eyes scornfully scanned his face and wavered at what she saw. He was indeed looking pale and drawn. Less indignant now, she asked, 'What was wrong with you?'

'I had the 'flu. This is my first time out in a week.'

'Could you not have got word to me some way?'

'How could I, Rebecca? I could hardly lift my head off the pillow, and as far as the world is concerned we hardly know each other. Imagine my mother or one of my sisters ringing your house and leaving a message that Desi McKernan was sick and couldn't meet you. What would your ones have thought of that, eh? Especially Rachel.'

She saw at once that he had been in a quandary and was quick to apologize. 'I'm sorry. I really am sorry, but I wasn't to know. I was worried stiff.'

'What's all this about you won't hang on where you aren't wanted? Don't you trust me, Rebecca? Have I not proved myself yet?'

Slipping her arm through his, she said placatingly, 'It's too cold to go for a walk. Let's catch the bus into town and go to the pictures.'

'To be truthful, I'd much rather go home to bed. I really don't feel well.'

Slowly she withdrew her arm. He hadn't seen her for a whole week and all he wanted to do was rush back home? Pushing self-pity aside she agreed with him. 'That's a good idea. You do look rather shaky. I'll wait at the bus stop with you till the bus comes. I hope one is due soon. As you know they're few and far between along here.'

He was so quiet and withdrawn she found herself babbling to fill the long gaps in the conversation. With an abrupt movement he silenced her. 'Look, Rebecca, we can't go on like this.'

'Like what?'

'For a start you don't trust me.'

255

'Oh, I do! I do!' she cried.

Sadly he shook his head. 'And you don't love me.'

He was trying to break it off! She went cold inside. How would she be able to face life without him? Calmly she replied, 'If that's how you feel there's nothing more to be said. After all, I'm not the one who has the reputation for loving and leaving them.'

She wanted to walk proudly away but her heart wouldn't let her. Tears spilled over and she kept her head bent so he wouldn't notice. A bus rumbled towards them and she said, 'Well, see you around,' and turned to go.

Lost in misery she was some steps away before she realized that he was behind her. She glanced over her shoulder. The bus was disappearing round the bend in the road. 'You've missed your bus,' she cried foolishly.

'I know! And God knows when there'll be another one. But we can't part like this.' Taking her by the arm, he drew her to a halt. 'Will you for heaven's sake stop for a minute, till we thrash this out!'

She stood and gazed up at him, unaware just how forlorn she looked. With a muttered exclamation he gathered her right up off the ground in a bear hug. 'Ah, don't look like that, Rebecca! I don't want to hurt you. I love you and I want the world to know it.'

Her voice muffled against his chest, she cried, 'I thought you were breaking it off?'

'Never! But we can't go on like this.'

'What else can we do?'

'I want us to get engaged at Christmas. Come out into the open. What do you think about that?'

She opened her mouth to speak but before she could utter a sound he warned, 'And don't say "What about our Rachel?" She's old enough to look after herself. Besides, she has been out with a couple of others since me.'

'Has she?'

'Yes, and made sure that I knew about it!'

'You're right,' she conceded, after a thoughtful pause. 'I've been a fool. I will be very happy to accept your backhanded proposal of marriage and get engaged at Christmas.'

'Ah, my love, my love.' He gripped her closer still and kissed

256

her, leaving her breathless. 'Come on . . . let's go for a walk. You've just given me a new lease of life.'

He led her across the road and turned up in the direction of the castle. She clung to his arm; she was going to become Mrs McKernan. Nothing else mattered. Tomorrow she would worry about how to break the news to her family. Tonight, she just wanted to be near him. To have him hold her close and kiss her.

Christmas was fast approaching; just a week away and Rebecca had still to break the news of her imminent engagement to Desi. He was very annoyed about it. In despair, she decided to get George and Josie's reaction first. She was looking after young Jamie tonight while they did some late-night shopping. She would invite Desi to join her.

Jamie was teething, and hot and bothered. He whinged constantly and Rebecca was at her wits' end as to how to soothe him. When he eventually arrived, Desi took the fretting child in his arms and, cradling him against his chest, walked the floor with him until his parents came home. Rebecca rose to her feet and stood close beside him when George and Josie entered the room. Josie's eyes went directly to her son and she cried in alarm, 'What's wrong with him?'

'Don't worry, Josie. He's all right! He seems to be teething. He was quite cross for a while but Desi has the magic touch. He soon nursed him to sleep.'

Only then did George realize a stranger was holding his son. He nodded at him in bewilderment and then at his wife for guidance. Did she know this young man? She took it all in her stride. Thrusting her hand towards him, she said, 'You must be Rebecca's mysterious friend. You're welcome to come here with her whenever you like. Here, let me take Jamie. He seems contented now. I'll try him in his cot again. Thank you for looking after him. Meanwhile—' she flashed a look at her husband— 'George, will you put the teapot on, please?'

Only then did it dawn on Rebecca that they had never met Desi before. Had they heard tell of him?

Following Josie into the nursery, she watched her place the child in his cot and tenderly tuck the bedclothes around him.

'Josie, have you ever heard the name Desi McKernan mentioned in our house?'

A slight frown puckered her brow as she pondered. Then it cleared as she said, 'Isn't he the young man who treated Rachel so badly?'

Rebecca closed her eyes and screwed up her face in despair. 'He didn't treat her badly! He just didn't fall in love with her. Is that such a big crime?'

Josie blinked in bewilderment and Rebecca cried, 'That's him in there. We're in love and he wants us to get engaged at Christmas.'

'So that's what all the secrecy was about. But surely Rachel won't object? She can't still be carrying a torch for him, can she?'

'Not really, but she will make a point of being a martyr, that you can count on. What am I going to do, Josie?'

'I don't see any problem, Rebecca. If you love him, and you're sure that he loves you, and you intend marrying him . . . well then, you have to tell the family. But don't wait until the last minute. Tell them before he lands down with the ring.'

'Me dad doesn't like him.'

'It's not your dad who's marrying him, so why worry? Besides, once he knows you're serious about him, Sean will come round.' Putting a comforting arm around her niece's shoulders, Josie led her from the room. 'Come on and introduce him to us. Let's see what we think of him.'

George and Desi were deep in conversation and when belated introductions were made, Rebecca could see that Desi's name did not ring any bells where her uncle was concerned.

He obviously enjoyed the visitor's company. 'This is a sensible young man you have here, Rebecca. See you don't let him slip through your fingers,' he jested.

'Oh, I'll not let her do that, George. As a matter of fact we're getting engaged at Christmas, so we are.' Desi fixed his gaze on Rebecca. There, the die was cast! There was no backing out now.

'That's wonderful news!' George cried, obviously delighted. 'Isn't that great, Josie? You'll have to bring him over to our New Year's Eve party, Rebecca. It's just a small family affair,

Desi, but sure you're going to become one of the family, aren't you?'

Tears pricked Rebecca's eyes as she thanked them for their kindness. It was great that they liked Desi! Perhaps her father would follow their lead?

The feeling of well-being had subsided somewhat by the time Rebecca arrived home. Desi had made her promise that she would delay no longer and she entered the living room with fear in her heart but determined to get it all out in the open. Everyone but Thomas, who retired early each night, was present. Her father and mother were engrossed in the TV and Rachel, as usual, had her head buried in a book. It was she who first noticed Rebecca.

Whatever she saw in her sister's face caused her to ask in concern, 'Is anything wrong, Rebecca? You look like you've just seen a ghost.'

This remark brought all eyes to focus on her and she quailed inside, heart thumping like mad.

Considering her inner turmoil, she was surprised by how calm her voice sounded when she at last managed to speak. 'I have some news for you. Now I know you won't be all that pleased but I beg you to give us a chance. We couldn't help ourselves.'

'What on earth are you talking about?' Annie asked in bewilderment. Remembering that not so long ago Josie had thought that Rebecca was unhappy over some boyfriend, she cried in alarm, 'You're not pregnant, are you?'

Rebecca was glad that she could honestly assure her mother that indeed she was not pregnant. 'No, I'm not! But I am getting engaged at Christmas.'

'Engaged?' Rachel was gaping at her in amazement. 'But you don't go with anybody.'

'I have been seeing someone for months now but due to circumstances beyond my control we had to keep it a secret.'

Slowly Sean rose to his feet. 'He had better not be divorced!' he thundered.

'No, he's never been married.' Rebecca threw her sister a look of entreaty before confessing, 'I'm marrying Desi McKernan.'

259

The silence was deafening. It was Rachel who broke it. 'Desi? I don't believe you! Why, I've been asking around and he hasn't even been dating anyone for months now. He's studying for his finals.'

'That's where you're wrong. We have been going out together but we kept it very quiet.'

'Are you saying, that knowing how your sister was breaking her heart over this . . . this twerp, for want of a better name, you were secretly seeing him?' Sean was trying to keep his cool. He waited patiently for her to deny the accusation.

'She wasn't breaking her heart. She's dated numerous boys since Desi.'

'Who told you that?' cried Rachel.

'Desi! He saw you.'

'I suppose it didn't dawn on him that I was trying to make him jealous? Of course it wouldn't, if he was looking for an excuse to skulk around with you. How could you be so devious? You did it to spite me, didn't you? The first time you set eyes on him, here in this very room, you set your cap at him. I remember thinking at the time you were acting very funny. And then the next day . . .' words failed Rachel for a moment at the very idea of it ' . . . you had the audacity to try and put me off him.'

'I was only thinking of you, Rachel. I had no designs on him, honest!'

'You're a rotten liar, Rebecca Devlin! You told me a pack of lies! Or, if he is such a womanizer and troublemaker – and these are your very own words, remember – how come you fell for him?'

'It was as you yourself said, he just hadn't met the right one.'

'And you're the one?' Rachel was on her feet. Glaring at her sister, she cried, 'Do you imagine for one minute that he didn't make each and every girl he met feel special? Come off it! He'll ditch you, like he did the rest of us. You mark my words.'

Tears spilled over and with a flounce Rachel left the room. Quietly, Rebecca clapped her hands. 'What an exit. There goes the next Scarlett O'Hara.'

'That's not funny, Rebecca,' Sean admonished. 'She's very

hurt and I can't say I blame her. How could you do this to her? Your own sister. I hope you're not serious about getting engaged, because I for one don't like that fellow! And this episode hasn't made me feel any friendlier towards him. In fact, it seems to me he's setting you two against each other.'

White with rage, Rebecca heard him out. 'I do intend to get engaged to Desi at Christmas and we hope to marry next year. I can't help it if you don't like him. If you want me to leave the house, so be it. Otherwise, he must be made welcome here.'

'Is that a threat I hear? What will you do if I don't make him welcome?'

'Like I said, I'll leave home.'

'You do that . . .'

'She'll do no such thing!' Annie cut in. 'She'll be given her chance like Rachel was. Time alone will tell whether or not Desi is serious. If not then you can gloat all you like, Sean. Meanwhile, I for one will make him welcome in this house.'

Sean gaped at her in amazement. 'You're taking her side?'

Slowly Annie nodded her head. 'I have no choice. Rebecca has done nothing wrong, so I don't see why she should have to leave home.'

'Then there is nothing more to be said.' Without a glance in his daughter's direction, Sean also left the room. The outer door slammed shut as he left the house.

'Ah, Mam, I'm sorry. I really tried to fight my feelings for Desi but I do love him. I didn't want to hurt anybody. You've got to believe me, Mam.'

'It's all right, love. As I said before, you must have your chance. Invite him here for his Christmas dinner.'

Relieved, Rebecca hugged her tight. 'Thanks, Mam. Thanks a lot.'

Returning her embrace, Annie assured her, 'He's your friend. Why shouldn't he come for his Christmas dinner? Your dad will come round once he gets to know Desi.'

'I hope so, Mam. But you know how stubborn he can be.'

'I know only too well, love. But we will just have to let things take their course and hope they turn out for the best all round. That's all we can do.'

Chapter 7

Instead of being a joyous occasion, Christmas was a time of false gaiety in the Devlin household. Loath to face Desi, Rachel had elected to spend the day at her friend's home and Sean accused Rebecca of depriving her sister of the company of her family at this holy festive time. The solitaire diamond ring that had just about emptied Desi's savings account was barely acknowledged by Sean and he deliberately refrained from congratulating them. He rarely spoke to Desi, in spite of his bending over backwards to be pleasant. Annie, in an effort to cover up her husband's rudeness, was too gushing and therefore sounded insincere. Desi took it all in his stride but Rebecca felt like weeping at the farce of it all.

In due course the arrival of Thelma, John, Rosaleen and her cheerful young daughter Patricia helped to ease the tension. Their congratulations and best wishes for the future warmed Rebecca's heart and she thawed a little. Without their company she very much doubted if she would have survived the day. She watched her father being nice to everyone else and resentment gathered like a great ball of fury within her, ready to erupt at the slightest provocation. How dare he treat her like this? She was his daughter and had done no wrong. Huh! She had little difficulty imagining that if the positions had been reversed and Rachel had managed to hang on to Desi, her father would have been all over them. The wonderful Rachel who was at Queen's and who would one day make her father very proud. She wished that she could shrug off the resentment that was gnawing away inside her but she couldn't; she hurt too much.

The day dragged on until at long last it was time for Desi

to make his farewells. Relieved, Rebecca pulled on a coat and said she would wait outside with him until the taxi arrived. He demurred at first, saying it was too cold, but seeing the misery in her eyes, he bit on his tongue and, tenderly wrapping his scarf around her head, led her outside.

They stood on the steps wrapped in each other's arms and gazed out over the beauty of the lough. The lights from the far shore twinkled like diamonds on the water and a deep frost gave everything in sight a fairyland appearance. A pale moon hung low in a starlit sky and an eerie silence filled the air. The tranquillity of it proved too much for Rebecca. She turned in his arms and buried her head in his chest. Great convulsive sobs wracked her body.

'Ah, now, love,' he chastised her. 'There's no need for this. Your dad will come round in time, I know he will.'

'He shouldn't need time!' she wailed. 'He should be happy for me. He's spoilt what should have been one of the happiest days in my life and I hate him for it! I'll never forgive him. Never!'

Cupping her face in his hands, Desi fixed a stern gaze on her. 'You don't mean that. If I thought for one minute that I was going to come between you and your father, I would walk away now. I know how much you look up to him.'

'And a lot of good it's done me! I've always been second best, Desi. Rachel is his favourite. She was encouraged to stay on at school, but me . . . I was allowed to leave. They pretended that they were annoyed at me but with a little persuasion I would have stayed on. I just didn't feel clever enough. Rachel was a hard act to follow. I needed them to show confidence in me. I needed a little push in the right direction. But I didn't get it.'

'Ah, love, I'm sorry to hear all this. I didn't realize that you felt that way. But you made your decision and it's water under the bridge now. Besides, you've done very well for yourself and I'm sure that your dad is proud of you. Just wait and see. In a few months' time we will have forgotten all this. Remember, your mother's on our side and that's half the battle.' The hoot of a car horn broke through his impassioned speech, causing him to tut with frustration. He didn't want to leave her in this state. 'Here's the taxi, love. I'll have to go.

263

But remember, tomorrow I'm showing you off to my family. I'll get Dad to run me over in the car to pick you up at about twelve. So come on now ... I want a nice big smile and a kiss before I go.'

'I love you, Desi! I love you so much I hurt inside.'

'And I love you, Rebecca. Remember, that's all that really matters. Good night, love.' He kissed her long and hard then gently eased her from him. With long strides he descended the steps and drive and with a final wave of his hand jumped into the taxi. She watched through a mist of tears until it was out of sight. Oh, how she wished she was going with him. How would she get through the rest of the evening without his support?

Seeing her young niece slip quietly upstairs on her return indoors, Rosaleen asked the question that had been hovering on her lips all day. 'Annie, why is Rebecca so unhappy when she should be overjoyed at winning such a fine young man? Is she pregnant? Is that why Sean can't look Desi straight in the eye?'

Annie threw her hands high at the very idea if it. 'Oh, thanks be to God, no, she isn't! That would be the final straw so far as Sean is concerned. It's a long story, Rosaleen. Come on in here with me and I'll tell you all about it.'

A glance round the company showed that everyone else was half asleep except for Patricia who was patiently helping Thomas with a large piece jigsaw. They were all feeling lazy after the big meal washed down by wine and beer. Annie led the way through the kitchen into the conservatory where they could talk in private. After pouring some drinks, she quietly brought her sister up to date on events.

'Isn't Sean being a bit unfair?' Rosaleen exclaimed. 'I mean, Desi seems a fine young man, and if he gets his degree he can go places. You'd think that Sean would be glad to have him as a son-in-law.'

'I know that, and you know that. And in his heart Sean must know it. But you see ... it was the deceit. They should have been open about their feelings for each other. Sean is feeling hurt for Rachel. All this secrecy has caused bad feeling. I

264

thought perhaps you might have known something was going on?' An inquisitive eye was fixed on Rosaleen.

'No, I never noticed anything different. But then, I haven't seen much of them lately. You know, since Pat McDade came on the scene. Does Rachel still care for Desi?'

'It's hard to tell. She hasn't mentioned him lately. But of course she couldn't bear to face him here today and pretend to admire the ring and all, and I don't really blame her. That's why Sean is acting so nasty. He's angry that I invited Desi here today. I suppose in a way he's right. After all, Rachel did meet him first.'

'But surely you don't really think that Rebecca should turn her back on love because Rachel saw him first?' Rosaleen asked softly. 'That would be wrong.'

'No, I don't, but everything is so mixed up. I only hope that Desi is serious and doesn't let Rebecca down.'

'I don't think you need worry on that score. He is obviously nuts about her.' Rosaleen sighed. She was remembering how, in the early days of her relationship with him, Sean had looked at her like that. What a fool she had been, insisting on going through with her marriage to Joe, and what a disaster that had been. Then, with war being imminent, Sean had rushed into marriage with Annie.

'Why the big sigh?' Her sister eyed her curiously and Rosaleen blushed as if she must surely be aware of these secret thoughts.

'I'm just envious of their commitment to each other.'

A toss of the head showed just what Annie thought of that. 'Commitment is all right but it isn't enough! You can't take your happiness at the expense of others.' An accusing look accompanied her next words. 'If people respected others' rights there would be less trouble in the world.'

'Perhaps it's better to cause pain now than to let things get out of hand?' Rosaleen said pensively. 'There was no point in Rebecca stepping aside if Desi didn't care for Rachel, now was there? That way everybody would have suffered.'

'You're right, of course,' Annie agreed with a sigh. 'I just hope Sean comes around to our way of thinking.'

To Rosaleen's relief Patricia entered the conservatory and brought the conversation to an end. All this was too reminiscent of her own life story for comfort. She for one would certainly encourage Rebecca to follow her heart. It was the only road to happiness. She squirmed restlessly. Too many memories were crowding her mind. Resolutely, she pushed them to one side and with a welcoming smile to her daughter, adroitly changed the subject.

However, during the course of the evening she found herself eyeing Sean covertly and wondering if he was happy with his lot. Lately, in repose there was a discontented droop to his mouth. She was the first to admit that a disabled child would likely put a strain on any marriage, but Annie and Sean seemed to be coping admirably. Thomas was such an affectionate young man and doing so well at school now, he was a credit to them. Still, recently Sean seemed abstracted. She could sense discord between him and Annie. Could he also be thinking of the past and, but for her stupidity, what might have been? That was hardly likely, she derided herself. He rarely paid any attention to her. Most likely he was worrying about Rebecca.

Suddenly, as if aware of her scrutiny, Sean raised his head and their eyes met. For some moments they gazed at each other enthralled. It was like the first time they had met on that fateful evening outside the Falls Flax Mill all those years ago. Hot colour washed over Rosaleen's face at what she read in his eyes, and even though Annie was present she could not tear her gaze away. Sean blinked in confusion; these emotions towards Rosaleen were alien to him now. He had been taken unawares. Guiltily his eyes sought Annie, thankful to see that his wife was busy passing round nuts and savoury dishes, and that none of the others seemed to have witnessed his discomfiture. He breathed a sigh of relief. He had disagreed with Annie about Rosaleen returning to her children in Canada. After all, he'd argued, children married and made lives of their own so why shouldn't Rosaleen stay where she was happy? Now he confessed to himself that it would be better if she did return to Canada. And the sooner the better! He would not have believed it possible but he surely had not imagined the emotion emanating from her? Her interest in him seemed to be reviving and must at all costs be averted. All she had ever brought him was misery.

New Year's Eve, spent at Josie's, was a much happier affair. Rachel turned up with a tall fair-haired young man in tow; Anthony Clarke was his name. When she removed her coat Rebecca stared in amazement. Her sister looked splendid in knee-length white plastic fashion boots that were all the rage at the moment, and a brief white mini dress that left nothing to the imagination. The outfit highlighted her wonderful colouring. Thick chestnut hair tumbled in disarray about her shoulders and the frosty air had reddened her cheeks and set her great wide thick-lashed eyes aglow. Sean frowned in disapproval at the sight of his daughter's bare thighs but managed to hold his tongue. Rebecca watched her father struggle for control and a grimace crossed her face.

'What was that for?' Desi whispered in her ear.

'I was thinking that if I had dared wear a dress like that, me dad would have landed on me like a ton of bricks.'

'Perhaps he's just trying to keep the peace, eh?'

'In my case it wouldn't have mattered. He would have let loose, no matter what!'

'Let's give him the benefit of the doubt, eh, love? You're not thinking straight at the moment. Besides, even I would have been a mite annoyed if you'd called attention to yourself like that.'

Rebecca smiled at him, reaching up to touch his face. 'Do you know something, Desi McKernan? You really are a very nice person and I'm a very lucky girl. You always say the right things at the right time.'

A rueful smile touched his lips. 'I remember a time when you thought I was a right tearaway.'

'I know that.' The light kiss she placed on his lips was full of apology. 'I'm only too glad that I realized your worth in time, or I might have lost you.'

'Not once I saw you! Believe me, you had no chance of escaping my evil clutches.'

'I think it's about time I congratulated you, Desi.'

Engrossed in each other, neither of them had noticed Rachel approach. Now she sidled between them and her arms went up around his neck. 'I hope you and Rebecca get all the happiness you deserve.' She stressed the word 'deserve' and a frown gathered on Desi's brow.

Realizing that she was the worse for drink he ignored it and suffered her kiss, then turned to her companion. 'Anthony, I think Rachel could do with some strong coffee and a walk in the fresh air, don't you?'

'Is that an invitation, Desi?' she asked coyly.

'Oh, behave yourself, Rachel,' Rebecca admonished scornfully.

A derisive eye passed slowly over Rebecca's red sweater and knee-length skirt. 'Do I detect a note of jealousy in your voice, dear sister? It wouldn't be the first time that Desi and I had walked out together, you know. Remember, Desi? We did have some good times, didn't we?'

The insinuation sickened Rebecca but before she could reply Anthony intervened. 'Come on now, love. I think coffee would be a good idea.' Putting an arm around her waist, he smiled indulgently down at her and, mollified, Rachel let herself be led away.

'She's been drinking.' Rebecca stated the obvious. 'That's not like her. That's why she's so brave!'

'Yes,' Desi agreed. 'Probably Dutch courage.'

'Will she be all right with him or should I rescue her?' Rebecca sounded troubled.

'She'll be all right with Anthony.'

'I hope she catches herself on and doesn't play up like that every time she sees us together,' Rebecca said ruefully. 'I don't think I could bear it.'

'Let's just be glad she has broken the ice. I think she was embarrassed. It should be all right in future.'

Holding his eye, Rebecca said softly, 'I'd probably be better not knowing . . . but did you two ever . . . you know?'

'No! No matter what she might have implied to the contrary, we never did! There's nothing for you to worry about. Please believe that, Rebecca.'

A soft sigh escaped on the breath she had been holding. 'I believe you.'

Desi was right. Rachel appeared to have buried the hatchet, and life became a lot easier at home. Both girls were out a lot but when under the same roof they managed to put on a show of camaraderie. Nevertheless Rebecca was aware that her sister had not forgiven her.

In mid-January, in spite of Annie's protests, Rosaleen returned to Orangeville with the intention of selling up and coming to live in Ireland. She had decided that life was too short to live by everyone else's rules and she would grab at any chance of happiness that come her way. Annie hoped and prayed that once back with her children and granddaughter she would change her mind and remain safely in Canada.

To help fill the hole left in his savings by the purchase of Rebecca's ring, Desi had managed to get himself a job as barman in a pub in the town centre. Thus, since he was also studying for his final exams, Rebecca didn't see as much of him as she would have wished. The weeks passed slowly and eventually the exams were upon them. Rachel lost weight as she swotted night after night and Annie worried about her.

As predicted, Desi passed his finals with honours and got his degree in economics. He felt that he was now in a position to pick and choose which firm he would work for and Rebecca saw the chance of an early wedding. However, as Desi had once explained to her father, his father's eldest brother, who was childless, had promised that if Desi got good results he would give him enough money to tour America for a year before settling down. Give him a chance to see just what could be achieved out there. Desi broached the subject with Rebecca and found her against the idea. He agreed not to go but she could see that he was restless and discontented. Nor was an early wedding mentioned. To Rebecca's dismay, he seemed content to drift.

To everyone's relief Rachel also passed her exams and Sean couldn't hide how proud he was of her. He bought her a beautiful gold wrist watch engraved with her name. Next year, he promised, when she got her final exams, it would be something even better. Rachel basked in all the admiration; she was in her glory and you couldn't have angered her if you had clobbered her over the head. In the swing of things at Queen's now, she was enjoying the popularity she craved. Boyfriends came and went but whether Rachel was serious about him or not, Anthony Clarke hung on and remained a welcome visitor

269

to their home. Rebecca managed to hide the hurt all this admiration of her sister caused her.

Terence O'Neill seemed to be dragging his feet about the promises he had made and both sides of the community were angry at him. Meanwhile, the Civil Rights Movement was gathering momentum. Desi was not finding it so easy to get a job as he had first thought, and to Rebecca's dismay threw himself heart and soul into the pursuit of Civil Rights for all. The right to a good high-paid job no matter what your religion, and the right to live where you chose. He swept Rebecca along with him to marches and demonstrations where she found herself chanting 'One man, one vote' with the rest of the throng. It was so easy to get carried away when feelings ran high. She could find no fault with the crowds who gathered to march. So far the protests were orderly and peaceful and most of the action was outside Belfast with the first big march being held in Coalisland in August.

However, in October, in Belfast itself, a march to the City Hall was arranged and over three thousand people gathered. At the allotted time they started in orderly procession on their journey to the town centre. Along the chosen route their way was barred by counter demonstrators and they sat down in Linenhall Street until forcibly moved. Two days later the People's Democracy was formed. It was stressed that this was a non-violent, non-political and non-sectarian party, and Desi became very much caught up in it. The founder members of the Democratic Party thought that direct action would be provocative and urged for restraint. In spite of their warnings, towards the end of October a group of activists took it upon themselves to occupy the Great Hall in Stormont; they were there for three hours. And so were the TV cameras. There it was! Headlines on the six o'clock news for all to see, and Desi a prominent figure.

'He's going to get into trouble, that one!' Sean stormed. 'You mark my words. You should finish with him before it's too late. He'll bring you nothing but heartache!' With a baleful glare at Rebecca, he left the room.

Appalled at the way things were getting out of hand, she sought ways to get Desi away from it all. Quietly, she told him that since he was unable to find a job suited to his qualifications, he should take his uncle up on his offer and go to America. She was convinced that all would be settled by the time he returned.

'What brought about this change of heart?' Desi was bewildered, could not understand her reasoning.

'I want you as far away from here as possible in case there's trouble.'

'You're over-reacting, love. There won't be any trouble. Not with the TV cameras there. The eyes of the world are on us, Rebecca.'

'Please, Desi. I've a bad feeling about this. I beg you to go.'

He gripped her by the shoulders and pulled her close to him. 'I'll go if you'll come with me. Eh, Rebecca? What about it? I've been saving like mad. Imagine us two touring America together. I'm sure I'll be able to get odd jobs to boost whatever Uncle Edward gives me. It's a chance not to be sneezed at. Will you come with me? We might even be lucky enough to get good jobs out there.'

'Now you're talking nonsense. You never wanted me to go before, so why now? Besides, I was under the impression you were saving so that we could get married.'

'Oh, but I *did* want you to come with me! Did you really think I could leave you alone here for a whole year?' He shook his head sadly. 'But you were so against the idea, I saw no reason to mention it. And if we don't go ... well then, of course the money I've saved will go towards our wedding. But we'll forfeit Uncle Edward's gift. It's up to you, love.'

Wide-eyed, she gazed at him. 'I thought that you meant to go alone?'

'Never, Rebecca. I need you by my side. I'd be lost without you. If I go, will you come with me?'

'My dad would hit the roof. He would never hear tell of it, you know that.'

'That's another reason I didn't ask you. I told you before that I wouldn't come between you and your dad. You would have to choose between us and I didn't want to start another row.'

'It's a big step, Desi,' she sighed. 'I'll be branded a bad woman, going away with you and us not married.' She paused,

271

hoping he would suggest a quick quiet wedding, But no, he remained silent, awaiting her decision. At last she asked, 'Can I sleep on it?'

'Of course you can. Take all the time you need. And remember, I'll always love you, no matter what you decide.'

Annie's prayers regarding Rosaleen went unheard and by June her sister had sold her house and its contents and was preparing to return to Ireland. It seemed that life was not going to be easy; not by a long shot. The idea of keeping Sean and his son apart should Liam decide to visit his mother was ludicrous. And as Annie had pointed out to Rosaleen, what about the rest of the family? In spite of all the objections August had seen Rosaleen, accompanied by Patricia, back at Orange Row. She immediately began looking at houses. True to her word she looked at them over in the direction of Dundonald on the opposite side of Belfast. As if that would make any difference, Annie fumed inwardly, if her son decided to pay her a visit.

Pat McDade became a permanent fixture by Rosaleen's side. She brought him up to renew Sean and Annie's acquaintance. Annie found that he had mellowed with age and quite liked him and Sean was polite but distant with him. But then, Sean was polite but distant with everyone nowadays. She could not fault his manners but there was no warmth there.

As Annie prepared the turkey for yet another Christmas dinner, she wondered if she would ever enjoy Christmas again. There would just be the four of them for dinner this year: Sean Rachel, Thomas and herself. Rebecca was spending Christmas Day at Desi's home. They saw so little of her these days Sean complained she might as well be living with Desi. His wife had been quick to point out, if that was the case, there was no one to blame but himself. The McKernan family welcomed their daughter with open arms, and she was happy there, but how did he treat Desi? The way he would an acquaintance. Desi would make a fine son-in-law. Why couldn't Sean accept him? Make him welcome. What if he was caught up in the Civil Rights Movement? That was just an excuse Sean was using! Wasn't most of the youth of Northern Ireland caught up in it one way or another?

To crown it all, Thelma and John were dining out with Rosaleen, Patricia and Pat. This idea had disgusted Annie. Imagine spending Christmas Day in a hotel. It was unheard of! Christmas was for families. It was supposed to be a holy, happy time when families forgave each other and goodwill was shared by all. Anthony Clarke had been invited to dine with them but a few days ago Rachel had informed them that he would not be coming after all. It seemed he had proposed to her and she had turned him down. This had infuriated Sean. Was Rachel daft, letting a fine young man like Anthony slip through her fingers? Annie, on the other hand, was glad to see him go. There was something about him that she couldn't cotton on to. Determined not to make the same mistake as her husband had regarding Desi, she had not aired her opinion that he did not come across as a sincere person to her.

Her mind drifted back over the past year. It hadn't been all bad. They had gotten out and about a lot and entertained in return so why was she feeling so down? The girls seemed to have buried their differences. Rebecca was saving like mad for her wedding although no date had yet been set. Tentatively, Annie had suggested to her husband that it was their duty to put on the reception and Sean had halfheartedly agreed that when the date was set he would make the offer. Until then he was able to hope that Rebecca would change her mind.

Why was Annie so restless and dissatisfied with her lot? When had all the joy gone out of her life? It wasn't so long ago that she had been thanking God for his goodness to them. What had changed? Was it because Rosaleen was here to stay? Not really. As promised, her sister had bought a house out at Dundonald and they saw little of her now. As for Liam, at the moment he was still safely tucked well way in Orangeville and was the least of her troubles. If he ever decided to come over, she would meet that problem when it presented itself. No, if she were truthful, she would admit it was Sean's unrest that was the cause of her unhappiness. No matter what she did to try and bridge the gap, he seemed so remote. Was it all in her mind? Was she being fanciful? Surely at this stage in their lives they should be able to expect some contentment?

As expected, Christmas passed quietly. The time had come for Rebecca to tell her parents of her plans. Everything was arranged. They would be leaving Belfast on New Year's Day and flying out from Shannon on the second of January. It was with trepidation that she prepared to break the news of her decision to accompany Desi to America. Hoping for some backing, she approached her mother first. She got no joy there.

'Go away with Desi and you not even married?' Annie cried in alarm. 'Are you daft? Your dad will never hear tell of it. He'll go berserk at the very idea of it.'

'Could you not persuade him, Mam? It would just be like going on a holiday, so it would. Lots of couples go on holiday together now, and they aren't all married.'

'Not Sean Devlin's daughters! Why don't you wait until you're married, for heaven's sake, and make it your honeymoon? Or does he not intend tying the knot? Eh, is that it? Is it a case of come with me or else?'

'No, it's not! If I don't go he'll stay here with me.'

'Well then, why not put the money towards a house? Make your dad eat his words. Once you set the date, you know, he'll come round and help out. We'll pay for the reception.'

'It's a bit late for that! If we had known, we would probably have been married by now. But you see . . . if Desi doesn't go he won't get the money. His uncle wants him to see the world before settling down. He has been to America and thinks Desi would love it. He said if Desi got a job out there he would be set for life. It's too good a chance to miss, Mam, and I'm going. With or without your blessing.'

'Rebecca, please don't do this. It will break your dad's heart.'

'Huh, you've got to be joking! It might hurt his pride, but it certainly won't touch his heart. As far as I'm concerned he just couldn't care less. All these months he hasn't even tried to get to know Desi, barely acknowledging him when he comes to collect me, but Anthony Clarke practically lived here. And look how that turned out,' she cried derisively. 'A waste of time, that's what it was! But of course Rachel can do no wrong so far as Dad is concerned.'

Sensing the deep hurt her daughter harboured, Anne inwardly grieved with her and sought to console her. 'Rebecca, to be truthful, I don't know why he's taking this stance with Desi. He just took an instant dislike to him and I have pleaded

274

until I'm blue in the face for him to back down, but Sean's stupid pride won't let him.'

'It doesn't matter any more, Mam.' The sadness in Rebecca's voice found an answering chord in Annie and she felt like weeping. 'I've reached the point where I don't care what he thinks. I'd just like to get away without a great big row. Do you think that's possible? Will you speak to him?'

'It's not fair, asking me to do your dirty work for you. God knows I've enough worries of my own.'

Rebecca drew back at these words and pondered inwardly for a few seconds. It was true that her mother hadn't been herself lately. 'You're right, Mam. I'll tell him myself. Can I do anything for you?'

'You could stay at home!' A sad shake of the head was her answer to this. 'If you really are determined to go, I think you should leave it until the last minute to tell him,' Annie lamented. 'Because there'll be no living with him once he knows.'

'We're leaving on New Year's Day.'

'What? So soon!' Annie was aghast. But why was she so surprised? The young ones nowadays didn't let the grass grow under their feet. 'Oh, Rebecca, I dread it, so I do. Your dad will hit the roof. Is everything arranged? You know, passports and money and all?'

'I'm afraid so. I'll tell him tonight.'

Annie nodded mournfully; she dreaded the revelation. She was also ashamed that her daughter had to make all her plans on the quiet. What must Desi's family think of them?

After dinner that night, dressed in her outdoor clothes ready to escape in a hurry should her father explode, Rebecca entered the living room. Standing just inside the doorway, she addressed him. 'Dad, I've some bad news, I'm afraid.'

Sean closed the book he was reading, fixed his gaze on her and waited in silence. He noted her pallor and saw her lick her lips nervously. Apprehension rose within his breast. He was aware in his heart that he was being unfair to this young daughter of his, but he just couldn't stand that big twerp she had given her heart to.

'In three days' time I'm leaving for America with Desi.'

'What do you mean, you're leaving for America?'

'Just that. Desi and I are going to tour America for about a year before settling down to married life.'

His voice still quiet, Sean said, 'Like hell you are! It'll be over my dead body.'

'Dad, it's all arranged. There's nothing that you can do to stop it. Please don't cause any trouble.'

'If you go . . . you don't ever come back into this house.'

'Ah, Dad. You can't mean that!'

'I mean it all right. If you think that Desi McKernan is going to take you and use you and make a laughing stock of you, and you can just waltz back in here when you return, you've another thought coming. If you go, I never want to see you again. It's as simple as that.' A movement from Annie brought his attention abruptly to her. 'And if you take her side in this, you can go too.'

Amazed silence reigned. Both Annie and Rebecca were at a loss for how to reply. The situation was saved by the arrival of Rachel. With one more quick look of appeal at her father, Rebecca took the opportunity to escape and without another word left the house. There was no turning back now; she only hoped her mother didn't suffer on her behalf.

Rachel looked from one to the other of her parents. 'What was all that about?'

'Nothing that concerns you,' Sean said abruptly.

Rachel gazed in mute appeal at her mother but Annie just shook her head warningly. She could practically feel the rage bubbling through her husband. Without another word he entered the hall, shrugged into his heavy outdoor coat and left the house.

When the door closed on him Rachel burst out, 'What's the matter, Mam? Is Rebecca pregnant?' Her eyes were agog with excitement.

In a flash, suspicion entered Annie's mind. Did Rachel know something? Was there an ulterior motive for this trip to America? 'Why do you ask that? Have you heard anything?'

'No, I haven't. But me dad is in such a temper I thought something awful must have happened.'

'Rebecca is leaving for America in a couple of days. Desi and she are going to see a bit of life before settling down.'

Surprise took the breath from Rachel and she sank down on

276

to the nearest chair. 'Oh, isn't she lucky? I'd give my eye-teeth to be in her place.'

'Oh, would you indeed! Just you keep your sights set on getting your final exams. Don't you disappoint your father too.'

A grimace twisted Rachel's mouth. What about all that wonderful understanding. That 'It won't matter if you fail' rubbish? she thought scornfully. It was going to be a long hard slog. With Rebecca in America, her father would be watching her even more closely. Not something to look forward to.

With feet like lead, Sean trudged his way up the Serpentine Road. He was heading for Hazelwood, that quiet peaceful haven where he usually went to be alone and sort out his problems. He walked until he came to a fallen tree trunk. Many a time over the years he had sat here and examined all the options open to him. But this time there were no options to examine. How could they expect him to give them his blessing? It was like condoning living in sin. And that he wouldn't do. Good God, Rebecca was his daughter! His flesh and blood. He knew how permissive the young ones were today. Didn't he have to listen to their escapades at work? He knew what went on all too well. But he expected his daughters to be above that kind of carry on. Why couldn't she have gotten married first? He groaned aloud as he admitted to himself that with a bit of help and encouragement from him they probably would have been married by now. Too late thinking like that, his conscience taunted him. Much too late.

With a sigh he sank down on the weather-beaten trunk and buried his head in his hands. Right from the beginning he had handled things all wrong. Why had he been so obstinate? If he had extended the hand of friendship to Desi, who knows how things might have turned out? Good God, he didn't have to love the man! Who knows, he might even have come to like him. They could have been married by now. Then this question of America wouldn't have come up.

It was because Rebecca had been so defiant! Threatening to leave home and all if Desi wasn't accepted. That had got his hump up. Still a year had elapsed since she'd first announced that she was marrying him. A whole year! And he had done nothing to bridge the gap between himself and his daughter.

277

Where had all that time gone? It seemed like a couple of months. True, Rebecca had spent a lot of it away from home; had just eaten and slept there. But that also had been his fault. And now she was going to America. He might never see her again. Another thing . . . Annie was sure to blame him for chasing her away. Another nail in the coffin of their teetering marriage?

He lost track of time until a chilly breeze rustling through the trees made him shiver. It was pitch black. Rising to his feet, he stretched frozen limbs. What in the world was he thinking about, sitting here like an eejit in the cold? He wasn't a young man any more and would suffer for his stupidity, that he could bank on. Perhaps if he tried to win Annie around he could find a way out of this predicament? Carefully he picked his steps over the frozen rutted ground and slowly descended on to the Antrim Road. He wasn't looking forward to the hours ahead. Humble pie was not something he digested easily.

During the evening Sean had tried to bridge the gap of silence but his wife remained aloof and the carefully rehearsed words remained unspoken. Now he lay in bed and watched as she went through her nightly routine. First she lightly creamed her face and throat, then lifting the hairbrush began to give her long thick hair its nightly one hundred strokes. Aware of his scrutiny Annie actually felt shy. It was a long time since he had examined her. What was behind his inscrutable eyes? Laying down the brush, she turned to face him.

'Well?'

He reached out a hand towards her. 'Come here, Annie.'

Slowly she approached the bed and stood gazing down at him.

Gripping her hand, he tugged at it. 'Sit down, for heaven's sake. I'm not going to bite you.'

She remained standing. 'What is it you want, Sean? I've to look in on Thomas yet.'

Reluctantly, he released his hold on her. 'It can wait. Away you go.'

Thomas was fast asleep. After straightening the bedclothes, Annie kissed him on the brow and returned to her own room in trepidation. What was Sean planning? There was no way she would agree with him if he wanted to throw a spanner in the works and try to prevent Rebecca going to America. That was something she just couldn't do.

'Don't look so worried, love. Come to bed. I want to talk to you.'

Shrugging out of her dressing gown, she slipped between the sheets, all the while eyeing him warily. Sean sighed and gingerly gathered her close. If she rebuffed him now, his chance to make amends would be gone forever. It was turning out to be much harder than he had anticipated. The words were sticking in his throat. He swallowed and began. 'Annie, I've had a good long think and I realize now how stupid I've been. Is there any way I can make amends before they go?' There, it was out! How would she react?

Unable to believe her ears, Annie just gaped mutely at him. Never in her wildest dreams had she expected this.

'Is it too late?' His look was anxious. 'Will you help me?'

'It is a bit late, but of course I'll help you all I can.'

'What can I do?'

'Well, we could have a bit of a "do" for them on New Year's Eve. Invite family and friends in to say farewell. Show them that you really have buried the hatchet. Can you do that?'

'That sounds wonderful, Annie. Do you think Desi will come at this late stage?'

'I think he will. He really is a very nice young man, you know.'

'So you keep telling me. But, you see, I can't help feeling that I'm condoning sin. Giving it my blessing, as it were.'

Amazed at his way of thinking, Annie had difficulty holding her tongue. How could he so easily forget the way he had betrayed her with Rosaleen? But she reasoned with him, 'Look, Sean, they don't have to go to America to get up to a bit of hanky-panky, you know. We have no control over our daughter's actions any more. She is a big girl now in case you haven't noticed.'

'That's what worries me, Annie. They're so permissive nowadays.'

'Really, Sean, it was almost as bad when we were young. Only it was done on the sly. Remember, you were no angel!'

'I wasn't all that bad surely?' he exclaimed, greatly affronted.

279

'Well, that's a matter of opinion. But let's not dwell on that now. Can we afford to give them any money?'

'Some. Not a lot. Remember, we will have a wedding to pay for when they come back.'

Annie sighed contentedly. So long as they gave them something and had a wee 'do' for them, she was happy. 'That's great, love.' Deciding to make the most of the situation, she pressed closer and offered him her lips. Thankfully, he claimed them. With her on his side it would be easier to eat humble pie. Why on earth hadn't he talked to her sooner?

To his relief, Annie took it upon herself to break the news of Sean's change of heart to Rebecca next morning. To her dismay her daughter was sceptical. 'What's the matter with you, Rebecca? I thought you'd be delighted, so I did,' Annie cried.

'I don't know how Desi will take this. I wouldn't blame him if he refused to come after all the grief me dad has caused.'

'Ah, Rebecca, you've just got to persuade him.'

'I'll do my best, Mam, but I won't hold it against him if he refuses. He would have every right to tell Dad to stuff his wee "do". But I'll do my best.'

Desi was only too glad to agree to anything that meant Rebecca wasn't leaving for America under a black cloud, so a small farewell party was arranged. He said unfortunately his parents and two sisters would not be able to attend as they had already made other arrangements to see the New Year in, some time ago. Annie took this at face value. She wouldn't hold it against his family if they decided not to bow to their wishes at this late stage. Not everyone was as forgiving as Desi.

However, she phoned around and in the end there was quite a crowd there. Besides the immediate family Moira Mullen came escorted by her latest boyfriend, and friends from Rebecca's work place arrived weighed down with gifts. Even Minnie Carson, who for the past year, because of ill health, had lived with her son, came to wish Rebecca farewell and present her with a cheque. Overcome at all this unexpected kindness, Rebecca blinked furiously to hold back the tears and fussed over Josie's baby girl, her little goddaughter Martha, to hide the emotion that threatened to engulf her. Her prayers had been answered; she would not be leaving under a cloud after all.

With a few drinks under his belt, Sean plucked up enough courage to approach Desi for a word in private. He had seen him leave the room and caught up with him at the foot of the stairs. 'Desi?'

'Yes, Mr Devlin?'

'I think I owe you an apology. I'm aware I've been a surly bugger and I honestly can't begin to explain what got into me. You were my daughter's choice and I should have respected that and made you welcome in my home.' Tentatively, he offered his hand. 'Can we start from scratch, do you think?'

Desi eagerly gripped the proffered hand and agreed. 'We certainly can, Mr Devlin.'

Sean smiled slightly. 'Now you're making me feel old. Do you think you could call me Sean?'

'Yes, Sean. And I know this can't be easy for you, so let's forget it ever happened. You probably still hate my guts, but I love Rebecca. I'll do all in my power to make her happy.'

Sean nodded and turned away. Maybe someday he might come to like this young man. Only time would tell. At least he had pleased Annie and Rebecca and at the moment that was all that mattered.

Everything went according to plan and as midnight approached the revellers moved outside into the crisp night air to welcome in the New Year. Church bells could be heard ringing out joyfully and the ships in Belfast harbour blasted their foghorns' mournful sounds across the lough. Greetings were passed among the happy crowd and hands were joined as 'Auld Lang Syne' was sung. Peace and contentment prevailed as they returned indoors. Hopefully 1969 would prove a happier year.

Shortly afterwards Rebecca climbed the stairs to attend to last-minute packing and then, amidst tearful farewells, she and Desi entered the waiting taxi and were whisked off.

It was after tea-time on New Year's Day that Annie called Sean from the garage where he had been changing the oil in the car. Silently she pointed to the television set.

Wiping his hands on a rag, he stood in the doorway and

281

listened to the newscaster. The news was tragic. That day Michael Farrell had led a People's Democratic march from Belfast to Derry. The marchers had been attacked at Burntollet. So much for a peaceful New Year.

'Thank God Desi is away,' Annie said softly. 'He would surely have been in the thick of that and might have been injured. I'm so glad, Sean, that you made the effort. Knowing how proud-necked you are, I realize it can't have been easy for you.'

'You're right there, Annie. It wasn't easy, but I did it to please you. To be truthful, I felt a real hypocrite, so I did! Saying one thing and thinking another. But no matter.' He gestured towards the TV set. 'Didn't I prophesy that no good would come of those marches? I'm glad that Desi is away from it all.'

A frown puckered his brow and Annie guessed what was troubling him. 'Sean, stop worrying about Rebecca. We've no authority over them now.'

'Don't be daft! How can I help worrying about her? What if she is foolish and becomes pregnant, and her on the other side of the world?'

'Desi will look after her, I know he will! Why can't you have faith in them?'

He shrugged, at a loss for words. Did he expect too much of his daughters? Perhaps, but he wasn't going to make excuses for feeling like that; any father would be the same. 'To be truthful, I don't know what's got into me lately.'

'Lately?' Annie failed to keep the scorn from her voice. 'You've always been the same! Sailing through life, doing what you wanted, and expecting everybody to forgive and forget, just because you say you're sorry.'

'Hey, that's a bit harsh, isn't it? Seems to me I'm the one who has always knuckled down to your wishes. Not so long ago we could have had a wonderful holiday in Canada, remember, but I gave in to your wishes and got the conservatory built instead.'

'Oh, if only you knew,' she fumed. 'If only you knew the truth.'

'The truth about what?' His bewilderment was apparent. 'Eh? I've always done what you wanted.'

'Are you joking? You've a short memory! Remember when, without so much as a thought for how desperately I wanted another child, you took that right away from me?'

His chin was thrust out and his eyes hardened. 'That was for your own good, Annie, and you know it!'

Tight-lipped, she didn't answer him. He was awakening old grudges and she wanted to lash out at him. But that could prove fatal. She wished he would take himself off somewhere until she was in control of her senses. Too many accusations were trembling on her lips, ready to spew out. Things that once said would be irreversible and fraught with danger.

Completely unaware of her simmering anger, he said gently, 'You know, I only want what is best for Rebecca. If I hadn't been so pig-headed they could have been married and then this uncle of Desi's wouldn't have wasted his money sending them off to the other side of the world.'

'It's no use mulling over that now. They'll manage all right. Just you wait and see.'

'I wish I could be as sure of that as you seem to be. But they're so far away.'

'Well, if we're needed in an emergency, we can scrape the money together and be with her in no time at all.'

'Huh, you never cease to amaze me, Annie. If it was someone else's daughter you wouldn't be so broad-minded about it.'

'Listen, Sean, if she does fall from grace, what about it, eh? She won't be the first, for heaven's sake.'

'That's not the point! She was brought up decently. We should be able to expect the best from her.'

Annie was at the end of her tether. 'Why? Tell me why? Are *we* so perfect that we can expect it in others?' she cried in exasperation. 'Didn't *you* fall by the wayside?'

Sean couldn't believe his ears. Imagine Annie throwing that in his face now. 'You're not harping back to me and Rosaleen surely? That was just a fling!' These words took him by surprise. Had he really convinced himself it had only been a fling? Hadn't she, for a long time, been the love of his life?

'Tell me, Sean, what's wrong with Desi? Just what did he ever do to make you dislike him so bitterly?'

'He was such a know-all! All mouth and poetry. And I didn't like the way he treated Rachel.'

'Did it never dawn on you that perhaps he was trying to make a good impression that first night he came? Have you never said or done something you later regretted? You didn't give him a chance. Most men would be delighted to have a young man with a degree interested in their daughter, but not you! Oh, no, Sean Devlin has to be different. As for Rachel . . . it's not the first time a man has fallen in love with his girlfriend's sister. It would have been different if they had been engaged or married, but Rachel hardly knew him.'

'Are you pleased they're away together then? Does it not worry you that they are probably sleeping together.'

'What makes you think that? Is this the voice of experience talking now?'

'Ah, come off it, Annie! Do you think they will just hold hands and recite poetry together? Of course they'll be at it!'

'You sicken me! You're such a sanctimonious prig. How long did we go out together before we got married, eh? And were we "at it", as you so crudely put it?'

'Things were different then!'

'So you keep telling me.'

'I bet she comes back with a child. How will you feel then?'

Drawing herself to her full height, Annie faced him. She was fed up with his 'Holier than thou' attitude. It was time that he faced the truth; realized just how fallible he was. Perhaps then he would stop pointing the finger. They were middle-aged people. If he couldn't face the truth now, he never would. She decided the time had come for a show-down.

For a moment she dithered, then flung the truth at him. 'A fling . . . or one-night stand, as you both so aptly put it, that left Rosaleen pregnant. She was left to carry on alone, with a child. And she managed. She managed very well indeed all these years.'

She watched fearfully as he digested these words. There was no vestige of colour in his face and his jaw muscles twitched erratically. Already she regretted her decision to speak out; wished that she had held her tongue. A shake of the head showed he didn't believe her and she sighed in relief. Perhaps it was just as well. She hadn't really meant to blurt out the truth like that. Not after all the trouble she had taken to keep it hidden all these years. It was because he had goaded her beyond endurance. She was sick, sore and tired of defending Rebecca's reputation.

He stood in a daze as memories from the past bombarded him. He distinctly remembered his dismay that a dying man like Joe could leave Rosaleen pregnant while he himself had been unable to give Annie a child. Had he been blind? Had that one encounter after Joe's death really resulted in a pregnancy? He just couldn't take it in.

In two strides he was on her and gripping her roughly by the arms, shaking her. 'Are you telling me that Liam is my son? Is that what you're saying?'

Uncertainty was now overwhelming her as she gazed fearfully into his eyes and admitted, 'Yes, I think it's about time you learnt the truth. Perhaps you won't be so bloody sanctimonious then.'

'Liam's really mine? My son?' His face widened with amazement, eyes practically popping out of their sockets. 'Why wasn't I told, eh? Why wasn't I?' The restrained anger in his voice brought fear to her heart.

'Because you didn't want to know, that's why!' she cried. 'You weren't blind. It was plain for all to see. I saw it! He's your double. Why do you think Rosaleen emigrated to Canada? It was because as the child grew older and the family saw you and him together, they would have put two and two together and guessed the truth. She left while you were still in the Merchant Navy to avoid that. And why do you think we never received any invitations to visit her in Canada? Eh? It was because your adultery would have become apparent to all concerned. 'You spoilt a lot of things for me, Sean Devlin, because you couldn't control your lust, so don't rant on at me about Rebecca. She's a far better person than you'll ever be. Liam is your double. You'd swear that you spat him out of your mouth.'

The anger that had spurred her on petered out and she continued more quietly, 'That's why Rosaleen never brought him over here on holiday, or sent any photos over for that matter. That's also the reason why we couldn't take that holiday to Canada. Did you really think I wanted to pass up a wonderful opportunity like that, Sean? I was made out to be an old stick-in-the-mud. The girls hated me for it! I would loved to have gone, but of course I couldn't. I was afraid of losing you when you learnt the truth. And you would have! Certainly George was gobsmacked when he first saw Liam when we were over for the funeral.'

All her accusations churned together in his mind. He latched on to the last one. 'George knows? George knows as well?' Incredulity spread through him at the very idea. 'Seems to me I should be the one to rant and rave. Good God, I was the one who was duped. I had the right to know, do you hear me? I had the right to know! I should have been told the truth.'

'What would you have done, Sean? Although you didn't know it at the time, I was expecting our first child. Would you have left me and gone off with Rosaleen? Did you still love her? Remember, I gave you the option all those years ago and you chose to stay. In fact, you convinced me that you loved me. So there!'

'But I didn't know the whole truth!'

'So you would have left me? Is that what you're saying?'

'How do I know what I would have done? You didn't risk it by telling me the truth so now we'll never know. I'm sure something could have been worked out. There was no need for her to take off like that. We could have worked something out between us. We were adult people, for heaven's sake! Not a bunch of kids.'

Annie's voice was sad. 'Don't be daft! She wouldn't have gone away if something could have been worked out. At least she was thinking of me. She didn't want to put you on the spot. Do you think I could have lived with Liam running around and everybody knowing you'd been unfaithful to me? Do you?'

He threw her roughly from him. This was all too much to take in so suddenly. He needed space to think this through. Without another glance at her he left the house. Slowly she sank down on the chair by the fire, hands cradling her head as she rocked to and fro in anguish. What would Sean do? She had never seen him so angry. A chill crept through her body. She shivered in foreboding. Would she ever feel warm again?

With great difficulty Sean controlled his anger as he eased the car from the drive. He wanted to put his foot down and roar away but common sense prevailed. This was a twisting road and he could cause an accident if he wasn't careful. His care continued along the Antrim Road but once through Glengormley, putting his foot down, he roared along the open country road, fields and farmland passing in a blur in the arc of the headlights.

Pictures from the past kept flashing through his mind. Joe had been buried on the very day Sean had at last managed to get home on compassionate leave. He had arrived in Colinward Street to find Annie in a right state. It seemed that Rosaleen had insisted on being alone in the house with just young Laura for company. Annie was worried about her and had urged him to go and make sure she was all right. He had been only too happy to oblige. When Rosaleen had opened the door to his knock she had looked so young and vulnerable, he had held her close. The way he felt about her, it was inevitable that she should end up naked in his arms. She had given her all in great abandon and he had been so happy. But not for long! She had convinced him that on her part it had been nothing but lust. That she was missing Joe so badly. She had sounded very convincing, and he had believed her.

Annie and he had been going through a rough patch at the time. All she could think of was having a child and apparently he was unable to give her one. He had tried to persuade Rosaleen to run off with him, picturing a life in England or America with her and young Laura. At that time he really had been convinced that Annie didn't love him. Rosaleen had refused. He remembered how, some weeks later, he had actually secretly cried when he'd heard that she was pregnant, bewildered that a dying man had given her a child while he, after years of marriage, was unable to make Annie conceive. What a fool he had been! Imagine not realizing that Liam was his. He had a son he hadn't seen since he was ten months old. Sean remembered the little boy toddling from one to the other of them, but could not recall his features. If Annie had guessed the truth, then how come he had been so blind? Was she right? Had he not wanted to know the truth?

He drew into a lay-by and, closing his eyes, tried to work

things out in the quiet insulation of the car. What difference would this make to their lives?

Could he and Annie carry on after all this deceit? Between them, she and Rosaleen had stitched him up good and proper; had made a right fool of him. He didn't take kindly to being duped. Bitterness was warping his judgement, making it difficult for him to think rationally. He sat for a long time reliving the past and at last came to a decision. It was time to bring it all out into the open. Tomorrow he would face Rosaleen and hear what excuses she had to offer.

It was late when he returned to the house. Annie lay with ears strained following his progress along the hall and into the living room. She heard the fire she had banked up for the night being poked into life again. Then all was silent and she guessed he would remain downstairs and sleep on the settee. For a long time she tossed and turned, unable to sleep. She lay envying the snores that rose from below, proclaiming that Sean was having no such difficulty. Eventually sleep also claimed her.

She slept late next morning. Starting up in alarm, she sank back when she realized it was still holiday time and she didn't have to rush to get Thomas off to school.

'It's not like you to have a lie in, Mam,' Rachel greeted her when she eventually ventured downstairs to face the world. 'You must have been tired.'

'Mmm. Where's your dad?'

Rachel shrugged. 'I thought he was still in bed. Can I get you some breakfast?'

'He got up early. Must have gone for a walk or something. Thanks. A glass of orange and some toast would be lovely.'

Rachel fussed over her and Annie's nerves, already on edge, were stretched to breaking point. Lifting her glass of juice and plate of toast with hands that shook, she said, 'Thanks, love. I'll just sit in the conservatory and have these.'

'It will be cold out there, Mam, so early in the day. It's January, remember.'

'I'll be all right. This dressing gown is nice and warm. Don't let me keep you, love. You do whatever you have to do.'

'I'm supposed to meet some friends in town this morning to

go round the sales.' Rachel eyed her mother keenly. 'Will you be all right? You look a bit off colour.'

'I'm fine, Rachel. Away you go and enjoy yourself.'

Later when Rachel, after more fussing and lamenting on her pallor, eventually left the house, Annie checked the garage. It was empty. Where had Sean gone so early in the day? He had arranged a few days off so that they could spend some time together. Why hadn't she kept her big mouth shut? This could have been a happy time; they could have taken Thomas out for the day if only she had kept quiet.

Sean sat outside the driveway to Rosaleen's new detached house, in two minds. Was he doing the right thing confronting her? Would it not be better to have it out with Annie first? Get all the ins and outs of it before facing Rosaleen. Did she need to know that he now knew the truth? Suddenly he came to a decision. Come what may, he just had to hear her side of it. Leaving the car on the road, he was halfway up the drive when the thought hit him that perhaps she might not be alone. He was aware that young Patricia was staying over in Bangor for a few days. She loved visiting Josie and the kids. What if, meanwhile, Pat McDade was keeping Rosaleen company? He'd feel a right fool bursting in on them at this hour of the morning. Still, that was a chance he would have to take. After all, Rosaleen was a free agent; she could entertain whomsoever she liked so there should be no embarrassment. If Pat was there, Sean would make some excuse and leave.

There was no answer to his ring on the bell so, circling the house, he knocked on the back door. Still no sign of life. Maybe Rosaleen was away somewhere with Pat for a few days. He was about to retrace his steps when he caught sight of her leaving the greenhouse at the bottom of the long back garden. He watched from the shadows of the patio as she walked towards him, still slim and beautiful in tight-fitting jeans and pale green cashmere sweater, her hair catching the pale winter sunlight. She really was holding her age well. He felt old and haggard in comparison.

Deep in thought, pausing to pull a weed here, gently touch a snowdrop there, she was almost upon him before realizing he was standing there. She stopped, hand on her heart, and gasped, 'You frightened the life out of me, Sean Devlin! Skulking there in the shadows. Why didn't you let me know you were here?'

He shrugged. 'I thought you saw me. I did knock on the door but got no reply.'

She eyed him warily. There was something different about him, but what? He appeared tense; not his usual relaxed self. 'I was seeing just what sort of shape the greenhouse is in. Pat has offered to clear it out and start afresh for me. What has you out so early in the day?' She unlocked the door as she spoke and led the way into a spacious kitchen. 'Have you eaten? I was going to fry myself some bacon and egg. Would you like some?'

Realizing that he had not eaten since tea-time the previous day, he nodded his head. 'That would be lovely.'

His eyes followed her every move as she flitted from cupboard to stove, remembering past romantic episodes. The thrust of her breasts against the fine cashmere wool and the slim buttocks in the tight jeans set him off. He grimaced wryly, resenting the fact that he could still be so aroused by her sensuality. She had deceived him, for heaven's sake! And here he was, longing to hold her close. At last, unable to bear his scrutiny, she cried restlessly, 'Why are you looking at me like that, Sean?'

'You used to like me looking at you, Rosaleen. But no matter.' He nodded towards the pan. 'That smells lovely. I didn't realize just how hungry I was. Let's eat first and talk later.'

He soon cleared the plate she put in front of him and pushed it to one side. 'Can I have a cigarette?

Under his intense scrutiny she fidgeted, pushing her food about the plate, eating very little. Now she looked up at him in concern. 'When did you start smoking again?'

'As from now. Give me one, please.'

'No, I will not. Annie will be after my blood if I start you off again.'

He reached over and gripped her wrist so tightly she cried aloud in pain. 'I think it's about time you and my dear wife let me make up my own mind about things, don't you?'

'I don't know what you're talking about.' He released her

and as she rubbed ruefully at her wrist she questioned him, 'Just what are you getting at?'

He rose to his feet and stood towering over her. 'I'm getting at the fact that between the pair of you, you decided I should live in total ignorance of the fact that I have another son.'

A lump gathered in her throat and threatened to choke her. Dear God, how had he found out? How she had longed for him to know. But not like this. Gulping convulsively to dislodge the lump, she said unsteadily, 'What in the name of heaven are you talking about?'

Leaning his hands on the table, he glared into her face and ground out through clenched teeth: 'You know very well what I'm talking about. What right had you to deny me the knowledge that I was the father of Liam? You, above all, Rosaleen, knew how tormented I was with Annie accusing me of being infertile. She made me feel half a man. Yet all the while you knew that I was the father of your child and you never once spoke up in my defence.'

She made to rise, to get away from the anger and hurt in his eyes, but he barked, 'Sit,' and like a whipped dog she obeyed.

'Why didn't you tell me?'

Slowly, anger built within her. What was he ranting on about? His pride! She was the one who'd had to leave her country, her family and friends. Until her marriage to Andrew, she'd had to raise the baby on her own. Now she hissed at him, 'How could I? Eh? You were married to my sister and she was nuts about you. How could I break her heart? And remember, I had Laura to consider. I couldn't run off with her wonderful Uncle Sean. She would have wanted to know where Aunt Annie was. Besides, I just couldn't have faced all the scandal it would have caused.'

'So you couldn't face living in sin. Is that what you're saying? You could, however, make mad passionate love to your sister's husband, so long as nobody knew about it. So long as no one guessed your guilty secret. What kind of woman are you, for God's sake? What about Andrew? Did you keep him in the dark as well?'

'No, he knew everything about me, and married me in spite of all my dark secrets. He was a wonderful man. I could talk

291

to him. I did what I had to do all those years ago. I had no one to turn to. Can you picture me asking Mam for advice? No, I think not! So I took the only option open to me, which turned out to be the right one.'

Like gas escaping from a balloon, all the tension left his body. Pulling a chair round beside her, he sat down. Clasping her hands between his, he gazed into bewildered green eyes. 'I realize that it must have been hard for you, Rosaleen, but you should have told me. We could have worked something out between us.'

She shook her head sadly and tears brimmed over and fell at the memory of it all. 'There was no alternative. I half hoped that you would realize the truth and the decision would be taken out of my hands. You didn't! But Annie did. She was heartbroken. We talked it over and I did what I thought was best for all concerned.'

Gently he wiped away her tears. 'I was a blind fool. But I should have been told the truth. You and Annie had no right to keep me in the dark. What happens now, Rosaleen? Are we supposed to carry on as if everything is still the same?'

'In reality, Sean, nothing has changed. It would ruin too many lives for the truth to be revealed at this late stage.'

'You mean, you expect me to sit back and do nothing?' He sounded scandalized.

Quickly she assured him, 'That's exactly what I mean! Can't you see? There's no other way. We can't turn back the clock.'

'We could be together, Rosaleen.' Agitated at the hope that leapt into her heart, her hands trembled in his. She tried to drag them away. She must be strong. But he defied her efforts and clung on. 'Listen to me, Rosaleen. I saw how you looked at me. I know I could make you love me again.'

Make her love him again? Was he so blind he couldn't see that she had never stopped loving him? Against her will she allowed him to draw her to her feet and into his arms. As always she trembled in anticipation. Only he had been able to arouse her like this. Andrew had been a wonderful fulfilling lover, but only Sean, her first love, could set her afire.

His mouth savaged hers and hungrily she responded, her arms gripping him close, as the old fire spread through her body. It had been so long since she had felt like this. Hadn't she, at the back of her mind, returned here to live, determined to grab any chance of happiness that fate offered her? She hadn't dared hope that Sean could be hers. But now, here was her chance of even greater happiness than she had ever anticipated. There was no need for Annie to know. She could see him now and again. That would be sufficient to keep everybody happy.

It was Sean who came to his senses first. Pushing her away so that he could see into her eyes, he muttered, 'Is this for real, Rosaleen? Are you going to live with me?'

She wanted to say, 'Yes, yes,' make him get on with it; she wanted him so, but common sense forbade it. He must come to her on her terms. A scandal was out of the question.

'You know I can't do that, Sean.'

'Why not, Rosaleen? Are you committed to Pat McDade or something?'

'No, I'm not. But what about Annie? And Thomas, and the girls! What about them? Aren't you forgetting about them?'

'You must have noticed by now that Annie and I have drifted far apart. I can't reach her any more. The girls are old enough to understand. As for Thomas, of course I'll provide for him.'

'Sean, Annie needs you. She can't rear him on her own.'

'Ah, come off it, Rosaleen. He's her whole life! He's all *she* needs.'

'No, Sean. That's where you're wrong . . .'

Her voice trailed off as once more he gathered her close and she succumbed to his desire. They clung together and she argued with herself. He was right! Annie was a foolish woman. If she had kept him contented he wouldn't be here now. Her sister had had him for over twenty years. He should be so devoted to her by now that he would never dream of leaving. But did that make it right? Of course it didn't!

Feverishly she twisted in his arms and broke free. Gripping the edge of the sink, she gazed blindly out of the window, gasping for air.

He watched her in silence, his face a tight determined mask. He would not be thwarted again. When at last she could trust her voice she said pleadingly, 'Sean, be reasonable. We can be together as often as you like. You can come here whenever you get the chance, but let's keep it quiet. Let's not cause a scandal. Our families would never forgive us and I couldn't live with that.'

'To hell with the families! I'm sick to the teeth bowing to everybody's whims. I'm a man, for God's sake, not some wee schoolboy who is expected to do everything he's told. Tell me this, do you love me or not?'

He had moved close to her and saw the love that would not be denied radiating from her eyes. 'Right, I'll explain it to Annie.'

'No, Sean. Look, let's talk this over. We just can't run into this with our eyes closed.'

'All right. Go ahead! I'm listening. But I warn you, my mind's already made up.'

Out of her depth, she groped for words that would make him see sense. He waited patiently, admiring the soft hair curling around her ears. The wonderful skin that would be the envy of any young girl. Tentatively, he touched her arm. 'Do you know something, Rosaleen? I really did believe that Joe was Liam's father. I was devastated that he could give you a child whereas I had failed Annie. I wasn't pretending, you know, to escape my responsibilities.'

She smiled slightly. 'I know that, Sean. Annie had you in a tizzy. You were easily duped.'

'Were you ever in any doubt as to who was the father? I mean, was it only when the child resembled me that you realized the truth?'

Softly, thoughtlessly, she assured him. 'Oh, no, how could I doubt it, with Joe the way he was? I always knew Liam was yours.'

'What do you mean, "With Joe the way he was"?'

He saw her eyes widen, saw colour flood her face as she floundered about searching for the right words to say. Gripping her arm, he exerted pressure. 'What do you mean?'

Unable to conjure up a suitable reply, she whispered, 'He was impotent.'

The words fell into a well of silence. It lasted so long she breathed a sigh of relief. He had not twigged. Her secret was still safe. The relief was short-lived.

He dragged her round to face him. 'Joe was impotent? Was he always impotent, or was it the effect of the war?'

Thankfully she grabbed at the excuse he afforded her. 'Just after the war. It was the war that caused it! Shell shock, I think they called it.'

He didn't believe her! He recalled the one and only other time that they had made love. He had persuaded her to go out with him one last time, hoping to change her mind about Joe. They had ended up at the Springfield Road dam and they had come together in a wave of uncontrolled passion that would not be denied. He had been elated; exulting in her love. To his great dismay and bewilderment, however, she had still refused even to postpone the wedding. This had been a mere week before her wedding day. He had been convinced that they were meant for each other and that she loved him almost as much as he loved her, but she had scorned him. She had insisted that they had not been thinking rationally and had behaved like animals. The following Saturday, while he had stood outside St Paul's church, broken-hearted, she had gone through with her marriage to Joe Smith. Now it all clicked into place. Had that first encounter at the dam also resulted in a pregnancy? Could Laura also be his?

'Is Laura mine too?' His voice shook at the very idea of what he was insinuating. She opened her mouth to deny this accusation but his grip on her tightened even more and he shook her so violently her teeth chattered. 'Tell me the truth! Or so help me I won't be responsible for my actions. She *is* mine, isn't she?'

Her face was a study in indecision and, releasing her, he groped blindly for a chair and sat down. Laura was his. What next? What else would crawl out of the woodwork?

That lovely young girl, who was now a mother herself, was his daughter. He was a grandfather, for heaven's sake!

'In the name of God, woman, what have you done to me? Does Annie know all this?'

These words galvanized her into action. On her knees beside his chair, she gripped his arm and cried beseechingly, 'No! And she must never find out. She would never believe that it had only happened twice. And could you blame her? She would think that we had been carrying on during the first seven years of your marriage. God, can't you see what it would do to her? She'd be devastated!'

295

'*She'd* be devastated? How the hell do you think I feel? I've a good mind to kill the both of you. It would be worth serving life for! You've played judge and jury with my life; made a real mug of me! Can't you see? If you had been truthful where Laura was concerned, I would never have married Annie.'

'How could I be? If Joe had been a normal man I would never even have guessed that you were Laura's father. She doesn't resemble you in the slightest. I would probably have had plenty of children and I wouldn't have been so foolish as to allow myself to be seduced by you a second time. I can tell you this, Sean Devlin, at the time I was glad of Joe's ring on my finger. You were somewhere in the middle of the Atlantic. I was only too glad that Joe was daft enough to believe that Laura was his.'

His hands cupped her face and he lamented, 'Ah, Rosaleen, it must have been awful for you. You're a very passionate woman and to have lived all those years with a man who couldn't perform . . .'

Annoyed that he had the audacity to pity her, she knocked his arms aside and retaliated. 'Oh, sex isn't everything, you know!' she said curtly. 'I managed. Joe was a kind, considerate husband and father. I wanted for nothing.'

'Nothing, Rosaleen? Nothing?'

'Am I interrupting something. Shall I come back later?'

Both of them swung round to face Pat McDade. He had entered the kitchen unnoticed. How much had he heard?

Slowly, Sean rose to his feet and helped Rosaleen to hers. Gaze intent, he said, 'I'm going home to see Annie, but I'll be back.'

With an abrupt nod to Pat he left the house.

Eyeing the high colour of embarrassment in Rosaleen's cheeks, Pat asked quietly, 'What was all that about?'

'All what?' Her voice was curt. Pat McDade had no right to enter her home without knocking first.

'You two looked real cosy a minute ago. What's going on between you?'

'Your imagination is running away with you, Pat. Believe me, we were anything but cosy. And anyhow, why didn't you knock?'

'Think back, Rosaleen,' he cried indignantly. 'A week ago

you told me not to stand on ceremony. To treat this as a second home. Now you're telling me I must knock before entering. I wish you would make your mind up!'

He was right of course. Not once had he put a foot wrong. She had encouraged him to feel at home. Hadn't she been, in a way, manoeuvring him towards the altar?

Now she placated him. 'I'm sorry, Pat. Sean had some bad news and I was trying to comfort him. I'm glad you came when you did. It was getting a bit embarrassing,' she lied.

He eyed her suspiciously. Something didn't quite ring true here. They had looked so guilty when he walked in on them. Was Rosaleen using him as a smoke screen so that she could carry on with her sister's husband?

'Rosaleen, you made a fool of me once before, all those years ago. I won't let you do it again,' he warned.

Slowly she approached him. 'I won't, Pat. I promise you I won't. I need you.' And she really did need him, if not for all the right reasons! If she could only persuade Sean to keep quiet and visit her whenever he got the chance, she would need Pat's friendship so that things would appear normal on the outside. Suddenly her conscience pricked her. What kind of devious creature was she becoming? Pat cared for her, and here she was planning to use him. Ruthlessly, she pushed this thought from her mind. Hadn't she vowed to grab any chance of happiness that ventured her way, regardless of who got hurt as a consequence? And didn't Sean Devlin figure most in her mind? Hadn't she always loved him? If he was careful, it could all be done on the quiet and no one would be any the wiser.

Hands on his chest, she offered Pat her lips. She put on a great act of returning his passion but he wasn't fooled. Nevertheless he took what she offered. He had made up his mind. Sean was a married man. A married man with a disabled son. If there was anything going on, the chances were that it wouldn't last, and Pat would make sure that he was around to pick up the pieces. He just had to persuade her to marry him. Without her, life would not be worth living.

Annie watched from the sitting-room window as her husband climbed slowly from the car and thought how the night's revelation had aged him. He looked about ten years older. If only she had resisted the impulse to tell him the truth! She waited patiently but he was such a long time entering the house, she went out the back to see what was keeping him. She found him slouched in one of the wicker chairs in the conservatory, head down on his chest. He made no effort to greet her.

'Have you been to see Rosaleen?'

'Yes.'

'And . . .?'

'I got her to admit everything.'

Nervously, she perched on the edge of the other wicker chair and asked, 'What happens now, Sean? Are you going to leave me?'

He hesitated. He had considered confronting her and then packing a bag and going to a guest house until things could be sorted out. However, on the way home from Rosaleen's, away from her overpowering presence, his thoughts had become more rational. He had gone over in his mind all the changes that would have to be made if he decided to leave his wife and handicapped son. The girls were adults, they would probably understand. But Annie and Thomas? Where would they end up?

Every stick and stone of the house and all its contents were paid for. He and Annie were not people to remain in unnecessary debt. That was one thing to be thankful for. Nevertheless, everything would have to be sold and the money split down the middle. There was no way he could just walk away and live off Rosaleen. So what should he do? They had told him so many lies between them, his mind was in complete turmoil. Did Annie really not know that Laura was his daughter? Was Rosaleen still trying to pull the wool over his eyes? He decided to find out. After all, why should his wife be shielded? Rosaleen had said that she would be devastated. Well then, that would make two of them.

'Did you know that Laura was my daughter?'

Obviously she had not. Her start of surprise almost brought her off her precarious perch. All vestige of colour drained from her face and a great moan of pain escaped her white lips. Not trusting herself to stand, she cowered back in the chair and hugged herself for comfort, all the time watching him with great haunted eyes.

He returned the look but could find no pity to offer. She had deceived him. Suddenly she was on her feet and in feverish haste entered the kitchen. Keeping all thought at bay she started to wash and chop vegetables with manic energy. Anything rather than face all the implications of what he had just said. Him and Rosaleen . . . together . . . before they were married! That meant that they were at it for years. Her mind boggled and refused to dwell on it. The vegetables got all her attention. How firm the carrots were; how dark green and flourishing the leeks. They would make a lovely pot of stew.

Thomas had followed his mother into the conservatory and had watched them with worried eyes. He was aware that she was angry, but couldn't understand why. When she left the room he followed her into the kitchen. Sean sat for some moments in thought, then he too followed her. He was sorry now that he had spoken out. Hadn't he betrayed Annie in the first place? It was his adultery that had started this deceit. However, she must be made to understand how all this had put a different complexion on things.

Thomas stood glaring at him and, ruffling his hair to show he understood how his son felt, Sean leant against the table and watched his wife. Anger was in every urgent movement she made. Unwillingly, he began to see things from her point of view. All these years she had been aware that he had a fine healthy son. How that must have eaten away at her. Now he had added to her pain by blurting out the truth about Laura. He should have heeded Rosaleen. With hindsight he now wished he had. No! His conscience disagreed with him. There had been too much deceit already. He had been right to speak out. Covering up all those years ago was the cause of all this misery now. But the sight of his wife's pain filled him with pity. After all, at the beginning she had been the innocent party. He tried to soften the blow.

'It's not what you think, Annie. We didn't have an affair. It only happened twice. And that's the God's honest truth!'

She turned and glared at him with baleful eyes. 'Aren't you just wonderful? You'll be telling me next you didn't even touch her! That you waved a magic wand or something.'

'I know it's hard to believe, Annie, but it's the truth, as sure as God's my witness.'

'You wouldn't know the truth if it was staring you in the face.' Abruptly she turned back to the task in hand. Leeks, carrots and onions were chopped with bitter thrusts and followed each other into a big saucepan. Tears poured down her face and dripped on to the draining board. She ignored him completely, afraid of what she might say once started. She was horrified to find that swear words were struggling to get out of her; she who never swore wanted to curse him to hell. No words would be bad enough to let him know just how she felt about him.

'Annie, stop that! We have to talk.'

'There's nothing to say.'

Going to the fridge, she removed some meat and reached for the sharpest knife. It slipped through the thick stewing steak like it was butter.

'Annie . . .'

She swung round to face him once more. 'There is nothing to say! Do you hear me? I don't want to listen to any more of your excuses. Get the hell out of here before I stick this bloody knife in you.'

With an angry exclamation he moved towards her. 'Listen, all this wouldn't have happened if you hadn't played God with my life. So don't you go threatening me.'

Terrified at the anger in his father's voice and his threatening attitude towards Annie, Thomas started to whimper, bringing her attention to him. 'Hush, son. It's all right.'

The next thing she knew Sean was impaled on the knife as Thomas, seeking to defend her, tried to push his father away. She saw her husband's face go slack with shock, his eyes staring in disbelief, then the knife was pulled from her hand by the weight of his body slumping to the floor.

For some moments she gaped down on him in horror. Then, falling to her knees, she cradled his head in her lap, all the while moaning aloud. His eyes, full of horror, accused her, and his mouth opened and closed like a stranded fish's, but no words came out. Then his eyes glazed over and with a long harsh shudder his body went slack.

'Sean! Sean, do you hear me? Don't leave me. Please, Sean, wake up.'

Memories from the past came to mind. Never let anyone

die in sin! But Sean wasn't going to die. She wouldn't let him. Nevertheless, thrusting her lips close to his ear she whispered an Act of Contrition. Just in case. Oh, God, please don't let him die, she begged. The ugly black handle of the knife was protruding obscenely from his body and a dark red stain crept slowly over his shirt. Grasping it, she pulled it free. Horrified, she watched as the released blood spurted everywhere in a great torrent. She felt it splash her face and saw her hands and dress turn bright red. She could hear Thomas's frightened moans but it was as if they were coming from another world.

It was Rachel's voice, rising in panic as she witnessed the scene in front of her, that penetrated the numbed layers of Annie's brain. 'Mam! Mam, what have you done?'

Relief flooded through her, leaving her weak and limp. 'Thank God you're here, Rachel! Get help. Quickly! Phone for an ambulance and the priest.' Rachel stood as if turned to stone and Annie's voice rose shrilly: 'For God's sake, get help. Get help! Do you want him to die?'

It seemed like an eternity that she knelt whispering endearments in his ear, begging him to hang on; assuring him that help was on its way. In reality it was but a few minutes before the ambulance arrived.

Someone gently coaxed her away from him and then they were working over him stemming the flow of blood; giving him oxygen; setting up a drip.

Rachel led her mother into the living room and pushed her into the armchair. She thrust a glass into her mother's blood-spattered hands. 'Here, Mam, drink this. It will help you.' Sinking down beside her, Rachel whispered in bewilderment, 'Mam, why did you do it?'

'It was an accident. He fell against the knife.'

Rachel's mind wouldn't accept this. Her father was not a clumsy man. 'That doesn't sound like Dad. Besides, I heard you threaten him.'

'He fell against the knife, I'm telling you!'

They heard a car screech to a stop and a commotion in the kitchen.

Rachel whispered, 'It's the police.'

'The police? Why did you send for the police?'

Before Rachel could assure her that she hadn't, two

uniformed men entered the room. They introduced themselves as Sergeant Walsh and Constable Nelson.

Sergeant Walsh was a tall thin man with a long face with drooping jowls that looked as if it had seen the sorrows of the world. It was he who removed the glass from Annie's hand and sniffed at it before putting it to one side.

'Have you been drinking much today, Mrs Devlin?'

'No, she hasn't! I just gave her that whiskey a few minutes ago to settle her nerves, so I did,' Rachel cried defensively.

The long sad face turned in her direction, as if seeing her for the first time. 'And just who are you?'

'I'm her daughter, Rachel!'

'And have you been in the house all day with her?'

'No, I just arrived after the accident happened.'

'Then you didn't witness it?'

'No.'

'So you don't know whether or not it was an accident. Is that right?'

'Of course it was an accident! What are you implying?'

'I wish to question your mother alone. Would you please wait in the other room?'

'I'm not leaving Mam.'

'Well then, be quiet,' he said curtly.

The conversation had gone over Annie's head; her thoughts were full of Sean. She could not forget the accusing look in his eyes before he lost consciousness. Was he going to die?

'Mrs Devlin.'

Her name repeated in a louder tone brought her back with a start of surprise. 'Is he dead? Is Sean dead?'

'They are taking your husband to the hospital, Mrs Devlin.'

'He's still alive then?'

'Yes, he's still alive. Does that worry you, Mrs Devlin?'

'Worry me?' She shook her head in bewilderment. What did he mean?

'Well, if he regains consciousness he will be able to tell us exactly what happened. It would be in your best interests to tell us the truth now.'

'It was an accident. He will tell you that! We were arguing and he was angry. He stumbled and fell against the knife.'

'What were you arguing about?'

'A private family matter.'

'And your husband was very angry?'

'Yes, very,' Annie whispered. She pictured Sean's face, convulsed with wrath as he came towards her, he was so very angry.

'You were afraid of him?'

'Afraid? Of Sean? No! No, Sean is a gentle man. He would never harm me.'

'But you said he was very angry. So you thought that he just might harm you. Is that right? Is that why you stabbed him with the knife?'

'No, I tell you, it was an accident. He fell against the knife.'

At a nod from the sergeant, the constable went to the door and beckoned to someone outside. A young police woman came into the room.

'Constable Newton, please take Mrs Devlin upstairs and help her change into clean clothes. Bag what she is wearing for forensics. And when we leave, don't let anyone into that kitchen until forensics have given it the once over.'

Rachel was on her feet at once. 'I'll look after my mother, thank you.'

'I'm afraid Constable Newton will have to accompany you.'

Tight-lipped, Rachel assisted Annie to her feet and from the room, closely followed by the police woman. A great fear was gathering within her. The police were treating her mother like a criminal. What had her parents been arguing about? Had Mam in a moment of anger stabbed him? She caught sight of Thomas huddled in a corner of the sitting room. He had witnessed it all! If only he could understand, he would be able to explain. Poor Thomas; he must be so confused. She would have to attend to him next.

As her mother removed each item of clothing, the police woman took it from her and dropped it into a plastic bag. Then she stood at the bathroom door while Annie took a shower. Rachel handed her mother a bath towel and stood between her and Constable Newton while she dressed. She wished they were alone and she could question her mother further. Her father's white stricken face swam before her eyes. What on earth had possessed her mother?

However, the closeness of the police woman prevented any further conversation.

When they descended the stairs Rachel was horrified to hear the sergeant requesting that her mother accompany them to the station to help them with their enquiries. They were taking her to York Street Police Station for further questioning.

Annie took all this very calmly. 'It's all right, Rachel. I'll soon make them understand. Ring George and ask him to come over. He'll know what to do.'

'George? Who George?' Sergeant Walsh suspiciously latched on to the masculine name. Was this the typical love triangle?

It was Annie who answered him. 'He's my brother.'

'Oh, I see.'

People had gathered outside; some standing in the drive of the Presbyterian Church across the road, some huddled in small groups along the road. All whispering and nudging each other, wide-eyed with anticipation. Nothing as exciting as this had happened since the woman in the White City was arrested for kidnapping a baby many years ago. Annie bowed her head. Sean would be so annoyed if he knew he was the centre of all this excitement. The ambulance door was open and she hurried towards it. Quickly Constable Newton pulled her back.

'Is he still alive? Please, find out if he's still alive.'

A young man whom she took be a doctor took pity on her. 'Yes, missus, he is still alive, but only just! It will be touch and go. He has lost a lot of blood.'

'Thanks be to God.' Her eyes sought Rachel's. 'Where is Father Malachy? Why isn't he here? Sean should have the last rites.' She turned to the police woman. 'Can I go with him?'

With a sad shake of the head Constable Newton answered her, 'No, I'm afraid you can't.'

The ambulance sped off with blue lights flashing and as Annie was about to be bundled into the back of a police car, Father Malachy's old banger drew up. In a flash Annie escaped the police woman's grip and was at the door of the car.

'What kept you? Sean needs you!'

'I was out on a sick call, Mrs Devlin.'

304

Quickly a red-faced Constable Newton regained her hold on Annie, more firmly this time, and tugged her back to the police car. Inspector Walsh climbed in beside the driver and they headed down the Serpentine Road, leaving Constable Newton standing guard at the front door.

As it left, a young couple approached Rachel. It was the man and wife who had bought Minnie's house some time ago, and had just moved in a few weeks back.

The man, voice full of compassion, said diffidently, 'Look, if we're intruding, just say so and we'll go away. But you seem to be alone and we thought you might need some help.'

'Oh, yes, thank you. Please come in. I'm at my wits' end what to do about Thomas.'

'We'll look after him for you. He's met us before so at least we aren't strangers to him. Will you not come in and sit with us?'

'Thanks. I appreciate the offer but I have some phone calls to make.'

She had been leading the way into the sitting room as she spoke, watched by the ever alert constable. 'Ah, Thomas. Thomas, love.'

Her brother was curled up in a ball on the armchair near the window and rocking himself as if in great pain, soft piteous moans issuing from his lips.

'Thomas, will you go next door with Joan and Freddy? They will look after you until I get Uncle George to come and fetch you. You'll like that, won't you, going over to Josie's?'

It was some minutes before she could persuade him to leave the sanctuary of his chair and accompany their new neighbours next door. Rachel was grateful for their kind consideration. They did not ask any embarrassing questions about what had happened. To be truthful, if they had there wasn't very much she could have told them. What did her father do to justify getting stabbed? She just couldn't understand it. Eventually she would find out, but meantime, she had to phone Uncle George.

Chapter 8

Slowly, Josie replaced the receiver on its cradle, a frown puckering her brow. She stood for a long time gazing at it, unable to take in what she had just heard. Annie arrested! Surely there must be some mistake? Quickly she made her way to the back of the bungalow and entered the spare room. Standing stock still inside the door she waited for her husband's undivided attention. George took no notice of her for a few moments, then becoming aware of her presence, glanced up from the strip of wallpaper he was pasting and looked askance.

'That was Rachel on the phone. But I must have somehow or other picked her up wrong. She's in an awful state! She says there has been an accident and that the police have arrested her mother. She's crying her eyes out. I told her that you would ring her back.'

Carefully, to avoid drips, George drew the brush back and forth across the string he had tied over the top of the paste bucket, before putting it to one side. Reaching for a rag, he wiped his hands. 'Arrested our Annie?' Laughter accompanied his words. 'You certainly must have gotten your wires crossed, Josie.'

He bent and kissed her furrowed brow as he passed by. 'Don't look so worried, pet. I'll soon get it all sorted out.'

The phone was answered on the first ring. It was Rachel. 'Oh, Uncle George, thank God it's you! I was so relieved when Josie said you were still on holiday from work – I'm at my wit's end. Don't know what to do. It's awful here, so it is. I don't know where to turn or what to do. I don't want to go down and upset Grannie until I hear how Dad is . . .'

Apprehensive now, George interrupted the garbled flow of his niece's words. 'Hold on a minute, love. Start at the beginning and tell me what happened.'

'That's just it! I don't *know* what happened. I went to town this morning to the sales. Mam was a bit off colour. A bit depressed, you know. I didn't want to leave her, but she insisted that I go. When I arrived home a while ago me dad was lying on the kitchen floor and Mam was hysterical. I couldn't get any sense out of her. There was blood everywhere. All over her face and hands and clothes; it's even splattered on the walls, and there's a pool of it on the kitchen floor. It's like something out of a horror movie! Mam was cradling Dad's head in her lap and begging him not to die, but I think he's dead already.'

Her voice rose shrilly and George said soothingly, 'It's all right, Rachel. Stay calm, love. We'll soon find out how he is.'

He heard her gulp for control and said, 'Good girl. You're doing fine.'

After a short pause she continued, 'Mam told me to phone for an ambulance and the priest. I dialled 999 and the police came as well as the ambulance. Luckily the ambulance was only minutes away, dropping a patient off at the Throne Hospital. It arrived in no time. Father Malachy came just as they were putting me mam into the police car. It was awful! Mam lashed out at him, accusing him of letting Dad die without a priest giving him the last rites. He had a talk with the officer in charge then followed the ambulance to the Mater Hospital. The police took Mam away. She told me to ring you.'

'Rachel, whose blood is it?'

'Dad's! I told you, I think he's dead.' Sobs tore at her throat. 'I think me mam killed him!'

'Steady on now, love, and don't talk daft. Where did they take her?'

'York Street Police Station.'

'Where's Thomas?'

'Our new neighbours took him in next door. He seems to be in a state of shock. They're getting the doctor out to him.'

'Why don't you join them, love? You shouldn't be on your own.'

'They wanted me to, but I prefer to stay here near the phone.

307

You know, in case anyone rings. Besides, I'm not on my own. The forensics people are here. They're all over the place.'

George was annoyed with himself. He should have realized that perhaps their conversation could be overheard. 'Listen, Rachel. I'll break the news to Thelma and John and get them to go up to you. You need company. I'll find out how your dad is too, and then I'll go to the police station. All right, love?'

'Thanks, Uncle George. Don't be too long. Sure you won't?'

'I'll be as quick as I can, love.'

It was John who answered the phone at Orange Row. Quickly George put him in the picture as far as he was able.

John was very calm, as if he received tragic news like this every day. 'Never worry about Thelma, George. She's stronger than you think. I'll break the news gently and we will go on up and keep Rachel company until you come. Thanks for ringing. See you later, son.'

Josie had followed her husband into the hall and listened to his side of the conversation. She knew something was seriously wrong. Fearfully she waited for an explanation.

'There has been some kind of accident,' he volunteered. 'Sean is in the Mater Hospital and Annie has been arrested.' He started thumbing through the telephone directory.

'What on earth do you think could have happened?'

'I wouldn't even try to hazard a guess, but it must be serious if the police have arrested Annie. They don't do that without some justification. Do you mind if I leave you alone, love? I know I was supposed to work wonders in the spare room today but this is an emergency.'

He was running his finger down a column of names as he spoke, not really listening to her reply. 'Ah, here's what I'm looking for. I must let Sean's parents know that there has been an accident. They'll want to go to the hospital to see him. Will you be all right, love? Patricia will help with the kids.'

'Of course I'll be all right. You must go to Annie,' Josie repeated. 'But first you had better change out of those old clothes. Have a quick wash and I'll get some decent clothes ready.'

Ten minutes later he was in the car, ready for the road. 'I'll ring you as soon as I know anything, Josie. I can't understand why they arrested Annie. Surely there must be some mistake?

I'll head away on, love. See you soon.' For the first time since they were married he forgot to kiss her goodbye. All his thoughts were on Annie.

Annie sat slumped on a bench gazing blindly at the dirty cream wall of the police cell. They had questioned her for hours and hours. The same questions over and over again. Surely they couldn't really believe that she would be capable of murder? It had been an accident! Thomas hadn't meant any harm when he had pushed his father. But then, they must never learn of Thomas's part in this. They would say he was dangerous and have him put away. That must never happen. They refused to tell her whether Sean was dead or alive. Was this a bad sign? She didn't know. Her only knowledge of jails was what she saw on TV. Had Rachel phoned George? Why wasn't he here?

In spite of trying to keep her thoughts occupied she found them returning again and again to the awful events of the day. In her mind's eye she relived over and over again the terrible scene. She saw Sean coming towards her, his face flushed with anger. Heard his cutting words as he lashed out at her, accusing her of playing God with his life. The next thing she knew he lurched towards her. She shivered as she recalled the sensation of the the knife jarring in her hand as it sliced through his clothes and into his body. In the confined space she hadn't stood a chance of avoiding him. Would they believe that? She remembered how the blood had turned her hands and clothes bright red, terrifying her. Stifled sounds had brought her attention to where her son cowered in a corner. He must be looked after. What was she going to do?

'Mam! Mam, what have you done?' The appearance of Rachel came as a great relief to Annie. The next thing she knew the police had come and arrested her. Why had Rachel sent for the police? Surely to God her daughter didn't think that she had deliberately stabbed Sean?

Aching in every limb, she wearily curled up on the hard wooden bench and closed her smarting eyes. If only she could sleep, but the image of Sean's deathly white face branded across her mind prevented it. Tomorrow she was to be taken to Chichester Street, and there she would appear before the Magistrates Court and be charged. The horror of it all made her body jerk in revulsion. Charged with attempted murder? Maybe murder? Oh, dear God, help me. Please help me, she entreated silently. Above all, please don't let Sean die.

George entered the Mater Hospital and after some interrogation was directed to the intensive care unit. That was as far as he got. A police constable sat outside the door.

Rising to attention the constable said, 'I'm afraid you can't go in there, sir.'

There was a small window in the door and George peered through it. The figure on the bed had an oxygen mask on and tubes protruded from his body. One was attached to a blood bag; what the others were for he had no idea. A nurse was monitoring the equipment beside the bed. From what he could see of Sean, he was a grey colour. The policeman moved closer, ready to stop him if he should attempt to enter the room.

'How is he?'

'You are . . .?'

'I'm his brother-in-law.'

'I'm afraid I can't discuss his condition with you, sir.'

'George! Thanks for phoning me. In the name of God, what happened, man?'

At the sound of his name George swung round and confronted a tall elderly man. It was Jim Devlin, Sean's father. They had only met a few times before at family gatherings but got on well.

'I don't know, Jim. They won't tell me anything because I'm not immediate family.'

'Well, I am! Is Sean in there?' Jim made to enter the room but the policeman quickly blocked his way.

'I'm afraid I can't let you go in there, sir.'

'I'm his father, for heaven's sake, man!'

'I'm sorry, but I don't have the authority.'

Jim swung on his heel and stamped down the corridor. 'Come on, George, let's find someone who *has* the authority.'

Some time and numerous phone calls later to different parts of the hospital, a small man came and introduced himself as John Carson, the consultant in charge of Sean's case.

'I'm afraid your son is not out of the woods yet. He has lost a lot of blood. Indeed, if an ambulance hadn't been nearby he would have surely died.'

'What are his chances, Doctor?'

'About fifty-fifty.'

'Can we see him?'

The surgeon considered for a moment. At last he muttered, 'He's unconscious. He won't know you're there. But yes, if it helps to set your mind at rest, you can see him for a minute. That is, if the police agree?'

Another phone call and the police constable on guard got permission for them to enter. George stood beside Jim Devlin, looking down on the bleached face of his brother-in-law. God, but Sean looked dead already. How had this come about? What had possessed Annie?

Jim turned to him in stunned bewilderment and for a moment George thought the man was going to pass out. And no wonder! Sean looked like a corpse. After a silent struggle, he regained his composure and, dropping to his knees, knelt in prayer beside the bed. Feeling that he was intruding, George quietly left the room.

Joining him some minutes later, a badly shaken Jim cried in anguish, 'He looks at death's door! What possessed Annie? Eh, George? Why, she idolizes him. Did she have a brainstorm or something?'

'I don't know, Jim. You know as much as me. I'm going to the police station now to see if they will let me talk to her. Like to come along?'

'I would, but first I must phone Jane. She's not in the best of health and I want to reassure her that Sean is still alive. I'll not admit he's only just alive, by the look of it.'

George gave his arm a sympathetic squeeze. 'This must be awful for you, Jim. I'll wait outside.'

At York Street Police Station they had another wait. At last a uniformed officer appeared and told them he was Sergeant Walsh. George introduced himself and Jim and they were then led into a small room and invited to take a seat.

George remained standing. 'I want to see my sister, please.'

'I'm afraid that won't be possible. She will be taken to the

Magistrates Court tomorrow morning and charged. You can see her then.'

'I demand to see her now!' He became belligerent. 'Do I need a solicitor?'

'You must understand that your sister stabbed her husband and the chances are that he could very well die. He has lost a terrible amount of blood. It's a wonder he survived at all. Your sister could well be facing a murder charge. At the very least she will be facing a charge of attempted murder.'

'He's not dead yet, and I want to see my sister! I'll phone my solicitor. I intend seeing her tonight.' George turned on his heel but with a motion of his hand the sergeant stopped him.

'I'm waiting for my superiors to arrive. They might let you see her. Meanwhile, would you like a cup of tea or coffee?'

Slowly George sat down and nodded his head. 'Yes, tea, please.' Jim followed suit but asked for coffee.

It was but a short time later that two plainclothes men bustled into the station, Detective Inspector Green and Detective Sergeant Benson.

They conferred for some minutes with Sergeant Walsh then agreed that George could see Annie once they had questioned her. Another hour passed and his temper was on a short fuse when at last he was was taken along a corridor and shown into another room. Jim was asked to remain behind.

Annie sat slouched on a bench, staring vacantly at the floor. She looked so forlorn and pathetic, George's heart went out to her. When she became aware of him she made no effort to rise but held out her arms. Tears welled up and ran down her face.

'What kept you? I thought no one cared. I thought you would never come.'

Disregarding the grubby floor, he was on his knees beside her, holding her close, mopping at her face with his handkerchief. 'How could you think such a thing, Annie? Of course I care. We all care. Because of red tape, I've been sitting in a room down the hall for the past couple of hours twiddling my thumbs. Sean's father's still out there. They wouldn't let him see you because he isn't immediate family. He sends his love.'

'Poor Jim. What must he think of me? Have you seen Sean? How is he? They won't tell me anything.'

'Yes, I've seen him, and he's holding his own,' George lied.

'You're telling me the truth?'

'He's lost a lot of blood, but hopefully he'll recover.'

'Thank God! And Thomas? What about him?'

'When I leave here I'm going up to see Rachel and will take Thomas home with me, so don't worry on that score.' He eased himself upright and sat down beside her. Taking her hand between his, he asked gently, 'Annie, what happened?'

Great green eyes looked piteously at him and tears brimmed over once more. 'I didn't do it deliberately, George.'

'Ach, Annie, that goes without saying! I know you wouldn't harm a fly. Tell me exactly what happened.'

In a low voice she began, 'Sean and I were arguing.'

'What about?'

Her lips tightened and she muttered, 'It was private.'

'You'll have to tell them, Annie. You'll be required to make a statement. They will want to know what you were arguing about. Every little detail, no matter how private.'

The tears overflowed and she wailed, 'I can't tell them! I'm so ashamed. To think that he could treat me like that.'

George's heart sank. What on earth had Sean done to have Annie in this state? 'Treat you like what? What did he do, Annie?'

'I can't tell you.'

'Well then, leave that for now. Tell me exactly what happened today.'

She sat in thought for some moments, then began. 'Sean came home and I knew he was upset.' She laughed hollowly and muttered, 'That's an understatement if ever there was one.'

George interrupted her. 'Home from where?'

'Rosaleen's, of course.'

Brows meeting in perplexity, he probed, 'Had he spent the night at Rosaleen's and that's why you were so upset? Is that it?'

'No, he spent the night downstairs on the settee.' She leant closer and confided in a whisper, 'You see, George, yesterday I told him about Liam and he took it badly.'

'Ah, Annie, what possessed you to do that?'

'I had to tell him! He kept going on and on about Rebecca and Desi. Acting as if he was a paragon of virtue. I thought it

313

was about time he faced up to the truth. I thought he was old enough and man enough to take it.' She sighed deeply. 'I wish now I had held my tongue. I was so wrong. He went berserk. Went out in the car and stayed away for hours. I went to bed but couldn't sleep. Kept picturing all kind of things, like his car in a crash and him lying somewhere unable to get help. I didn't know what to do for the best. Eventually, he came home and slept on the settee. Early this morning, before I had a chance to talk to him again, he went over to see Rosaleen. She told him it was true.'

Annie fell silent. After a few moments he prompted her. 'And when he came home what happened?'

Annie's face blanched when she thought of Laura's being Sean's daughter. She couldn't ever tell anyone that terrible thing. Not even George. They would all know that he and Rosaleen had been carrying on under her very nose for years. Why hadn't Sean married her? Her lips tightened as she said, 'Nothing happened. He was angry because Rosaleen and I had deceived him. Later, when I was preparing the stew, he followed me into the kitchen. We argued, and when I turned to face him he fell on the knife.'

'Just like that?'

She avoided direct eye contact and answered tersely, 'Yes. Just like that.'

George rubbed a hand wearily over his face. He was aware that Annie was holding something back. However, they had only allowed him ten minutes alone with her so he changed tactics.

'Annie, listen to me! Tomorrow morning I'll be at the Magistrates Court and I'll have a solicitor with me. Meanwhile don't offer any information and don't sign anything unless a solicitor is present.' With more confidence than he felt, he added, 'And don't you worry too much. We'll have you home in no time at all.'

The door opened and he knew his ten minutes were up. She rose with him and clung to him in terror. 'Don't leave me, George. Please! I dread the night. It will be full of terror.'

'I have to go now, Annie, but tomorrow we will get you out of here. All right, love?'

He put her forcibly from him and walked out of the door

without a backward glance, her sobs echoing in his ears. He didn't want to break down in front of her.

Outside dusk was falling and a chill wind had risen. Before parting company in the sheltered confines of the station doorway, Jim questioned George. 'Well, did you find out what happened?'

'She says Sean fell on the knife.'

'Do you think she's telling the truth, George?'

'She's holding something back, Jim, but I don't for one minute believe that she deliberately stabbed him.'

'To tell you the truth neither do I, son. She thinks the world of him. Do you mind if I go back to the hospital now?'

'Not at all, Jim. I'm only sorry your journey here was wasted. I thought they would have allowed both of us in to see her.'

'Never worry about that, George, though I would dearly have liked to have seen her. It was worth a try. Let me know of any further developments, won't you?'

'Of course I will, Jim. See you soon.'

They hurried to their respective cars and headed off in opposite directions.

Night was now descending with a vengeance, with gale-force winds that cut right to the bone. To crown it all, rain began as George left the Shore Road and turned up the Whitewell Road. It came down in torrents, obscuring his vision still further. The icy wind came down from the hill with such force that when he left the shelter of the car it buffeted his body, tugging at his open Crombie overcoat as if trying to wrench it from him. Pulling it close and sinking his head deep into the protection of the thick collar, he fought against the wind and struggled up the steps to the big oak door, his outer clothes saturated by the torrential rain in such a short space of time.

Before he had time to knock the door was pulled open and Rachel threw herself at him.

'Here, love. Let's get in out of the rain. No need for you to get wet.'

Gently he pushed her inside and closed the door. Removing his coat and shoes, with a word of thanks he took the towel John thrust at him and rubbed vigorously at his thick mop of hair. Then, putting a comforting arm around his niece's shoulders, he gently led her into the living room.

Here, Thelma, looking pale and frail, greeted him plaintively. 'It's been a long day! We thought you'd never get here.'

'I came as soon as I could. Did you think I was enjoying myself?' His reply was more curt than he'd intended and she drew back, a hurt look on her face. To take the sting out of his words he asked in a gentler tone, 'Have forensics gone?'

It was Rachel who answered him. 'Ages ago. The three of us have scrubbed out the kitchen. You should have seen it. It was awful, wasn't it, Grannie?' Thelma nodded her head in agreement and Rachel asked, 'How is Mam? We phoned the hospital and they said Dad was stable and that we could see him tomorrow morning. But we can find out nothing at all about Mam. She must be in an awful state, worrying about me dad and Thomas.'

'I've just left her. She's bearing up well in the circumstances. Where's Thomas?'

'He's asleep. The doctor gave him something to settle his nerves and Freddy, our new neighbour next door, carried him in and put him to bed.'

'Thelma, I haven't eaten anything since breakfast this morning. Will you boil me an egg or something? Then I'll tell you everything I know. But I warn you, it's not much!'

Glad of something to do, she rose quickly to her feet. 'I'll put the pan on. I'm sure Annie will have some bacon and eggs in the house.' She looked inquiringly at Rachel who nodded assent.

'While you do that, I'll phone Josie and bring her up to date. I'm sure she thinks I'm lost.'

It was Josie who, once she was put in the picture, asked if Rosaleen had been notified of events. Assuring her he would find out, George told her he would be home as soon as possible and hung up.

Putting his head into the kitchen where Rachel and Thelma were busily cooking, he inquired, 'Has anyone let Rosaleen know what's happening?'

Thelma and Rachel gaped at each other in dismay and shook their heads. 'I never thought to phone her, Uncle George. My mind is all mixed up.'

'Nor I!' Thelma admitted. 'Perhaps John did. Ask him.'

It was quickly apparent that he had indeed spoken to Rosaleen on the phone.

Looking embarrassed at the question, he beckoned George into the living room and asked, quietly, 'Did I do wrong?'

'No, of course not. I'm surprised no one else thought of it.'

John closed the door and lowered his voice before confessing, 'George, I phoned Rosaleen shortly before you arrived. She's on her way over. I never mentioned it to Thelma and Rachel because I'm a bit worried by Rosaleen's reaction to the news. She practically accused Annie of deliberately stabbing Sean. Kept repeating, "He shouldn't have told her! I told him not to tell her. I knew she'd go berserk." When I asked her what she meant, she just said, "Oh, nothing. Nothing." What do you make of that?'

'Sounds ominous to me. But no matter what she implied, I don't think Annie is capable of deliberately hurting anyone. Let's wait and hear just what Rosaleen has to say.'

He had finished eating and was making motions that indicated it was time he made tracks when a loud urgent knock on the door heralded the arrival of Rosaleen. George opened the door and she burst into the hall and stood there like a drowned rat: breathless, her hair soaked and rain dripping off her mackintosh, a mangled umbrella clutched in her hand. 'What a night! The heavens have truly opened.' Removing her coat, she retired to the bathroom to repair the damage to her hair and face. They waited in silence for her to return. It was some minutes before she eventually reappeared.

'I feel a bit more respectable now.' She got her own question in first. 'How's Sean? They wouldn't tell me anything at the hospital when I phoned.'

'He's holding his own. We can but wait and see.'

'He's so impetuous! I warned him that Annie would be devastated.'

'You think that maybe she stabbed him deliberately?' George asked soberly.

'Why not? I would have done the same in her place. How she must hate me! But poor Sean. He didn't deserve this.'

Outraged, Rachel cried bitterly, 'A fine sister you are! No

matter what it looks like, my mam wouldn't hurt a fly. Regardless of the circumstances.'

Shame-faced, Rosaleen flopped down on the settee and with a grateful glance accepted the cup of coffee that John handed her. 'I'm sorry, Rachel. You're right, of course. That's your mother's weakness. She's too good. Trusts everybody.'

'What made you think Annie might have deliberately stabbed him?' George asked.

Rosaleen sat in deep thought for some time. Obviously they didn't yet know the truth. Well, Liam's parentage would soon be common knowledge. It would be safe to confess to that, but best to keep quiet about Laura in case Sean hadn't mentioned it to Annie. 'Because she was stupid enough to tell Sean that he was the father of my Liam, and he took it very badly.'

Thelma's mouth gaped at this but it was Rachel who cried aloud, 'Liam! My cousin?'

'Your half-brother.'

'You mean . . . you mean . . .' Thelma's voice trembled and she found it hard to form the words of condemnation. To think that one of her own daughters could carry on like that, and with her sister's husband of all people.

It was Rachel who cried bitterly, 'She means she had an affair with my father. Isn't that right? No wonder Mam was devastated. It should have been you she went for. You should have stayed in Canada!'

'Hold on now, Rachel,' George said sternly. 'It takes two! And it all happened a long time ago. Hardly justification for killing anyone now.'

'She has just accused Mam of trying to kill Dad, so she has!' Rachel cried indignantly.

Rosaleen shook her head. 'You don't understand. There's more to it than that.'

'What do you mean?' George asked quickly.

'I'm not at liberty to say. I have to see Sean first.'

'What if he dies, eh, Rosaleen? What then? Have you evidence that can put your sister behind bars for the rest of her life? If he dies, would you want that?'

Rosaleen's eyes widened and fear showed in their depths. Her voice shook when at last she could get her tongue around the words. 'There isn't really any chance of his dying, is there?

318

No, he can't die! You're just trying to frighten me, George Magee. Aren't you?'

'You listen to me, Rosaleen! All of you, listen.' His voice was full of authority. 'This isn't some game we're all caught up in. Sean might very well die, and if the worst comes to the worst . . . Annie could spend a long time behind bars. Is that what you want?' His eyes held Rosaleen's.

'If Annie's guilty she should pay the price!' his sister cried defiantly. 'You just can't stab someone because they've had it off with someone else. Think how many murders there would be if all cheated wives took the law into their own hands.' More quietly, she added, 'He told me he was going to leave her and come to me. That must be why she stabbed him. I begged him not to tell her, but he wouldn't listen!'

'If I know Sean, he wouldn't turn his back on his responsibilities. Walk out on Thomas, just to be with you?' A light scornful laugh accompanied George's words. 'No! Not Sean. Not even in the knowledge that he had fathered Liam.'

Her pride stung, Rosaleen retaliated swiftly. 'It's not just a matter of Thomas and Liam! Sean and I go back a long way. Before he even met Annie. Even before I married Joe! He's Laura's father too. I've always loved him, but I lied to him because I couldn't bear to see Annie so unhappy. If I hadn't been such a fool we would have been married years ago then none of this would ever have happened.'

A stunned silence reigned as the implications of this began to sink in. It was Thelma who broke it. 'Did Joe Smith know this?'

'No, he was naive enough to accept that Laura was his. He wanted to appear normal, you see. But he wasn't! He was impotent. He must have had his doubts but he never voiced them. I tried to ask *you* for advice before Laura was born. Do you remember at all? But you didn't want to know and I'd nowhere else to turn.' Rosaleen's voice was resentful and hot colour flooded Thelma's face.

George got her off the hook. 'Did Sean know about Laura?'

Rosaleen looked guiltily at him. She hadn't meant to reveal so much. The flood gates had just opened. In a low voice she admitted, 'He does now. I didn't mean to tell him, but in the upheaval about Liam, it slipped out.'

'How did he take it?'

'At first he ranted and raved. I've never seen him so upset. Then, when he calmed down, he said that this proved we were destined to be together. Said he would talk to Annie ... make her see that it would be for the best in the long run. I tried to talk some sense into him. I warned him that she would be devastated, and that there was no telling what she might do, but he just wouldn't listen.'

'Do you think he told Annie about Laura?'

Rosaleen shrugged her shoulders slightly. 'How can I know? He left me with that intention but he might have had second thoughts.'

A great tide of compassion welled within Rachel as she pictured how hurt her mother would be if she ever learnt her husband and sister had been deceiving her. If she had known, it would have been enough to make her lash out in anger. And if this was so, it was her aunt's fault. She who had everything had taken what was most precious to Annie. Rachel came to a quick decision. This was no place for her aunt. 'I think you had better leave this house, Aunt Rosaleen. My hands are itching to strangle you.' With these words she entered the hall and came back with Rosaleen's mackintosh.

Rosaleen threw her a look of contempt. 'Oh, don't be so silly! Act your age! This is the nineteen sixties we're in, in case you didn't know. If things had been as permissive before the war this would be an entirely different story.'

'Well, they weren't, and you should have known better. I want you to leave now. I don't want the air in my home contaminated by the likes of you.'

George, for the first time in his life that he could remember, stood tongue-tied. His mind could not take in what he had just heard. No wonder Annie was devastated. This was a whole new kettle of fish altogether. His sister was so proud! Had she lost control completely? Had she deliberately stabbed Sean? In the name of God, where was all this going to lead?

With difficulty, he brought his mind back to the present situation. 'I really think you should do as Rachel suggests. Annie wouldn't want you here at this moment. How she will feel later on is another matter. In my opinion, she seems to have been very forbearing where you're concerned.'

'Hah! Have you all gone daft? She's my sister, for heaven's sake!'

'A pity you didn't think of that years ago!' Rachel retorted bitterly.

As usual, John tried to pour oil on troubled waters. 'Look, it's too bad a night to travel home, Rosaleen. Why don't you come down and spend the night with us?'

She threw her mother a look of contempt. 'And have me mam look at me like that all night? You'd think I was something the cat brought in. No, thank you, John. I'll go home. I'd rather face the elements.' Her eyes raked them scornfully. Then she faced George. 'But mind, I intend seeing Sean. You can be sure of that. I'll be at the hospital first thing tomorrow and I won't leave until they let me talk to him.'

No one bothered to inform her that Sean was in no fit shape to talk to her and that she wouldn't be allowed into the ward anyway. Shrugging into her mac, she threw them one last baleful glare before storming from the house.

Rosaleen drove recklessly up Serpentine Road and along the Antrim Road in the blinding rain. At Carlisle Circus, on a sudden impulse, she decided to go to the hospital and demand to see Sean. Swinging the car right, she headed up Crumlin Road. She pulled into the small parking lot in front of the hospital and sat for some moments to compose herself. Then, protecting her hair with a newspaper held aloft, she made a mad dash for the reception hall. It was deserted. She approached the desk and rang the bell. A nurse immediately appeared from a small office.

'Can I help you?'

'I wish to see my brother-in-law, Sean Devlin.'

The nurse ran her finger down a chart, stopping near the bottom, before replying, 'I'm afraid you have had a wasted journey. Did no one explain to you that only immediate family are allowed in?'

Rosaleen smiled grimly. 'No, they neglected to tell me that. Could I not slip in for a moment?' she wheedled.

'You don't understand. There's a police constable at his bedside. There's no way he would let you near him.'

'Is he really that bad then?'

'I'm sorry, but I am not at liberty to talk about his condition.'

Seeing that she would get no joy here, Rosaleen gave in and with a muttered, 'Thank you' left the hospital.

On leaden feet she went forth into the elements again. Uncaring now about the wind and rain, she slowly crossed to her car and climbed inside to sit in stupefied silence. Was there really a chance that Sean might die? It would be all her fault if he did. She found herself praying and broke off on a sob. Wasn't her lust the cause of all this? How could she expect divine help now?

After some time she felt composed enough to drive. Leaving the car bay, she edged out on to the Crumlin Road and headed for home. Pat McDade was waiting for her when, wet and disgruntled, she arrived at the house. 'I used the spare key,' he explained.

Shrugging her coat from her shoulders she let it slip to the floor and thankfully entered his arms, burrowing close, glad to feel the heat of his body against the chill of hers. 'You heard?'

He nodded. 'I went across to the Beehive for a drink and couldn't believe my ears when someone said Jim Devlin's son had been stabbed. How bad is he?'

'I don't know. They wouldn't let me see him. But they say he could die. Did you hear that our Annie has been arrested?'

Again he nodded and drew her into the sitting room where a fire burned brightly. He gently pushed her down on to the settee and knelt to remove her boots. Next he poured her a stiff whiskey and sat beside her to hold her close.

'Oh, Pat, this is all my fault,' she wailed. 'I should have stayed in Canada and then none of this would have happened.'

'Hush, love. Don't talk nonsense!' he admonished her. 'You didn't stab him.'

'I may as well have. I'm to blame.'

He brushed the damp hair back from her brow. Rosaleen grimaced and exclaimed, 'I must look awful.'

'You look fine. Just relax. Tomorrow we will go to the hospital together. I'll look after you, Rosaleen.'

Gratefully she offered him her lips. Aware that she was in a vulnerable state, he nevertheless took them.

Friday the 3rd dawned dark and miserable. After breakfast, as promised, Pat drove Rosaleen across town to the Mater Hospital. She sat beside him, deep in thought.

She was all mixed up while Pat was quietly confident today. And why not? she derided herself. Hadn't she willingly gone to bed with him last night? What was she coming to? Sean was lying at death's door because of her, and last night, for the first time, mind, she had lain in Pat McDade's arms.

At the hospital, he sought out the sister in charge. As before she was unable to help them. Pat asked to speak to someone who could. With a slight shrug the nurse said she would take them to the intensive care unit, but that was as far as they would get. They thanked her warmly and followed her along corridors and up stairs until they arrived at the door of the ward. With a brusque 'Good luck' she took leave of them.

The constable on guard that morning was young and cast an approving eye over Rosaleen.

Seeing his interest, she was all smiles and asked winningly if she could speak to her brother-in-law.

'He hasn't regained consciousness yet.'

Taken aback, Rosaleen asked if she could at least see him, only to be told that it was as much as his job was worth to let anyone enter the room without higher authority.

'Couldn't you turn a blind eye for a moment?'

'I'm sorry but no. The nearest you'll get is that window.'

Rosaleen moved close and peered through the tiny window. She didn't recognize the figure on the bed for all the tubes and a mask. With a strangled sob, she turned and pressed close to Pat.

'Oh, Pat, he looks dead already.'

Over her shoulder he gazed in at the figure on the bed. Perhaps Sean would die. If he did it would surely be the end of all his problems. Where else would Rosaleen turn if not to him?

Friday the 3rd was even more dark and miserable from Annie's point of view. Friday the 13th would have been more apt, she thought sadly. She was awakened early and taken to a washroom where she was left to freshen up. Constable Newton asked what she would like for breakfast but she declined the offer, saying she wasn't hungry. The young police woman stressed that she had a long arduous day ahead of her and would be wise to eat something. Not wanting to offend this young woman who had shown her great kindness, Annie relented and asked for tea and toast. Unable to stomach even that light meal, after a few nibbles she pushed the plate to one side and, wrapping her hands around the cup for warmth, she sat like that until they came and took it away from her. Having slept all night in her clothes, she still felt dirty and smelly. She longed for a hot bath and a change of clothes. To her great relief Constable Newton solved her problem by bringing her a parcel.

'I got permission to call and fetch some fresh clothes for you, Mrs Devlin. Your daughter also enclosed some cosmetics. She sends her love.'

Annie received the parcel gratefully. 'Thank you. Thank you very much indeed.'

At nine o'clock she was formally cautioned and charged, then taken in a police car to Chichester Street Magistrates Court. The car circled to the back of the building where the cells were. Annie's nose wrinkled in distaste at the fusty odour. They were dirty and smelt of stale sweat and tobacco. Eventually she was ushered to a room at the front of the building and here George was waiting with a tall, dark-haired man whom he introduced as Phillip Bradley. 'He is going to represent you, Annie.'

She was allowed fifteen minutes to confer with her solicitor and inwardly thanked Constable Newton for her thoughtfulness; thanks to her she at least looked presentable. Phillip leant across the table and, taking her hands in his, said earnestly, 'Annie, when we come before the magistrate, you will be charged with attempted murder. You must plead not guilty. You understand?'

She returned his gaze steadily and nodded her head. 'It was an accident!'

'Yes, but just answer "not guilty". Now, with such a serious charge the procedure is that you will be remanded for trail in the High Court. Whether on bail or in custody will depend on the magistrate. I will try to get you out on bail but I must warn you that I am not very optimistic. You see, your husband is not out of the woods yet. The magistrate will be thinking along the lines that this could very well turn into a murder charge and you might prove a threat to others.'

'Me? A threat? You can't really think I deliberately stabbed Sean?' Annie's voice was scornful at the very idea.

'What I and your family think doesn't count. You see, all the newspapers are carrying the story this morning and the magistrate must be very careful. He can't afford to be lenient, in case your husband dies.'

Wide, haunted green eyes sought George's. 'Is it really in all the papers?'

He nodded. 'I'm afraid so. Luckily, because of the trouble in Londonderry last night, it hasn't made the front page. There is, however, a write up on the inside page.'

'Is Sean going to die?' she asked fearfully.

'We don't know, Annie. We honestly don't know. Let's concentrate on you for the moment. There's not much time. Please listen to Phillip and do as he advises.'

Reluctantly, she brought her attention back to the solicitor who smiled kindly at her. 'They will probably remand you in custody until they see how your husband fares.'

'How long do you think that will be for?'

He shrugged. 'The magistrate will decide that.'

'Will I have to stay in York Street Police Station?'

'I'm afraid not. If I fail to get bail for you, you will be taken to Armagh Prison.'

It seemed impossible that Annie could go any paler but she did. Her face blanched. Thinking she was about to faint, George moved to her side but she quickly regained control of herself and whispered, 'I'm all right! I'm all right.'

'It won't be for long, Annie,' he assured her. 'Phillip will get you out in no time.' A glance at the solicitor asked for backing.

Phillip Bradley wished he could second George, but he remained silent. He was aware that if Sean Devlin died, his wife could be facing a long term behind bars.

After listening to the police version of events and to Phillip's plea for clemency, the magistrate did take the view that this could well become a murder trial. Refusing the plea for clemency that Phillip put forward on the grounds of her handicapped son, he remanded her in custody for a week. On legs that shook, Annie followed the police woman through a door at the side of the courtroom and along a corridor. Suddenly a door at the end burst open and she found herself blinded by flashing lights as reporters clambered in and bombarded her with questions.

'Why did you do it?' one shouted.

'Was he a brutal husband?' asked another.

'Was another woman involved?'

Quickly the police had things under control and the reporters were escorted noisily from the premises. Then George and Phillip were by her side, sheltering her from any further surprises until at last a door closed behind her and she was amazed to see her mother, John and Rachel.

Rachel gripped her close and their tears mingled. 'Where's Thomas?' Annie asked anxiously. 'It seems ages since I last saw him. Is he all right?'

'He's a bit confused at the minute, but otherwise fine. Josie and George are going to look after him until you come home, Mam.'

'They're very kind. I'll never be able to repay them.' Gently, she touched her daughter's cheek. 'Are you all right, Rachel? You look pale.'

'Yes, Mam, I'm fine. Don't worry about me. Just think of yourself. I'll look after the house for you. But I was wondering if we should let Rebecca know?'

'No! Wait and see if it's necessary. Have you seen your father? Is he improving? Besides, we don't know just where Rebecca is at the moment.'

'All right, Mam. Yes, Grannie and John and I were allowed to see Dad early this morning.'

'How is he?'

'He doesn't look too bad.'

Tentatively Annie asked, 'Did he ask about me?' Why should he? she derided herself. Hadn't she almost killed him?

A great lump in Rachel's throat threatened to choke her as she lied, 'He was asleep, Mam. We didn't get speaking to him.' Remembering the colourless face, the limp form and numerous tubes, she very much doubted that her father would ever speak again.

Pushing forward, Thelma edged her granddaughter aside

326

and took her daughter in her arms. 'What happened, Annie? Why did you do it? You shouldn't have let him goad you into it. To think that our Rosaleen is the cause of all this . . .'

John whispered urgently, 'Hush, Thelma. Are you trying to get her put away?'

'Mam, don't blame her. It takes two. Besides, it was an accident. Honestly!'

Unconvinced, Thelma said, 'Just you stick to that, love. Look, they gave us a list of things you would need. Just essentials. You know, face cloth, soap, toothpaste. They said anything else would be confiscated and sent home again. Annie, how are you going to bear it? Oh, God, how I wish I could take your place.'

'Ah, Mam, don't worry, I'll be all right.'

John took Thelma by the arm. 'Come outside, love. Let Rachel say goodbye to her mother. They'll have things to discuss. Given the chance, we'll come and see you, Annie.'

Gripping her close, Thelma promised to pray for her. Then she let John lead her from the room.

Alone with her mother, Rachel confided. 'Mam . . . Aunt Rosaleen told us about Liam. It must have been awful for you all these years.'

'Yes, it was. What else did she tell you?'

The fear in her mother's voice made Rachel draw back in alarm. George had admitted knowing about Liam but had warned her to take anything else Rosaleen had said with a pinch of salt and not to mention anything at all about Laura to her mother. Now she said softly, 'Nothing. She seems to think that Dad didn't know about Liam. But, Mam, I've been thinking about it and I don't see how he couldn't have known.'

'He didn't, Rachel. Believe me, he didn't know. Rosaleen and I duped him completely. That's why he was so angry.'

Rachel longed to question her about Laura. All the indications were that her mother was aware of that too. But what if she didn't know? Best to keep quiet. 'Mam, I don't know whether or not I should tell you this, but Aunt Rosaleen says Dad was going to leave us and go to her. She says that must be why you stabbed him. He wouldn't do that, sure he wouldn't?'

Fear clutched at Annie's heart like an iron fist. Was this

327

true? 'I don't know, Rachel. I just don't know what he intends to do. I don't know anything any more.'

She sounded so wounded, looked so wretched, that for a moment Rachel was sorry she had spoken. But she found she couldn't let it pass. She had to know! Wrapping her arms around her mother's neck and burying her head close to her ear, she mumbled, 'Is that why you did it? Is that why you stabbed him?'

Pushing her away, Annie gazed earnestly into her eyes and stressed, 'It was an accident, Rachel! You must believe that. I love your father very much. I would never deliberately harm him no matter what he did.'

Great haunted blue eyes searched for the truth. 'Mam . . . I heard you threaten to stick the knife in him.'

Annie's mouth gaped. The opening of the door came as a great relief to her. Gently she put Rachel from her. 'Goodbye, love. And remember, I would never deliberately do anything that would bring shame on you. It was a terrible accident. And that's the God's honest truth, so it is!'

Unconvinced, Rachel nevertheless hung on. 'Ah, Mam, I love you. I'll come and see you, no matter what.'

About to leave the room, Annie turned and said quietly, 'Please tell Rosaleen I don't want to see her.'

'I've already put her out of the house, Mam. I didn't think you'd want her there.'

These words brought a wan smile to Annie's lips. 'Good for you, love. Good for you.'

George and Phillip were allowed to speak with her for a few minutes and then, to her great shame, she was assisted into the back of a Black Maria and started on her journey South to Armagh Prison.

For some minutes the four of them stood at the back of the court at a loss as to what to do but not wanting to part company. The women were in tears and the men were trying to keep a stiff upper lip. It had been horrendous seeing Annie being put into the Black Maria. She had looked so lost. How on earth would she cope? George suggested that he phone Josie and warn her to expect them for lunch, but first they must stop off and see how Sean was faring. This suggestion was greeted with relief. Anything, so long as they stuck together, gleaning comfort from each other. George also knew that by returning to his home they could talk things over and Josie wouldn't feel left out. He knew that he had been neglecting his wife lately. Just popping in to eat and sleep and out again. Not taking the time to confide how worried he was about Annie.

At the hospital they found Sean was still in intensive care with his father and sister at the bedside. A police officer now sat inside the room, ready to take a statement should Sean regain consciousness. To Rachel, her father looked no better. They were, however, told that he had improved slightly. An infection that had festered in the wound was now under control. His recovery looked more hopeful.

Tears blinded her as she stood praying by the bedside. Oh, God, please let him live. He was good man. Stern and a bit stubborn, but a good father. Then she remembered. How could he be good if he'd been having an affair right under her mother's nose for years? Still, her Aunt Rosaleen was right. He didn't deserve to be lying at death's door because of his adultery.

Leaving the women together, Jim followed George and John out into the corridor to find out about the court hearing.

'In the name of God, they didn't?' he cried when George told him that Annie had been remanded in custody for a week. 'Do they think she's going to run off or something?'

George smiled wryly. 'They think she may be a danger to others,' he confided.

'Never!'

'I'm afraid so.' George was grateful to this big man for his attitude towards Annie. He could so easily be blaming her. He was in danger of losing his only son but still showed nothing but compassion towards Annie.

Jim's attitude changed. Learning forward, he confided, 'Sean opened his eyes today. Just for a few seconds, but it looks promising.'

'That is good news. I just wish this was all behind us.'

'So do I, son. So do I. But it's going to be a long uphill struggle,' Jim replied philosophically.

They stayed at the hospital for an hour and then, bidding

Jim and his daughter farewell, continued on their journey to Bangor.

Rachel was glad she wasn't going to her own home to face the neighbours. She had been appalled to read about her mother in the newspapers that morning. *'Crime passionnel!'* *'Woman stabs husband in fit of jealousy!'* were but two of the headings that she had seen. No doubt the rest followed suit. That morning she had gone down to the Spar grocery shop for a loaf of bread and all conversation stopped when she entered the shop. Obviously her family was the subject under discussion. Most of the women there had, after the initial embarrassment died down, nodded and kindly inquired after her health. Her parents had not been mentioned. Well, they were unlikely to inquire after her father, and they couldn't very well say, 'Has your mother settled down in Armagh?' could they?

After paying for the bread, head held high, she had bravely addressed the small group. 'May I tell everyone who's interested that it was an accident. Tragic, but an accident nevertheless. I'm afraid the newspapers have once again got it wrong.' She had left the shop followed by the buzz of renewed excited gossip.

Suddenly, as she approached George's home, she found herself surrounded by reporters. One minute the road was empty and the next they were swarming all over her. Tight-lipped, she had elbowed her way through them and slammed the door in their faces. Would they still be hanging about when she eventually returned home? Perhaps she would take Grannie up on her offer after all and sleep in her house at night.

To her surprise, the lovely aroma that permeated from Josie's kitchen made Rachel's mouth water. Since the arrest of her mother, she had been picking at her food, every morsel tasting like sawdust. Now she realized how hungry she was and immediately felt guilty.

Josie, who had been watching the different expressions flit across her face, asked gently, 'What's the matter, Rachel?'

'That lovely smell has made me realize how hungry I am, and I feel guilty because of it. You know . . . with Mam being in prison and Dad at death's door. I've no right to be hungry!'

Josie laughed aloud at this. 'I don't think for one minute either of them would want you to starve. Come and help me set the table.'

As they laid out the cutlery, Josie gently questioned her. 'How did things go this morning? George only gave me the bare details on the phone.'

'It was awful! The magistrate was adamant that Mam should be remanded in custody. He treated her like a murderer. What happened to British justice? "Innocent until proven guilty." Eh, Josie? I thought Mam was going to collapse. Then we had to watch her being put into that great van, the Black Maria. It will be a week before she appears in court again. And then, if Dad dies or can't remember what happened, or worst of all accuses her of deliberately stabbing him, she will be tried before the High Court. I'm so afraid, Josie. I don't know where all this is going to end.'

Holding her close, her aunt tried to be reassuring. 'Don't be daft now, love. Your mother would never have deliberately stabbed Sean, so once he's out of danger, she'll be released. Just wait. You'll see.'

'I hope you're right, Josie. Oh, I hope you're right, but something else has cropped up, you know! If the police get hold of it, Mam won't stand a chance.'

'What's happened?'

'Did Uncle George not tell you?'

Slowly, Josie shook her head. Since Annie's arrest he had barely talked to her at all.

'It's me Aunt Rosaleen. Last night she came over to our house and confessed that her and me dad had been having an affair. She even said that Laura and Liam are his children.'

Josie drew back and gazed at her in amazement. 'I knew about Liam, but Laura too?'

'Who told you about Liam?'

'He's the picture of your dad. I saw the resemblance when we went over to Laura's wedding and remarked on it to George. He put me in the picture but warned me to keep quiet about it.' Struck by a sudden thought she exclaimed, 'Why, your dad is a grandfather now!'

'Is the lunch nearly ready, Josie? I'm starving!' George called from the other room.

331

'Yes, we're just about to dish it out. Tell the others to come in.' Giving Rachel a comforting squeeze, she said, 'We can talk later, love.'

The dish of lamb casserole Josie had prepared, accompanied by a mixed salad and soft bread rolls, soon disappeared and they retired to the living room to discuss the events of the day and decide who should visit Armagh Prison tomorrow.

The Black Maria travelled smoothly along country roads but Annie took no notice of her surroundings through the darkened windows. Forty-eight hours ago her great worry had been how to cope with Sean's condemnation of Desi and Rebecca's holiday in America. Why hadn't she left well alone? So much had changed in such a short space of time. Was Sean suffering much? Would he survive? If he did, would she still be charged with attempted murder? Whenever she had read of people charged in this way, she had pictured hardened criminals and had often expressed the opinion that she hoped they got their just desserts. Would she get hers? Would it matter? Whether he lived or not, Sean was dead to her anyhow. If he was going to Rosaleen, what did it matter whether she was put away or not? Her life wouldn't be worth living.

Now she was being selfish, she admonished herself. She had Thomas and the girls to think about. She remembered how, when Thomas was a baby and she had so desperately wanted another child, Sean had pointed out to her that they needed to plan for the time when they would no longer be here to care for Thomas. Had his renewed passion for Rosaleen blinded him to this obligation?

How it hurt to think that he and Rosaleen had deceived her all that time. Once had been hard enough to endure, but years of carrying on behind her back? And what about since Rosaleen came back? Had they taken up where they'd left off? She must have been blind all those years ago! Everybody must have known. Up in Colinward Street, where you couldn't even sneeze without everybody knowing about it, there must have been talk. Just like everywhere else, the neighbours there thrived on bits of scandal. So how come she hadn't noticed? Certainly she had been aware the time there was talk about Rosaleen and some man. Hadn't she herself condemned her

332

sister? There had been speculation that the man had been on the scene before Joe's death and that the child Rosaleen was expecting was his. That man had turned out to be George, her half-brother. Their mother's health had been failing since Da's death during the blitz and Rosaleen had been afraid to break the news that he had spawned an illegitimate child. When George was eventually introduced to the family, Anne had been so ashamed for doubting Rosaleen she had gladly accepted that Joe must be the father after all.

Never dreaming that all the time Sean was the culprit. That he had been getting his leg over! And not just once, as he had led her to believe. That she had managed to live with all these years. What really hurt was her own willingness to believe his lies. How many years had it gone on? Her mind refused to go any further. Suffice to say that two children had been born of his adultery. If the newspapers got hold of all this slimy scandal, they would have a field day. She could imagine the headlines. *'Woman admits having two love children to sister's husband.'* Would Rosaleen have the sense to keep quiet? Annie didn't know how long had passed as she mulled over the events but became aware that the van had entered a courtyard surrounded by high walls. It continued around to the back of the building and came to a halt.

She stumbled as she descended from the van and one of the prison wardens waiting to receive her roughly steadied her. Police Constable Newton, who had become rather fond of this quiet unassuming woman, glared at the warden. With a 'Keep your chin up', she squeezed Annie's arm gently and left her.

Hustled into a small room, she had no time to take stock of her surroundings. To her great dismay she was strip searched. 'Is this really necessary?' she cried in alarm. Never in her life had she felt so degraded. She was assured that everybody was strip searched when they first arrived: prostitutes, shop-lifters, thieves – it made no difference. There was no exception made for would-be murderers. On a great wave of raucous laughter she was handed a uniform and told to get dressed. This consisted of a green polka dot blouse and green herringbone skirt made of cheap material. It was two sizes too big and Annie felt lost in it. Then she was led down a long corridor to a cell.

The cell was already occupied by a woman of about thirty-five years. She nodded to the top bunk, 'That's yours,' then returned to the magazine she was reading.

Annie felt tears threaten, and stubbornly defied them to fall. She would have to learn to be tough if she was to survive at all.

She jumped when the woman spoke to her again. 'I'm Nellie Gorman. Got any fags?'

'Sorry, no, I don't smoke. I'm Annie Devlin.'

'I know. Stabbed your husband, didn't you?'

'It was an accident. But how did you know?'

'Visitors sometimes slip in newspapers. See!'

A newspaper was thrust under Annie's nose and she recoiled when she read the headlines. '*Woman attempts to murder husband!*'

'That's not true! It was an accident!'

'That's what we all say. In here we're all innocent.'

Nellie thawed enough to inform her that all meals were eaten in the cells. Apparently, Annie had missed dinner which was served at noon every day. At four-thirty, tea was brought round on trolleys. She found the food tasteless and not very warm. After tea the prisoners were allowed to mix in the TV room.

Here Annie discovered that there were different uniforms. She questioned Nellie, who had reluctantly taken her under her wing, about this. She explained that there were different categories of prisoners, depending on age, or how many times you had been in before, or the severity of the offence.

Some of the women ignored Anne completely. Others laughingly congratulated her on her attempts to get rid of her 'old man'. The hours passed slowly and Annie was glad when it was time to return to her cell. She undressed and put on the pyjamas provided. They were miles too big and she saw Nellie suppress a smile when she looked at her.

'You'll get used to it in here. Most of the girls are all right.'

'How long have you been in here, Nellie?' Annie asked tentatively.

'Three months. I've another three to do.'

'Can I ask what you're in for?'

'Soliciting!'

Annie's eyes widened in amazement. Nellie gave a wry

laugh. 'I know what you're thinking. With an ugly mug like mine, who'd have me? Well, you'd be surprised. They don't have to look at your face, ye know.' She thrust out her bust. 'I've a good pair of tits, and my legs aren't bad either. That turns some men on.'

The look on Annie's face brought forth a cry of anger from Nellie. 'Don't you dare pity me, Annie Devlin! I do it from choice. I bet you stabbed your man because he was unfaithful. Am I right? Was he playing the dirty on you? Maybe with someone like me?'

'I didn't stab him! He fell on the knife.'

'Hah! Pull the other one. Don't expect the jury to believe that. If he dies, you'll be in here for a long, long time, Annie. And now it's time you were up on that top bunk. And I sure as hell hope you don't snore or I'll be tempted to smother you!'

Annie doubted very much that she would sleep, never mind snore. However her body had taken enough abuse during the last couple of days and to her great amazement the next thing she knew it was seven o'clock and time for slop out.

After breakfast, disappointment lay in store for her. There would be no visitors for her today. The procedure was that she let the governor know who she wanted to visit her and a permit would be sent out to them. No permit, no visit. It would be Monday before she would see any of her family. Annie almost wept with frustration. How would she get through the weekend? Why hadn't someone explained to her?

Three visitors were allowed each day for remand prisoners, one solicitor and two family members or friends. She arranged for Philip Bradley to come on Monday morning, and George and Rachel in the afternoon.

The permits arrived in Monday morning's post and in spite of Josie's concerned gaze, George phoned work and managed to get another week of his holidays brought forward. His boss was proving very considerate. Studiously avoiding his wife's eye, George phoned and arranged to pick Rachel up about noon for their journey to Armagh.

It was a bright crisp day and on any other occasion he would have delighted in driving along these country roads. Today his mind was in turmoil. On visiting the hospital that day he'd learnt that Sean was slipping in and out of consciousness but had yet to speak. On his return home from Armagh that morning Phillip Bradley had phoned him with more bad news. He told him that Annie was putting up a brave front but he feared for her health. He also said that she had requested that they bring sixty cigarettes with them this afternoon. It seemed that although Annie didn't smoke herself, a number of women would be very grateful if she asked for her quota of cigarettes.

The beauty of the countryside had a soothing effect on him. There were high grassy banks, tall hedges and trees all along the route. The fact that everything was covered in frost only added to the splendour of the scene. Dark clouds scudded across a pale blue sky and against this background the trees looked truly majestic in their silver coating; spiky branches stretched against the blue of the sky. The last time he had travelled this way he and Josie had been going to a wedding in Armagh's great Cathedral. The route then had held an entirely different beauty. Armagh was famous for its great and many orchards and the apple blossom had been in bloom; the sun had blazed down and the smell of newly cut grass had spiced the air. Against a background like this, what wedding photographs could be anything but beautiful?

They left the motorway at junction eleven and turned right, eventually crossing over the River Bann where below could be seen the slow-moving, slate-grey water. At this time of day Portadown town centre was busy and they passed through it at a crawl. Eventually the town was left behind and they increased speed as they headed for Armagh City.

Armagh too was busy and it was some time before George found a parking space in a side street close to the Mall where the prison was situated. They had allowed for delays and were still early. South of the Mall, the County Gaol ran the length of one side of the huge square. Facing it at the north end was the County Court. The gaol was an impressive building, three storeys high, with long, narrow, barred windows. To the right of the building an arched doorway led to a courtyard. Slowly they made their way past impressive houses, most of which were now offices.

They entered through the main gates and, as directed, made

their way to a wooden hut which served as a reception area. Here they had to sign in and were relieved of their gifts for which they received a receipt. Their permits also were taken. They were then led across an open courtyard to another door which was opened by a guard. The warden left them here. Once they were admitted the great door clanged shut and was locked behind them. A cold chill hung in the air and Rachel shivered, not from the cold alone. George smiled encouragingly at her. A stretch of corridor led to a waiting room about six feet by four. A dull grey room with two doors, one table and one chair. Rachel started in surprise when a warden body searched her; a guard did likewise to George.

Through yet another door and at last they were in the room where they would see Annie. Facing the door were three rows of plastic tables and chairs. Five or six tables in each row; four chairs to each table. Some were already occupied by other visitors. Not once were they left alone. Always two guards or wardens were present. In this room, one stood watch at the top and the other patrolled randomly between the tables, alert for any signs of underhand activity. Seated at one of the tables, George reached out and squeezed Rachel's hand. 'Don't look so scared, love. Remember, we're supposed to cheer your mother up.'

With an apprehensive glance at the other visitors, some of whom looked like thugs, Rachel whispered, 'Look at them, Uncle George. And they're only the visitors. We must get her out of here. This is an awful place.'

Following the direction of her gaze, George smiled wryly. 'These are ordinary people, Rachel. Your imagination is highly coloured at the moment. But I agree that we must get your mother out as soon as possible.'

At the allotted time, the prisoners' numbers were called out and they were brought to the room in groups of six. Annie was in the second batch.

As soon as she saw her, Rachel was on her feet and moving forward, arms outstretched in greeting. 'Mam! Mam, how are you?' The patrolling warden quickly stepped between mother and daughter and warned Rachel to be seated. With an angry scowl, she ungraciously did as she was told.

Taking the chair facing them, Annie said, 'Don't look so worried, Rachel. I'm all right. It's not as bad as it looks.'

'Oh, I hope it's not.'

'We handed in your gift, Annie. Do you intend to take up smoking, then?' George teased her, trying to ease the tension.

Leaning across the table, with a sidelong glance at the warden, she whispered urgently, 'Hush! Don't let them hear you. My cell mate asked me to get them. She says it will keep me in favour with the rest of the girls since I don't smoke. You don't mind, do you?'

'No, I don't mind in the slightest. It will be my pleasure to do anything that makes your stay in here easier. I'll make sure you get your quota, while you're here.' With a smile he added, 'But for heaven's sake, don't take them up yourself.'

He was blustering to hide his dismay at the change in her. Inside a few days she seemed to have shrunk and had obviously lost weight. Great dark shadows ringed her eyes and she constantly twisted her hands. 'Are you not eating, Annie?'

Her mouth twisted in distaste but she said, 'I get what does me.'

'Mam, will we try to slip something tasty in to you?'

Annie smiled wanly. 'Not unless you want to join me. You'd never get away with it. Look, let's not waste time talking about me. We only have a half hour. How's Sean?'

'No change, Mam,' Rachel answered truthfully. 'Me Grandad Devlin sends his love. He and Grannie Devlin and Aunt Betty take it in turns to sit by Dad's bed all day long. The other aunts and their husbands come when they're able. Everyone is in an awful state, but no one blames you. They say to keep your chin up. Uncle George and I go to see Dad twice a day.'

Tears came to Annie's eyes. 'The Devlins are so kind. I'm sorry to have caused all this trouble. If I had kept my big mouth shut none of this would have happened.'

'That's water under the bridge now,' George said consolingly. 'Did Phillip advise you about your statement?'

'Yes, George. I am to say nothing about Liam or . . .' She stopped herself in the nick of time. She had been on the verge of saying 'Laura' and no one must ever know about her part in all this.

338

George and Rachel exchanged a glance. Obviously Annie knew about the second child too.

'Annie, we know that Sean is Laura's father,' George confessed. 'You'd be as well telling us everything that happened.'

'Did Sean tell you?' All colour drained from Annie. Her face looked like a mask made from *papier-mâché*.

'No, I told you, he hasn't spoken yet. It was Rosaleen who told us.'

Eyes closed, Annie rocked back and forth. 'How could I have been so blind? So stupid! I'm so angry with myself.' Tears squeezed from tightly closed eyelids and trickled down ashen cheeks.

Rachel reached across and gripped her hand tightly. 'Ah, Mam, please don't let it get to you like this. It all happened so long ago. And me dad has been a good husband in all other ways, hasn't he?'

'I keep telling myself that it's all in the past. That it doesn't matter. But it still hurts. And all these repercussions will change our lives. There's no way we can go back to how we were. Even if your father decided to stay with us . . . it wouldn't work. How could I stay under the same roof as him? I just couldn't! My flesh creeps every time I think of him and her together.'

George listened to this tirade in dismay. 'Annie, I hate to ask you this, but when you found out about Laura, did you lose your head and stab Sean?'

'No, George, I didn't! He fell on the knife.' Her gaze wavered; she could see that her brother was unconvinced. She muttered so low they had to lean across the table to catch her words, 'That's not really the truth. If I tell you what really happened, do you promise never to breathe a word of it?'

George and Rachel exchanged a worried glance. 'What do you mean, Annie?' George asked.

Voice still low, she explained, 'It was Thomas's fault. We were arguing and Sean came towards me. He was in a terrible temper. Thomas was upset.' She looked appealingly at Rachel. 'You know the way he acts when anyone even pretends to hurt me? He tried to push Sean away, but he took him unawares and instead Sean fell towards me. On to the knife. There was no way I could have avoided him.'

They gazed at her in silence and she asked, 'Don't you

339

believe me? I'm not deliberately putting the blame on Thomas, you know. I would never do that.'

George shook his head. 'I know you wouldn't.' He could only too easily picture the scene she had just painted. It made sense. In his own way, Thomas was very protective of his mother. And hadn't he known in his heart that Annie was incapable of deliberately wounding another? Urgently, he beseeched her, 'Annie, the police must be told about this.'

'No, you promised! They'll say Thomas is unstable and have him put away. Can't you see that? I couldn't live with that! His part in this must never be revealed.'

'Listen, Annie, you must tell the truth. You owe it to yourself and the girls! Do you want to spend years in here?'

She shivered, but her eyes blazed anger at them and she whispered furiously, 'I told you about Thomas in confidence. If you tell anyone, I will deny it. I'll say you are making it up to try to get me off.'

'All right, all right! But you must tell Phillip and be guided by him,' George urged. 'When will you see him again?'

'Thursday.'

'Annie, promise me you will tell him about Thomas?'

Her lips a straight line in her face, she said stubbornly, 'No. I'm all Thomas has to shield him from the world. I won't risk his being put away.'

'What kind of a life do you think he'll have if you're convicted and have to spend years in here? Eh, Annie? Have you thought about that?'

'My days are full of "what ifs!" I have plenty of time to think. But one thing I'm determined about is that Thomas won't be put away. It would kill him. Now let's talk of something else. Any word from Rebecca?'

The return home was quieter than the journey down to Armagh. Even the beauty of the passing countryside with its pink-tinged sky failed to command George's attention. He was lost in deep thought.

It was Rachel who broke the strained silence. 'What do you intend doing, Uncle George?'

He sighed and glanced sideways at her. 'I haven't a clue,

340

Rachel. A promise is a promise . . . but I don't intend to let Annie be put away for something that wasn't her fault.'

'Do you think Thomas would be taken into care?'

'I don't know. I can't see it, but I just don't know how the authorities would view things. Perhaps Josie will be able to find out . . .'

'But you can't ask her! What about your promise to Mam?' Rachel cried in alarm.

'It will go no further than Josie, that I can safely promise. And, she just might have connections in the right places. You know she still helps out at Fulton House when they're short-handed. People who work there might be able to advise us. We can only play it by ear, Rachel.'

That evening at dinner George broached the question of Thomas's fate should the truth be revealed. He found Josie distant and uncommunicative. He couldn't understand her attitude. Had she expected him to sit back and throw Annie to the wolves? All right, so he was using up all his spare holidays and he might have to foot the bill for expenses incurred. So what? His sister's freedom was at stake here.

With puckered brow, he looked across the table at her. 'So you have no idea what would happen in those circumstances?'

'For heaven's sake, George! I only worked at Fulton House, I wasn't their solicitor. This is entirely different from anything I ever came across. It's Phillip Bradley you should be talking to. He's the law man.'

'I can't do that! I've been sworn to secrecy.'

'So you told me!'

'I felt it was safe to tell you. I tell you everything, so I do.'

'Hah! That's a laugh. Since the day Annie was arrested you've hardly opened your mouth. You talk all right – about everything, anything, but Annie! Now I find that peculiar, so I do. Do you not think it strange? You eat breakfast and dinner here, but it may as well be a café for all the private conversation we have. You're like a zombie! I'm your wife, for heaven's sake. Is it expecting too much to want to be kept up to date on how things are going?'

'What's got into you, Josie? I tell you everything.' His voice was stubborn. Didn't he phone her regularly? Explain what was going on.

'Huh! The bare details. Why, you haven't even time for the kids. They're asleep by the time you come home at night and you're away before they wake in the morning. Don't you miss them? Tell me, just why do you have to be away so often? What good is it doing? It won't speed up proceedings.'

George was gaping at her in amazement. 'Surely you understand that I have to do all I can for Annie,' he ground out through clenched teeth. 'She's my sister, for pity's sake! She depends on me.'

'So do we.' Josie gave a sad nod of her head. 'So do we. And, remember, I have Thomas to see to. It's no picnic, you know, getting two young children ready every morning and seeing that he eats enough and is washed and dressed. God love him, he's no bother but he does need a lot of attention. And no one . . . not Thelma or Rachel . . . has phoned to ask how I'm coping and could they take him away for a few hours to give me a break. What are they all doing to pass the time while they wait for reports about Annie, eh, tell me that? They probably think, "Oh, good old Josie will be only too glad to help. It might even make her feel part of the family at last." But I have things to do as well, you know! I can't cope with two young children and Thomas in the car, so I'm stuck here, day in, day out. You expect the impossible from me.'

George couldn't believe his ears. He would never have dreamt that easy going, compassionate Josie could spit such venom. He heard her out in silence. 'And here was me thinking that you would be glad to be involved,' he reproved her. 'If it was someone at Fulton House that was in need you'd be off like a shot to see how you could be of assistance.' The look he threw her was full of disgust.

She was on her feet glaring at him. 'Involved? You call this being involved? I'm being used! That's what the lot of you are doing to me.' Feeling tears threaten, she turned on her heel and left the room.

He rose to follow her but hearing the bathroom door open and close and the bolt being shot home, he sank down again. What had he done that was so wrong?

Josie stood dry-eyed before the bathroom mirror, the threatening tears held in check. She did not weep easily and had no intention of starting now. What had possessed her to rave and rant like that? Was jealousy at the bottom of all her resentment? What if Sean died? Poor Sean ... it seemed to her that Annie was getting all the attention, all the sympathy, when it was Sean who was at death's door. If he died Annie would surely be tried at the High Court and how many months would that last? Trials had been known to go on for years. Could their marriage survive? She leant closer and examined her face. Her eyes were too big, her nose too short and her mouth too wide. She remembered Annie's honey-coloured skin and high cheek-bones, the great green dark-lashed eyes, all this framed in wonderful chestnut hair. She grimaced at her own reflection. She had always known how George felt towards his sister, even if he had never admitted it to himself, so why was she griping now? What annoyed her most was the fact that Annie and Thelma had been slow to receive her into the family group. If it hadn't turned out to be a blessing her starting to work in Fulton House, she might never have been accepted. Indeed, Thelma still had reservations about her. And all the while they had their own skeletons in the cupboard. *She would not allow them to use her!*

When she returned to the dining room the table had been cleared and the dirty dishes were steeping in hot water in the sink. Of George there was no sign. Belatedly she remembered that he had said he was picking up Thelma and John to take them to the hospital. As yet, no one had asked her if she would like to visit Sean, but then, she was Josie, the outsider! Something else for her to grouse about. And he had left without seeking to bridge the rift between them.

The shrill ringing of the phone brought her out of her self-pitying thoughts and to her feet. Grateful for its intervention, she quickly went into the hall and lifted the receiver. It was Rachel.

'Josie, I was wondering if I might come over for a while? Just for a natter. I feel so alone.'

Her usual compassion coming to the fore, Josie cried, 'Of course you can! I'll be delighted to see you. But George has gone out and I can't leave the kids so you will have to make your own way over here.'

'Oh . . .' There was a pregnant pause, then, 'Ah, to hell with poverty. I'll ring for a taxi. See you soon.'

Rachel arrived thirty minutes later, a bottle of wine under her arm. Josie had been listening for the taxi and opened the door before she had a chance to knock. Hugging the girl, she closed the outer door and led the way into the living room.

'I hope you don't think me cheeky for inviting myself over, Josie, but I need to talk to someone.'

'To be truthful, I'm glad of your company, Rachel. I see very little of George these days.'

Removing her coat, Rachel said, 'I feel guilty about Thomas. We just plonked him on you and abandoned him. He's not your problem. I'll take him home with me for a few days. Where is he?'

Now that someone was actually admitting that she was being used, Josie felt ashamed. It was as if Rachel was telepathic. 'He's in his bedroom. I borrowed some occupational toys for him and he spends hours putting them together. He's very good at it. Jamie and Martha are sleeping. Have you been talking to George?' she asked apprehensively. Surely her husband hadn't let Rachel know that she was griping?

'Not since yesterday. Why? Does he want to speak to me?'

'No, no. I just thought that perhaps he had phoned you tonight.'

'No. Poor Uncle George. He's worried stiff about me mam. She looks awful, Josie. Skin and bone. Worse even than me dad. Thank God he looks a bit better. But now we've something else to worry about . . .'

'Hang up your coat while I fetch some glasses and then you can tell me all about it.'

Josie poured some wine and handed Rachel a glass, then pouring one for herself, joined her on the settee. 'So, tell me what's worrying you?'

Rachel raised her glass. 'To Dad's recovery.'

Again shame smote Josie. Obviously Rachel was concerned for her father's welfare. They were probably all out of their minds with worry and she could only feel sorry for herself.

Touching her glass to Rachel's, she said softly, 'I second that. And to your mother's release.'

'Dad does seem to be improving, thank God. However, there's always a policeman sitting in the ward and if me dad wakes and tells how he happened to arrive on the end of Mam's knife, they might put Thomas away.'

Josie blinked in bewilderment. 'But if he doesn't tell the truth, your mam could be put away for a very long time. Is that what you want?'

'Of course not! But she says she'll take the blame to safeguard Thomas. If only Dad realized how things stood he could say that he stumbled.'

'Perhaps he will.'

'I'm not very hopeful, Josie. Another thing, I've been thinking about our Rebecca ... surely she has the right to know what's going on?'

'What difference would it make? She'd just be another worrier.'

'I suppose you're right, but I know she'll never forgive me if Dad dies and she can't get home in time.'

'Give it another couple of days, Rachel. Then, if your dad hasn't recovered, ask George to set things in motion to contact Rebecca.'

'You're right, Josie. We must look on the bright side. And thanks for letting me come here and talk to you. You're always such a comfort. I really don't know how we would manage without you. I'll go and have a chat with Thomas now.'

'I'll make a pot of tea and something to eat.'

It was while she was brewing the tea that Josie heard the car draw into the drive. Quickly she went to the door to warn her husband not to put the car away as Rachel would need a lift home.

George saw her, and coming forward drew her into his arms. 'I'm so sorry, Josie. I've been an unfeeling brute. Can you forgive me, love?'

'Yes, yes.' Sensing his rising emotions, his need to make amends, she hurriedly warned him, 'Rachel's here, so don't put the car away.'

'Has anything happened?' he cried in alarm.

345

'No, she just wanted to talk. She's taking Thomas home for a few days to give me a break.'

'I'm glad to hear it. I intended to ring her and ask her to do just that. I've been very remiss towards you.'

Slightly placated, Josie said, 'Go and talk to her while I make some sandwiches.'

'Can I have a kiss first?'

He pursed his lips. Planting a light kiss on them, she gave him a gentle push towards the living room. 'Go entertain our visitor. We can talk later.'

Josie was in bed when George returned from running Rachel and Thomas home. Quietly he locked up and made his way to their bedroom in a thoughtful mood. What had possessed him lately? He hadn't realized just how much he was shutting Josie out until she had let go at him earlier that evening. She was such an understanding person he could have discussed all that had happened with her. Why hadn't he? For the life of him he didn't know! But from now on things would be different, he silently vowed.

Thinking that his wife was asleep, he removed his pyjamas from under the pillow and headed for the bathroom to undress.

'You can switch on the light, George. I'm awake.'

'Did I disturb you, love?'

'No, I've been lying here thinking about us.'

'What about us?'

He climbed into bed beside her and, propped on one elbow, looked gravely at her. In the dim bedside lamp her skin glowed and her mouth looked very inviting. However, when he would have kissed her, she turned aside.

'I was wondering if you regretted marrying me?'

His mouth dropped open and he gasped in amazement, 'What brought this on?'

She remained silent and at last he queried, 'Is it because I've been so preoccupied lately?'

'Partly, I'm no oil painting, and I've always wondered what you saw in me. Lately we seem to be drifting apart.'

'Josie, if I've been absent-minded it's because I've been out of my mind with worry about Annie and Sean. Surely you realize that?'

346

She examined him and was worried by what she saw. There were deep lines etched down each side of his mouth and dark shadows under his eyes. Instinctively, she reached out and gently touched them. At once he grabbed her hand and kissed it.

'Do you not care for me any more, Josie?'

'Of course I do!'

'Then be kind, love. Please be kind. I need you so much.'

She thought of all the questions to which she needed answers but pushed them to one corner of her mind. George needed her and at the moment that was all that mattered. She moved closer and thankfully his arms crushed her to his chest. 'Ah, Josie. Josie.'

Pushing away from him, she looked solemnly into his eyes. 'Tomorrow night we must talk. All right?'

'Tomorrow night I'll come home early and we'll thrash this out, Josie. You have my solemn word on that.'

With a sigh she cuddled close, and reaching across her George turned out the bedside lamp.

But things seldom work out as planned. The following morning he was called into the office to sort out a problem. He was gone all day and that evening asked Josie if she would like to go and see Sean. Glad that at last she was being included, she agreed to ask Rachel to sit with the children for a few hours. Thus her own worries had to be set aside till a future date.

Chapter 9

Awareness came slowly to Sean. His eyelids were so heavy it was too much of an effort to raise them. Where was he? Memories nudged at the edge of consciousness and he saw Annie; saw the glint of the big knife she held in her hand; remembered his horror at the sharp pain as the knife pierced his body. Was he dead? Had his eyelids been weighted with pennies to hold them down until rigor mortis set in because they thought he was dead? Wasn't that how it was done? Was there a book under his chin to keep his mouth closed? He tried to raise his arm to investigate but failed to move it. Terror gripped him. Were they about to bury him? Panic sent his heart thudding against his rib-cage. It sounded like a Lambeg drum being beaten. No obvious response. Surely if he was alive someone must come to investigate the racket it was making? Apparently not. No one paid any attention. Panic deepened; he just had to make them understand that he was still alive!

He lay tense and worried, unable to move, ears strained to catch muted voices. The speakers were too far away for him to hear what was being said. Was it a funeral service? He pictured himself lying in a satin-lined coffin, dressed in a brown shroud and clasping a rosary to his chest. If this was the case, he couldn't feel the beads. He could feel nothing! But then ... he wouldn't, if he was dead. Was the lid still off the coffin or was it already screwed down? No, he was letting his imagination run away with him! There was still plenty of air circulating about him. Suddenly the voices drew nearer until they seemed to be be coming from directly above him. Once more he attempted to open his eyes, but in vain. His father's deep drawl came to his ears.

'If only Sean would come round, perhaps he would be able to clear the air.'

Come round from where? Could they not see him lying here? Was he a ghost and just didn't realize it? A hand gently touched his face. 'He looks much better today, if only he would wake up.' Relief flooded through him. At least they knew he was still alive. He recognized the voice that answered his father – it belonged to George. 'It's been a week now. Annie comes before the magistrate again tomorrow. What do you think they will do, Jim?'

'Remand her in custody again, I suppose, poor girl.'

'It will be the death of her. She looks awful.'

A week? Had he been unconscious for a whole week? Why was Annie in custody? Didn't they know that it was Thomas who pushed him? Once again he tried to force open his eyes but the effort proved too much and although he fought against it, he found himself floating away, further out of control, into a deeper sleep.

Thelma wept softly as she gazed at the haggard face of her son-in-law. To think that all this was Rosaleen's fault. How could a daughter of hers have been so deceitful? True, Sean was as much to blame, but Rosaleen should have left well alone. She should have had more sense! She had everything going for her. But she had been weak, just like her father. Would Sean recover? Why . . . his eyelids had twitched there. Was it wishful thinking or her imagination? No! They just moved again! She glanced at John at the other side of the bed and by the quick startled look he gave her, realized that he too had noticed.

Suppressing her excitement, she motioned for him to follow her and quickly moved out into the corridor to where George and Jim stood conversing quietly. 'George, I think Sean is about to wake up,' she whispered, emotion making her voice shaky. 'What will we do?'

With a warning finger to his lips George cast a covert glance in the direction of the police constable sitting just inside the door of the room, engrossed in a newspaper. Quietly he passed him and walked to the bedside, followed by Jim.

Seeing that his brother-in-law's eyelids were indeed fluttering and that he looked to be about to waken, George addressed Jim Devlin in a low conspiratorial voice. 'Jim, if Sean were to wake and say that he fell on the knife, then Annie wouldn't have to worry about Thomas being put away.'

Taking his cue from George, Jim whispered back, 'It would be a godsend if only it were to happen that way. Otherwise God alone knows what will happen. If Thomas is taken away it will be the death of Annie and she has enough on her plate, God help her.'

With a superhuman effort, Sean at last managed to get his eyelids open. He looked blankly at them and muttered, 'I'm so tired.' His voice came out in a thin rasp, bringing a bewildered look to his face.

Immediately, the police constable was on his feet and reaching for his notebook and pen.

'I must ask you to leave the room please, while I take Mr Devlin's statement.'

Ignoring him, Jim gripped his son's hand. 'Welcome back, Sean. God, but I'm glad to hear your voice. Even if it is only a croak. Your mother will be delighted. She hasn't been off her knees all week, praying.'

George also grasped his brother-in-law's hand. 'Glad you're conscious at last, Sean.'

Angrily elbowing him out of the way, the policeman looked down on Sean. 'Mr Devlin, I must ask if you remember what happened on the afternoon of Thursday the second of January?'

Sean opened his mouth to try and oblige but before he could utter a sound a nurse bustled into the room.

'Ah, so you're awake at last, Mr Devlin.' She cast a reproving eye around the room. 'And no one thought to enlighten me. The doctor will want to examine you first thing.' She turned a stern eye on the constable. 'I'm afraid you will have to wait a little while longer to get your statement, constable. The doctor will want to see Mr Devlin as soon as he can. Meanwhile, I must ask you gentlemen to leave the room. The patient is very weak. He will need peace and quiet until he recovers more fully. Meanwhile, he will want to be freshened up. So if you will just excuse me?'

She stood patiently waiting, hand outstretched, indicating the door, as if they might have difficulty finding it, until George and Jim, with a last worried look in Sean's direction, quietly filed from the room. Unwillingly the constable returned to his seat. He was in two minds as to whether or not he should insist on getting a statement, but these nurses were so officious. And after all, the man wasn't going anywhere. Drawing a screen between the bed and the door, the nurse proceeded to attend to her patient.

Outside in the corridor, George and Jim exchanged worried glances. Had Sean been conscious enough to understand what they were saying? They had done their best; now they could but wait and see.

Washed and comfortable, Sean managed to eat some thin soup, spoon fed to him by the nurse. Then, to the frustration of the police constable, he feigned sleep again. He wanted time to think before making a statement. The doctor had come and examined his wounds and congratulated him on his return to the world, as he laughingly put it. He had explained to Sean just how near to death he had been. It had been all explained in medical jargon; the knife just missing this organ but glancing off another had resulted in internal injuries which had become infected. That, and the loss of so much blood, had kept him hovering between life and death.

He had also learnt that Annie was in Armagh Prison. The very idea of her in a place like that made his blood run cold. From what he had gathered from the message his father and George had managed to get across to him earlier as he recovered consciousness, if he implicated Thomas the lad might be taken into care. Surely not? He was harmless. It had been an accident. Thomas wouldn't hurt a fly. If anyone was to blame it was Sean himself. He remembered the anger that had seethed within him as he'd confronted Annie. So much wild emotion directed at her. He recalled her pale, tear-stained face as she'd proudly berated him. No wonder Thomas had been frightened. If anything, he had got his just desserts for being so high-handed and expecting Annie to understand his feelings.

Accusing her when most of the fault was his! Annie had indeed threatened him, and who could blame her? He would have done the same had their positions been reversed. But she would never have carried it through. He had felt the thrust of a hand on his back, and young Thomas had been the only other person there.

What a mess everything was! The family disrupted and Annie locked away. She had been so hurt when he had challenged her about Laura. The shock and pain had been so apparent, it was obvious she had not known. It must have seemed to her that he was taunting her with his past exploits. He had been ashamed, so great was the pain he had obviously inflicted. But it hadn't stopped him from continuing to vent his anger on her. Oh, no! He had ranted on and on. After all . . . he had been deceived. There was no getting away from that. But did that make what he intended doing right?

Was he wise, wanting to start a new life with Rosaleen at his age? Maybe he would have no choice now. Annie would never let him near her again after he'd admitted that he was Laura's father too. Who would blame her if she couldn't be persuaded that it had only happened twice? After all the lies she had been told. First things first. He must make a statement to the effect that he had stumbled. Annie must be set free as soon as possible. He opened his eyes and weakly raised his head from the pillow. Immediately the young copper was at the bedside, pen poised over his notebook.

Annie gazed gratefully up into the kind rugged face of Phillip Bradley. 'Thank you. Thank you very much. I must owe you a lot of money.' They were still in the Magistrates Court. She had just been discharged.

Gripping her hand warmly between his, he smiled down at her. 'I didn't really do much. It was Sean's statement that got you off the hook. Still, I'm afraid you will eventually receive my bill. Goodbye, my dear, and steer clear of knives in future.'

George also gripped Phillip's hand. 'Thank you from the bottom of my heart. I'll be in touch with you soon about settling the account.'

'Goodbye, George.'

Going over to where Annie was being consoled by the rest

of the family, he cried, 'Well, what are you all waiting for? Let's get her home.'

'No! I don't want to go home.'

A startled silence followed this outburst and they all stared at her in consternation. Then Rachel looked understandingly at her mother. 'You want to go and see Dad first. Isn't that right, Mam?'

'No. I can't face your father at the moment. He's the last one I want to see. I'd like to see Thomas.' Her eyes sought George. 'Is that possible?'

'He's with Josie and the kids. Let's go see him.' He glanced around the group. 'Is everyone coming?'

Thelma and John declined, and Rachel said she would go home with them and do some shopping in the village. He offered to drop them off first but they insisted on getting a taxi and urged George to get Annie away as quickly as possible from this Godforsaken place.

There were reporters milling around outside hoping for a statement from her. Brushing roughly past them, George quickly guided her to the car. Soon they were on their way to Bangor.

Annie sat gazing down at her hands, clasped tightly together in her lap. 'I'll never be able to thank you and Josie enough for all the trouble you have taken. I don't know what I'd have done without you.'

'Catch yourself on, Annie. We're family and that's what family are for.'

'Still, I feel so ashamed when I think of how I treated Josie at the beginning of our acquaintance. I was a fool not realizing her worth. She really is an angel for caring for Thomas and all. I don't deserve her kindness.' She hesitated and then said tentatively, 'Perhaps you should have let her know that I'm coming?'

George had been thinking along the same lines. What if Josie thought that he was using her again? He gave a shrug and assured his sister, 'I'm sure she won't mind.'

There was no sign of life when they arrived at the bungalow. However, once George had opened the door it soon became obvious that the house was occupied. Squeals of laughter were coming from the direction of the kitchen. Quickly George passed down the hall, followed closely by Annie.

'Hello there,' Josie greeted them from where she sat at the table blowing up a balloon.

Gazing at the dishes of crisps and sweets and soft drinks that were spread on the table and the balloons that floated in the draught from the open door, George cried, 'What on earth is going on here?'

'We are having a little party,' his wife cried gaily. 'Here, Jamie, catch.' A balloon was thrown and the chuckling child chased it across the kitchen with raised arms. 'Rachel phoned to warn me that you were on the way and Thomas was so excited when I told him that his mother was coming home he couldn't be still. I decided to keep him occupied by preparing a welcome home party for Annie.' Hiding her dismay at the change in her sister-in-law's appearance, she came round the table and warmly embraced her. 'Welcome home, Annie. Somebody has been missing you very much.'

Thomas hung back, eyeing his mother from under lowered brows. Slowly Annie moved towards him and held out her arms. 'Come here, love.' Then he was in her arms and clinging to her as if he would never let her go. 'Ah, Thomas, I've missed you so. I'll never leave you again.' Stretching on tip-toe, over his shoulder her eyes met Josie's. 'Thank you for looking after him. Thank you for everything you've done for us.'

Feeling a hypocrite, she repeated her husband's words. 'Ah, it's what families are for.'

When the reunion between mother and son was over, Josie said, 'First I'm going to make some lunch and then, if you don't mind my saying so ... I think you should take a nap, Annie.'

'You don't know how wonderful that sounds, Josie. I haven't slept much this week and I really am exhausted.'

Annie found that although she was hungry, the emotional state she was in prevented the food from going down her throat. She struggled gamely for a while, then with tears of frustration in her eyes, apologized for not eating more of the delicious meal.

'I understand, Annie. It's a good rest you need. Come on, I'll show you the way. You can have a nap on Thomas's bed.'

Tired though she was, sleep eluded Annie. Her thoughts went round and round in circles and she tossed restlessly. What was to become of her and Thomas, and the girls for that matter? The house would have to be sold. Tears smarted in her eyes at the thought of losing her beautiful home, after all the years of hard work both she and Sean had put into it. Still, painful though it may be, there was no other way. She could not afford to buy his half of it, so it would have to go on the market, and the sooner the better. It was no use prolonging the agony. They had lived there for nearly twenty-three years. Sean had bought it off a mate in the Merchant Navy just after the war, and for a quick sale had got it at a bargain price. The market value today should be very high. Eventually her half of the money would be enough to buy a small house somewhere, but meanwhile where would they live?

She would have to go up to the house some time soon, before Sean was released from hospital, and pack all her and Thomas's belongings. And Rebecca's things would have to be seen to as well. It was all so frustrating. There was so much to think about. Where would she take everything? What about Orange Row? Her mother and John were kind but she didn't want to intrude in their lives. Even so, their house was too small to accommodate them all.

Rachel would probably stay at home until Sean managed to sell the house and it would be over eleven months before Rebecca came home from touring America. Sadly Annie thought of the changes her youngest daughter would find on her return. Meanwhile, where would Thomas and herself go? She couldn't face going back to the house to live and Sean was bound to want to stay there until it was sold. Under no circumstances at all did she want to be under the same roof as him. If it was in her power, she would never set eyes on Sean Devlin again. He had hurt her too much. In the region where her heart should be there was a great aching sore festering away. Their divorce would have to go ahead without her approval. The church would frown on it, of course, but it was out of her hands. Sean would want his freedom to marry Rosaleen and there was nothing she could do about that. He could make whatever arrangements he thought fit and she would fall in with them. Rosaleen could have him and good riddance! The deceitful pair deserved each other. Meanwhile, she needed to talk to someone who would advise her what to do in such circumstances. A face floated across her thoughts. A kind rugged face . . . Phillip Bradley's. Would he be able to help her?

Josie listened attentively as George explained how Annie had refused to see Sean. 'Well, I for one don't blame her. He has deceived her all these years, so how could she ever trust him again? One child was bad enough . . . but two? It's mind-boggling. And with her own sister? That's unforgivable. And seven years between them? Well now, that's enough to kill even the most ardent love.'

'Don't be so quick to condemn Sean. It appears to me that there was deceit on both sides. After all, Sean must have gotten an awful shock. He didn't even know about the kids.'

'Sorry, but I'm having great difficulty believing that. One, yes. But two? Sean's no fool, he must have known!'

'Well, it appears that he didn't. Between the pair of them they certainly managed to pull the wool over his eyes. That's why he was so angry.'

'If Sean had been fair with Annie from the first, she wouldn't have had to deceive him. Why on earth did he marry her when he was in love with Rosaleen? That's what I can't understand. Obviously she must have turned him down. It seems to me to be a case of wanting the best of both worlds. Someone to give him children and satisfy his needs, while he could still keep in touch with and admire Rosaleen from afar. Believe you me, that's very hard to live with and I have nothing but admiration for Annie. In my opinion, she's the one who was hard done by.'

'Given time, it will all blow over. She won't be the first woman to forgive and forget! It happens all the time.'

'Truly spoken like a man! *She* will be expected to forgive and forget. I only hope she sticks to her guns.' George was surprised to note a sneer in his wife's voice. 'Besides, aren't you jumping the gun? Has Sean said he wants her to take him back? Isn't Rosaleen using all her wiles to try to tempt him away from Annie? Wasn't that the idea of suddenly

356

revealing all these dark skeletons that have been hidden away for so long in your closets?'

'What do you mean . . . *my* closets? I knew nothing about Laura. Why, it's only recently I learnt about Liam. But you're probably right. Rosaleen hasn't been allowed in to see Sean yet. No doubt, now he's conscious, she'll manage to get into the ward. I wish she'd take herself away back to Canada, then this would all die down.'

Josie gave a small scornful laugh. 'No chance! It's too late for that. She's trying to hold on to the past. She probably thought that she had lost all chance of ever having Sean and now, suddenly, there's a chance that they can spend the rest of their lives together. Just like a romantic fairy-tale. She's living in fantasy land, but she can't see it. You can never recapture the thrill of past love. Especially at the expense of others' happiness. Annie's a fool! She's playing right into Rosaleen's hands by refusing to return to the house. I'd fight them every step of the way, so I would!'

This was a new side to Josie that George was seeing and he wasn't sure that he liked it. Why was she so bitter? Perhaps he should wait until she was in a softer frame of mind before broaching what he had in mind. But he couldn't wait. He needed to know now! 'Again, you're probably right,' he agreed. 'But meanwhile Annie has nowhere to go. So . . .'

Josie's heart sank. She actually felt it slip down. Surely he wouldn't . . . couldn't have the audacity . . . to expect . . . 'Yes, George?'

The sudden quietness of her tone should have warned him, but it didn't. She discovered that indeed he could and did have the cheek! 'I was wondering if perhaps she could stay here for a few nights?'

'George, there's only three bedrooms,' she pointed out reasonably. 'Where would she sleep? We're already over-crowded as it is.'

'I thought that perhaps Thomas could sleep on the settee and Annie could have his room.'

'It wouldn't work. He goes to bed early every night and it would be unfair to keep him up to all hours.'

'Well then, what if we brought a mattress from Annie's

house and Thomas slept on the floor of her room? It wouldn't be for long, Josie.'

Obviously he had been giving it a lot of thought. A great ache gathered inside her. He would do anything for Annie. But what about her? Did her feelings not count? Could he not see that she was against this mad idea of his? Didn't she deserve some consideration? If she agreed, where would it all end? Annie might even become a permanent fixture and how would she be able to cope with that? If she didn't agree would he hold it against her? That was a chance she would have to take. Sadly, she put him off. 'No, George, I don't think that would be a good idea at all. Sean is still in the hospital. There's no chance that he will be out for a while. So Annie can safely return to her own home for a few days and make her arrangements from there.'

A long searching look seemed to see into her very soul. Then, with an abrupt nod, he left the room. Josie felt like weeping but couldn't afford even this luxury. At the moment, her home wasn't her own and there was nowhere private to hide and lick her wounds.

Rosaleen paused at the door of the small ward that Sean now occupied. He was asleep and she tip-toed across to the bed and stood gazing down at him. How she loved him! She couldn't believe that at last he was to be hers. To have and to hold, forever and ever.

Her perfume wafting on the warm air made Sean aware of her presence. His mind recoiled. He needed more time to think. Unwillingly, he opened his eyes and greeted her. 'Hello, Rosaleen.'

'How are you feeling, love?'

'I'm coming on all right. Another couple of days and I'll be home.'

'You will come to me, of course.' She was matter of fact, and a cool hand with pink-tipped fingers rested on his with assurance.

'No, I'll return to my own home. I've a lot of thinking to do.'

She bent over him, great green eyes shining, and red lips inviting. All this framed in a bell of silver hair was a beautiful picture to behold, as Sean was the first to admit. She was a beautiful woman. 'Sean, I love you,' she reminded him softly. 'I have always loved you. You don't know how happy I am that at last you know the truth.'

'Rosaleen, I'm . . .'

'Hush. No need to talk now. The Sister warned me that you are very weak and need to rest. We can make our plans later.'

He smiled at her, relieved that no decision was expected from him right away. His feelings were all mixed up. Annie had yet to come to see him.

The problem of where Annie would stay was taken out of George's hands. When she arose from her nap she announced that she had decided to return home for a few days to pack her clothes and personal belongings.

'Annie, is there no chance of a reconciliation?' he asked tentatively.

A sad shake of the head. 'There would be more chance of a snowball surviving in hell than Sean and I coming together again. How long do you think he'll be in hospital?'

'He won't delay long, Annie. If I know him, as soon as he is able he will discharge himself. He'll probably be out in a day or two.' George wanted to inquire what her plans were, and bitterly resented the fact that Josie had effectively sealed his lips. He could not offer his sister sanctuary.

'I agree. And that's all the more reason why I should go home now, today. Can I ring for a taxi, Josie?'

'Don't be silly! George will drive you home.'

'I've been taking up a lot of his time lately, but if you're sure you don't mind?'

'I'm sure.'

'I'll pack Thomas's clothes. And thanks again, Josie, for all your help.'

'I'll show you where Thomas's clothes are kept,' she volunteered, and avoiding her husband's eye, followed her sister-in-law from the room.

Sean couldn't understand why Annie's refusal to visit him caused him so much pain. Wasn't it all the better to make a clean break? It would be easier to come to a decision if he didn't have to face her. Still, he was contrary enough to resent her lack of interest. Good God, she could have come to view her handiwork! Make sure he really was on the road to recovery. Had she no feelings left for him at all?

On the other hand, Rosaleen haunted the hospital. She spent every available minute there, fussing over him; only slipping away from the accusing eyes of her niece and brother when they came visiting. Sean began to derive comfort from her attention. At least she wanted him; cared about his welfare. However, he was uneasy that given the opportunity she insisted on talking about the wonderful future they would have together. His parents, who had by now gleaned something of the reason behind Sean's stabbing, certainly did not make it easy for her.

On the third day he was allowed to walk the corridors for exercise. She walked with him, eyes defying Jim Devlin to accompany them. Regretfully he sank back in his seat and watched them leave the room. Why couldn't that woman leave his son alone?

Glad of the chance at last to talk to Sean in private, Rosaleen slipped her arm through his and, hugging it close to her side, whispered, 'I've been thinking that perhaps we should go back to Canada, Sean. Make a complete new start out there. You'd love it, I know you would. Here we run the chance of meeting members of the family every time we go out. It could prove uncomfortable.'

'Still worried about a scandal, Rosaleen?' he taunted her.

'No, Sean. Not any more.' She nuzzled her head against his arm. How she longed to be alone with him. Recapture all the excitement they had once known. 'I've been foolish long enough. I just want us to be together, no matter what. And I thought it would be better for you too.' She drew him into a small annexe and stood close to him. Too close for comfort, her lips inviting, her breast brushing lightly against his arm.

Restlessly he moved away and continued walking along the corridor. 'Rosaleen, at my age I would have no hope of getting a job out there.'

She stared up at him in amazement. 'Don't be silly! I've plenty of money. You wouldn't have to work. We would have a wonderful time, playing golf and skiing. Why, we can tour the world if we want.'

The idea of a life of leisure, living off Andrew Mercer's money, didn't appeal to him. 'No, Rosaleen. I've worked hard all my life.'

'Well then, you could work in the publishing house. I'm sure Laura would be glad, once she knows that you're her father.'

'You haven't told her?'

'Not yet. I want to explain to her, face to face. Make sure she understands why I didn't marry you all those years ago.'

'It will come as a shock to her. What makes you think she will welcome me as her father? Will you tell her she came about from a one-night stand up at the Springfield Road dam a week before you married Joe Smith, the man she always regarded as her da?'

Slowly her arm was withdrawn from his and distance was put between them. 'That's a very cruel thing to say.'

'Nevertheless, it's the truth. As I recall, you derided me when I said I loved you. You said that it wasn't love. That we had behaved like animals. Will you tell her that?'

Her eyes clouded in bewilderment and tears glistened. 'Why are you doing this, Sean? You're deliberately hurting me. I don't understand. You know how I was situated back then. There was no way I could put off the wedding.'

'I'm sorry.' He grimaced and shrugged. 'I don't know what's got into me lately.'

Tight-lipped, she received his apology. 'I'll leave you now but I'll be back this evening. Perhaps then you will be in a better frame of mind.'

She swung away from him but he reached out and gripped her arm. 'I'm sorry. Don't go, Rosaleen. It's just . . . I'm not as sure as you are that Laura will accept me.'

'Of course she will! They both will. Liam will be delighted to have a father again.'

Sean didn't agree. Why should Laura want to get to know him even? She was a mature woman with a husband and child, and she had been very close to her stepfather. As for Liam? Well, teenagers could be very obstinate at times. He obviously doted on his mother. Who knew what his reaction would be?

361

'Look, Rosaleen, I don't feel up to making decisions at the moment. I need more time.'

'Huh! It was you who brought things to a head. I've covered up the truth of Laura's parentage all these years, but you ... you caused an explosion inside a few hours of knowing the truth, and almost lost your life because of it! But for that, no one need have been any the wiser. But there's no going back now, Sean. I know our Annie. You're living in cuckoo land if you imagine she would ever take you back. Besides, you do love me, don't you?'

He was evasive, asking plaintively, 'What about Pat, eh? Do you not owe Pat McDade some loyalty?'

Hot colour swept in a tide from her jaw to her hairline. 'What do you mean?'

He noted the blush and drew his own conclusions. 'He's apparently been faithful to you for a long time. Have you given him reason to think you care? Will our getting together affect him badly? Do you not think you owe him some consideration, Rosaleen?'

Her colour deepened but she insisted, 'I don't know what you're playing at, Sean. If you love me, Pat doesn't enter into it. I'll deal with him. It's you I love. I've always loved you and I certainly won't let Pat, or anyone else for that matter, come between us. Don't back out now,' she warned. 'I couldn't bear it.'

He smiled grimly. What more could she do to him? Why couldn't she have been as strong as this when he had begged her not to marry Joe Smith? How different their lives could have been then.

'Look, I don't understand you at all today. I'd better go now before we both say something we might regret later. I'll come back this evening. Perhaps you'll be more amicable then. Can you make your own way back to the ward alone?'

He nodded and without another word she left him. He watched her walk the length of the corridor, saw heads turn to look after her. Without a doubt, Rosaleen was still a beautiful woman. Why was he acting like this? If he wasn't careful he would drive her away and then he would have nothing but a lonely old age to look forward to. She turned the corner

362

without a backward glance and slowly Sean made his way back to the ward.

George confided in Sean about Annie's endeavours to find somewhere to live before he left the hospital. This saddened him greatly.

'Tell her not to worry, George. I'll go and stay with my parents until I get things sorted out. Me ma will be glad. Tell her she can stay in the house without fear. I won't bother her.'

'Sean, aren't you being an awful fool?'

'What do you mean?'

'Well . . . aren't you a bit long in the tooth to go gallivanting off with Rosaleen? I know sometimes first loves come together in their twilight years, but it's usually after both their partners have died. But you! You're breaking up a good family. And for what? I know Rosaleen's money doesn't enter into it. And after all, she's just a woman. You're being plain stupid, if you don't mind my saying so.'

Sean rounded on him in anger. 'Oh, but I do mind. I mind very much indeed! You make us sound ancient. Good God, there's plenty of life in the old dog yet, and in case you haven't noticed, Rosaleen is a beautiful woman. Any man would be proud to possess her.' He flashed a belligerent look at his brother-in-law. 'Besides, what right have you to tell me what I should or shouldn't do? From what I've heard, your infatuation with a married woman nearly ruined your life. So don't you preach to me, George Magee! It's the pot calling the kettle black.'

George gaped at him as if he was indeed an idiot. 'What on earth do you mean, my infatuation for a married woman? I've never even had any unworthy thoughts towards anyone else's wife.' But colour flooded his neck and face as he realized that this was not wholly true.

Sean noted it and taunted, 'Oh, no?'

'No! And I still think you're a fool.' Rising to his feet, George shrugged his shoulders. 'But have it your own way. Be a mug if you must. Just remember, Annie's worth a dozen Rosaleens!' With a final baleful look he left the room.

Try though he did to put Sean's words from his mind, George

found that they still rankled. He had visited Sean during his lunch hour and all afternoon had difficulty keeping his mind on his work. He had never seriously had designs on Annie, and no one at all had known how he felt, least of all her. She was his sister, for heaven's sake! After the war, when he had arrived on Rosaleen's doorstep, he had been overjoyed when his two half-sisters had welcomed him into their lives. There was barely six months between him and Annie and to him she had seemed vulnerable, so it had been natural to be closer to her than the older, stronger Rosaleen. Widowed and the mother of a seven-year-old girl, she had seemed competent and remote. Even when she had confided in him that she was pregnant, and her husband but a week buried, he had admired her strong spirit and had looked up to her, never dreaming then that Sean was the father.

Still, he had to admit that he had become very fond of young Annie. Until he realized how much Josie meant to him, all other women were insignificant compared to his sister. He had thought her wonderful.

Look how Mary Mitchell had lost her appeal. He had been daft about her, had almost married her, but something had held him back. That was what had made him think he was a lost cause; that he could never care for anyone else the way he did for Annie. How wrong he had been. It had taken his deep feelings for Josie to put things into their proper perspective.

He dragged his mind back to the present. Who had told Sean? Nobody, just nobody knew! He had confided in no one at all. Had Sean guessed? No! His brother-in-law would have been unable to hold his tongue.

George was in a pensive mood the remainder of the day. That evening as he helped Josie to prepare the children for bed, he eyed her speculatively. Could she ever have guessed? But then, she would never have told Sean. Besides, as he well knew, Sean was not the man to keep quiet about a thing like that.

'Why are you looking at me like that, George? You've been acting funny ever since you came home from work. And I warn you . . . don't expect me to change my mind about putting up

364

Annie and Thomas. To be truthful, I've enjoyed having the house and my own children to myself today.'

He grabbed the opening given to him. 'Yes, I agree it is nice to have the house to ourselves. To tell you the truth, I'm glad of the chance to talk to you.'

Josie was determined not to be sidetracked and insisted, 'No, George! Forget it. I'm not having Annie staying here.'

He eyed her thoughtfully. 'Josie, tell me, is there any ulterior reason why you don't want her here?'

She went very still. What was he getting at? Holding his eyes she challenged him. 'What do you mean?'

'I thought you liked Annie?'

'I do, but I don't want her living here.'

'Why not?' he persisted.

'Because it wouldn't be natural. That's why!'

'Why would it not be natural, Josie? My sister, your sister-in-law? What could be wrong with that?'

She turned aside and with a toss of the head, retorted, 'That's why.'

'That's not an answer, Josie. I want to know what you mean.'

'I don't want to talk about it.' How could she put her worst fears into words? Awaken misgivings that she had thought buried forever. Had she been kidding herself? Had he at last admitted to himself how he felt towards his sister? What effect would it have on their lives?

'Talk about what? You're losing me, Josie. Explain yourself!'

Suddenly her temper flared, and throwing discretion to the wind, she flung at him, 'Because of how you feel about Annie!'

'How do I feel about her?' he asked softly, his eyes intent.

Suddenly Josie felt unsure of herself. Could she possibly be wrong? Her eyes filled with tears and she made to brush past him, seeking to leave the nursery and his intrusive questions. She didn't want to make a fool of herself.

His arms closed about her and he clasped her close. 'We have to get all this straightened out, Josie. Do you agree with me?'

'I don't know,' she wailed. 'It depends on how you feel about Annie now. I don't want things to change.'

'I care for her like the sister she is. I can't, for the life of me, think what made you think otherwise.'

365

'Ah, George, this is me! Your wife! I can read you like a book and I *know* you were in love with Annie. Don't deny it. I *know*. I've always known. Why do you think it took so long for me to agree to marry you? I was afraid that some day she might need you. And now she does.'

'You don't for one moment think that she is a threat to our marriage?' She looked at him and he saw by the fear in her eyes that indeed she did. 'Ah, Josie, how could you?' Gently he led her along the passage to the living room. Sitting on the settee, he drew her down beside him. 'I see I've a lot of explaining to do. Although, to be truthful, I certainly wasn't doing anything wrong.'

He sat in thought for some moments and she waited with bated breath. 'First, tell me this. Have you ever said anything that might have given Sean the impression that I was interested in Annie?'

She vigorously shook her head. 'No, never!'

'What made you think that I was ... huh!' He shook his head in disbelief, 'I can't believe I'm saying these things. How could you ever think that about me? Eh, Josie? You make me feel unclean.'

'Oh, no! No, I never thought you lusted after her. It seemed deeper than that. More spiritual. That was why I wouldn't marry you. I knew you could never really care for me because of your deep commitment to her. But I also realized you weren't exactly panting after her. So, as time wore on and I realized that life was passing me by, because no other man could hold my attention for more than a few days, I agreed to marry you.'

He looked perplexed. 'I thought you eventually gave in and accepted my proposal because you were afraid to trust younger men and regarded me as a safe father figure?'

'Oh, George, you can be as thick as two short planks at times!' she cried in exasperation. 'I've always loved you, right from the very first. But for a long time I was afraid to take a chance. You see, I knew you only wanted to marry me because time was getting on and you wanted children. And then, I've always been aware of the threat of Annie in the background.'

'It seems to me that we have both been under a misapprehension. I love you! You're everything to me. I can't believe you didn't know that.'

'You never said.' Her voice was sad. 'And you are a good husband and father, so I had no complaints. Until this happened. Now you're completely wrapped up in Annie.'

'Only because she's in trouble. Look, let's get this clear once and for all. I love you dearly, and as far as I'm concerned, no one, not Annie or anyone else, can ever come between us.' He hugged her close. 'Ah, Josie, I'm sorry if I've been a stupid fool, but it will be different from now on, I promise.'

They sat for a long time, contended and happy, savouring the joy of knowing that their love was mutual. Suddenly George moved restlessly. 'There's still one thing that bugs me,' he admitted.

She gazed at him wide-eyed as he continued, 'What on earth was Sean on about today? He said he was aware that I had almost wrecked my life because of my love for a married woman. What on earth did he mean? I've never, ever looked at a married woman.'

'I think perhaps I know what he was getting at,' she whispered softly.

'You do?'

'Yes. He once asked me why I didn't marry you and I told him you were already in love with someone else. He asked why you didn't marry this other woman and I told him she was already married.'

'Josie, you never did!'

'I'm afraid so. But of course I wouldn't reveal the other woman's name. Shortly afterwards you proposed to me yet again and I said yes. That was the end of it. It was never mentioned again.'

'Ah, Josie, my love. My dearest love.'

It was heart breaking for Annie, gathering together her personal belongings and packing them away. George had brought her some tea chests and tears trickled down her cheeks as she carefully wrapped her best dinner service and ornaments in newspapers and packed them away.

Rachel watched her unnoticed from the doorway. In her opinion, her mother was being daft. She should fight to keep her husband. And if not that, she should at least fight to keep the house. After all, Aunt Rosaleen had plenty of money. And there was always a chance that her father might change his mind. Oh, if only he would! If only he would, surely things could be worked out and they could all be together again. Much as she sided with her mother, she still loved her dad and the idea of his going to the other side of the world devastated her. And to a ready-made family too. He would probably forget all about them in no time. So far she had managed to hide her feelings from her mother.

'Mam . . .' At the sound of her daughter's voice, Annie surreptitiously wiped her cheeks with the back of her hand before turning to face her. 'Would you not fight Dad for the house? Aunt Rosaleen has pots of money.'

A grim smile twisted Annie's lips. 'You don't know your father very well, Rachel. He would never go to Rosaleen empty-handed. He's too proud. And, to be fair, the house is more his than mine. He put every spare penny he earned into making it comfortable.'

'And you devoted your life to keeping it comfortable. It's not fair!'

'Life isn't fair, Rachel. The sooner you accept that, the easier it will be to compromise.'

'Where will we live, Mam? Have you thought of that?'

'I've thought of nothing else. I've been wracking my brains ever since I got out of Armagh. I'm seeing Phillip Bradley tomorrow afternoon. Perhaps he'll be able to advise me. Meanwhile, let's get stuck in here and get as much packing done as we can. Your father might just change his mind and return here and I want to be long gone when he does.'

'Mam, would that be such a bad thing?' Rachel's longing came across on her words. 'Perhaps if you saw him he would consent to stay with us?'

Annie gaped at her daughter in amazement. 'Consent? Do you think that would be good enough for me? Hah! You can put any notions you have of reconciliation from your mind. I'll never take him back! Never!'

'Ah, Mam. Must you be so stubborn? Do you not miss Dad at all? Could you not at least see him? Talk to him?' Her voice broke and, not waiting for an answer to her outburst, she ran for the stairs and the refuge of her bedroom.

Annie gazed after her in dismay. She rose to follow her daughter but sank down again, burying her aching head in her hands. Of course she missed her husband! Missed all the normal things that being with him meant. For the first time she admitted to herself that she was afraid to face Sean. What if, in spite of all he had done to hurt her, she was tempted to attempt to win him back? The humiliation of his still preferring Rosaleen didn't bear thinking about. It was a risk she wasn't prepared to take.

It was the following morning that Annie's prayers appeared to be answered. It was Rachel who opened the door to the knock, mid-morning.

'Mam, it's someone to see you.'

Dismay crumpled Annie's face. 'It's not another one of them reporters, is it?' They still came, offering money for her story.

'No, Mam. No! He says it's a private matter he wants to discuss with you. I've put him in the sitting room.'

Annie paused at the hall mirror and smoothed her hands over her hair. She looked a mess, gaunt and ugly. Great dark rings around her eyes told of worry and sleepless nights. She squared her shoulders and entered the sitting room.

There was something very familiar about the man who rose, hand outstretched, to greet her but she was sure that she had never met him before. 'I'm sorry for disturbing you, Mrs Devlin but I didn't know what else to do. I'm Matt McKernan.' When she continued to look blankly at him he, prompted, 'Desi's father?'

Embarrassment caused her to blush bright red. 'I should have guessed!' she apologized. 'He resembles you a lot. Won't you sit down, please?'

He chose a straight-backed chair and, sitting down, examined her gravely. 'I've been reading in the newspapers about your recent trouble, Mrs Devlin. I would have got in touch sooner to see if I could be of any help to you but, never having met, I was afraid you might think me nosy.'

'Annie. Please call me Annie. And I certainly wouldn't have thought you nosy.'

He nodded. 'Annie, I don't want to intrude at this troubled time but I received a letter from Desi this morning. They expect to be in Los Angeles today and he says he will ring the first opportunity he gets, to hear all the news. It is obvious from his letter that they know nothing of recent events, so I was wondering if you want me to keep quiet about all the trouble? Or perhaps you want them to know about your husband's accident?'

'I'd much rather they didn't know. Rebecca would want to rush straight home and there's no need. It would be a shame to spoil their holiday.'

'I thought that's how you would see things, but I had to be sure.'

'It was kind of you to come. Would you like a cup of tea or coffee?'

'Coffee would be lovely, thank you.'

'Excuse me. I won't be a moment.'

In the kitchen Rachel had already boiled the kettle. 'Does he want tea or coffee, Mam?'

'Coffee. He's Desi McKernan's father, so he is.'

'I guessed that much. Desi resembles him. What does he want?'

'They had a letter from Desi. He's phoning home soon and his father wants to know whether or not to relay the news about your dad.'

'What did you say?'

'I told him not to. They may as well have their holiday in peace.' She put the two steaming cups on a tray and added a milk jug, sugar bowl and plate of biscuits. 'Will you not join us, Rachel?'

'While he's here, Mam, I'll nip down to the shops and get a few messages, and see if I can get some cartons to pack books and small things. OK?'

'That's fine by me, love.'

Matt was standing by the window, gazing out over the lough. He turned and took the tray from Annie. 'No sugar and very little milk, thank you,' he said in answer to her query.

They sat and sipped their coffee in silence. It wasn't a strained silence. Annie felt very much at ease with this man.

370

It was he who spoke first. 'This is a lovely place you have here, Annie. It's very well located. That's a wonderful view of the lough you have.'

She sighed. 'Yes, I'll miss it. The house will be on the market soon.'

He gazed at her in concern but was too much of a gentleman to probe.

'My husband and I are separating,' she went on.

'I'm very sorry to hear that. You must have been married a long time.'

'A very long time.'

'Oh, that's sad. Very sad. Where do you plan to live?'

To her great dismay tears threatened to fall, taking her unawares. Blinking furiously to hold them back, she wailed, 'I don't know! I don't know what's to become of us.'

Embarrassed, he rose to stand awkwardly beside her, patting her on the shoulder. 'There now. There now.' With a couple of convulsive sobs Annie managed to stifle the tears. Once she had control of herself, he returned to his seat.

She blew her nose soundly and managed a watery smile. 'I'm sorry. I'm so ashamed. This isn't like me, you know. To break down in front of a stranger.'

'You've been through a rough patch lately. I've visited Armagh Goal, Annie, and I wouldn't fancy being confined there. You have every right to be upset.'

He sat sipping at his coffee. Once he had finished, he continued to sit thoughtfully, toying with his empty cup. She watched him, and tried to think of a way to get him to leave without giving offence.

Suddenly he raised his head and caught her eye. 'I have something to suggest, Annie, but if I'm out of order please just say so. Right?' Bewildered, she nodded and he continued, 'As I'm sure you're aware, I live in Dunmore Street.'

Once more she nodded in response. 'Well, my sister died almost a year ago and left me her house just round the corner in Oranmore Street. I'm in the house repair business and I'm modernizing it at my leisure. At the moment it's quite habitable but I'm in no hurry to sell. There's always the chance that Desi and Rebecca just might hate America.' He smiled at the idea.

'Some people do, you know! They might want to settle here, and then the house would be there as a starter home for them.'

Annie wondered where all this was leading. It was coming up for twelve o'clock and she would soon need to get ready for her appointment with Phillip Bradley.

'It's very kind of you to think of them,' she murmured.

He laughed. 'I'm going about this all wrong. You were saying that you had nowhere to go. So, if you're interested, you can stay in the house until you find something more suitable.'

Annie blinked at him in amazement. Imagine a stranger, for that's what he was after all, offering her the use of a house!

Mistaking her silence for consternation, Matt rose to his feet and placed his cup on the table. 'I know it's far removed from here,' he said, with an expansive wave of the hand. 'But it is partially furnished and quite comfortable. However, I do understand you might find it restricting. It was just an idea. Forget it.'

Embarrassed, he glanced at her, preparing to make a quick retreat. To his great dismay, tears were slowly rolling down her cheeks. 'Ah, now, there's no need for that!' he cried in concern.

'Matt McKernan, you are the answer to my prayers. God must have sent you to me this day. I'd be delighted to accept your kind offer.'

'Grand!' he bellowed. 'That's great. I'd better get a move on then. Get my wife to go round with the vacuum cleaner and polish. Can I bring some of those boxes up for you now?'

'Yes, please. And I'll do any cleaning that is necessary.'

'When would you like to move in?'

'Is tomorrow too soon?'

'No. Not at all. And don't you worry about transport. I've a van. I'll come back in the morning and move you up.'

'Thank you, Matt. I'll be forever grateful.'

'You can't possibly move up to Oranmore Street!' Rachel wailed in dismay.

'Why not? It's an answer to my prayers. Why wouldn't I go?'

'Isn't there only two bedrooms in those houses? What about me? Where will I go? And they have only outside toilets, Mam.'

'That won't worry me. I was reared with very few modern

facilities, remember. However, I do understand you might find it quite daunting. I thought perhaps you would stay here until the house is sold? If I'm not here your father will probably move back, so you won't be alone.'

'And what are Dad and I going to find to talk about, eh? I despise him for the callous way he has treated us, so how can I possibly live under the same roof as him?'

'Ah, Rachel, don't be like that. He's your father. He loves you and I know you love him. He's always been good to you. All this trouble is between me and him. Don't let it come between you two. I would be very hurt if I thought I was causing a rift between you. At all costs you must keep in touch with your father.'

'But if I stay here, you'll only have Thomas for company. You'll be lonely, Mam.'

'After Armagh Gaol, I'll be glad of a bit of solitude. You needn't worry about me. Thomas will be company enough.'

'I'll stay here for a while, Mam, but I intend looking for a flat out near the university. I'll have to learn to be independent from now on. You'll have enough on your plate without worrying about me.'

'I'll still worry about you, Rachel. Wonder what you'll be getting up to.'

She threw her arms around her mother and hugged her close. 'Just think of the good time I'll be having without you breathing down my neck,' she jested, but Annie felt the tears on her cheek nevertheless. God forgive Sean Devlin, she thought, for treating his lovely daughter like this. She had done nothing wrong.

The house in Oranmore Street was beyond Annie's expectations. When she had lived up the Springfield Road in Colinward Street, as a young girl, she had often visited a school friend in one of these houses and had expected it to be the same. However, she was pleasantly surprised to find that Matt had indeed modernized it. The small entrance hall was still the same, with the stairs rising steeply opposite the outer door. A door half panelled with frosted glass to the left of the hall led to what used to be called the kitchen but was now regarded as the living room. Facing the door, a fire burned brightly in a small black and white kitchenette grate. The door that had at one time led into the 'wee room', as it had been called, had been blocked off. This wall was now panelled in pale oak wood and there were three shelves stretching the length of it. Annie could picture all her ornaments displayed there.

Through the remaining door she discovered that the wall between the 'wee room' and the scullery had been knocked down. It was now one spacious room with modern kitchen units, and a dining table and four chairs at one end. She could see that there was both hot and cold taps in the stainless steel sink unit and a modern stove graced the wall beside it. And, to her great delight, wonder of wonders, a bathroom had been built on to the back of the house.

She turned to Matt. 'Ah, this is lovely. I'll only stay as long as is necessary. I'm indebted to you. Meanwhile, we will have to decide how much I pay you a week.'

Embarrassed at her obvious sincerity, he gruffly assured her that she could stay as long as she wished, but insisted that he wanted no money off her. Said she could consider herself a live-in caretaker. The way things were at the moment people were desperate to leave districts of mixed denominations. He didn't want squatters taking over the house.

'Oh, but I insist, Matt. I couldn't live rent-free. Sean will have to arrange some kind of allowance for me and the kids, so I will have some money coming in and I'll be only too glad to rent this lovely house.'

To please her he agreed on a nominal figure and started to unload the van.

Sean heard the news about where Annie was living from Rachel. Aware that he was leaving hospital, she had visited him with this information. She explained that her mother had moved out and that his home was empty and he could return to it as soon as he liked.

'Where is she living, Rachel?'

'Oranmore Street.'

'Oranmore Street? Who on earth does she know up there?'

'Desi McKernan's father is renting her a house. I would like to stay on in Serpentine Road until you manage to sell the house. Is that all right?'

'Certainly! But . . .' he hesitated. 'Will you be all right on your own for a short time? Mother has everything prepared for me to stay with her for a while. I don't want to disappoint her. You know how it is.'

'I'll be all right, Dad.' Rachel gripped his hand suddenly and cried, 'Don't do this to us. Do you not love any of us?'

'Rachel, my dear, how can you think that? I love you all dearly, but sometimes husbands and wives drift apart and the obvious solution is to separate. But that doesn't change my love for you and Rebecca and Thomas.'

'Will you not give it another try?'

'There would be no point, Rachel. Ah, don't cry, love. It's all for the best.'

'Do you love Aunt Rosaleen so much, then?'

He was embarrassed. He could hardly explain to his young daughter how Rosaleen had captured his affections as a young man; how he had married her mother on the rebound. It made it seem that he hadn't loved Annie, when he had. A very different love but strong and sincere nevertheless. And they had been happy. If only the women hadn't deceived him! That was what was really bugging him. One was as bad as the other for keeping information from him.

Rosaleen's temper was still simmering on a back burner when she left the hospital. Sean had really been in a foul mood. Was he having second thoughts? Surely he realized that it was too late for that? Annie would never take him back now. She crossed to the car park and looked in distaste at Pat McDade. He was leaning against her car, smoking a cigarette. He was always following her about like a lap dog. Every time she visited the hospital, he was there waiting for her to come out. She couldn't see him far enough! True, for a time she had been grateful for his company. He had helped her through some rough patches, but at the moment she needed to be alone; needed seclusion to plan her next course of action. Things were not working out as she had planned. Sean seemed to be cooling off.

Now she greeted Pat irritably. 'You shouldn't have come here. Stop hounding me!'

'You don't mean that, Rosaleen. You know you need me.' He peered intently at her. 'You look upset. Shall I drive?'

Really, she should be discouraging him, but he was right. At the moment she needed his company. She nodded and he hid a smug smile as he opened the passenger door for her. When she was settled in her seat he set off.

'What's wrong, Rosaleen?'

They had been driving in silence for five minutes or more. 'Nothing! Why should anything be wrong?'

'You're not usually so quiet. Shall we take a drive along the coast and have lunch at Carrickfergus?'

'That's a good idea, Pat. It will help me unwind.'

He gave a smug contented smile. He hadn't given up hope yet.

The move to his parents' house over at Beechmount brought home to Sean just how much he missed his own big spacious house. This house of his parents had been built to replace the one that had been bombed during the blitz. Actually, the night the house was flattened was the very night that Annie's father, Tommy Magee, had perished, caught in the same blast. It had been a great shock to everybody.

Although bigger than the other houses in the street, it was still small compared to his own home. His firm had proved very understanding and had granted him a month's leave with pay to recuperate. Of course they had no idea that he planned to go to Canada. He found the days tedious and, picturing the house on the Serpentine Road, longed for the peace and seclusion of it. Here neighbours were always popping in and out. There was never a quiet moment.

With Annie in Oranmore Street and Rachel preparing to move to a flat near the university, the house was standing empty. Only one thing stopped him. Rosaleen would be sure to come to him there and he would have no excuse to keep her at arm's length. But why did he want to keep her at arm's length? He was a contrary bugger! Always wanting what he couldn't have. Here in his parents' home there was no privacy for *tête-à-têtes*. His mother or father was always hovering about and his sisters dropped in at all hours of the day to see how he was faring. To be truthful, they were beginning to get on his nerves. He couldn't even get his thoughts in order.

Sometimes he went out for a drive in Rosaleen's car with her. One night, after a meal and a few drinks in the Chimney Corner Hotel, they ended up at her house. It had been an enjoyable evening and they were both a bit tipsy and had touched and cuddled in the car for a while before heading home. Sean admitted to himself, that 'tonight's the night!' They got as far as the hall and were in a passionate embrace when the light was switched on. They drew apart, dazzled by the bright light, and squinted at Pat McDade. He stood in the doorway to the living room, looking very much at home in slippers and cardigan, a drink in one hand and a cigarette in the other.

'Oh, I do beg your pardon. I didn't realize you had company back with you, Rosaleen.'

To say that she was annoyed would be putting it mildly. She looked as if she could throttle Pat. Her face crumpled in dismay and she actually stamped her foot. Quite an act! But as Sean asked himself, how did Pat get in if Rosaleen hadn't given him a key? He bade them both good night in spite of her pleas to him to stay and have another drink. He declined and left the house, determined to catch a taxi at the corner. That was the last time he had set foot in her house.

The Democratic Party was still very much in the news and meeting with obstructions at every move. They were fighting for one man, one vote, and although Sean did not think this an unreasonable request, he did not see that they stood much of a chance of obtaining it. Unemployment continued to rise and discontented youths stood around at street corners. Sean had to admit that he had only noticed these things since moving back to his old home ground. It was not so apparent in Greencastle. Unemployment seemed to be higher, up here on the Falls Road. With no jobs, no money and no place to go, young lads had no other choice but to hang about all day.

Although Sean sympathized with them, he didn't like the idea of Annie and Thomas living in Oranmore Street. However, he knew better than to dictate to Annie what she should or should not do. Tensions were running high in the community;

had been for a long time now. A slow fuse was burning and it would take very little to cause an explosion.

At bedtime every night he had taken to going for a walk, hoping the exercise would help him to sleep. In spite of warning himself not to be a fool, and to put the past behind him, he still found his footsteps led him along Beechmount Avenue, down Oakman Street and Iris Street. From there it was but a stone's throw to Oranmore Street. From the corner, he eyed the row of houses and wondered which one his wife and son lived in. He could very easily find out and confront Annie; say he wanted to see Thomas. But his wife had put no obstacles in the way. A phone call to John and Thelma and he was at liberty to see his son where and whenever he chose. The only stipulation Annie made was that she need not be present. Loneliness was eating away at him, and in spite of Rosaleen's painting wonderful pictures of his family in Canada he could not work up any enthusium to go over and meet them.

It was late as Annie climbed the Serpentine Road. It was a cold miserable evening that sent a chill to the very core of her. She had deliberately waited for dusk; there was less chance of meeting any of her neighbours at this time of night. To converse with anyone would have distressed her. She picked her steps carefully. It had snowed earlier that day and the icy wind coming down from the hill made the footpaths treacherous. As she slithered along she questioned herself. Was she a fool coming away out here to say goodbye to a house? No! This was her last chance to look around the home she'd loved so much. How on earth could Sean bear to part with the house he loved so dearly? But then, he loved Rosaleen more.

Funny, beautiful though it was, she couldn't picture him in that big ranch-style house Rosaleen owned in Canada. She had heard from George that Rosaleen had taken the house off the market and planned to return and live there. Well, no one had said outright that they had left for Canada. After all, she had requested that they weren't mentioned in her company, it hurt too much. Still all the signs pointed that way. The For Sale sign had been taken down from their house and Sean had been more than generous in his financial offer to her. Phillip Bradley had stressed that he had given her about two-thirds of the value of the house, and had paid all expenses.

She had been surprised but not unduly worried about receiving the money. She couldn't afford to be proud and insist on taking only half of it. After all, she had to buy and furnish a house for herself and Thomas, and Sean certainly wouldn't go short. Rosaleen was a rich woman and must have persuaded him that they had more than enough. All Annie's dealings with Sean had been conducted through Phillip Bradley. She had steadfastly refused to face him herself. Had signed any papers that Phillip put in front of her; trusting him to look after her interests. She didn't want to listen to the excuses her husband would make for all the heartbreak he was causing. It was Phillip who had warned her that if she wanted a last view of her home, she should go tonight.

Her footsteps faltered as she approached the bend in the road. What if the new owners were already in the house? Well then, she would walk on past. Make her way up to and along the Antrim Road and go down Gray's Lane. Then back to Orange Row where Thomas was waiting with his grannie and John.

The house came into view and she breathed a sigh of relief; it was in darkness. Her fingers curved around the torch she had in her coat pocket. The electricity was probably cut off but even without a torch she would be able to find her way about. She knew that house like the back of her hand. The slope up to the house was icy and she floundered about helplessly for some moments before managing to negotiate a path to the steps. These were hazardous and she almost turned away in defeat, but stubbornly she carried on and at last arrived at the door itself. For a moment she paused in concern. What if the locks had been changed? She had not considered that possibility. Was she still to be thwarted? Carefully, she slid the key into the lock. It turned easily and she quickly entered the hall and closed the big oak door with a sigh of relief, very much aware that she was trespassing.

Standing with her back against the door, she gazed around her in the dim light afforded by the street lamps. To her amazement the hall was the same as she had left it. The large mirror and the paintings still adorned the walls, and the hallstand was

379

still in place. Bitterness swamped her. Sean must have sold the house as it stood. He had no right to! She should have been allowed to choose the pieces she wanted. She had taken so little with her when she left. It was a cruel thing that he had done. But then, she had refused to meet him. If she had consented they would have discussed things like this. And really, she shouldn't complain. He had been more than generous money wise. It was her own stupid fault that she had missed out on keeping some of the furniture.

Slowly she made a tour of the ground floor and through the conservatory to stand outside and gaze up at the black mass of the hill outlined against the paler sky, saddened to think that no more would she sit in the sun and admire this view. Returning indoors, she locked up and made her way through the house along the hall to the stairs. It depressed her to think that so much of what she and Sean had saved for and chosen with such loving care was about to pass to strangers.

Climbing the stairs, she entered the room she had shared with Sean for most of their married life. This had been their first and only home. The first years of their marriage, during the war when Sean was away at sea most of the time, they had lived with her mother in Colinward Street. The bed was still there but stripped and pushed against one wall. Rachel had stripped all the beds and brought the bed linen, together with the curtains, table cloths and cushion covers, to Annie. At the time she had been against receiving anything but now she was glad. Strangers would have got all those too with the house otherwise. She should have asked for more. This dressing table, for instance. Her hand lovingly caressed it. And the hall-stand. There was room in Matt's house for those, and he had advised her to share the furniture with Sean; said he would remove anything of his from the house to make room for hers.

Perhaps she should not have been so proud? Perhaps she should have asked Phillip to negotiate for her? Thank God Rachel had not been so silly! She had taken the bedroom suite out of her room, a chest of drawers, a small bureau, and the two easy chairs out of the sitting room, when she moved into the flat she now shared with another student on Malone Road. To Annie's knowledge, Sean had taken nothing. But then, what would he want with it? He was going to a whole new way of life out in Canada. As far as she was aware he had never even returned to the house at all.

With a sigh of regret for things lost, she left the bedroom and entered the smallest room. This had been the nursery when the children were young. Then in later years it became Thomas's room. Skirting the single bed, she stood at the window looking out over the lough. She missed the views from this house. Missed the peace and quiet of the nights. There were no views in Oranmore Street except into someone else's backyard. Still, she had a lot to be grateful for. Their moving to that house had been a blessing so far as Thomas was concerned. Matt McKernan had discovered that the lad was quite useful with his hands. Thomas seemed to sense which tool Matt would need next and always had it ready for him.

Matt was amazed but Annie explained that Thomas had always been observant. At school he had helped with arranging stage settings for the small plays that were put on regularly. He had also watched all the jobs Sean had done about the house and he obviously remembered what each tool was used for. This made her more bitter still towards her husband. Why hadn't he spent more time with his son? Now he would never be able to build up a relationship with him.

Matt was patient with and encouraged Thomas. He took him out on small house repairing jobs with him at weekends and gave him a wage. Thomas was in his glory. Yes, she had a lot to be thankful for. The McKernans did all in their power to make her feel welcome without intruding too much into her private life. However, nothing could fill the vast hole created by Sean's betrayal.

Against her will thoughts of him bombarded her mind. Was he in Canada yet? She would probably never see him again. Well, that was the way she wanted it. Would he settle to a life of luxury? Why not? He'd had very little luxury so far. All his time and money had gone to making his family as happy as possible. Rosaleen would be sure to pamper him. In spite of herself, the pain grew more acute when she thought of him and her sister together.

She wished now that she had confronted Sean when she'd learned about Liam. Perhaps then things would have worked

381

out all right. Who knew what choice Sean would have made? At that time he had seemed to love her.

Oh, stop torturing yourself, she lamented inwardly. It's too late now. Pressing her forehead against the window pane, she gazed out over the lough with unseeing eyes. Pictures from the past kept flashing before her eyes. Sean happy and contented; Sean tender in love making. Thomas and Sean rolling about on the grass, laughing and playing games. Poor Thomas, he was so confused. She had explained to him that his father was going away but she knew that he didn't understand. Where had she gone wrong? Was it all her fault?

A noise brought her upright, ears strained. There it was again: a footstep. She hadn't heard the outer door open. It must be the new owners. How would they receive her presence here? Would they understand? Perhaps they would not come up the stairs. Her straining ears told her it was only one person.

What if it was an intruder? She looked wildly around but there was nothing about that she could defend herself with. Withdrawing the torch from her pocket, she stood to one side of the window, in the shadows. It was not a very heavy torch but if he or she entered the room she would flash it full in their face and if it was an intruder perhaps they would turn tail and run.

Breathlessly she waited, torch poised. The footsteps were anything but stealthy so she was convinced that it was the new owner. She hoped that he or she would understand. The figure turned into the room where she stood and a gasp escaped her lips. Even without the help of the torch she recognized who it was. The light from the street lamp outside fell full on Sean's face.

They gazed at each other in the dim light and then he slowly approached the window. As he drew near she moved to one side. Sitting down on the window seat, he smiled grimly. 'You needn't be afraid. I'm not going to touch you.' He sounded as if he wouldn't even touch her with a barge pole and she felt colour rush to her face. Ah, but then, she didn't expect him to want her. He had the beautiful Rosaleen. 'I would, however, like to talk to you and since you kept refusing to meet me . . . well, Phillip was kind enough to set this up.'

'He had no right!' she cried in outraged dignity.

'You must agree that he has been very helpful in every other way,' Sean said quietly.

'Well, yes, still . . .'

'Sit down, Annie. I won't bite.'

He made room for her on the window seat but she chose to sit on the end of the bed, her mind in a whirl. She had been mistaken in thinking they had already left for Canada. Why had he gone to all this trouble? What on earth was there to talk about at this late stage?

He sat silent and she examined him covertly. He had lost weight; his cheeks were hollow and he looked quite ill. The silence stretched and she felt compelled to talk. 'How are you?'

He gaped at her in mock amazement. 'You care?'

'Of course I care. I never meant to harm you. I don't wish you ill.'

'Why didn't you come to see me in the hospital then?'

'Why would I? There was nothing to say. It would have been a slanging match! You had made your decision and that was that.'

'I wanted you to come.'

'Why, Sean? You had what you wanted. Did you want to gloat as well?'

'Oh, don't be silly!'

She shrugged; why else would he have wanted to see her? 'I'm here now. What do you want to talk about?' she asked quietly.

'You sure as hell don't make it easy, do you?'

She shrugged again and fell silent. It was his turn to examine her. Even in the dim light the dark rings under her eyes were obvious. He had brought her to this state. Was she glad to be rid of him? Very possibly. He had brought her nothing but grief. To think that she had known all these years about Liam and had managed to keep quiet about it. She, with her fiery temper, had managed not to throw it in his face. But then, she had deceived him too. She had something to hide. She didn't want it all to come out.

'Why did you not tell me about Liam?'

'Look, Sean, that's all water under the bridge. It's all so long ago. I don't want to talk about it.'

'Please, Annie, before we go our different ways, tell me why.

Surely that's not asking too much?' She remained tight-lipped and he continued, 'I remember the shock I got when Rosaleen told me that you had found out about us. I couldn't imagine how. It wasn't as if we'd had a long drawn out affair.'

'Oh, no?' she cried in disbelief.

'We hadn't! That's why I was so surprised. Was it because you realized that Liam was mine?'

She sat silent.

'Come on, Annie, please talk to me.'

Suddenly she flared up. 'All right! If you must know. One night, there was Liam lying on the rug looking up at me with these great big blue eyes and I realized how much like you he looked. If you remember I was desperate for a child and it just wasn't happening. Even then I didn't twig. Ah, no . . . I was laughing when I said in all innocence that wanting a baby so much must be affecting my mind as I could actually see you in the child. I can't believe that I was so gullible! If Rosaleen's guilt hadn't been written all over her face, I would never have guessed. That's how naive I was. But then, there was an excuse for me. I trusted you. I never dreamed you would do a thing like that. Strange, isn't it? However, she convinced me it was a one-night stand, and because I loved you, God help me, I believed her.'

'Annie, it *was* a one-night stand,' he said softly, a plea in his voice. He could imagine how hurt and shocked she must have been.

Suddenly she was on her feet, clenched fists in the air as if to strike out at him. He waited breathlessly. If she came close enough to hit him, he would be able to grip her in his arms and maybe, just maybe, would be able to make his peace with her. It had become imperative that she forgive him or he would be unable to live with himself.

It was not to be. As quickly as she had erupted, her temper subsided and she sat down again. In control once more, she said, 'Don't you patronize me. I was gullible then, but not any more.'

'Annie, it was just like I said. It happened the night of Joe's funeral.'

'Sean, stop it! Stop, for heaven's sake. What about Laura?

Are you saying that Rosaleen lied and you are not the father? Why would she lie?'

'No.' The admission came out on a sigh. 'She was telling the truth. But I didn't know a thing about Laura, until that day you stabbed me. I was convinced you also knew about her. That you had both been hoodwinking me. That's why I was so demented. That's why I blurted it all out.'

'Your pride was hurt, eh?' she cried scornfully. 'Big deal! Well, then, we both know now. So why rake over all these ashes? Are you deliberately trying to wound me?'

'I'm trying to explain that, once again, it was a one-night stand.'

'Oh, spare me, Sean. You make our Rosaleen sound promiscuous and whether or not she's that way inclined now, I don't know. But then, she was innocent. She wouldn't even listen to smutty talk. If she hadn't loved you there was no way she would have conceived a child outside marriage. So don't you try to tell me otherwise.'

'I was certainly in love with her. I wasn't using her, you know. I thought she loved me too. But she went through with the wedding to Joe Smith.'

Annie moved restlessly. Where was this all leading? 'I don't understand. Once Rosaleen was married to Joe, why did you seek me out, Sean? What did you hope to achieve?'

'I wanted to find out how Rosaleen was faring. Joe came across to me as a cold fish and I was worried about her. I wanted to find out if she was happy. I didn't think a few dates would do either of us any harm.'

'You cared for her that much?'

He bowed his head in shame. The hurt in Annie was apparent. The pain in her heart was so great she wanted to sob in anguish. He had used her! Right from the very start. Pride held the tears at bay.

'Why did you marry me, Sean? Was it necessary to go that far?'

He wanted to tell a lie; say that he had fallen in love with her, but he hadn't, not then. That came later. And there had been too many lies told already. Gently, he said, 'I was very fond of you, Annie. You were lovely and caring, and the war

385

showed no signs of abating. I wanted someone to come home to.'

He was fond of her! He hadn't even the decency to pretend that he loved her. What kind of a blind fool had she been? Her chin tilted and she forced a laugh. 'Ha, ha! And then when the war was over you came home and discovered that Joe had died and Rosaleen was a free woman. How you must have regretted our marriage! So much so, you rushed straight into her arms.'

'I did no such thing! You did it! You, pushed me out into the street, remember? It was you who sent me to her.'

'Oh, yes, let me think.' She put a hand to her head as if to recall. 'I remember. I said "Sean, I'm worried about our Rosaleen. She shouldn't be alone in that house with just Laura for company. It's not right. She's just buried her husband today. Go down and see her. Oh, and by the way! Get your leg over while you're at it." Yes, I remember.'

'Don't be so crude! It's beneath you.'

'Me crude? It was you who did it. But then, I was such a fool I was easily hoodwinked. How the two of you must have laughed up your sleeves at my stupidity.'

He thumped his forehead with his fist. 'We didn't! Oh, God, this isn't going as I intended.'

'Huh! I'll bet it isn't!' she jeered.

'You're twisting everything I say.'

'What did you expect? Understanding? Maybe my blessing? Catch yourself on! Surely you didn't really expect my forgiveness? All the talking in the world isn't going to make any difference, so why don't you just go off to Canada with Rosaleen and leave me in peace?'

Sensing that he was fighting a losing battle, fear entered his heart. He changed tactics.

With a glance around him, he said, 'I wasn't surprised to find you in this room. It was always your favourite, right from the very first.'

She eyed him warily. What was he up to now?

'Do you remember the great big row we had when you found out about Rosaleen and me?'

As if it was yesterday, her mind shouted, but her tongue remained still.

'I thought I'd lost you and I came up here to plead my case. It was snowing then as well. Remember? That was when I discovered how very much I loved you. I realized how much I needed you, that I couldn't live without you if I was to have any happiness. I was over the moon when you told me you were pregnant. Do you remember, Annie? We were both so happy that day!'

He willed her to remember. They had been lifted from the depths of despair to cloud nine that day. In the dim light he couldn't be sure but he thought her features softened and he pressed on. 'Annie we've had a turbulent marriage and here we are again in this very same room, at loggerheads. We've come full circle. Do you not fancy another circuit with me?'

Her mouth dropped open. 'Are you daft? Do you think I would ever risk trusting you again, after the way you've behaved?'

He smiled slightly. 'I've mellowed, Annie. I'd be afraid to do anything wrong in case you and Thomas came after me with a knife.'

Confused, she shook her head and stumbled towards the door. Why was he saying all these things? What was the point? Suddenly the penny dropped. He and Rosaleen must have had a disagreement. Ah, yes. That must be the reason. Well, he wasn't going to make a mug of her again. That's for sure.

'I'll have to go now. Me mam will think that something must have happened to me, and it's way past Thomas's bed time.'

He was on his feet and slowly shortening the distance between them. 'Annie, I'm serious! Will you not give me another chance?'

Utterly bewildered, she cried in frustration, 'Has our Rosaleen given you the brush off?'

'No, I declined to go to Canada. I find my only chance of happiness lies here with you and Thomas. I've missed out on a lot of things where my son is concerned . . .' He held up a hand to stave off any comments she might be tempted to make on that score. 'All my own fault, I know. I want a chance to put things right.'

'Sean, I find this change of heart too much to take in.'

'I'll not rush you, Annie. But I want to make it clear that Rosaleen and I haven't . . .' He paused. He didn't want her imagination running wild. 'You know what I mean. We haven't been together since the night Joe Smith was buried.'

The look of disbelief on her face was comical. 'You expect me to believe that? What do you take me for, Sean? Some kind of eejit?'

'I know! I know how it looks, but nevertheless it's true. Only if you believe that it just happened twice will we be able to find happiness together. Otherwise, you must send me away.'

'Huh! You've a cheek! Now you're giving me an ultimatum. Well, so far as I'm concerned . . . you can go. I'll have you know that Thomas and I are quite settled in Oranmore Street.' She couldn't resist taunting him. 'Matt McKernan is great with your son. He makes time for him!'

He winced as if she had struck him. 'What about you, Annie? Does he make time for you too?'

This time she really did strike him, with such force he staggered back. Then he was gripping hold of her, shaking her roughly. 'I'm fighting for my happiness here, Annie. I want to know if that's why you never came to see me in the hospital? Are you attracted to McKernan?'

At last the floodgates opened and she sobbed and spluttered against his chest. 'Matt McKernan is a very happily married man, I'll have you know, and I won't hear a word said against him. He is a true friend. He urged me to agree to see you. He wanted me to have my share of the furniture. It's breaking my heart to think of all my lovely things going to strangers.'

'Hush, love. The house is still mine. All your lovely things are safe. No matter what we decide, you shall have anything you want.'

Pushing herself back, she gazed up at him in wonder. 'But . . . you gave me two-thirds of the value of it. Where did you get all that money? Was it from . . .'

'No, I didn't get it from Rosaleen. I remortgaged the house.'

Head bowed, she pondered on this. He was taking too much for granted. Now she eased away from him. 'Look, Sean. I really must go. Me mam will be frantic with worry.'

'I've the car outside. I'll run you down.'

'No, I'll walk, thank you.'

'Be sensible, Annie. I'll run you down. It will only take a couple of minutes, and it's snowing again.'

388

In the car she was ashamed to find herself wondering how it would be if she took him back. Everybody would know about Laura and Liam. They would all be talking behind her back. They would think her a fool for letting him return.

Suddenly, as if reading her thoughts, he said, 'You know, Annie, very few know the whole story. Just the family, Thelma and John, and Rachel. And then of course Josie and George. And they're not going to broadcast it, are they?'

He drew the car into the side of the road at Orange Row and turned to face her. 'I don't want to face Thelma now. I'll wait here and run you and Thomas home.' She hesitated and he pleaded, 'Please, Annie?'

'Well, don't you think for one minute that it means I'm taking you back, Sean Devlin! Far from it.'

'Is that a yes, then?'

With an abrupt nod she left the car and hurried to her mother's door, glad he wasn't coming in. Explanations were out of the question at the moment.

Alone in the car, Sean relaxed with a sigh of relief. He ran a hand wearily over his face. He felt as if he had just done a couple of rounds with Henry Cooper. He had passed the first hurdle and was aware there was a hard uphill struggle ahead, but there was hope in his heart. It was up to him now to really win her back.

Rosaleen had been very angry when he told her of his decision. She had warned him that she wasn't going to hang around to see if Annie proved willing. She had threatened him with a picture of her and Pat McDade enjoying themselves in Canada. But what good would Canada be to him without Annie?

Seeing the door of the house open, he left the car and went to assist Annie and Thomas down the path. Thomas's face was alight with joy and he clung to Sean's arm. In the background, he saw Thelma staring in amazement; saw her turn to John who gave him a huge smile and the thumbs-up sign.

As Sean eased the car away from the kerb, he said, with laughter in his voice, 'You didn't tell them we were back together again, then?'

'I did nothing of the sort!' Then, realizing that he was teasing her, she smiled slightly. 'And don't you dare take anything for granted, Sean Devlin.'

'I won't, Annie. I certainly won't. I've too much to lose.'

Reaching over, he squeezed her hand and was happy when she didn't pull it directly away. It wouldn't be easy, but then, he liked a challenge.

Thomas stood up in the back of the car with his arms around their shoulders, a huge grin on his face. 'Are we going home, Daddy?' The words came out distinctly. Plainer than ever before. They both glanced at him in wonder. Then, with a sideways look at her, Sean said, 'I'll let you answer that one, love.'